ALICE LECCESE POWERS

Ireland in Mind

Alice Leccese Powers is the editor of the anthology *Italy in Mind*, and coeditor of *The Brooklyn Reader: Thirty Writers Celebrate America's Favorite Borough*. A freelance writer and editor, she has been published in *The Washington Post*, *The Baltimore Sun*, *Newsday*, and many other newspapers and magazines. Ms. Powers also teaches writing at the Corcoran College of Art and Design. She lives in Washington, D.C., with her husband and three daughters.

Ireland in Mind

Ireland in Mind

AN ANTHOLOGY

Edited and with an Introduction by

Alice Leccese Powers

VINTAGE DEPARTURES

VINTAGE BOOKS

A DIVISION OF RANDOM HOUSE, INC.

NEW YORK

A VINTAGE DEPARTURES ORIGINAL, MARCH 2000
FIRST EDITION

Copyright © 2000 by Alice Leccese Powers

All rights reserved under International and Pan-American
Copyright Conventions. Published in the United States
by Vintage Books, a division of Random House, Inc.,
New York, and simultaneously in Canada by Random House
of Canada Limited, Toronto.

Vintage is a registered trademark and Vintage Departures and
colophon are trademarks of Random House, Inc.

Pages 329–332 constitute an extension of this copyright page.

Library of Congress Cataloging-in-Publication Data
Ireland in mind : an anthology / edited and with an
introduction by Alice Leccese Powers.
p.   cm.
ISBN 0-375-70344-6
1. Ireland—Literary collections.   2. English literature—
Irish authors.   3. Ireland—Description and travel.
4. American literature.   5. English literature.
I. Powers, Alice.
PR8835.I75   2000
820.8'032417—dc21   99-39790
CIP

Book design by JoAnne Metsch

www.vintagebooks.com

Printed in the United States of America
10 9 8 7 6 5 4 3 2 1

For Alison, Christina, and Brenna

Acknowledgments

WITH GRATEFUL ACKNOWLEDGMENT to my editor, LuAnn Walther, her associate, Diana Secker Larson, and my agent, Jane Dystel; to my family, both Italian and Irish; to Erich Parker, Jane Vandenburgh, Kem Sawyer, and Pat Taylor for their counsel and friendship, and, as always, to my husband, Brian Powers.

Contents

MUNSTER

LEINSTER

Introduction

Towards the end of his life, James Joyce was asked if he might ever return to Dublin. He always gave the same reply. "Have I ever left?"

Leaving Ireland. Millions have, but something primal keeps a hold on them, their children, and even those who simply come to visit. Sentiment plays a part, but the country cleaves to the body as well as to the heart. Perhaps the Shannon leaves a watermark on the skin or the flame of a peat fire burns a brand into the retina. Maybe Dublin infects the brain—as it did Joyce—so that after thirty years its streets are recalled fresh as yesterday's evening stroll.

The writers in *Ireland in Mind* look at the country through telescopes, each fitted with a different eyepiece. The emigrants see through a lens of physical distance; the visitors, through a lens of psychological distance. Included in this anthology are the celebrated expatriates such as James Joyce, Samuel Beckett, and George Bernard Shaw and the famous travel writers such as Jan Morris, H. V. Morton, and Paul Theroux. Some, like Frank McCourt, wrote from decades-old childhood memory; others, like Virginia Woolf, recorded their impressions with the instantaneousness of a Polaroid.

The perspective of physical and psychological distance is the central conceit of *Ireland in Mind*. This is not the Ireland of native writers such as William Butler Yeats, Sean O'Casey, or Roddy Doyle, who stayed and produced passionate work based in reality, not memory. The margins of time and space create a different literary genre—one filled with longing, wonder, sometimes anger, and often bemusement. *Ireland in Mind* is an amalgam of the work of the Irish émigré and the foreigner. Both try to find the real Ireland; each brings too much of himself to the journey. Individually, no one succeeds. Collectively, these writers create a kaleidoscope of a land and her people.

An anthologist is more archaeologist than writer. Years are spent reading, choosing, discarding, and sifting, putting together different parts to complete the puzzle, the portrait of a place. Because I thought that many would use *Ireland in Mind* as a literary travel companion, the selections represent the four provinces, Leinster, Munster, Ulster, and Connaught. I sought writers of different views, styles, and epochs, creating a rich cacophony of voices—whispers of sentiment, shouts of judgment, songs of praise, chortles of recognition. Beneath this veneer of science, my work was ultimately subjective. William Trevor's short story "Autumn Sunshine" moved me to tears. It is here. Heinrich Böll surprised me with his delightful travel book, *Irish Journal*. An excerpt is, of course, here. Eric Newby's *Round Ireland in Low Gear* was so disarming, so funny that I not only wanted a chapter for the book, but also wished he would come around for Sunday dinner. Like many, I had enjoyed Jonathan Swift's *Gulliver's Travels*, but I did not know about his brave championship of the Irish cause. Such heroism deserves recognition. His poem "An Answer to the Ballyspellin Ballad" is here.

Ireland in Mind is my attempt to find the mysterious and elusive Ireland. *Mysterious* and *elusive* are words not often applied to Ireland. The people seem so friendly; life is lived so much in the open, in shops and pubs. Conversation is the national currency, and no one spends as freely as the Irish. Many have been seduced by Irish talk. The British travel writer H. V. Morton wrote, "Talk matters. Wit matters. Laughter matters. And the man who has something interesting to say has more platforms than he can occupy." But do not be fooled by conviviality; intimacy is harder won in Ireland than anywhere on earth. The country is a clan, one that is impossible to join and difficult to leave.

Many writers who did leave found that, whether they were in London, Paris, or New York, their best work was about Ireland. Oliver Goldsmith's poem "The Deserted Village" was, in part, based on his hometown of Lissoy. Like many, Goldsmith wrote letters promising to return to West Meath, but never did. Nor did Joyce, who left Dublin in his twenties and spent the rest of his life mining her streets for his stories. He never got closer than London's Euston Station, the terminus for Irish immigrants who got off the boat-train for England. Shaw also left in his twenties and only returned in his old age.

But they were all adamantly and fervently Irish. They left for reasons economic, political, and personal, but there is something in their core that belongs to their birthplace. It is like uranium with a half-life so long that it becomes part of the genetic makeup, passed down two, six, ten generations. It is that DNA that makes the American who is one sixteenth Irish, whose great-great-grandparents came to America during the Famine, who has never set foot in Dublin, wear green on March 17.

Shaw wrote, "Eternal is the fact that the human creature born in Ireland and brought up in its air is Irish. Whatever variety of mongrel he or she may derive from, British or Iberian, Pict or Scot, Dane or Saxon, Down or Kerry, Hittite or Philistine: Ireland acclimatizes them all. I have lived for twenty years in Ireland and for seventy-two in England; but the twenty came first, and in Britain I am still a foreigner and shall die one."

Balancing the Irish expatriates are the travel writers. Their telescopes put them at a psychological rather than a physical distance. They tiptoe around the country, half expecting to be bored or blown to bits. Cautious at first, they try to find the familiar. Do the mailboxes look like those in Britain? Are Dublin's streets as wide as those of Paris? Does Guinness taste the same as it does in New York? Virginia Woolf thought the country a "mixture of Greece, Italy & Cornwall; great loneliness; poverty & dreary villages like squares cut out of West Kensington." Those who stay long enough find what every good travel writer concludes: Ireland is Ireland.

In this contrary country opposites thrive: Catholic and Protestant, poverty and wealth, rigid religious adherence and complex superstition, North and South, peace and war, hope and despair. There are few places that are safer—hitchhiking is epidemic, locks go unbolted, honesty is a national virtue. Yet, until recently, a Protestant risked his life in the wrong part of Belfast and a Catholic, the same.

Ironically, David Wilson observed, both Catholics and Protestants are threatened minorities, Protestants in Ireland and Catholics in Ulster: "It's like living in a world of mirror images where each side sees the image, but neither sees the mirror." After finding Belfast hospitable beyond its reputation, Niall Williams wrote, "Was *this* Belfast then? Was this what it was like here? It was—and it wasn't. For such is the complexity of the tragedy of Northern Ireland that scenes of absolute tranquillity are quite possible and even normal only minutes away from places where the blackened shells of houses, barred gates, and barbed wire bear testament to a state of war. . . . Was Belfast, perhaps, the friendliest city in Ireland?"

Rhetorical questions abound when one attempts to solve the Irish puzzle. "A strange country—but how strange?" asks Paul Theroux. "One where the sun bursts through the clouds at ten in the evening and makes a sunset as full and promising as dawn . . . Ancient perfect castles that are not inhabited, hovels that are . . . Stone altars that were last visited by Druids, storms that break and pass in minutes."

Like those violent storms, Ireland demands competing emotions. The country is so beautiful, so dazzling that, to see it from a plane circling Shannon airport after an all-night flight, its intensity hurts the eyes. Memory cannot diminish the image of variegated green punctuated by miles of fuchsia hedges and ancient stone walls. "How can anyone leave this place?" is always a visitor's first question. Followed by "How can anyone stay?" Heinrich Böll, fresh from postwar Germany, surveyed an abandoned village and concluded, "No bombed city, no artillery-raked village ever looks like this, for bombs and shells are nothing, but extended tomahawks, battle-axes, maces, with which to smash, to hack to pieces, but there is no trace of violence; in limitless patience time and the elements have eaten away everything not made of stone, and from the earth have sprouted cushions on which these bones lie like relics, cushions of moss and grass."

Ireland is not in my bones, it is not in my DNA, but it is part of my children and so much a part of my husband, their father. Anthony Burgess once wrote, "Any man, whatever his nationality, has a right to admire and to propagandize for Irish literature, but it helps if he possesses Irish blood or a mad capacity for empathizing with Ireland."

Like many Irish-American families we went back to Roscommon where my mother-in-law was born. We had vague directions—ask at the pub, you'll see it from the road. But what pub? What road? Our relatives, the Martins, had no phone. They lived on a 75-acre farm near the Shannon River, a portion of the original 400 acres that the family had owned a hundred years ago. As we got closer, my husband became uncharacteristically timid. He must have felt the same kind of reluctance that adoptees have in meeting their biological families, for returning to Ireland is like finding a severed past. We can't find the place, he insisted. We're too late to call (although we had written to expect us "sometime in August").

Down the road at last and we were welcomed as if we had just returned from a fortnight sojourn in Dublin. Uncle Batty, at ninety-nine, was the image of my husband, plus more than fifty years. My middle daughter looked so much like her second cousin Judith that even her parents got them momentarily confused. My eldest child has the Martins' oval fingernails; my youngest, the resolute stance of both her father and her great-great-uncle. The Martins have scattered to Australia, America, Canada, England, but they return to those 75 acres on the Shannon. That is home.

Times have changed in Ireland. The economy is booming. Ireland's best export is no longer her children, but Ireland herself. Enormous tour buses lumber along roads scarcely wide enough for a man and a cow walking abreast. It is not uncommon for an Irishman to give his cell phone and fax number. Ireland's heritage centers make it easier for the descendants of the diaspora to find their Irish families, or what is left of them. Emigration is slowing and, in time, Irish mothers may no longer need to calculate the distance of their children by time zones or continents. But for every Irishman at home, there are twenty of Irish blood who are not. Brian Moore calls them "the wanderers." "There are those who choose to leave home vowing never to return and those who, forced to leave for economic reasons, remain in thrall to a dream of the land they left behind," he wrote. "And then there are those stateless wanderers who, finding the larger world into which they have stumbled vast, varied and exciting, become confused in their loyalties and lose their sense of home. I am one of those wanderers."

Ireland in Mind is for those Irish wanderers and for those, like me, with a "mad capacity" for Irish literature. It is for those who tour Ireland once and for those who return there every night in their dreams. And it is for those who travel there and feel at home and for those who travel everywhere else in the world and find that home is only Ireland.

Connaught

HEINRICH BÖLL

(1917–1985)

In the 1950s the German author and Nobel laureate Heinrich Böll must have been an unlikely Irish tourist. He began Irish Journal, *his memoir of the trip, with this disclaimer: "This Ireland exists; but whoever goes there and fails to find it has no claim on the author." Böll found the Irish unfailingly trusting—from the train conductor who let his whole family travel on credit to the bank manager, reached at home, who simply gave them two pound notes. Shortly after his arrival, Böll encountered another facet of Irish life—an abandoned village, evidence of the poverty that had driven the Irish to emigrate.*

Böll was called the conscience of postwar Germany. Wounded repeatedly during fighting on both the Eastern and Western fronts, he was finally taken prisoner by the Americans. His war experiences left him cynical of government, religion, and bureaucracy, and all of his novels reflect his strong antiwar feelings. Irish Journal, *from which these excerpts are taken, is atypical of Böll's work, most of which is devoted to the absurdity of war and the dehumanization of the individual in postwar Germany.*

MAYO—GOD HELP US

from IRISH JOURNAL

In the center of Ireland, in Athlone, two and a half hours by express from Dublin, the train is split up into two. The better half, the one with the dining car, goes on to Galway; the underprivileged half, the one we remain in, goes to Westport. We would be watching the departure of the dining car, where lunch was just being served, with even more painful emotions if we had any money, English or Irish, to pay for breakfast or lunch. But as it happens, since there was only half an hour between the arrival of the ship and the departure of the train and the exchange bureaus in Dublin do not open until 9:30, all we have is flimsy notes, useless here, just as they come from the printing presses of the German Federal Bank, and central Ireland knows no rate for these.

I still have not quite got over the scare I had in Dublin: when I left the station to look for a place to change some money, I was almost run over by a bright-red panel truck whose sole decoration was a big swastika. Had someone sold *Völkischer Beobachter* delivery trucks here, or did the *Völkischer Beobachter* still have a branch office here? This one looked exactly like those I remembered; but the driver crossed himself as he smilingly signaled to me to proceed, and on closer inspection I saw what had happened. It was simply the "Swastika Laundry," which had painted the year of its founding, 1912, clearly beneath the swastika; but the mere possibility that it might have been one of those others was enough to take my breath away.

I could not find a bank open and returned discouraged to the station, having already to let the train for Westport leave as I could not pay for the tickets. We had the choice of taking a hotel room and waiting till the next day, till the next train (for the afternoon train would be too late for us to make our bus connection)—or in some way boarding the Westport train without tickets; this "some way" was found: we traveled on credit. The stationmaster in Dublin, touched by the spectacle of three tired children, two dejected women, and a helpless father (escaped only two minutes earlier from the swastika truck!), worked out that the night in the hotel would cost as much as the whole train journey to Westport: he wrote down my name, the *number of persons traveling on credit,* shook my hand reassuringly, and signaled to the train to leave.

So on this strange island we managed to enjoy the only kind of credit which we had never been given and never tried to obtain, the credit of a railway company.

But unfortunately, there was no breakfast on credit in the dining car; the attempt to obtain it failed: the bank notes, in spite of the crisp new paper, did not convince the headwaiter. With a sigh we changed the last pound, had the Thermos flask filled with tea and ordered a package of sandwiches. The conductors were left with the stern duty of writing strange names down in their notebooks. It happened once, twice, three times, and the alarming question arose for us: shall we have to pay these unique debts once, twice, or three times?

The new conductor, who joined the train at Athlone, had red hair and was eager and young; when I confessed to him that we had not tickets, a ray of recognition crossed his face. Clearly he had been told about us, clearly our names and our credit together with the *number of persons traveling on credit* had been telegraphed through from station to station.

For four hours after Athlone, the train, now a local one, wound its way through smaller and smaller stations farther and farther to the west. The highlights of its stops were the towns between Athlone (9,000 inhabitants) and the coast: Roscommon and Claremorris, with as many inhabitants as there are people living in three city apartment blocks; Castlebar, capital of County Mayo, with four thousand; and Westport with three thousand inhabitants; on one stretch, corresponding roughly to the distance between Cologne and Frankfurt, the population dwindles consistently, then comes the great water and beyond that New York with three times as many inhabitants as the whole Republic of Ireland, with more Irish than there are living in the three counties beyond Athlone.

The stations are small, the station buildings light green, the fences around them snow-white, and on the platform there usually stands a solitary boy who has taken one of his mother's trays and hung it around his neck with a leather strap: three bars of chocolate, two apples, and a few rolls of peppermints, chewing gum and a comic; we wanted to entrust our last silver shilling to one of these lads, but the choice was difficult. The women were in favor of apples and peppermint; the children, of chewing gum and the comic. We compromised and bought the comic and a bar of chocolate. The comic had the promising title of *Batman,* and the cover showed a man in a dark mask climbing up the outsides of houses.

The smiling boy stood there all alone on the little station in the bog. The gorse was in bloom, the fuchsia hedges were already budding; wild green hills, mounds of peat; yes, Ireland is green, very green, but its green is not only the green of meadows, it is the green of moss—certainly here, beyond Roscommon, toward County Mayo—and moss is the plant of resignation, of forsakenness. The country is forsaken, it is being slowly but steadily depopulated, and we—none of us had ever seen this strip of Ireland, or the house we had rented "somewhere in the west"—we felt a little apprehensive: in vain the women looked left and right of the train for potato fields, vegetable plots, for the fresh, unresigned green of lettuce, the darker green of peas. We divided the bar of chocolate and tried to console ourselves with *Batman,* but he was really a bad man. Not only, as the cover had promised, did he climb up the outsides of houses; one of his chief pleasures was evidently to frighten women in their sleep; he could also fly off through the air by spreading out his cloak, taking millions of dollars with him, and his deeds were described in an English such as is taught neither in Continental schools nor in the schools of England and Ireland; *Batman* was strong and terribly just, but hard, and toward the wicked he could even be cruel, for now and again he would bash in someone's teeth, a procedure fittingly rendered with the word "Screech." There was no comfort in *Batman.*

A different comfort awaited us: our red-haired conductor appeared and wrote us down with a smile for the fifth time. This mysterious process of frequent notation was now explained. We had crossed a county borderline again and were in County Mayo. Now the Irish have a strange custom: whenever the name of County Mayo is spoken (whether in praise, blame, or non-committally), as soon as the mere word Mayo is spoken, the Irish add: "God help us!" It sounds like the response in a litany: "Lord have mercy upon us!"

The conductor disappeared with the solemn assurance that he would not have to write us down again, and we stopped at a little station. Here they unloaded what had been unloaded at all the other stations: cigarettes, that was all. We had already acquired the habit of estimating the size of the hinterland according to the size of the bales of cigarettes unloaded, and, as a look at the map proved, our calculation was correct. I walked through the train to the baggage car to see how many bales of cigarettes were still left. There was one small bale and one large one, so I knew how many more stations were ahead. The train had become alarmingly empty. I counted eighteen people, of whom we alone were six, and we seemed to have been traveling for an eternity past peat stacks, across bogs, and still there was no sign of the fresh green of lettuce, or the darker green of peas, or the bitter green of potatoes. Mayo, we said under our breath. God help us!

WE STOPPED, THE large bale of cigarettes was unloaded, and looking over the snow-white fence of the station platform were some dark faces, shaded by peaked caps, men who seemed to be guarding a column of automobiles. I had noticed these at other stations too, the cars and the waiting, watching men; it was only now that I remembered how often I had already seen them. They seemed familiar, like the bundles of cigarettes, like our conductor and the little Irish freight cars, which are scarcely more than half the size of the English and Continental ones. I entered the baggage car where our red-haired friend was squatting on the last bale of cigarettes; using the English words with care, like a novice juggler handling china plates, I asked him the significance of these dark men with the peaked caps, and what the cars were standing there for; I anticipated some kind of folkloric explanation; a modern version of an abduction, a highway robbery, but the conductor's answer was disconcertingly simple:

"Those are taxis," he said, and I breathed a sigh of relief. So whatever happens there are taxis, just as sure as there are cigarettes. The conductor seemed to have noticed my suffering: he offered me a cigarette, I accepted it gladly, he lit it for me and said with a reassuring smile:

"We'll be there in ten minutes."

Right on schedule we arrived ten minutes later in Westport. Here we were given a ceremonial reception. The stationmaster himself, a tall, dignified elderly gentleman, took up a position in front of our compartment, a friendly smile on his face, and by way of welcome raised a large engraved brass baton, symbol of his office, to his cap. He helped the ladies, helped the children, signaled for a porter, guided me deliberately but unobtrusively into his office, wrote down my name, my address in Ireland, and advised me in fatherly fashion not to depend on being able to change my money in Westport. His smile became even gentler when I showed him my German bank notes, and he said, "Nice, very nice," adding kindly:

"There's no hurry, you know, there's really no hurry, you'll pay all right. Don't worry."

Again I quoted the rate of exchange, but the dignified old man merely waved his brass baton gently from side to side, saying:

"I shouldn't worry." (And all the time the billboards were exhorting us to worry. "Think of your future. Safety first! Provide for your children!")

But I was still worrying. Our credit had brought us this far, but would it take us any farther, a two-hour stop in Westport, two and a half hours by bus to our destination, across County Mayo—God help us?

I WAS ABLE to rouse the bank manager at his home; he raised his eyebrows, for it was his afternoon off. I was also able to convince him—and he lowered his eyebrows—of the relative diffi-culty of my position: quite a bit of money, and not a penny in my pocket! But I could not convince him of the credit standing of my bank note collection. He must have heard something about East and West German marks and of the difference in cur-rency, and when I pointed to the word "Frankfurt" on the note he said (he must have had an A in geography): "There's a Frank-furt in the other half of Germany too"; I had no choice but to play off the Main against the Oder, which I didn't like doing, but he evidently had not had *summa cum laude* in geography, and such subtle differences, even after looking up the official rate of exchange, were too slender a foundation for a sizable credit.

"I'll have to send the money to Dublin," he said.

"The money," I said, "just the way it is?"

"Of course," he said. "What good is it to me here?"

I bowed my head: he was right, what good was it to him?

"How long will it take," I said, "for you to hear from Dublin?"

"Four days," he said.

"Four days," I said, "God help us!"

One thing at least I had learned. Could he then let me have a little credit on the basis of this bundle of bank notes? He looked thoughtfully at the bills, at "Frankfurt," at me, opened the cash drawer and gave me two pound notes.

I said nothing, signed a receipt, got one from him, and left the bank. Of course it was raining, and my family were waiting trustfully for me at the bus stop. There was hunger in their eyes, almost a yearning, the anticipation of powerful masculine, pow-erful paternal aid, and I made up my mind to do something which is the basis of the myth of masculinity: I made up my mind to bluff. In a grandiose gesture I invited them all to tea, to ham and eggs, salad—wherever did that come from?—to cook-ies and ice cream, and after paying the bill was happy to have half a crown left. That was just enough for ten cigarettes, matches, and a shilling in reserve.

I still did not know what I found out four hours later: that you can give tips on credit, and not until we had arrived, at the outer edge of County Mayo, from where there is nothing but water all the way to New York—did credit come into its full glory. The house was painted snow white, the window frames dark blue; there was a fire burning in the grate. The welcoming feast consisted of fresh salmon. The sea was pale green, up front where it rolled onto the beach, dark blue out toward the center of the bay, and a narrow, sparkling white frill was visible where the sea broke on the island.

That evening we were given something worth as much as cash—the storekeeper's account book. It was a fat book consisting of nearly eighty pages, solidly bound, with a very permanent quality about it. We had arrived, we were in Mayo—God help us?

SKELETON OF A HUMAN HABITATION

from IRISH JOURNAL

Suddenly, on reaching the top of the hill, we saw the skeleton of the abandoned village on the slope ahead of us. No one had told us anything about it, no one had given us any warning; there are so many abandoned villages in Ireland. The church, the shortest way to the beach, had been pointed out to us, and the shop where you can buy tea, bread, butter, and cigarettes, also the newsagent's, the post office, and the little harbor where the harpooned sharks lie like capsized boats in the mud at low tide, their dark backs uppermost, unless by chance the last wave of the tide had turned up their white bellies from which the liver had been cut out—all this seemed worth mentioning, but not the abandoned village. Gray, uniform, sloping stone gables, which we saw first with no depth of perspective, like an amateurish set for a ghost film; incredulous, we tried to count them, we gave up at forty, there must have been a hundred. The next curve of the road gave us a different perspective, and now we saw them from the side: half-finished buildings that seemed to be waiting for the carpenter: gray stone walls, dark window sockets, not a stick of wood, not a shred of material, no color anywhere, like a body without hair, without eyes, without flesh and blood—the skeleton of a village, cruelly distinct in its structure. There was the main street, at the bend, by the little square, there must have been a pub. A side street, another one. Everything not made of stone gnawed away by rain, sun, and wind—and time, which patiently trickles over everything; twenty-four great drops of time a day, the acid that eats everything away as imperceptibly as resignation. . . . If anyone ever tried to paint it, this skeleton of a human habitation where a hundred years ago five hundred people may have lived: all those gray triangles and squares on the green-gray slope of the hill; if he were to include the girl with the red pullover who is just passing along the main street with a load of peat on her back, a spot of red for her pullover and a dark brown one for the peat, a lighter brown one for the girl's face, and then the white sheep huddling like lice among the ruins—he would be considered an unusually crazy painter: that's how abstract reality is. Everything not made of stone eaten away by wind, sun, rain, and time, nearly laid out along the somber slope as if for an anatomy lesson, the skeleton of a village: over there—"look, just like a spine"—the main street, a little crooked like the spine of a laborer; every little knuckle bone is there; there are the arms and the legs: the side streets and, tipped slightly to one side, the head, the church, a somewhat larger gray triangle. Left leg: the street going up the slope to the east; right leg: the other one, leading down into the valley, this one a little shortened. The skeleton of someone with a slight limp. If his skeleton were exposed in three hundred years, this is what the man might look like who is being driven by his four thin cows past us onto the meadow, leaving him the

illusion that he was driving them; his right leg has been short-
ened by an accident, his back is crooked from the toil of cutting
peat, and even his tired head will tip a little to one side when he
is laid in the earth. He has already overtaken us, already mur-
mured his "nice day," before we had got our breath back suffi-
ciently to answer him or ask him about the village.

No bombed city, no artillery-raked village ever looked like
this, for bombs and shells are nothing but extended tomahawks,
battle-axes, maces, with which to smash, to hack to pieces, but
here there is no trace of violence; in limitless patience time and
the elements have eaten away everything not made of stone, and
from the earth have sprouted cushions on which these bones lie
like relics, cushions of moss and grass.

No one would try to pull down a wall here or take wood
(very valuable here) from an abandoned house (we call that
cleaning out; no one cleans out here); and not even the children
who drive the cattle home in the evening from the meadow
above the deserted village, not even the children try to pull
down walls or doorways; our children, when we suddenly found
ourselves in the village, tried it immediately, to raze to the
ground. Here no one razed anything to the ground, and the
softer parts of abandoned dwellings are left to feed the wind,
the rain, the sun, and time, and after sixty, seventy, or a hundred
years all that is left is half-finished buildings from which no car-
penter will ever again hang his wreath to celebrate the comple-
tion of a house: this, then, is what a human habitation looks like
when it has been left in peace after death.

Still with a sense of awe we crossed the main street between
the bare gables, entered side streets, and slowly the sense of awe
lifted: grass was growing in the streets, moss had covered walls
and potato plots, was creeping up houses; and the stones of the
gables, washed free of mortar, were neither quarried stone nor
tiles, but small boulders, just as the mountain had rolled them
down in its streams into the valley, door and window lintels were
slabs of rock, and broad as shoulder blades were the two stone
slabs sticking out of the wall where the fireplace had been: once

the chain for the iron cooking pot had hung from them, pale potatoes cooking in brownish water.

We went from house to house like peddlers, and every time the short shadow on the threshold had fallen away from us the blue square of the sky covered us again; in houses where the better-off ones had once lived it was larger, where the poor had lived it was smaller: all that distinguished them now was the size of the blue square of sky. In some rooms moss was already growing, some thresholds were already covered with brownish water; here and there in the front walls you could still see the pegs for the cattle: thighbones of oxen to which the chain had been attached.

"Here's where the stove was"—"The bed over there"—"here over the fireplace hung the crucifix"—"over there a cupboard": two upright stone slabs with two vertical slabs wedged into them; here in this cupboard one of the children discovered the iron wedge, and when we drew it out it crumbled away in our hands like tinder: a hard inner piece remained about as thick as a nail which—on the children's instructions—I put in my coat pocket as a souvenir.

We spent five hours in this village, and the time passed quickly because nothing happened; we scared a few birds into flight, a sheep jumped through an empty window socket and fled up the slope at our approach; in ossified fuchsia hedges hung blood-red blossoms, in withered gorse bushes hung a yellow like dirty coins, shining quartz stuck up out of the moss like bones; no dirt in the streets, no rubbish in the streams, and not a sound to be heard. Perhaps we were waiting for the girl with the red pullover and her load of brown peat, but the girl did not come back.

On the way home when I put my hand in my pocket for the iron wedge, all my fingers found was brown dust mixed with red: the same color as the bog to the right and left of our path, and I threw it in the bog.

No one could tell us exactly when and why the village had been abandoned; there are so many deserted houses in Ireland,

you can count them on any two-hour walk: that one was aban-
doned ten years ago, this one twenty, that one fifty or eighty
years ago, and there are houses in which the nails fastening the
boards to windows and doors have not yet rusted through, rain
and wind cannot yet penetrate.

The old woman living in the house next to us had no idea
when the village had been abandoned; when she was a little girl,
around 1880, it was already deserted. Of her six children, only
two have remained in Ireland: two live and work in Manchester,
two in the United States, one daughter is married and living
here in the village (this daughter has six children, of whom in
turn two will probably go to England, two to the United States),
and the oldest son has stayed home: from far off, when he comes
in from the meadow with the cattle, he looks like a youth of six-
teen; when he turns the corner and enters the village street you
feel he must be in his mid-thirties; and when he finally passes
the house and grins shyly in at the window, you see that he is
fifty.

"He doesn't want to get married," said his mother, "isn't it a
shame?"

Yes, it is a shame. He is so hard-working and clean; he has
painted the gate red, the stone knobs on the wall red too, and
the window frames under the green mossy roof bright blue;
humor dwells in his eyes, and he pats his donkey affectionately.

In the evening, when we go to get the milk, we ask him
about the abandoned village. But he can tell us nothing about it,
nothing; he has never been there: they have no meadows over
there, and their peat cuttings lie in a different direction, to the
south, not far from the monument to the Irish patriot who was
executed in 1799. "Have you seen it yet?" Yes, we've seen it—
and Tony goes off again, a man of fifty, is transformed at the
corner into a man of thirty, up there on the slope where he
strokes the donkey in passing he turns into a youth of sixteen,
and as he stops for a moment by the fuchsia hedge, for that
moment before he disappears behind the hedge, he looks like
the boy he once was.

THOMAS FLANAGAN
(1923 –   )

Thomas Flanagan is one of the best-known historical novelists of his generation. He has spent so much time in Ireland that he said, "Maybe I've become a bit Irish myself, though not for ancestral reasons, but because I've lived there so long, because I go so often." Ireland "somehow liberated" his imagination and has become the inspiration for his fiction.

The Year of the French *is Flanagan's first and arguably his most popular novel. Published in 1979 at the height of "The Troubles," it put the Irish conflict in historical perspective. Part documentary, part narrative, it is a fictionalized retelling of the Irish uprising against British rule in 1798, from many perspectives—loyalists, rebels, soldiers, clergy. The* Year of the French *is not a thinly veiled call to arms. Newsweek wrote that Flanagan's intentions were "to convince us of the inevitability of this useless confrontation, to expose for our sympathetic consideration the roots of this hatred, this despair, this fanaticism that spurs honorable or ignorant men to throw away their lives without hope of anything gained."*

Flanagan continued the story of the Irish struggles with the novels The Tenants of Time *(1988) and* The End of the Hunt *(1994).*

From An Impartial Narrative of What Passed at
Killala in the Summer of 1798, *by Arthur
Vincent Broome, M.A. (Oxon.)*

Some years ago, when I first took up the pastoral care of the
wild and dismal region from which I write, I was prompted to
begin a journal in which would be set forth, as I encountered
them, the habits, customs, and manners of the several social
classes, with the thought that it might someday furnish the sub-
stance of a book with some such title as *Life in the West of Ireland.*
I rightly feared that time would otherwise hang heavy on my
hands, and I have long been aware of a capacity for slothfulness
which can reveal itself when my life lacks order and direction.
And it was clear to me that few portions of His Majesty's realms
are less known than this island, which might for all purposes be
adrift on the South Seas, rather than at our doorstep. Before set-
ting forth from England, I had made it my business to read Mr.
Arthur Young's *Tour in Ireland,* a sage and clear-headed book,
bountiful in its information, liberal and enlightened in its tem-
per, but being nevertheless exactly what its title claims to be, the
account of a tour. My work would have the advantage of a pro-
longed and steady contemplation of the scene, a natural history,
as it were, of life in County Mayo.

Alas for good intentions! The journal did have for a time a
spare existence, scattered notes set down in the excitement of
my encounters with novel scenes and faces, and with a society at
once picturesque and alarming. But like others of my projects, it

stumbled to a halt after some months, and long lay gathering dust upon a shelf in my library. Where these notes are now I cannot say; perhaps they served to start a fire, this being a fate which locally befalls loose sheets of paper. They would have served no large purpose, however, for my early impressions were all, as I now know, misleading, this land being as treacherous as the bog which stretches across much of its surface. It is, in a most exact sense of the word, an outlandish place, inhospitable to the instructions of civilization.

My present purpose, more practical and limited, is to offer as fully and as impartially as I can, yet without idle digression, a narrative account of those events which, a few years ago, bestowed upon our remote countryside a transient celebrity. Those events, however, were given their particular shape by the collision of an extraordinary event with an extraordinary society. It is therefore necessary that I present at the outset my own halting and puzzled sense of that peculiar world which was to provide a theater and actors for my drama.

A map reveals Mayo as a county on the western extremity of what has been, for the past several years, the United Kingdom of Great Britain and Ireland. At the time of which I write, of course, Ireland was in theory a separate nation, possessing its own parliament, yet sharing with England King George as its sovereign ruler, and being much under English influence. Of its illusionary and fictitious "independence" I shall have something to say hereafter. It is more to the present point to observe that the events which I propose to unfold played their part in bringing down the much-boasted but trumpery "Kingdom of Ireland." Thus do large and stately changes have at times their origins in crude and remote circumstances.

Were I to have the coloring of that map of Ireland, Mayo would appear upon it in browns and blues, the brown of hillside and bogland, arched over by an immense sky of light blue. Save when it rains, which, alas, is often. It is raining as I write these words, steadily and copiously, and shrouding from view the bay toward which my library faces. My parish is centered upon the town of Killala in the barony of Tyrawley, once a bishop's see and a prosperous community of coastal traders, but for decades past in a state of sore decline and disrepair. There are other towns in Mayo, of course: Ballina, our successful rival to the south; Westport on the western coast, the seat of the Marquis of Sligo and graced by his elegant mansion. But there is only one town of true consequence, Castlebar, the capital of Mayo as it is grandiloquently termed, and the town toward which all the roads of Mayo lead. A Muscovite garrison placed upon the border of Siberia must have a similar appearance, although, like all the towns of Ireland, it is built entirely of stone, save for the mud cabins of the very poor. It has streets, a courthouse, a church, a gaol, a market house, a military barracks, the houses of prosperous merchants. And yet all seems provisional, gaunt, slender buildings huddled together against the immensities of sky and land. For to speak of County Mayo in terms of its towns is entirely deceptive. The impression which it first makes upon the eye and mind is that of limitless and inhospitable space, the vast, dreary expanse of bogland westward from Crossmolina, the steep and lonely headlands and peninsulas. It is its own huge and somber world, and by contrast with it, the flanking counties of Galway and Sligo present a civilized aspect which is, unfortunately, entirely spurious.

Neither is it a populous world, if we restrict our consideration to what would in England be termed "the county families." Within a morning's or a day's ride, I could then have claimed as neighbors some fifty or sixty families of the gentry and the near-gentry, these latter being locally termed "half sirs," or "half-mounted gentlemen." Close at hand, within the Killala and the Kilcummin boundaries, I had as neighbors, among others, Peter Gibson of The Rise, Captain Samuel Cooper of Mount Pleasant, George Falkiner of Rosenalis, my special friend, as these notes will reveal, and, on the Ballycastle road, Thomas Treacy of Bridge-end House. At a greater distance, involving arduous travel along wretched roads, stood the estates of George Moore of Moore Hall, Hilton Saunders of Castle Saunders, Malcolm

Elliott of The Moat, and a score of others. All of them, save only Moore and Treacy, were members of my parish, for it is one of the most notorious facts of Irish life that those who own the land and those who till it are severely divided by sect, the landlords being Protestant almost to a man, and the tenants and laborers being Papists.

To speak thus of our county society is to ignore its absent center, for dominating over our barony and those adjoining it are the estates, imposing and at first sight endless, of Lord Glenthorne, the Marquis of Tyrawley, or as he is called here, in a phrase taken from the Irish, "the Big Lord." The term falls with a faint blasphemy upon the ear, and Lord Glenthorne does resemble our Creator in that, having this vast domain at his disposal, he has elected to absent himself from it. In this there is nothing unusual, for the resident Irish landlords are for the most part the smaller ones, with estates of a thousand acres or less, while the great men of property are absentees, a circumstance which may hold to be contributory to our manifold woes. Lord Glenthorne, however, has chosen never to reveal himself, not even for brief visits, and yet so vast and so eminent is his place in our scheme of things that he has achieved on peasant tongues a legendary stature, a fathomless creature, beyond good or evil. In point of fact, before taking up my present charge, I was presented to him in London, where I found him to be a small, mild man of middle years, simple and unaffected in manner, and attentive to religious duties. I was to meet him also a second time, much later, on which occasion I was to form a more distinct impression of him, perceiving then that he was in every sense a lord.

To ride from here to Ballina is to ride for mile after mile beside the walls of his principal demesne, walls so high that a man on horseback can scarcely see over them, and all of cut stone. On occasion, the road will rise, and the traveler can glimpse in the distance, beyond sheltering plantations, the lovely form of Glenthorne Castle, a vast Palladian mansion which will seem to have floated down upon these inhospitable lands by some magical feat out of the *Arabian Nights*. And this illusion will be heightened if he reflects that this palace, for it is nothing less, stands waiting, staffed and doubtless furnished with unknown splendors, for a prince who has never visited it. It was far different in the days of his father, who indeed resided there from time to time, and who has left behind him most exotic and disreputable legends. But the traveler afoot sees nothing of Glenthorne Castle. He sees only the high, endless walls, and he may be pardoned for thinking that an army labored to put them into place, or such nameless legions of slaves as built the Pyramids of Egypt.

And such legions there are. In speaking as I have done of the "society" of Mayo, I have used the word in the common but un-Christian manner which excludes all whom we do not choose to see. If we admit to view the peasants, and that multitude of laborers who are infinitely more wretched even than the peasants, ours is not at all a lonely world. It is a populous, even a teeming one. They swarm like bees from their cabins, of which the meanest are made of mud, as a child builds by a riverbank, and they are everywhere, for they fasten upon every unclaimed acre which can sustain a blade of grass or a potato bed, and the hills are crisscrossed and crosshatched by fences made of the boulders which have been carried away by hand so as to expose every inch of arable land. Some few are prosperous, although precariously so—graziers and strong farmers and middlemen, but what of the numberless thousands of their coreligionists? It will be noted that here I have stumbled into the common Irish practice of confounding a social and a sectarian division. For beyond dispute there are here two worlds, "our" small Protestant world of property and their multitudinous Papist world of want.

I affirm most sincerely that distinctions which rest upon creed mean little to me, and yet I confess that my compassion for their misery is mingled with an abhorrence of their alien ways. Begin then with creed, but add to this that most speak a tongue not merely foreign, but as grotesque as the prattle of Sandwich Islanders, that they live and thrive in mud and squalor with

THOMAS FLANAGAN 21

dunghills piled before their windowless cabins, that their music, for all that antiquarians and fanatics can find to say in its favor, is wild and savage although touched upon occasion by a plaintive, melancholy beauty, that they combine a grave and gentle courtesy with a murderous violence that erupts without warning— pates smashed for pleasure on a fairday, cattle barbarously mutilated, bailiffs put to death with crude tortures—that they worship fetid pools as holy wells and go on pilgrimage to clumps of rock, that their eyes look toward you with an innocence behind which dances malevolence. Yet I avow my sympathy for them, and wish that I might serve them better, or at all.

How else can they live, poor creatures of the Father? The peasant has his few cows and pigs, his brief crops, but all must go to pay the landlord, every forkful of beef, every grain of oats, and he himself and his family must live on potatoes and milk. And he is fortunate, for worse there are who hold no land at all in the law's eyes, but crouch upon the mountainside or huddle near the bog. They travel with their spades to the hiring fairs, where they stand like slaves upon the block. In late winter, when the potatoes have been exhausted, they wander the roads to beg. And what of those who hold a bit of land but cannot meet the rent? A good landlord, like my dear friend Mr. Falkiner, will let it hang for a season or two, provided that he himself is solvent, but many landlords are mortgaged heavily to the Dublin banks and moneylenders and they too are pressed down by the system. Many others are not true landlords at all, but middlemen to whom the land has been set for reletting, and many of these employ the barbarous practice of the "rack rent." And there are many landlords great and small who, like Captain Cooper, when grazing proves more profitable than letting, will turn out his tenants to beg or starve upon the roads. I have myself seen families huddled in the sides of hills where they had hewn out holes, entire families, the small ones cowering and rooting beside the gaunt form of the woman.

A system more ingeniously contrived, first for the debasement, and then for the continuance in that debasement of an entire people, cannot easily be imagined. On this subject I lack both the eloquence and the lucidity of George Moore of Moore Hall, a most astonishing man to discover in such parts as these, being an historian of some note, enlightened and humane in his views, and a friend of Burke, Fox, Sheridan, and other notabilities. To attend to his acerb, sardonic voice as he discourses upon the ills of Ireland is to be confirmed in one's despair, for he has never a remedy to suggest. And yet despair is rightly held the one unforgivable sin, and I have striven mightily against it.

I have striven also to find common ground with this multitude, but with scant success. I except here Mr. Moore and also Thomas Treacy of Bridge-end House, for these are accounted gentlemen, and I have always regarded their Papistry as chivalrous adherence to a persecuted sect. And I except also, strange though this may seem, Mr. Hussey, the priest in Killala, for he is himself almost a gentleman, being the son of a prosperous grazier in the midlands. Often, it has seemed to me, he has been more dismayed than I am myself by the barbarous life and manners of those to whom he ministers. I sought, though, in my first year, to make the acquaintance of the scattering of Papist "half sirs," such men as Cornelius O'Dowd and Randall Mac-Donnell, but these two in particular, to speak bluntly, I found to be irreligious men, unless we account fidelity to whiskey, horses, and wanton women to be a form of devotion; and this sorry estimation of their characters was amply vindicated by the violent courses of action which they took in the events which I shall narrate. Beneath that level, of course, were farmers and servants who both understood and spoke English, indeed some who had mastered the art of writing it. But always, below the surface of our pleasant interchanges, I could feel the tremblings of the great chasm which separated us, as though we met to parley on the quaking face of a bog.

I propose to set forth in this narrative whatever I have learned of that singular and most unfortunate man, Owen Ruagh Mac-

Carthy. He once came to me at my bidding, for I wished to dispose of some books, and believed that he might make use of them in his "classical academy," a kind of hedge school in which children were given the rudiments of an education and older boys were prepared for the seminaries. I confess that I had my misgivings, for I had often seen him in the village, a tall, wild red-haired creature with a loping stride, notoriously given to drink and bad company. His earlier reputation was equally daunting, for it was said that he had wandered, or more exactly had been swept, northward from his native Kerry to Cork and thence through Clare and Galway into Mayo, flitting from troubles with the law, some said, but according to others pursued by posses of outraged fathers and husbands and brothers, for he could keep neither his eyes nor his hands from any woman of appropriate age and here his tastes were catholic in the nondenominational meaning of the term. And yet this was a man who possessed fluent Latin and had a good knowledge of Virgil, Horace, and Ovid. More astonishing yet, I have been informed by Treacy of Bridge-end House, a fanatic upon the supposed accomplishments of his race, that MacCarthy was a poet not lacking for fame, his verses being memorized and circulated in manuscript from Donegal to Kerry. I asked Treacy to render several of these into English for me, but he replied that the rhythm and meters, if such be the proper terms, could not be accommodated to English, so that words and sounds would be quarreling together like husband and wife, an instructive view into Irish attitudes toward matrimony.

At any event, and to end this digression, MacCarthy may for all one knows have been a second Ovid, but his words are locked forever within a barbarous language, which history has sentenced to silence and the plow. Upon this occasion, I assured him that I felt keenly the unhappy lot of his fellow countrymen, and suggested that this might somehow be improved if they were able to experience more completely the safeguards of English law. He responded with the verses of some other poet, which he then put into English for me, Treacy notwithstanding: "Troy and Rome have vanished; Caesar is dead and Alexander. Perhaps someday the English too will have their day."

I challenged him as to the meaning that he derived from this dark utterance, and he replied it meant only that Greece and Rome had once been empires, and England was now in its turn summoned to greatness. I told him that I did not for a minute suppose it to mean any such thing. Rather did it express the sullen vengefulness which the Irish peasantry notoriously nurse, and which, like their superstitions, distracts them from seeking proper and rational solutions to their problems. Then I reflected: What solutions? Well-meaning Protestant clergymen write books and tracts for them, urging them to dress neatly, when in fact they are half naked; to tell the truth, when only a lie will shield them from a rapacious landlord; to be sober, when the only comfort lies drowned in a bottle.

He then smiled at me, as though he had read my thoughts, and the smile altered his coarse, heavy features, suggesting a lively if sardonic intelligence. In an obvious effort to change the subject, he picked up a small book from the pile which I had set before him, a translation of Le Sage's romance of *Gil Blas.* "It is well I know this one, Your Reverence. I had it in the tail pocket of my coat when I was on my ramblings, years ago. No better book for the task." I discovered then that he had in fact a smattering of French, as was not uncommon, apparently, among the schoolmasters of his native Kerry, where there had earlier been much traffic with France. It was from Kerry and Cork that, until some ten years before, lads were shipped off to the seminaries at Douai and Saint-Omer or as recruits for the Irish brigades in the French army, and there was also a brisk smuggling trade. Not merely the last but all three of these enterprises were forbidden by law, but this seemed not to trouble MacCarthy at all. Herein may be discovered yet another sorry consequence of those abominable penal laws by which, for a century, the Papists were kept in a condition of semi-outlawry.

I found it curious in the extreme, this conjunction of *Gil Blas* and the French language with the coarse-molded cowherd who stood before me in his long-tailed coat of rain-colored frieze. Upon this occasion and those others when I talked with Mac-Carthy I was most favorably impressed by his transparent love of words and of books, though doubtless he apprehended these latter in a crabbed, provincial manner, and by his bearing, which was easy but at no time offensively familiar. And yet there was also about him something which did give me offense, a sly, slight mockery as though he knew, as well as I did myself, that we used the same words in quite different ways. How little we will ever know these people, locked as we are in our separate rooms. And often I have glimpsed him in another mood, stumbling drunkenly homeward, more beast than man, toward the bed he shared with some young slut of a widow. The course which he later followed saddened but did not surprise me. He dwelt deep within the world of his people, and theirs is an unpredictable and a violent world.

What most weighed down upon me in my first years in Mayo was that all seemed agreed, rich and poor alike, that the dreadful circumstances to which I have alluded were changeless, woven from a history of so thick a texture that it could never be pulled or tugged to a more acceptable shape. I am no manner of a radical. I know that the laws of human economy, like those of astronomy, are inexorable and strict. Yet I cannot escape the feeling that here these laws have been pulled awry, as comets and meteors are pulled down upon the earth. The poor we shall always have with us, but need we have them in such numbers, accounting at the very least for a simple majority of the population?

But the few remedies which have been proposed are more hideous than the disease which they affect to cure. Thus I have heard it proposed, by men no more inhumane than most, that the recurrent famines are Providential, and will in time bring down the population to a proper size, but this I hold to be blasphemy. Or, again, take the matter of the Whiteboys, which has its role to play in my narrative. For some thirty years these agrarian terrorists had been a scourge upon the land, ravaging countrysides, murdering bailiffs, maiming or killing cattle, pulling down the fences which enclose pastures, inflicting crude and loathsome punishment upon enemies and informers. In some few places their ambitions were satisfied; rents were lowered, or the expansion of grazing was halted. But in most, the Whiteboys were hunted down as stags and wolves are hunted, and were then destroyed. As destroyed they had to be, for civilization cannot abide such savagery. Famine or terror: what a fearful brace of proffered remedies!

And of what assistance is religion itself? I shall say little about the Church of the people. Doubtless it has been deformed and brutalized by the century or more of persecution which it has endured, and doubtless too it exercises a moderating influence upon its children, and yet I cannot profess to a great sympathy. Mr. Hussey, as I have remarked, is a man of education and good manners. Few sights were more ludicrous than that of Mr. Hussey in his silver-buckled shoes, picking his way into some cabin where his presence was required, all but holding his nose against the stench. In his chapel, which had been erected with the assistance of Mr. Falkiner and other of the more liberal-minded Protestant gentry, I believe that he inveighed steadily alike against Whiteboys and against the superstitious practices of his auditors. And yet far more typical of the Roman clergy was his curate, the egregious Murphy, the son of peasants and a peasant himself, a coarse, ignorant man, red-faced, young, stout, with the voice of a bull calf. Risen from the people, he could offer no example to them. And when the crisis fell upon us, he demonstrated that he shared to the full their darkest passions. Neither was he cleanly in his habits, and of his fondness for the bottle there is abundant evidence.

But of my own Church, what can I say, save that it is the Church of a governing garrison? My Church, unlike those in many other parishes, is well attended, and here I claim some credit for my sermons, which are not empty vaporizings upon obscure Scriptural texts, but are addressed to the daily business of life. And yet when I look to the bare white walls and slender windows, to the two battleflags which Mr. Falkiner's great-great-grandfather brought home from the wars of Marlborough, to the plaques erected to those who fell serving our sovereign on the fields of France and Flanders, when I look to my parishioners, stiff and erect as turkeycocks or conquistadors, then the troubling thought occurs to me that I am less minister to Christ's people than I am priest to a military cult, as Mithra was honored by the legions of Rome. Here, I think at such truant moments, is an outpost stationed in the land by the perpetual edicts of Elizabeth and James and Cromwell and William and charged to hold this land for our lord the King.

Why else does the Protestant gentry of Ireland send forth its young men into the British army and the army of the East India Company if not from an instinct bred in the bone, bred perhaps of childhoods of Sundays spent staring at battleflags? And yet one thing is certain: that if England advances upon a land with the sword, there follow soon after the arts and benefits of civilization, an orderly existence, security of person and property, education, just laws, true religion, and a hopeful view of man's lot on earth. Only here have we failed, in the very first land we entered, for reasons which were in part our fault and in part the fault of the natives. But I think it pernicious to rummage over the past, sorting out wrongs and apportioning guilts.

Perhaps I can see the more clearly for being English born and English bred and therefore not enmeshed by the ancient prides and hostilities of this land. Pride: above all else pride. For in the final quarter of the century, as the world knows, the Protestants of Ireland declared themselves to be a separate nation, owing allegiance to the King of England only in his capacity of King of Ireland. Nay, more, they had come to think themselves a separate people, neither English nor Irish, yet vowing the most utter loyalty to the British Crown, from which their rights, privileges,

possessions first flowed. A prodigious and ludicrous creature it
was, this "Nation of Ireland," from which the great mass of the
Irish were excluded upon the open ground of religion and the
covert ground of race. Its capital of Dublin was as fair a city as
these islands can boast, a city of warm, wine-colored bricks and
cool gray stones, dominated over by the severe, lovely lines of a
parliament house in which were seated the exclusively Protes-
tant representatives of an exclusively Protestant electorate. And
yet this vaunted independence was a mockery, for the governors
and administrators of the island were still appointed from Lon-
don, and the Parliament itself reeked with a corruption which
many of the purchased members scarcely deigned to conceal. I
yield to none in my admiration for Mr. Grattan and the other
"patriots" who labored to give Ireland true and honest gover-
nance, to reform Parliament, and above all, to stroke the chains
from their Papist fellow countrymen. And yet their efforts were
as futile as their oratory was glittering and enflowered.

We knew little of such matters in Mayo, and we cared less.
The interests of the landlords were well served in Parliament
by Dennis Browne, Lord Sligo's brother and High Sheriff of
the county, a clever and high-spirited man, bluff and hearty
when the occasion demanded, but with a mind as subtle and as
insinuating as mountain mist. If in these pages I shall have
much to say that is harsh in its judgment of Mr. Browne, I do
indeed believe that his love of Mayo is most sincere, although
it was to assume a terrible shape. I do confess that my feeble
understanding of these people falters entirely when it con-
fronts such families as the Brownes. Papists until well into the
eighteenth century, they retained their property by a variety of
ruses, and then, these being exhausted, they conformed to our
Protestant Church of Ireland. They, and they perhaps alone,
seem able to move at ease between our two worlds, great and
powerful personages in our Protestant world, yet the native
musicians and poets are made welcome by them, and songs and
poems are composed in their honor. Or were until very recent
years, for now the Brownes have a dark and somber reputation,

and for reasons that my narrative will make clear. If I could but understand the Brownes, I would understand much about the tangled roots of the past, its twisted loyalties and bloody memories. But I will never come to such understanding. The meanings of this land are shrouded from the eyes of strangers. Truth, like Viking treasure, lies buried in the bogs.

Boglands and rings of mountains sealed us off in Tyrawley, and left us facing the gray ocean. But by 1797, we knew that elsewhere in Ireland events were drifting toward rebellion. The wicked and seditious Society of United Irishmen, a band of unscrupulous city radicals in Dublin and Belfast, were bent upon an insurrection, and had chosen as their instrument an unnatural alliance of the Papist peasants of the south and the Presbyterian peasants of the north. Their agent abroad, the deist and madman Wolfe Tone, had secured the assistance of regicide France: the year before a formidable invasion fleet had been beaten back from the Kerry coast only by what the peasants called "the Protestant winds." Then, in the spring of 1798, we heard, aghast, of the dreadful rebellions in Wexford and Antrim, a murderous and insensate peasantry ravishing the countryside before being put down with great brutality. There followed then a dreadful pause, for although the rebellious counties had become vast charnel houses, the networks of the hellish conspiracy survived in the midlands and in parts of Munster. A second flotilla of invasion, it was said, was being assembled on the French coast, and Wolfe Tone hovered, a stormy petrel, above its masts. It is in this moment of dreadful pause that my narrative will open.

But all of this came to us as tidings from a different land. Our local corps of yeomanry, an exclusively Protestant body under the command of Captain Samuel Cooper, drilled more frequently, but less to defend our shores than to remind the Papist peasantry that the present order of things was changeless. There was first one, then several, then numerous instances of cattle maiming, by those calling themselves "the Whiteboys of Killala," but Whiteboyism was one of our old, familiar evils. The distant United Irishmen preached insurrection in the name of a desired "Republic of Ireland," but the word *republic* has no existence in the Irish tongue, and far less had the meaning of the word any existence in the minds of our peasantry. To be sure, there were some among the peasants, schoolmasters and tavern-keepers and the like, who, upon hearing of the Wexford rising, spoke in lofty terms of "the army of Gael." And many among the Protestants, in particular those of the more narrow and ignorant sort, spoke in fear and fury of a servile insurrection. But all was far distant from Mayo.

I have once and again sought to imagine myself as present in one of the taverns frequented by the peasantry, a low, vile cabin choking with smoke and rank with odors. Someone describes for those present the Wexford insurrection, not as the butchery which in fact it was, but as a glorious hosting of "the army of the Gael," with banners and bards, like a passage in Macpherson's Ossian poems. I seek to imagine in that setting the faces which I know only from roadside or field or stable, white skin, black hair, dark eyes. With what power would not the speaker's words burst upon such an assembly, for the native Irish, as has been remarked since the days of the Elizabethan Spenser, are easily overwhelmed by high-flown rhetoric. But imagination fails me. They are an alien people.

Once, at the home of Mr. Treacy, I heard Owen Ruagh Mac-Carthy recite his poetry. He was visiting the servants, and Treacy, being informed of this, brought him to the dinner table, where he stood before us and spoke a poem for which he was requited most generously with silver coins and two tumblers of brandy. It was of a kind called an *aisling,* Mr. Treacy informed me, a poem of vision, in which the poet, wandering in a meadow, encounters a maiden who speaks to him in cloaked and guarded terms of her present sorrows and prophesies some event of great good fortune for the Gaelic people—perhaps the Young Pretender sailing to the coast with swordsmen and casks of wine and French coins. The poem that night differed from others of its kind only in that it was not the Stuart Pretender who was invoked, but some nameless, cloudy deliverance. It is apparently a difficult and a metrically complex form, for all its conventionality, and MacCarthy's celebrity among other native poets was said to rest upon his mastery of its techniques. It was delivered with much florid vehemence of voice and body, but I do not pretend to admire what I cannot understand.

Leaving Bridge-end House some hours later, and walking toward the boy who held my horse, I passed the open door of one of the outbuildings, and again hearing MacCarthy's voice, I looked within. A number of the servants were gathered there, and MacCarthy, very drunk, was standing with one foot upon the bench. A girl was standing beside him, and his free arm was curved around her waist, his hand fondling her bosom. I needed no cicerone to explain to me the meaning of the song he was singing. As I rode off, the song ended, but the air was then filled with the sound of a violin, playing a most engaging air, very quick and lilting, as though for a dance.

Music and dance. What I have written must surely suggest a people cursed by Heaven, men sullenly in movement beneath a lowering sky. And yet most, were they to hear my words, would deny them utterly. For if the mind's eye perceives the grinding poverty, the ear of the mind hears music. No people on earth, I am persuaded, loves music so well, nor dance, nor oratory, though the music falls strangely upon my ears, and the eloquence is either in a language I cannot understand or else in an English stiff, bombastic, and ornate. More than once I have been at Mr. Treacy's when, at close of dinner, some traveling harper would be called in, blind as often as not, his fingernails kept long and the mysteries of his art hidden in their horny ridges. The music would come to us with the sadness of a lost world, each note a messenger sent wandering among the Waterford goblets. Riding home late at night, past tavern or alehouse, I would hear harps and violins, thudding feet rising to frenzy. I have seen them dancing at evening on fairdays, in meadows decreed by custom for such purposes, their bodies swift-moving, and their faces impassive but bright-eyed, intent. I have watched them in silence, reins held loosely in my hand, and have marveled at the stillness of my own body, my shoulders rigid and heavy.

Darkness hides them from me, and my sympathy is un-Christian and chill. We fear the unknown. Most earnestly do I wish to enter their lives, yet everywhere my wish is mocked, by Captain Cooper's complacent swagger, by the memory of Mac-Carthy's foot upon a bench, by a cabin bursting with music, by the thronging foreign faces at markets and fairdays, by dancers in a meadow, by the sounds of an alien speech. Yes, and by the very look of the land itself, the forbidding hills, the monotony of brown moorland, the small lakes set like watchful eyes upon the bog. It seems to me a land furiously guarding its meager secrets, gloating over its incomprehensibility. Whether it seems so to the people themselves, I cannot say. They are an ancient people, and possess an ancient knowledge which, because it falls short of wisdom, is frightening to a stranger.

And thus, in the narrative which I shall now commence, many of the actors come from a world which is recognizably my own, however altered by local conditions. Mr. Falkiner, my dear friend, might well be found in my native Derbyshire, arguing crops or politics with my brother. And Mr. Moore of Moore Hall would surely be more at home in London than in Mayo. Nor can England boast that it lacks such men as Captain Cooper, village Caesars and Hannibals, doughty captains of Sunday soldiers. But there my pen pauses, for one at least of Cooper's feet rests upon the bog. And when my thoughts move from him to the native Irish, to O'Dowd and to MacDonnell, to MacCarthy and above all to Ferdy O'Donnell, I feel them slipping toward the unknown, toward men whose actions and passions issue from that fearsome world of hillside and bog, choked with the petrified roots of the past. And beyond such men lies the multitudinous world of the peasantry, the dark sea which swept up upon us so suddenly that we were almost covered by its waves.

I shall nonetheless strive to present those events with such understanding of them as I have come to possess, and with an attempt at a strict impartiality. I fear in advance that I shall fail, for my knowledge of events is not matched by an understanding of their causes. But yet I hold it almost sinful not to seek after causes, the black roots of flowering passions. The rain has ceased to fall, and beneath a sky suddenly bright and almost cloudless, fields of a most intense green stretch northward toward the bay.

ERIC NEWBY

(1919–   )

> *In the autumn of 1985, more or less on the spur of the
> moment, we decided to go back to Ireland. We were
> not going to travel in the guise of sociologists, journal-
> ists or contemporary historians. We were not going
> there, we hoped, to be shot at. We were going there to
> enjoy ourselves, an unfashionable aspiration in the
> 1980s.*

*So begins Eric Newby's account of a bicycle tour of Ireland with his wife
and skeptical companion, Wanda. Loaded down with maps, long under-
wear, spare parts, and books, the Newbys set off at an unlikely time for a
bike trip—December. Predictably, they were lashed by storms, forced off
the road by aggressive lorries, beset by mechanical problems, and fueled
by Guinness. Although he comes dangerously close to being murdered by
Wanda, Newby never loses what one critic calls his "gusto."*

*Eric Newby has had many journeys. At nineteen he joined the four-
masted Finnish barque* Moshulu *and sailed in the last* Grain Race *from
Australia to Europe. Either on his own or as travel editor for the London*
Observer, *Newby is an indefatigable traveler. His accounts are literate,
sophisticated, but always buoyant. Newby has never lost his zest for
adventure. "Where others flutter on impressionistic wings, tread self-
consciously across unpeopled wastes, or muse lyrically and sometimes dis-
proportionately about the past," wrote Geoffrey Moorehouse in the
London* Times, *"Newby barges into everything with relish and mock-
ery in the very opposite of the grand manner."*

TO THE ARAN ISLANDS

from ROUND IRELAND IN LOW GEAR

The Islands of Aran (Ir. Ara-Naoimh, Ara of the Saints) are still believed by many of the peasantry to be the nearest land to the far-famed island of O'Brazil or Hy Brasail, the blessed paradise of the pagan Irish. It is supposed even to be visible from the cliffs on particular and rare occasions.

—*Murray's Handbook For*
Travellers in Ireland, 1912

As we worked out into the sound we began to meet another class of waves, that could be seen for some distance towering above the rest. When one of these came in sight, the first effort was to get beyond its reach. The steersman began crying out in Gaelic *"Siubhal, siubhal"* ("Run, run"), and sometimes, when the mass was gliding towards us with horrible speed, his voice rose to a shriek. Then the rowers themselves took up the cry, and the curragh seemed to leap and quiver with the frantic terror of a beast till the wave passed behind it or fell with a crash behind the stern.

—*J. M. Synge,* The Aran Islands

By the time we got back to Galway it was pouring with rain and the streets were almost deserted. We were ravenous. By a miracle we not only found a wine merchant's that was still open but also a shop in which the assistant sold us half a pound of delicious smoked salmon, soda bread, and butter, throwing in a lemon for luck, and allowed us to sit down and eat the lot on the premises, something that would be unthinkable in England.

Because of all this we felt a bit silly when we got back to Frenchville House to find that Mrs Robinson—whom may the Saints preserve—had prepared a substantial and delicious repast.

This we ate in the company of two mature and highly entertaining students from Dublin who had just returned from a long day's excursion to the shores of Lough Corrib on a couple of hired bikes and the air fairly rang with the "I tinks" and "I tought" of these hopes for the future of Ireland.

"I was doin' philosophy, den I heard that if I did Welsh it would be easier to get a good pass, so now I'm doin' Welsh," said one.

"Oim workin' to be a ship's radio operator, loike they had on the Titanic," said the other, "but by the toime I get me pass with luck there won't be any ships to operate in."

That evening some extra-sensory information was fed into Wanda's brain box informing her that the strawberries were ripe for picking back in the beds in Dorset and a telephone call to a friendly neighbour confirmed that this was so. We had agreed before setting out that in what seemed the unlikely event of them ever ripening, Wanda should return and set in train the manufacture of a year's supply of strawberry jam.

So on Tuesday morning, after bidding a melancholy farewell to Wanda (melancholy because I am of a gregarious nature), I set off alone in good time to catch the steamer to the Aran Islands. But nobody had bothered to tell me that the boat only sailed on Tuesdays to one island, Inishmore, so what followed was another *dies non,* the high point of which was putting my feet up that evening back at Mrs Robinson's and watching someone else's death throes in *Dynasty.*

On Wednesday I tried again. I got to the dock so early that there wasn't anyone in the ticket office to welcome me, take my money or clip my ticket, so I went aboard and waited. I must say

I hadn't expected luxury, having travelled this way twenty years before, but it did seem pretty sparse accommodation; there was no seating of any kind and a hellish wind blew through the whole boat, which on this dark, grey morning was more like a marine version of a house of horror than a passenger vessel. By around 08:45, with the boat due to sail at 09:00 and with no one else in sight, I began to experience sensations of unease. At 08:50 I went down into the deep-frozen bowels of the vessel where I eventually met an enormous ginger-headed man encased in bright orange plastic who informed me I was aboard not a passenger ship, but a deep-sea trawler which was about to leave for the Porcupine Bank, 180 miles out in the Atlantic, or thereabouts, where they would be fishing for prawns for an indefinite period. He went on to explain that the Aran steamer at this time of year left from quite another part of the docks, some 700 yards away round the opposite side of an eight-sided basin. As the gangway was so narrow that I had had to unload the bike completely to get it aboard, he very kindly helped me carry the bags ashore. I caught the boat, the *Naomh Eanna,* after the bow and stern lines had already been cast off.

There are three main Aran Islands, Inisheer, Inishmaan and Inishmore, and the boat called at all three. There were few other passengers and because the weather was still beastly most of us sat below in the austere bar/tea room, looking out through the portholes at the Burren, grey and ghostly away to port. I sat opposite a rather lugubrious islander who watched me with unblinking gaze while I put a shine on my camera lens, and finally asked me to take a picture of him. His reason for wanting me to do so was unusual. Some time previously he had picked up a bottle that had been thrown up on the foreshore of his island, which was Inishmaan, the middle island of the three. The bottle contained a message written by the barman of the Midships Bar on the QE2, which he had thrown overboard in mid-Atlantic. The islander now wanted to send him a likeness of himself that would, presumably, encourage him and other members of the crew and passengers to write more messages, seal them in bottles and throw them overboard in the hope that they, too, would be washed up on a beach at Inishmaan.

At this point the ship sailed out of the gloom that enveloped the Burren and the greater part of Galway Bay. The wind, instead of being easterly, was now warm and blew softly from the west-south-west and the sun shone down from a cloudless sky of the deepest imaginable blue. Summer had come. It was a day in a million. Another twenty minutes and the *Naomh Eanna* was lying off Inisheer. Apart from the lack of trees we might have been off Tahiti.

I had been here before, with Wanda, in the autumn of 1966. We had even travelled there in the same ship, or one that looked remarkably like it, which sailed to the islands twice a week, "weather and circumstances permitting" as the timetable stated, returning to Galway the same evening, just as it would today.

Of the islands, Inishmore was then the most developed for tourists and the most self-conscious; it was said that its people had never recovered from the pride of taking part in O'Fla-herty's film, *Man of Aran,* filmed there in 1934. At Kilronan, the principal town on Inishmore, passengers disembarked from the ship at a jetty, while on Inisheer and Inishmaan landings were made in *currachs.* On Inisheer the landing took place on a sandy beach and the chances of being weather-bound were less than on Inishmaan, the least visited of the group, where the landing place was a stone slip on the east side. On the ship we saw island people for the first time, returning after a few days on the main-land. Their shore-going clothes were unremarkable, although the women still wore the shawls which by then were a compara-tive rarity on the mainland. The men were mostly tall, and they gave the impression of being quiet people, speaking mostly in undertones.

We had planned to stay a week. There were no hotels and only the largest island, Inishmore, had guest houses; otherwise the only accommodation was in private houses and in the sum-mer months these were always very booked up. At that time, at the end of September twenty years ago, we had been told that we would find rooms but that we would have to be prepared to stay on one island only: in October the inhabitants began to lift the potato crop and were reluctant to cross the sounds to the other islands because they were too busy, and there were often dangerous shifts of wind. We had no idea on which island we wanted to stay, but the first stop was at Inisheer and when the ship lay off the shore and the *currachs* came racing out to her, as they did now, twenty years later, we found the place irresistible.

There was a storm beach with some vestiges of pale grass among the dunes and a settlement of low houses, most of them roofed with slate, some still thatched and others, roofless ruins. Behind the houses rose tiers of dry-stone walls which enclosed the "gardens" and the fields, and to the left, on a rock, was a fifteenth-century castle of the O'Briens, ruined by Cromwell's soldiers. There was a cemetery on a huge dune which concealed a prehistoric midden full of limpet shells and bones that had been broken for their marrow; and a long house from which donkeys were carrying quantities of *laminaria,* the long, sjambok-like sea-rods, down to the shore in sacks. They were ferried to the ship in *currachs,* and sold to iodine extraction factories on the mainland at £10 a ton.

The *currachs* are between 19 and 20 feet long. The hulls consist of a light framework of laths covered with tarred canvas; long ago they were made of cowhide. They have square counters and prows which turn up sharply, which are good in the surf. The oars are tapered, their laths almost bladeless, and they fit over a single thole pin, which enables them to be left unshipped in the water while the crew are fishing. Most of them have three oarsmen. They are very deep and can carry almost anything in good weather: up to twelve persons; more than a ton of potatoes; pigs, sheep, beds, mattresses, even tombstones. Larger livestock such as cows still have to swim to the ship when being embarked for the market at Galway, and very few actually drown. If one does inadvertently swallow a lot of water and looks about to sink, it is winched up by the hind legs and given the kiss of life on board. If that fails, its throat is cut and it is sold unofficially on the mainland, for meat. When fully loaded there is not much more than an inch of freeboard in the stern of a *currach*. Empty, they float like corks and are very volatile—too hard a pull on one oar is enough to send them spinning round and in inexpert hands they can be extremely dangerous.

Almost all the men in the boats at that time, young and old, wore the costume of the islands: very thick tweed trousers, split up the side seams so that they could be rolled up when the boats were launched through the surf, finger-braided woolen belts in colours made from natural dyes which ended in tassels, called *criosanna,* large tweed caps, thick indigo blue flannel shirts with stand-up collars and leg-of-mutton sleeves, and waistcoats made from a hairy, grey-blue tweed in which the ribbed pattern became more pronounced as the nap wore off. Some wore heel-less shoes of raw cowhide with the hair on the outside, which are very pliable when wet. Until recently all the wool for the flannel and the tweed had been woven at a mill in Galway, but the mill had been burned down and in 1966 the costume seemed doomed to die out in a few years, when any stocks of material on the islands had been exhausted.

When the pandemonium of the disembarkation through the surf had abated, the various goods and chattels had been carried away, and the *currachs* had been carried up the beach, upside down over the heads of rowers so that they looked like strange six-legged monsters, a peace descended on Inisheer that was to remain unbroken until the boat returned five days later.

The following day was Sunday. The people were all Irish-speaking and the Mass was in Irish. The men wore their uniform and sat or stood at the back of the church, the women and children were in the front. The older women wore deep, full red flannel skirts which they had dyed a shade of madder and which positively glowed in the pale autumn light. Some had shawls to match, or had rare brown ones from the Galway mainland that were beyond price. It was a wonderful sight to see, the costumes. When the Mass was over the young men and boys left first, the

old men and women last. Then the priest was rowed a couple of
miles across An Sunda Salach, otherwise Foul Sound, for the
service on Inishmaan.

Inisheer, only 1400 acres in area, is a table-land of bare sheets
of limestone slanting from north to south and dropping away
completely into the sea where the lighthouse stands. From it the
herculean labour of successive generations had removed millions
of stones, which had been piled up to form great cairns and
labyrinths of high dry-stone walls. In the thousands of stone
enclosures so formed, which acted as windbreaks, here and on
the other islands, the soil had been man-made too, by laying
down alternate levels of sand and seaweed ferried in panniers on
the backs of donkeys. The principal crop was potatoes (a boiled
Aran potato is one of the most delicious culinary treats), but
oats, cabbages and carrots were also grown. The grass was excel-
lent, which is why cattle fattened so well, and in October giant
daisies appeared in the fields. There were hardly any trees except
a few osiers, growing in sheltered places, which were used to
make baskets and panniers for the donkeys. There were no gates:
the walls were knocked down to let the animals in and out, after
which they were rebuilt. On the two smaller islands everything
was carried down the *boreens,* the little lanes that on the two
smaller islands run parallel to one another the length of them
from north to south. Everywhere were the remains of the kilns
in which seaweed was burned to make kelp, the rock-hard sub-
stance from which iodine is extracted, and the circular seaweed
stands and lengths of wall for drying the sea-rods.

Down at the south-western end of Inisheer near the light-
house, towards sunset, alone in this world of stone, 1650 miles
from St John's, Newfoundland, give or take a few miles, we
really felt that we had come to the end of the road so far as
Europe was concerned—at that time we had not ventured as far
west as the Great Blasket. For five days we stayed in a house in
Baile an Lurgain, one of the five villages on Inisheer and of the
twenty-six villages on the three islands, all of which have the
most intricate boundaries which were already in danger of

being forgotten. During this time I managed to wangle myself into a *currach* as a third member of the crew, having satisfactorily demonstrated that I was a fairly skilled oarsman, and went lobster-potting with them around the west side of the island. They had some good catches. The weather was calm so I shall never know now how good I would have been as one of the crew in bad weather. To prove what the sea can do in these parts was the wreck of the freighter *Plassy*, which went on the Carraig na Finnise reef in March 1960 and was later thrown high up on the shore, well above normal high tide level, where she remains to this day. What we both remember most about Inisheer was the intense cold in our bedroom. The only dishes we can recall were the amazing potatoes and the endless dollops of Birds custard.

Our host was an archetypal islander, very tall, with a large, long nose and grizzled straight hair, and he spoke *veery* slowly in beautiful English for our benefit, as if it was caviar not words he was dealing in. Every night we were there—there was no such thing as television on the island—he grilled me about New York, having heard that I had been there on several occasions, questioning me *veery, veery* slowly in his beautiful English, and *veery, veery* thoroughly. On the day we left he let us know that he had been janitor of a building on Lexington Avenue for something like fifteen years. I could gladly have murdered him.

In summer the islanders did well out of lobster fishing and tourism. In winter, even then, many of them were on the dole; but they had strong links with the United States (as I now well knew), to which many of them emigrated, and they had rent-free houses and a grant for speaking Irish, for this part of the world is regarded as one of the founts of the language. In fact it is thought they may be descended from an English garrison that was maintained there in the seventeenth century, but, nevertheless, must also have links with people who inhabited the islands much further back in time. Perhaps their lineage stretches back to when the Duns, the great stone forts of Aran, were built, the oldest in the Iron Age: Dun Aengus, Dun Oghil, Don Onact and Dubh Cathair (the Black Fort) on Inishmore; Dun

An Mothar and Dun Conor on Inishmaan; and Dun Forma on Inisheer. Or to the time when the churches, chapels and oratories of early Christian anchorites flourished, some of which are buried in the sand, and the holy wells, saints' beds of stone, caves, pillar stones, *clochans,* altars, cross slabs and monastic settlements. Notable among early Christians was St Eanna, otherwise Enda, the first to introduce monasticism in the severest sense of the word into Ireland. Here he lived and worked, giving St Brendan his blessing before he set off on his perilous voyage. And here he was buried in about 530, surrounded, it is said, by the 127 saints whom he had taught. Eanna's Household, Tighlagheany, is the holiest place in Aran, its great church surviving until it was destroyed by the Cromwellians.

Whatever their antecedents, the Islanders, at least the male ones, can be almost breathtakingly venal. On the day in October 1966 that we left Inisheer for the mainland it turned out that the only *currach* at that moment available to take us out to the ship was the one in which I had gone out fishing on several occasions with the two-man crew, with whom I had struck up what seemed a pleasant relationship. I had also treated them with considerable generosity in the pub each time we came ashore without, as I recall, ever being given a drink in return. In spite of this they now demanded something in the region of £5, which was at that time an outrageous sum, to take us 100 yards to the ship, which they did with the air of men who had never set eyes on either of us before. Not only this but our host, the ex-janitor from Lexington Avenue, who was down on the beach to see us off, did nothing whatever to dissuade them. There was nothing to do but pay up.

Altogether, at that time, the islanders were the envy of many people on the mainland who did not enjoy the same subsidies. They themselves, however, did not think themselves particularly lucky: "Ach," they used to say, in voices as soft as the wind, "that's how it goes."

*   *   *

NOW, IN 1986, things were different; but not all that differ-
ent. The skyline was the same, although there were now tractors
down on the beach and souvenir ships and craft shops, and a
craft kitchen, whatever that was, and a restaurant and two pubs
with shops attached, and a camping gas shop, and a public con-
venience and a camp site and an air strip with daily flights from
Galway city, and a co-operative weaving venture; and television
ruled the waves. A *currach* now cost £500; many of them were
fitted with outboards and you were still grossly overcharged to
ride in one. No one wore the costume anymore, as far as I could
see, with the exception of the caps. I didn't see a single donkey
but I expect they were there all right, working away up in the
boreens. I got my biggest shock as soon as I embarked in Galway,
on seeing the entire upper deck space of the ship forward was
taken up with plastic sacks filled with Dutch potatoes, bound for
Inishmore.

This was the week in which fishermen in eight *currachs* off
Inishmaan, wearing balaclavas and carrying sacks of stones, con-
fronted three Irish fishery protection vessels which were forced
to withdraw from the scene after their crews had been pelted
with stones "as there was a serious threat to life and limb." The
islanders were protesting against the confiscation of their illegal,
small mesh monofilament drift nets with which nearly 90 per
cent of all salmon reaching the Irish coast were being caught
and which the Western Regional Fisheries Manager described
as "a threat to salmon angling and spawning." One islander was
said to be earning £17,000 a year fishing from his *currach* with
these nets. Their right to fish was defended by the local curate,
Father Liam MacNally, who said that it was a question of sur-
vival for the Inishmaan men, who needed the summer salmon
and lobster season to put food in their children's mouths and
were entitled to use the best nets available. It was unfair, he said,
that large trawlers could put down three and four miles of drift
netting, while smaller, local boats were being interfered with.
When I left the dispute was still continuing.

Off Inishmaan we went through the whole paraphernalia of

putting passengers and freight ashore by *currach* and then loading up again—one *currach* put off for the shore with all the window frames for a house on board. Then we sailed on past what must be one of the most beautiful white sand beaches, the water turquoise in the shallows under a blazing sun. At 2:45 we berthed alongside the jetty at Kilronan on Inishmore, and really it looked just as attractive as it had all that time ago. There were still the horse-drawn carts to take you about the island and now a brisk business was being done in bike hire; but I had my own bike.

The Captain told me he was sailing at 4:45, even if I wasn't back, and I set off at a terrific rate to visit the greatest of the duns of Aran, Dun Aengus, using the Shimano oval chainwheels to some effect and glad, really, that Wanda wasn't there to be told that she was in the seventies gearwise when she urgently needed to be in the thirties. For the last part of the way you cannot ride even a mountain bike, so I left mine in a ditch and continued on foot. I'd decided I wasn't mad about mountain bikes. When you get to an Irish version of Kilimanjaro you have to carry them anyway.

To attempt to write about Dun Aengus and bring some sort of freshness to it is rather like trying to perform a similar service for Stonehenge: so many people have attempted it before that one is tempted to give up. What one is looking at is not only one of the wonders of Ireland, but of the entire western world. It is the greatest of the Irish stone forts; George Petrie, the nineteenth-century Irish landscape painter and antiquary, thought it "the most magnificent barbaric monument now extant in Europe" when he visited it in 1821.

It stands on the edge of a sheer 270-foot cliff which overhangs the sea, on a sheet of the bare limestone of which the islands are composed. Approaching it along the one road that spans the entire length of Inishmore it loomed on the skyline to the west, a sombre cyclopean mass with a single cyclopean eye, an entrance gateway through which the light of day was shining.

The walls are dry-stone, built of unworked blocks laid in

courses, some of them up to 7 feet long. I went through the now ruined outer walls into an enormous enclosure, the first of three, all roughly concentric, the innermost of which is the citadel. In this first enclosure one is faced with what looks like a dense forest of fossilized tree stumps up to 3 feet high which seem to grow from the living rock or else sprout from the wall in which they have been immovably planted. This abbatis, or *cheval-de-frise* (although the use of cavalry at such a time and in such a situation can scarcely have been envisaged) extends outwards from the wall for a distance of 80 feet in some places and beyond this are the remains of other walls, which formed outworks. Through these defences a sloping pathway leads into the second, middle enclosure through a gateway surmounted by a huge lintel stone. Beyond this middle enclosure is the citadel, an astonishing construction with walls 18 feet high in places and nearly 13 feet thick. All the walls have terraces, reached by steep flights of steps. A low gateway leads into the heart of Dun Aengus, which one would expect to be a claustrophobic enclosure, hemmed in as it is on all sides, with perhaps an Irish version of the Minotaur roaming in it. In fact there is nothing. Just the enclosure, with the walls terminating at the edge of the great cliff, and below and beyond it to the Atlantic, stretching away to what the islanders believed was Hy Brasil, the enchanted island of the west.

Back on board, everyone sunbathed on deck until Black Head on the coast of County Clare was abeam and there we once more entered the realms of rain and suicidal darkness. Fortunately, it was only necessary to look astern to see the islands still swimming in a glittering sea to remember that the day had not been simply some extravagant dream.

WILLIAM MAKEPEACE THACKERAY
(1811–1863)

Novelist, satirist, and travel writer, William Makepeace Thackeray was born in India, studied in England, tried his hand at art in Paris, met Goethe in Germany, and dabbled in law and journalism. He might have continued the life of a dilettante, but his family money was lost in the Indian bank collapse of 1833 and his mentally unstable Anglo-Irish wife was institutionalized. Thackeray was thus forced to make his living as a popular writer.

Thackeray's first works were sketches and reviews, often written under the pseudonyms "Charles James Yellowplush" or "Michael Angelo Titmarsh" or "George Savage Fitz-Boodle." After the publication of his first real novel, Barry Lyndon, *Thackeray turned to travel writing, producing* The Paris Sketchbook *(1840),* The Irish Sketchbook *(1843), and* Notes of a Journey from Cornhill to Grand Cairo *(1846).*

Overshadowed by his contemporary, Charles Dickens, with whom he feuded, Thackeray built his reputation on his novel Vanity Fair. *But his travel writing—now almost forgotten—also displays his skill in vivid characterization, humor, and irony.*

FROM GALWAY TO BALLINAHINCH

from THE IRISH SKETCHBOOK

The Clifden car, which carries the Dublin letters into the heart of Connemara, conducts the passenger over one of the most wild and beautiful districts that it is ever the fortune of a traveller to examine; and I could not help thinking, as we passed through it, at how much pains and expense honest English cockneys are to go and look after natural beauties far inferior, in countries which, though more distant, are not a whit more strange than this one. No doubt, ere long, when people know how easy the task is, the rush of London tourism will come this way: and I shall be very happy if these pages shall be able to awaken in one bosom beating in Tooley Street or the Temple the desire to travel towards Ireland next year.

After leaving the quaint old town behind us, and ascending one or two small eminences to the northwestward, the traveller, from the car, gets a view of the wide sheet of Lough Corrib shining in the sun, as we saw it, with its low dark banks stretching round it. If the view is gloomy, at least it is characteristic: nor are we delayed by it very long; for though the lake stretches northwards into the very midst of the Joyce country (and is there in the close neighborhood of another huge lake, Lough Mask, which again is near to another sheet of water), yet from this road henceforth, after keeping company with it for some five miles, we only get occasional views of it, passing over hills and through trees, by many rivers and smaller lakes, which are dependent upon that of Corrib. Gentlemen's seats, on the road from Galway to Moycullen, are scattered in great profusion. Perhaps there is grass growing on the gravel-walk, and the iron gates of the tumble-down old lodges are rather rickety; but, for all that, the places look comfortable, hospitable, and spacious. As for the shabbiness and want of finish here and there, the English eye grows quite accustomed to it in a month: and I find the bad condition of the Galway houses by no means so painful as that of the places near Dublin. At some of the lodges, as we pass, the mail car-man, with a warning shout, flings a bag of letters. I saw a little party looking at one which lay there in the road crying, "Come, take me!" but nobody cares to steal a bag of letters in this country, I suppose, and the car-man drove on without any alarm. Two days afterwards a gentleman with whom I was in company left on a rock his book of fishing-flies; and I can assure you there was a very different feeling expressed about the safety of *that*.

In the first part of the journey, the neighborhood of the road seemed to be as populous as in other parts of the country: troops of red-petticoated peasantry peering from their stone-cabins; yelling children following the car, and crying, "Lash, lash!" It was Sunday, and you would see many a white chapel among the green bare plains to the right of the road, the court-yard blackened with a swarm of cloaks. The service seems to continue (on the part of the people) all day. Troops of people issuing from the chapel met us at Moycullen; and ten miles farther on, at Oughterard, their devotions did not yet seem to be concluded.

A more beautiful village can scarcely be seen than this. It stands upon Lough Corrib, the banks of which are here, for once at least, picturesque and romantic: and a pretty river, the Feogh, comes rushing over rocks and by woods until it passes the town and meets the lake. Some pretty buildings in the village stand on each bank of this stream: a Roman Catholic chapel with a curate's neat lodge; a little church on one side of it, a fine court-house of gray stone on the other. And here it is that we get into the famous district of Connemara, so celebrated in Irish stories, so mysterious to the London tourist. "It presents itself," says the guide-book, "under every possible combination of heathy moor, bog, lake, and mountain. Extensive mossy plains and wild pastoral valleys lie embosomed among the mountains, and support numerous herds of cattle and horses, for which the district has been long celebrated. These wild solitudes, which occupy by far the greater part of the centre of the country, are held by a hardy and ancient race of grazing farmers, who live in a very primitive state, and, generally speaking, till little beyond what supplies their immediate wants. For the first ten miles the country is comparatively open; and the mountains on the left, which are not of great elevation, can be distinctly traced as they rise along the edge of the heathy plain.

"Our road continues along the Feogh river, which expands itself into several considerable lakes, and at five miles from

Oughterard we reach Lough Bofin, which the road also skirts. Passing in succession Lough-a-Preaghan, the lakes of Anderran and Shindella, at ten miles from Oughterard we reach Slyme and Lynn's Inn, or Half-way House, which is near the shore of Loughonard. Now, as we advance toward the group of Binabola, or the Twelve Pins, the most gigantic scenery is displayed."

But the best guide-book that ever was written cannot set the view before the mind's eye of the reader, and I won't attempt to pile up big words in place of these wild mountains, over which the clouds as they passed, or the sunshine as it went and came, cast every variety of tint, light, and shadow; nor can it be expected that long, level sentences, however smooth and shining, can be made to pass as representations of those calm lakes by which we took our way. All one can do is to lay down the pen and ruminate, and cry, "Beautiful!" once more; and to the reader say, "Come and see!"

Wild and wide as the prospect around us is, it has somehow a kindly, friendly look; differing in this from the fierce loneliness of some similar scenes in Wales that I have viewed. Ragged women and children come out of rude stone-huts to see the car as it passes. But it is impossible for the pencil to give due raggedness to the rags, or to convey a certain picturesque mellowness of color that the garments assume. The sexes, with regard to raiment, do not seem to be particular. There were many boys on the road in the national red petticoat, having no other covering for their lean brown legs. As for shoes, the women eschew them almost entirely; and I saw a peasant trudging from Mass in a handsome scarlet cloak, a fine blue-cloth gown, turned up to show a new lining of the same color, and a petticoat quite white and neat—in a dress of which the cost must have been at least £10; and her husband walked in front carrying her shoes and stockings.

The road had conducted us for miles through the vast property of the gentleman to whose house I was bound, Mr. Martin, the Member for the county; and the last and prettiest part of the journey was round the Lake of Ballinahinch, with tall mountains rising immediately above us on the right, pleasant woody hills on the opposite side of the lake, with the roofs of the houses rising above the trees; and in an island in the midst of the water a ruined old castle cast a long white reflection into the blue waters where it lay. A land-pirate used to live in that castle, one of the peasants told me, in the time of "Oliver Cromwell." And a fine fastness it was for a robber, truly; for there was no road through these wild countries in his time—nay, only thirty years since, this lake was at three days' distance of Galway. Then comes the question, What, in a country where there were no roads and no travellers, and where the inhabitants have been wretchedly poor from time immemorial—what was there for the land-pirate to rob? But let us not be too curious about times so early as those of Oliver Cromwell. I have heard the name many times from the Irish peasant, who still has an awe of the grim, resolute Protector.

The builder of Ballinahinch House has placed it to command a view of a pretty melancholy river that runs by it, through many green flats and picturesque rocky grounds; but from the lake it is scarcely visible. And so, in like manner, I fear it must remain invisible to the reader too, with all its kind inmates, and frank, cordial hospitality; unless he may take a fancy to visit Galway himself, when, as I can vouch, a very small pretext will make him enjoy both.

It will, however, be only a small breach of confidence to say that the major-domo of the establishment (who has adopted accurately the voice and manner of his master, with a severe dignity of his own which is quite original), ordered me on going to bed "not to move in the morning till he called me," at the same time expressing a hearty hope that I should "want nothing more that evening." Who would dare, after such peremptory orders, not to fall asleep immediately, and in this way disturb the repose of Mr. J——n M——ll——y?

There may be many comparisons drawn between English and Irish gentlemen's houses; but perhaps the most striking point of difference between the two is the immense following of the

Irish house, such as would make an English housekeeper crazy almost. Three comfortable, well-clothed, good-humored fellows walked down with me from the car, persisting in carrying one a bag, another a sketching-stool, and so on. Walking about the premises in the morning, sundry others were visible in the court-yard and near the kitchen-door. In the grounds a gentleman, by name Mr. Marcus C——rr, began discoursing to me regarding the place, the planting, the fish, the grouse, and the Master; being himself, doubtless, one of the irregulars of the house. As for maids, there were half a score of them scurrying about the house; and I am not ashamed to confess that some of them were exceedingly good-looking. And if I might venture to say a word more, it would be respecting Connemara breakfasts; but this would be an entire and flagrant breach of confidence, and, to be sure, the dinners were just as good.

One of the days of my three days' visit was to be devoted to the lakes; and, as a party had been arranged for the second day after my arrival, I was glad to take advantage of the society of a gentleman staying in the house, and ride with him to the neighboring town of Clifden.

The ride thither from Ballinahinch is surprisingly beautiful; and as you ascend the high ground from the two or three rude stone-huts which face the entrance-gates of the house, there are views of the lakes and the surrounding country which the best parts of Killarney do not surpass, I think; although the Connemara lakes do not possess the advantage of wood which belongs to the famous Kerry landscape.

But the cultivation of the country is only in its infancy as yet, and it is easy to see how vast its resources are, and what capital and cultivation may do for it. In the green patches among the rocks, and on the mountain-sides, wherever crops were grown, they flourished; plenty of natural wood is springing up in various places; and there is no end to what the planter may do, and to what time and care may effect. The carriage-road to Clifden is but ten years old; as it has brought the means of communication into the country, the commerce will doubtless follow it;

and in fact, in going through the whole kingdom, one can't but be struck with the idea that not one hundredth part of its capabilities are yet brought into action, or even known perhaps, and that, by the easy and certain progress of time, Ireland will be poor Ireland no longer.

For instance, we rode by a vast green plain, skirting a lake and river, which is now useless almost for pasture, and which a little draining will convert into thousands of acres of rich productive land. Streams and falls of water dash by everywhere—they have only to utilize this water-power for mills and factories—and hard by are some of the finest bays in the world, where ships can deliver and receive foreign and home produce. At Roundstone especially, where a little town has been erected, the bay is said to be unexampled for size, depth, and shelter; and the Government is now, through the rocks and hills on their wild shore, cutting a coast-road to Bunown, the most westerly part of Connemara, whence there is another good road to Clifden. Among the charges which the "Repealers" bring against the Union, they should include at least this: they would never have had these roads but for the Union: roads which are as much at the charge of the London tax-payer as of the most ill-used Milesian in Connaught.

A string of small lakes follow the road to Clifden, with mountains on the right of the traveller for the chief part of the way. A few figures at work in the bog-lands, a red petticoat passing here and there, a goat or two browsing among the stones, or a troop of ragged whity-brown children who came out to gaze at the car, form the chief society on the road. The first house at the entrance to Clifden is a gigantic poorhouse—tall, large, ugly, comfortable; it commands the town, and looks almost as big as every one of the houses therein. The town itself is but of a few years' date, and seems to thrive in its small way. Clifden Castle is a fine château in the neighborhood, and belongs to another owner of immense lands in Galway—Mr. D'Arcy.

Here a drive was proposed along the coast to Bunown, and I was glad to see some more of the country, and its character.

Nothing can be wilder. We passed little lake after lake, lying a few furlongs inwards from the shore. There were rocks everywhere, some patches of cultivated land here and there, nor was there any want of inhabitants along this savage coast. There were numerous cottages, if cottages they may be called, and women, and above all, children in plenty.

At length we came in sight of a half-built edifice which is approached by a rocky, dismal, gray road, guarded by two or three broken gates, against which rocks and stones were piled, which had to be removed to give an entrance to our car. The gates were closed so laboriously, I presume, to prevent the egress of a single black consumptive pig, far gone in the family-way—a teeming skeleton—that was cropping the thin, dry grass that grew upon a round hill which rises behind this most dismal castle of Bunown.

If the traveller only seeks for strange sights, this place will repay his curiosity. Such a dismal house is not to be seen in all England: or, perhaps, such a dismal situation. The sea lies before and behind; and on each side, likewise, are rocks and copper-colored meadows, by which a few trees have made an attempt to grow. The owner of the house had, however, begun to add to it; and there, unfinished, is a whole apparatus of turrets, and staring raw stone and mortar, and fresh ruinous carpenters' work. And then the court-yard!—tumbled-down out-houses, staring empty pointed windows, and new-smeared plaster cracking from the walls—a black heap of turf, a mouldy pump, a wretched old coal-scuttle, emptily sunning itself in the midst of this cheerful scene! There was an old Gorgon who kept the place, and who was in perfect unison with it: Venus herself would become bearded, blear-eyed, and haggard, if left to be the housekeeper of this dreary place.

In the house was a comfortable parlor, inhabited by the priest, who has the painful charge of the district. Here were his books and his breviaries, his reading-desk with the cross engraved upon it, and his portrait of Daniel O'Connell the Liberator to grace the walls of his lonely cell. There was a dead crane hanging at the door on a gaff: his red fish-like eyes were staring open, and his eager grinning bill. A rifle-ball had passed through his body. And this was doubtless the only game about the place; for we saw the sportsman who had killed the bird hunting vainly up the round hill for other food for powder. This gentleman had had good sport, he said, shooting seals upon a neighboring island, four of which animals he had slain.

Mounting up the round hill, we had a view of the Sline Lights—the most westerly point in Ireland.

Here too was a ruined sort of summer-house, dedicated "DEO HIBERNIÆ LIBERATORI." When these lights were put up, I am told the proprietor of Bunown was recommended to apply for compensation to Parliament, inasmuch as there would be no more *wrecks* on the coast: from which branch of commerce the inhabitants of the district used formerly to derive a considerable profit. Between these Sline Lights and America nothing lies but the Atlantic. It was beautifully blue and bright on this day, and the sky almost cloudless; but I think the brightness only made the scene more dismal, it being of that order of beauties which cannot bear the full light, but require a cloud or a curtain to set them off to advantage. A pretty story was told me by the gentleman who had killed the seals. The place where he had been staying for sport was almost as lonely as this Bunown, and inhabited by a priest too—a young, lively, well-educated man. "When I came here first," the priest said, *"I cried for two days"*: but afterward he grew to like the place exceedingly, his whole heart being directed toward it, his chapel, and his cure. Who would not honor such missionaries—the virtue they silently practice, and the doctrines they preach? After hearing that story, I think Bunown looked not quite so dismal, as it is inhabited, they say, by such another character. What a pity it is that John Tuam, in the next county of Mayo, could not find such another hermitage to learn modesty in, and forget his Graceship, his Lordship, and the sham titles by which he sets such store.

A moon as round and bright as any moon that ever shone, and riding in a sky perfectly cloudless, gave us a good promise of a fine day for the morrow, which was to be devoted to the lakes in the neighborhood of Ballinahinch: one of which, Lough Ina, is said to be of exceeding beauty. But no man can speculate upon Irish weather. I have seen a day beginning with torrents of rain that looked as if a deluge was at hand, clear up in a few minutes, without any reason, and against the prognostications of the glass and all other weather-prophets. So in like manner, after the astonishingly fine night, there came a villainous dark day: which, however, did not set in fairly for rain, until we were an hour on our journey, with a couple of stout boatmen rowing us over Ballinahinch Lake. Being, however, thus fairly started, the water began to come down, not in torrents certainly, but in that steady, creeping, insinuating mist, of which we scarce know the luxury in England; and which, I am bound to say, will wet a man's jacket as satisfactorily as a cataract would do.

It was just such another day as that of the famous stag-hunt at Killarney, in a word; and as, in the first instance, we went to see the deer killed, and saw nothing thereof, so, in the second case, we went to see the landscape with precisely the same good fortune. The mountains covered their modest beauties in impenetrable veils of clouds; and the only consolation to the boat's crew was, that it was a remarkably good day for trout-fishing—which amusement some people are said to prefer to the examination of landscapes however beautiful.

O you who laboriously throw flies in English rivers, and catch, at the expiration of a hard day's walking, casting, and wading, two or three feeble little brown trouts of two or three ounces in weight, how would you rejoice to have put an hour's sport in Derryclear or Ballinahinch; where you have but to cast, and lo! a big trout springs at your fly, and, after making a vain struggling, splashing, and plunging for a while, is infallibly landed in the net and thence into the boat. The single rod in the boat caught enough fish in an hour to feast the crew, consisting of five persons, and the family of a herd of Mr. Martin's who has a pretty cottage on Derryclear Lake, inhabited by a cow and its calf, a score of fowls, and I don't know how many sons and daughters.

Having caught enough trout to satisfy any moderate appetite, like true sportsmen the gentlemen on board our boat became eager to hook a salmon. Had they hooked a few salmon, no doubt they would have trolled for whales, or for a mermaid; one of which finny beauties the waterman swore he had seen on the shore of Derryclear—he with Jim Mullen being above on a rock, the mermaid on the shore directly beneath them, visible to the middle, and as usual "racking her hair." It was fair hair, the boatman said; and he appeared as convinced of the existence of the mermaid as he was of the trout just landed in the boat.

In regard of mermaids, there is a gentleman living near Killala Bay, whose name was mentioned to me, and who declares solemnly that one day, shooting on the sands there, he saw a mermaid, and determined to try her with a shot. So he drew the small charge from his gun and loaded it with ball—that he always had for him for seal-shooting—fired, and hit the mermaid through the breast. The screams and moans of the creature—whose person he describes most accurately—were the most horrible, heart-rending noises that he ever, he said, heard; and not only were they heard by him, but by the fishermen along the coast, who were furiously angry against Mr. A——n, because, they said, the injury done to the mermaid would cause her to drive all the fish away from the bay for years to come.

But we did not, to my disappointment, catch a glimpse of one of these interesting beings, nor of the great sea-horse which is said to inhabit these waters, nor of any fairies (of whom the stroke-oar, Mr. Marcus, told us not to speak, for they didn't like bein' spoken of); nor even of a salmon, though the fishermen produced the most tempting flies. The only animal of any size that was visible we saw while lying by a swift black river that comes jumping with innumerable little waves into Derryclear, and where the salmon are especially suffered to "stand": this animal was an eagle—a real wild eagle, with gray wings and a white

head and belly: it swept round us, within gunshot reach, once or
twice, through the leaden sky, and then settled on a gray rock
and began to scream its shrill ghastly aquiline note.

The attempts on the salmon having failed, the rain continu-
ing to fall steadily, the herd's cottage before named was resorted
to: when Marcus, the boatman, commenced forthwith to gut
the fish, and taking down some charred turf-ashes from the glaz-
ing fire, on which about a hundredweight of potatoes were
boiling, he—Marcus—proceeded to grill on the floor some of
the trout, which we afterwards ate with immeasurable satisfac-
tion. They were such trouts as, when once tasted, remain forever
in the recollection of a commonly grateful mind—rich, flaky,
creamy, full of flavor. A Parisian *gourmand* would have paid ten
francs for the smallest *cooleen* among them; and, when trans-
ported to his capital, how different in flavor would they have
been!—how inferior to what they were as we devoured them,
fresh from the fresh waters of the lake, and jerked as it were from
the water to the gridiron! The world had not had time to spoil
those innocent beings before they were gobbled up with pepper
and salt, and missed, no doubt, by their friends. I should like to
know more of their *"set."* But enough of this: my feelings over-
power me: suffice it to say, they were red or salmon trouts—
none of your white-fleshed brown-skinned river fellows.

When the gentlemen had finished their repast, the boatmen
and the family set to work upon the ton of potatoes, a number
of the remaining fish, and a store of other good things; then we
all sat round the turf-fire in the dark cottage, the rain coming
down steadily outside, and veiling everything except the shrubs
and verdure immediately about the cottage. The herd, the herd's
wife, and a nondescript female friend, two healthy young herds-
men in corduroy rags, the herdsman's daughter paddling about
with bare feet, a stout black-eyed wench with her gown over her
head and a red petticoat not quite so good as new, the two boat-
men, a badger just killed and turned inside out, the gentlemen,
some hens cackling and flapping about among the rafters, a calf
in a corner cropping green meat and occasionally visited by the

cow her mamma, formed the society of the place. It was rather a strange picture; but as for about two hours we sat there, and maintained an almost unbroken silence, and as there was no other amusement but to look at the rain, I began, after the enthusiasm of the first half-hour, to think that after all London was a bearable place, and that for want of a turf-fire and a bench in Connemara, one *might* put up with a sofa and a newspaper in Pall Mall.

This, however, is according to tastes; and I must say that Mr. Marcus betrayed a most bitter contempt for all cockney tastes, awkwardness, and ignorance: and very right too. The night, on our return home, all of a sudden cleared; but though the fishermen, much to my disgust—at the expression of which, however, the rascals only laughed—persisted in making more casts for trout, and trying back in the dark upon the spots which we had visited in the morning, it appeared the fish had been frightened off by the rain; and the sportsmen met with such indifferent success that at about ten o'clock we found ourselves at Ballinahinch. Dinner was served at eleven, and, I believe, there was some whiskey-punch afterwards, recommended medicinally and to prevent the ill effects of the wetting: but that is neither here nor there.

The next day the petty sessions were to be held at Roundstone, a little town which has lately sprung up near the noble bay of that name. I was glad to see some specimens of Connemara litigation, as also to behold at least one thousand beautiful views that lie on the five miles of road between the town and Ballinahinch. Rivers and rocks, mountains and sea, green plains and bright skies, how (for the hundred-and-fiftieth time) can pen-and-ink set you down? But if Berghem could have seen those blue mountains, and Karel Dujardin could have copied some of these green, airy plains, with their brilliant little colored groups of peasants, beggars, horsemen, many an Englishman would know Connemara upon canvas as he does Italy or Flanders now.

ANTHONY TROLLOPE

(1815–1882)

Anthony Trollope's mother, Frances, rescued the family fortunes by starting a career in travel writing when she was fifty-two. Her Domestic Manners of the Americans *was a best-seller and lifted the family out of genteel poverty. She wrote forty books in the next twenty-five years and inspired the writing careers of two of her six children, Anthony and Thomas.*

Initially, Anthony Trollope showed little inclination for a literary career. He left school at nineteen and became a civil servant. At twenty-six he volunteered to go to Ireland and ended up organizing the district postal service, a job of importance that involved national and international travel. Trollope married an Irish girl and wrote his first novel, The Macdermots of Ballycloran *(1847), from which this excerpt is taken. After more than fifteen years in Ireland, Trollope returned to Britain and settled there for the rest of his life.*

The Macdermots of Ballycloran *is the story of a doomed Irish family. Trollope's second novel, a historical romance,* The Kellys and the O'Kellys, *was also set in Ireland. It was not until his novels about the fictional "Barsetshire" (*The Warden, Barchester Towers, Doctor Thorne, *and others) that he achieved real success. Fifty more books followed—novels, short stories, and travel books. Trollope's Irish novels, not as well recognized as those set in England, are notable as the work of a young writer and early chronicler of Irish life.*

from THE MACDERMOTS OF BALLYCLORAN

In the autumn, 184——, business took me into the West of Ire-
land, and, amongst other places, to the quiet little village of
Drumsna, which is in the province of Connaught, county of
Leitrim, about 72 miles w. n. w. of Dublin, on the Mail Coach
Road to Sligo. I reached the little inn there in the morning by
the said Mail; my purpose being to leave it late in the evening by
the Day Coach, and as my business was but of short duration, I
was left, after an early dinner, to amuse myself. Now in such a
situation, to take a walk is all the brightest man can do, and the
dullest always does the same. There is a kind of gratification in
seeing what one has never seen before, be it ever so little worth
seeing, particularly if the chances be, that it will never be seen
again; and in going where one has never been before, and
whither one will never return. Now Drumsna itself is on a bend
in the Shannon; the street leads down to a bridge, passing over
which we find ourselves in the County Roscommon, and the
road runs by the well wooded demesne of Sir G—— K——;
moreover, here is a beautiful little hill, from which the demesne,
river, bridge and village can all be seen; and what farther agré-
mens could be wanted to make a pretty walk than these things?
but alas! I knew not of their existence then. One cannot ask the
maid at an inn to show you which way to find the beauties of
nature; so, trusting to myself, I went directly away from river,
woods, and all; along as dusty, ugly, and disagreeable a road, as is
to be found in any County in Ireland.

After proceeding a mile or so, taking two or three turns to
look for improvement, I began to perceive evident signs on the

part of the road, of retrograding into lane-ism; the county had
evidently deserted it, and though made for cars and coaches, its
traffic now appeared confined to donkeys carrying turf home
from the bog, in double kishes on their back: presently the frag-
ments of a bridge presented themselves, but they too were
utterly fallen away from their palmy days, and now afforded but
indifferent stepping-stones, over a bog stream, which ran, or
rather crept, across the road. These, however, I luckily traversed,
and was rewarded by finding a broken down entrance to a kind
of wood on the right hand. In Ireland, particularly in the poorer
parts—to rank among which, County Leitrim has a right which
will not be disputed—a few trees together are always the recog-
nised sign of a demesne, of a gentleman's seat, or the place
where a gentleman's seat has been, and I directly knew that this
must be a demesne. But ah! how impoverished, if one might
judge from outward appearances. Two brick pillars, from which
the outside plaster had peeled off, and the coping fallen, gave
evidence of former gates; the space was closed up with a loose
built wall, but on the outer side of each post was a little well
worn foot path, made of soft bog mould. I of course could not
resist such temptation, and entered the demesne. The road was
nearly covered with that short dry grass, which stones seem to
throw up, when no longer polished by the wealthier portion of
man or brutekind.

About thirty feet from the gap, a tall fir had half fallen, and
lay across the road; you would have to stoop to walk under it; it
was a perfect barrier to any equipage, however humble, and the
roots had nearly refixed themselves in their reversed position,
showing that the tree had evidently been in that fallen state for
years.

The usual story, thought I, of Connaught gentlemen; an
extravagant landlord, reckless tenants, debt, embarrassment,
despair and ruin. Well, I walked up the deserted avenue, and
very shortly found myself in front of the house. Oh, what a pic-
ture of misery, of useless expenditure, unfinished pretence and
premature decay.

The house was two stories high, with large stone steps up to the front door, with four windows in the lower, and six in the upper story, and an area with kitchens, &c. below. The entire roof was off; one could see the rotting joists and beams, some fallen, some falling, the rest ready to fall, like the skeleton of a felon left to rot on an open gibbet. The stone steps had nearly dropped through into the area, the rails of which had been wrenched up. The knocker was still on the door; a large modern lion-headed knocker; but half the door was gone; on creeping to the door-sill, I found about six feet of the floor of the hall gone also—stolen for fire wood. But the joists of the flooring were there, and the whitewash of the walls shewed that but a few, a very few years back, the house had been inhabited. I leaped across the gulph, at great risk of falling into the cellar, and reached the bottom of the stairs; here my courage failed me; all was so damp and so rotten that was left, so much had been gradually taken away, that I did not dare go up: the doors on the ground floor would not open; the ceiling above me was all gone, and I could see the threatening timbers of the roof, which seemed only hanging till they had an opportunity of injuring some one by their fall. I crept out of the demi-door again, and down the ruined steps, and walked round the mansion; not only was there not a pane of glass in the whole, but the window frames were all gone; every thing that wanted keeping was gone; every thing that required care to preserve it had perished. Time had not touched it; Time had evidently not yet had leisure to do his work. He is sure, but slow; Ruin works fast enough unaided, where once he puts his foot. Time would have pulled down the chimneys, Ruin had taken off the slates; Time would have bulged the walls, Ruin brought in the rain, rotted the timbers, and assisted the thieves. Poor old Time will have but little left him at Ballycloran! The gardens had been large, half were now covered by rubbish heaps; the other half, potato patches; and round the out houses I saw clustering a lot of those wretched cabins which the poor Irish build against a deserted wall, can they find one, as jackdaws do their nests in a superannuated chimney. In the front there had been, I presume, a tolerably spacious lawn, with a drive through it, surrounded on all sides, except towards the house, by thick trees: the trees remained, but the lawn, the drive, and the flower patches, which of course once existed there, were now all alike, equally prolific in large brown dock weeds and sorrels: there were two or three narrow foot paths through, and across the space, up to the cabins behind the house, but other marks of humanity were there none.

A large ash, apparently cut down years ago, with the branches still on it, was stretched somewhat out of the wood: on this I sat, lighted a cigar, and meditated on this characteristic specimen of Irish life. The sun was setting beautifully behind the trees, and its imperfect light through the foliage gave the unnatural ruin a still more singular appearance, and brought into my mind thoughts of the wrong, oppression, misery and despair, to which some one had been subjected, by what I saw before me.

I had not been long seated, when four or five ragged boys and girls came through the wood, driving a lot of geese along one of the paths. When they saw me, they all came up and stood round me, as if wondering what I could be. I could learn nothing from them—the very poor Irish children will never speak to you—but a middle aged man soon followed them. He told me the place was called Ballycloran: "he did not know who it belonged to; a gintleman in Dublin recaved the rints, and a very stiff gintleman he was too; and hard it was upon them to pay two pound tin an acre for the garden there, and that half covered with the ould house and the bricks and rubbish, only on behalf of the bog that was convaynient, and plinty of the timber, tho' that was rotten, and illigant out houses for the pigs and the geese, and the ould bricks of the wall wor good manure for the praties (this, in all my farming, I never dreamt of); but times was very hard on the poor, the praties being ninepince a stone in Carrick all last summer; God help the poor, the crayturs, for the gintlemin, their raal frinds, that should be, couldn't help thimselves now, let alone others"—and so on, now speaking of his sorrow and poverty, and again descanting on the "illigance" of

his abode. I could only learn that a family called the Macder-
mots had lived there some six or seven years back, that they were
an unfortunate people, he had heard tell, but he had not been in
the country then, and it was a bloody story, &c. &c, &c. The
evening was drawing on, and the time for my coach to come
was fast approaching, so I was obliged to leave Ballycloran,
unsatisfied as to its history, and return to Drumsna.

Here I had no time to make further enquiries; for Mr. Hart-
ley's servants always keep their time, and very shortly the four
horses clattered down the hill into the village. I got up behind,
for McC——, the guard, was an old friend of mine: and after
the usual salutations and strapping of portmanteaus, and shifting
down into places, as Mc—— knows everything, I began to ask
him if he knew anything of a place called Ballycloran.

"'Deed then, Sir, and I do," said he, "and good reason have I
to know; and well I knew those that lived in it, ruined, and
black, and desolate, as Ballycloran is now": and between Drumsna
and Boyle, he gave me the heads of the following story; and,
reader, if I thought it would ever be your good fortune to hear
the history of Ballycloran from the guard of the Boyle coach, I
would recommend you to get it from him, and shut my book
forthwith.

T. H. WHITE

(1906–1964)

Born in Bombay, Terence Hanbury White had an unhappy childhood. After his parents' divorce in 1920, he was sent to Cheltenham College in England, a training academy for the military. Harshly disciplined by both sadistic teachers and upper-class students, White sought refuge in books. From Cheltenham College he entered Queens College and discovered Thomas Malory's Morte D'Arthur, the fifteenth-century account of King Arthur and his court. At thirty, a professional writer with a best-selling book of essays, he returned to the Malory book. White's version, The Sword in the Stone, was a success in both England and America. White wrote of it, "It is more or less a kind of wish-fulfillment of the things I should like to have happened to me when I was a boy."

From 1939 to 1946 T. H. White lived in Ireland to work on the sequels to The Sword in the Stone. Wartime paper shortages delayed their publication, and the public lost interest in the fortunes of a long-dead monarch. All five books of White's Arthurian legend were not published as a set until 1957. White's idyll in Ireland did not end happily. After nearly six years, he still felt like a stranger, and some locals thought that he might be a spy. In 1946 he was asked to leave the country. He resettled in the Channel Islands. White died during a transatlantic voyage, when he was returning from an American speaking tour to promote Camelot, the musical version of The Sword in the Stone.

LETTER FROM A GOOSE SHOOTER

from THE GODSTONE AND THE BLACKYMOR

I felt lonely standing on the white sand in the twilight. The rowers in the currach cried a farewell to me as they left. Then, in the quickly falling darkness, shot with the goose cries, I went into the broken house on man's first duty—to make fire. When this was burning with wreckage, I set out to search for the well. But it was dark now, and the electric torch had broken somehow, so I could not find it. I went to the drinking place for cattle and got water there.

I was alone on the island, and it was mid-winter.

The Inniskeas are islands off the west coast, once inhabited by men. But ten were drowned in 1927, in what was called the Inniskea Disaster, and—the land being too exhausted by a thousand years of "sea-manure" (sea-weed) to grow potatoes any longer—they had been abandoned. The little village stood quite silent beside its anchorage, the roofs fallen, the stones of the walls in the street. In twelve years it seemed to have lost all human origin. No people were expected by its broken doors. A few black bullocks sheltered there at night, the seals came into the harbour, two small black birds visited it in the mornings, two ravens cronked higher up, and all the time you heard the eternal geese, which, driven away during man's thousand years of residence, had now returned.

The people in the currach had been afraid to leave me, because it was a bad coast. There was a chance that they might not be able to come back in six weeks, as sometimes happened

on the next-door neighbour, the Black Rock Light. Also they
feared the dead of the disaster and perhaps a certain old god of
the island, venerated until the last generation, of whom I was to
hear more.

Brownie, the red setter, kept me awake for all but two hours,
the first night, shivering. Such bed as we could make was
strange. The feelings and thoughts have gone with people about
me. But if I had had paper, and could have written, it would
have been a fountain of feeling about eternal things. I did write
on an envelope, during the strange and sleepless night, a message
of propitiation to the god. The romancing mainlanders had told
me about him already, and I had seen some Inniskea stones in
the Dublin Museum, and I believed what I had been told.

> On Inniskea, long before Patrick came,
> Stood the stone idol of the secret name:
> The magic people made him. No surprise,
> No threat, no question lit his two round eyes,
> Nor had he other features. Consciousness
> Was all his feeling, all his creed "I wis."
> He watched the wild geese twenty centuries.
>
> Inniskea is an island. Ten years gone
> The human race lived here, the windows shone
> With candles over the water, and men
> Fished currachs, women wellwards went from ben.
> There was a King to rule the island then,
> Chosen for might, who had his admiral
> Of all the Inniskeas. The priest's sick call
> Was this cold pasture's only festival.
>
> Mass was so far off, with such storms between,
> And in the dark nights moved so much unseen
> On the wild waters, that Man's beating heart
> Still sometimes turned towards the old God's art.
> Much magic was made with the dew. The wells
> Secretly stirred with strange internal spells.

To keep the Agent off, or the Excise,
Fires were lit before the God of Eyes
And dances made around his stone, sunwise.
Their old cold Godstone they, for comfort, dressed
In one new suit each year: his Sunday best.

Then the remorseless sea, the all-beleaguering,
The crafty, long-combed sea, the stark and whistling,
The savage, ancient sea, master at waiting,
Struck once.

        Two hours later the mainland
Received one man, a saucepan in his hand,
Astride an upturned currach. At the Inn
They gave him clothes without, whisky within,
Such as they could: but he nor left nor right
Altered his eyes. Only, with all his might,
This man bailed with his saucepan all that night.
In half one hour of squall, from calm to calm, the Main
Holding his ten mates drowned had fallen on sleep again.

Nobody painted the houses after.
The islanders lost all heart for laughter.
Work was a weariness, dances were done,
On the island whose pride of Man was gone.

Now I am all alone on Inniskea,
All alone with the wind and with the sea.
The corrugated iron, rusted brown,
Gives a burnt look to the abandoned town.
The roofs are ruins and the walls are down.

The Land Commission took the people ashore.
King Phillip Lavell is here no more.
They have even taken away the God Who Saw,
To stand in Dublin Museum. From ten till four
He eyes the opposite wall.

> Oh God of Eyes,
> Bound there in darkness and deprived of skies,
> Know that your Geese are back. Know that their cries
> Lag on the loud wind as, by candlelight,
> At Inniskea's one fire, I, your last subject, write:
> Lulled by their laughter, cradled in their night.

It was something I can't explain now, to write this by the popping of the salty firelight, in the one-roomed house, alone. The crayfish pots were piled high in the corner, with spherical lobster pots on top of them, twisted out of heather roots. A bed of hay stood in another corner with damp quilts on it. The room was crammed with wreckage (there was a goodish roof to keep it dry). There were two wooden stools, some seine nets, a bag of flour hanging in the window for castaways, a billy-can, a candle stuck in a bottle, the trembling dog. And outside, within twenty yards, there was the lonely sea, the goose music, the heathen god, the winter night of stormy solitude.

The flames of the fire in this primeval cave shone on a brown ceiling of boards.

Three mildewed religious pictures, without frames or glass, hung from a piece of timber beside the bed of straw. They were as necessary to the place, when two or three of the islanders slept there, waiting for wreckage, as lifeboats are necessary to a liner. But to a soul alone, possibly to stay six weeks if the weather broke, beleaguered by cold and ghosts and darkness and the sea of night, they were the lifebelt itself. One was of the Sacred Heart, in the middle of a cross. One was of some choristers singing with unnaturally goody-goody faces. And one, in colour, was of Joseph holding lilies and the Infant Christ. His beard was cut like mine. Brownie, a pagan, could find no comfort in these, and that was why she trembled. I stoked the fire and laid her before it, stretching my body across her to give by contact such Christian safety as I could. We slept, in three plaids, on the stone floor, two hours—waking at intervals to keep the fire bright.

At half past five it was too much trouble to pretend sleeping. I brewed tea in the billy-can, with a tot of fiery west-coast rum, and ate slices of bread and butter. The tea, boiled together with sugar, was fine. Then, a little after six, we opened the windy door and stepped into the night.

This door had opened itself once in the middle of the night, and once the candle and fire had simultaneously burned low for a moment, and the spirits, whistling like otters, had swung round the deserted homes.

Now, stepping out, I found myself face to face with the Devil.

He was black, motionless, a darkness silhouetted against the darkness, considering me with ears and horns. I stopped also, and considered him. The horns took shape against the night.

When the door had opened itself, I had stood for two heart-beats, then firmly shut it. When the lights had dimmed, I had sat for two heart-beats, waiting for them to burn again. To the cries of otters I had turned a defiant ear. Now, face to face with Satan, I stood as quietly as himself, for many heart-beats.

We watched each other with curiosity, in the calm of aidless spirits. You can only be afraid when you are clothed with civilization, when you have liens of succour. You can only be frightened when you have a chance of escape. Now that I had no human ties, no roof over my head, no means of escape, I had no fears. The Devil, with the same dignity as I felt myself, moved off quietly in the shape of one of the few black bullocks which were left all winter on the island. I had not frightened him—he did not gallop away with the sudden panic of half-wild cattle—and he had not frightened me.

I stepped on slowly over the fallen stones of the village walls, stones which man could hardly detect except by touch and by the wild sense of animals. The thing was to walk with the patience of prehistory, moving with a balanced body between shapes, at half a mile an hour, knowing only the stones, the fallen roofs, the choked drains, the wreckage, the rocks, and the feeling pace of night.

I was half-way to the place which I had chosen, imagining landmarks which themselves consisted only of the dark, when a thing flew up from under our feet. It circled two or three times invisible, braying like a donkey. The strange cry of the ass does have some quality of levitation about it, and perhaps the ruined walls may have reflected the noise in various directions. There were donkeys on the island, too—but my heart knew it was not these. With the beads in my pocket and the magnum in my hand, I did not fear it. It was possibly a shearwater.

By seven o'clock we were at the fallen gable, and, almost simultaneously, almost directly overhead, there was the first low quack of the geese. I could not see them.

The sun, when he was eventually resounding on Achill and Duvillaun and Innisglora and the distant kingdom of Erris, found us collecting six dead Barnacles and chasing two runners. We were sated with what then seemed a glorious victory, the first time we had killed so many at one flight. Fixed in the memory, now, is the first meteor of a darker darkness, streaking down out of the superb squadron—the soul-satisfying Thump with which he bounced upon the salty land. Then, as the light grew, there had been the crouching under the wall, the white breasts advancing with their thrilling cries and ordered ranks, Brownie ruthlessly held down in cover, the body straightening and the two bangs, the second almost coinciding with the thump of the first goose. This was the first time, out of some three hundred sunrises or sunsets, that I had had what I could truly call a left-and-right at geese. Those two White-Fronts on Carrowmore the previous week, for instance: I had been between them and the wind, had had time to reload, and had killed two geese out of four shots. But today, for the first time in my life, it was Bang-Thump, Bang-Thump—the real McCoy. Twenty years later, I can add with pleasure that it was also my last left-and-right.

The Barnacle Goose was a species I had not handled before. She was earlier in her flight than the grey ones. She had a lower, more monotonous, taciturn, disyllabic, quacking note. She had great vitality from the killing point of view, was as cunning as the grey goose, but did not raise herself in the air when shot at with the same rapid climb as her cousins. This heaviness in soaring was one of her chief differences. In appearance she reminded me of the sixty-year-old spinster aunts who used to frequent England in my childhood. She had the same black shiny gloves, the jet beads, the dress of black and dove-grey garnished with white, the high collar which was introduced by the wife of Edward VII, and she probably kept her toque on with a long black hat pin. The average weight of eight birds—I gave one away and did not weigh it—was four and a half pounds. You thought of her as female, but of all the other geese as male. In the hand she was female. In the air, like all these grand creatures, at whom I could not bear to shoot nowadays, she was a male.

Sleepy and satisfied with murder, we plodded the clean sand back to our burrow, and made more tea and bread and butter. The interior of the little house was a surprise in daylight, for, as the bullocks were liable to break glass windows, the owners of this, the soundest building on the isle, had covered the windows with corrugated iron. It was dark inside, both day and night, a sort of cave-life refuge among the straw and looming lobster pots and smoke.

The forenoon passed pleasantly in a long but profitless stalk of a large party on the other side of the hill. I was filled with happiness, watching them for half an hour. With a good appetite from this, we came back to dinner, which was to be a cold roast chicken we had brought. I had a bite from the breast and plenty of bread and tea, but Brownie had the two legs, the two wings and the carcase. I could not persuade her to eat bread and butter. So, as she had had an unhappy night, I let her have the meat we owned. Chicken bones are not so bad for dogs as people say.

Eating the good bread by the quayside, I heard geese taking a trip, and ducked into a broken door. Peering out with one eye, I saw the main party turn back. But one, evidently a raw recruit, came on over my head. I was half ashamed at killing so many in the morning, and, thinking that there was moderation in all things, particularly in regard to Edwardian spinsters, I had

decided to slay no more. But this was too much of a temptation.
I stood up, pointed the gun at him with a second's hesitation,
saw every feather of his breast in the frosted winter sunlight, and
the white-scarfed head turning hither and thither as he looked
about to discover why he was alone. Then the temptation was
too great, and, taking my finger from the choke trigger to the
cylinder (where I knew there was a small cartridge of No. 2
shot) I let him have it with the proper lead. Smack! He struggled
madly in the air, with one wing broken at the elbow, turned
four or five somersaults, and landed thumping on the white sand
of the harbour—where Brownie was waiting to receive him.
She brought him to me, his live snake head curling upright on
one side of her mouth, and, hating the business of screwing the
tough neck, I thumped his head on the door post to break his
brains.

These geese had been sent over by two men in a currach,
who, in fishing the bay, had made a visit to the North Island to
brew tea. Now, when I wanted to snatch an hour's sleep, the two
rowers of the currach arrived to pay a visit. They were Irish-
speakers. They apologized for having the English badly. They
danced round me like pleased dogs, delighted by the strange
beard-man who had dared the ghosts, giving loud joyful cries of
hospitality to their old kingdom, where they had been born in
the last century. They had been born on the flat North Island,
however, and disapproved my choice of the featured south.

We had high pleasure with each other. I bid them welcome to
the south with a glass of rum. They watched me finish my din-
ner, sitting interested in the dark den, watching my eating man-
ners. We made long talk. The elder of the two always addressed
me affectionately, laying his hand upon my sleeve, as "my *good*
man."

I was told about the Godstone, his yearly suit of new
clothes—I gathered they were of blue serge—and how the
South Island, once growing jealous of the North's holy posses-
sion, stole him away to the South in a currach on a dark night.
At about this time a barrel of paraffin was washed ashore, and

the King of the South had it brought into the house where the Godstone stood, hidden away behind a curtain at the hinder end. They were experimenting with the paraffin—a novelty to them—in the hope that it would be something to drink, when a child let fire to it, and the house was consumed. One man was burned to death in the flames. But the fire halted at the curtain of the Godstone, and he was untouched. "You may say what you like, my *good* man, but there was something strange about that, wasn't there?"

I expressed my indignation at his having been taken in chains to Dublin, and asked what he was like. "We do not know," said the elder man (Reilly). "He was in my father's time. A priest," he added indignantly, "then came and broke him. But the Godstone hurted his foot, and he was dead within the twelve-month." "Do you mean that it fell on the priest's foot?" "No, no," cried Reilly testily: "it hurted his foot." I was left with a confused guess that there might have been a verse of Scripture, distorted by translation from Irish into English, at the back of his strong mind. He probably had no idea about its being in the Bible: "Thou shalt bruise his head, but he shall bruise thy heel."

"Where," I asked, "was the Godstone kept when they stole him?" "Why, in the house you are in now, my *good* man; did you not hear anything last night?"

In the course of great compliments upon staying alone with the spirits, the younger man said strongly: "If they were to offer me three million pounds, I would not stay alone on the islands. If I had travelled the world a bit" (here he bowed courteously to me) "perhaps I would stay. But in my present state I would not stay a night alone, no, not for three million pounds." He giggled at the thought of anybody offering him this sum.

We discussed the thing which brayed, from under my feet. The whistling, they thought, was otters or seals. I whistled in imitation, and the old man, cocking his head on one side, said "Otters" emphatically. But the braying stumped them. Donkeys could not fly over your head, geese did not bray, and the God-stone would have been too heavy to fly. Anyway, he was supposed to be in Dublin, though I doubted whether he spent the nights there.

Were there any other stones on the island? Yes, plenty. There was a very good one quite close to here, which they would show me when they were showing the well after I had finished dinner. It had photographs on it.

The photograph stone was a thin slab of limestone stuck upright above the harbour. It had a circular cross, like a consecration cross, upon it, and underneath, beautifully carved, the kind of wriggle which you find in the Book of Kells.

There followed conversation about the North Island, dear to them, as yet unvisited by me. They eagerly urged me to come across to it in their currach, but I would not go. A currach is a primeval water vehicle with no keel, kept upright in the sea by faith. It is said to be safe. But I did not care for it, after coming in one of them on this long-rolling sea the day before, and I thought the motor-boat might arrive to take me home while I was away, and at any rate I had taken a dislike for the North Island. It seemed too flat to be interesting. Trying to provoke my interest they pointed out one high, symmetrical, lonely sand-hill—the landmark of the island. What did I think it was made of? It was not a sandhill at all. It was made of three things, with the sand piled round them: the three things were stones, shells and bones. "Bones of what?" I asked, thinking of some prehistoric kitchen midden. "Men's bones, of course." "Good gracious, what sort of men?" "Oh, it would be those Danes, I suppose," said the elder Reilly off-handedly. "A lady came here in the summer," he added, "from Dublin. She was digging them up, you know." Considering the matter, he reported with awe: "She put a wire fence all round them."

We had other interesting talk, about the two public houses there had once been (one was a shebeen), and about the dragging home of brides—how only the younger people could go to Mass, and then only on fine days, because it was not safe to take the old people in boats for fear of storm—about the last King of the Island, a big man with a voice like thunder, who was killed by drinking crude rum washed ashore, who spent a month in the Belmullet hospital, but was brought back to his island to die—about a man who had hanged himself from a rafter—about Columkille's church on the North Island—about the whaling station which the Norwegians once made here, and the great Iron they had left.

Then, seeking a little information for themselves, the old man mentioned that the Germans were very thorough men. I agreed. Was I an Englishman, he asked, with hesitation. "My mother was certainly an Englishwoman," I said, "and I was educated in England." "Well, that's the way it goes," said he, rubbing his hands together with delight. A man who could bring himself to live alone with the spirits of Inniskea was to Reilly worth considering.

We arranged to come out to the North Island in a three-man currach in January, there to spend some weeks together in amity. They promised to give me the Gaelic properly ("Fuil Gaedhilge agat?" they had inquired, and I, with stammering tongue and shame, had wrongly made up an answer, "Ní ta agam"). I was to give them change of thought I suppose. Then, waving their caps gaily in farewell, they pulled out of the harbour, and the currach dwindled over the sea.

The barnacles made no evening flight that sunset. They were upset by the moon, now growing. I guessed that on moonless nights they spent the day on the South Island, the night on the lake of the North, but that when the moon was strong they would fly at whim. I had caught the flight in the morning partly because it was the first quarter of a growing moon—they were not yet taking it for granted—and partly because the clouds had killed the light. Or did the sea-geese have no regular hours?

In our dark home I carefully dried two of the fishermen's quilts before a big fire, hard-boiled four eggs, of which I chopped up two for Brownie (who thought me no cook), drank tea, and made a bed with loving thought. Then I put the beads over my head, to wear them as a talisman which would not need holding, and slept in their protection, half believing. After an hour's deep unconsciousness I woke at eight o'clock, in an agony of cramp. Disposed again in better position—the priest's position for sleep, called "in Grace"—we sank into the deep world again till midnight: then woke with the roar of the wind outside, and its whistle under the door.

I revived the fire in the now freezing room, and lay listening. They had not wanted to leave us on the island, and I had been forced, pointing to the sack which bulged mostly with the rugs and two saucepans, to say that I had food for a fortnight. But there were only four loaves of bread, two pounds of butter, and a little sugar and tea, with twelve eggs and a pot of Bovril. Brownie was too pampered for these things. I was not troubled about starving, but the dog would lose condition, and a long stay might be a bore. These were enough geese to live on for the rest of the winter. Considering how I would fix up a wooden spit to roast the birds, and how I could eat a green plant from one of the streams, which looked a little like watercress, I fell into a blissful sleep for the third time, till I had slept eleven hours.

I had no geese the third day. The moon had put them off. With so many dead, it did not seem right to stalk them. Going out to the morning flight, I found the wind had dropped. In the afternoon the motor-boat called for us, on her way from relieving the lighthouse at Black Rock. By the evening I was back in a hot bath at our village of five hundred souls on the mainland, feeling as if I was in London, but feeling also a sense of loss in Bedlam. The equanimity and reality which I had collected on the last day, exploring the caverns and strong promontories of the west coast of the island—all the deep racial thoughts I had felt there and a temporary conviction of the relation of God to man—the cairn I had made for the bodies of two of my shot geese, which had been found by the herring gulls before I found them—all the hours on high places, with only a pair of ravens above me: all my strength was momently crumbling away. I can only remember that the North Island was said to be inhabited by one cat, and that, on the last morning, when I was standing by the glorious, lonely Atlantic harbour, wondering whatever other Christmas-present God could think of for me, I had looked up to find a pair of young ravens playing a few feet above my head. They were quite small, only about the size of jackdaws, and every feather on their bodies was perfect. I watched in rapture, admiring the strong re-curve of their glossy primaries and the way they wagged their feather-perfect tails. I thought how strange that young ravens should be as small as jackdaws, that they should have this thin and almost curlew beak. I looked earnestly upon the beak, and upon the feet. My heart bounded as I distinguished the redness, even against the sky. No wonder they were so trim, so much lovelier than any of the black-guard I had previously known. They were not ravens at all. They were the red-beaked choughs of legend, looking on Man for the first time—as I on them.

OSCAR WILDE

(1854–1900)

"Though by culture Wilde was a citizen of all civilised capitals," wrote
George Bernard Shaw, *"he was at root a* very Irish Irishman, *and as
such a foreigner everywhere but in Ireland."* *With the notoriety that sur-
rounds the life of poet and playwright Oscar Wilde, his Irishness is often
overlooked. Although most of his writing career was spent in England,
Wilde himself considered his nationality essential to his character.*

*Born in Dublin to Sir William Wilde and Lady Jane Francesca
Wilde, Oscar Fingal O'Flahertie Wills Wilde was exposed to the writ-
ing life at his mother's literary salon. The family had quite a different life
at Moytura House in County Mayo, a fishing lodge built by Wilde's
father that had a view of Lough Corrib. The following letters were writ-
ten either from or about Moytura House. Wilde left Ireland—and Moy-
tura House—for Oxford, where he became notorious for his espousal of
the aesthetic movement's theory* *"art for art's sake"—and for his dandy
dress. After his marriage to a wealthy Irishwoman, Wilde devoted him-
self to writing.*

*Wilde's trial and conviction for homosexual acts has overshadowed
his often brilliant writing: four comedies, still crisp and fresh after more
than a century,* Lady Windermere's Fan, An Ideal Husband, The
Importance of Being Earnest, *and* A Woman of No Impor-
tance; *his only novel,* The Picture of Dorian Gray; *and the power-
ful* The Ballad of Reading Gaol, *a portrait of prison life. When Lord
Chamberlain refused to license Wilde's play* Salome, *Wilde wrote, "I
will not consent to call myself a citizen of a country that shows such nar-
rowness in its artistic judgment. I am not English—I am Irish—which
is quite another thing."*

from THE LETTERS OF OSCAR WILDE

This excerpt was written to Oscar Wilde's friend Reginald Harding in August 1876 from Cong, County Mayo. It paints a concise portrait of life at Moytura Hall, built by Wilde's father, Sir William Wilde. Sir William himself wrote a book about Moytura Hall in 1867.

Dear Kitten, Have you fallen into a well, or been mislaid anywhere that you never write to me? Or has one of your nine lives gone?

Frank Miles and I came down here last week, and have had a very royal time of it sailing. We are at the top of Lough Corrib, which if you refer to your geography you will find to be a lake thirty miles long, ten broad and situated in the most romantic scenery in Ireland. Frank has done some wonderful sunsets since he came down; he has given me some more of his drawings. Has your sister got the one he calls "My Little Lady"—a little girl's face with a lot of falling hair? If she has not got it I would like to send it to her in return for her autograph on the celebrated memorial.

Frank has never fired off a gun in his life (and says he doesn't want to) but as our proper sporting season here does not begin till September I have not taught him anything. But on Friday we go into Connemara to a charming little fishing lodge we have in the mountains where I hope to make him land a salmon and kill a brace of grouse. I expect to have very good sport indeed this season. Write to me there if your claws have not been clipped. Illaunroe Lodge, Leenane, Co. Galway.

Best love to Puss. I hope he is reading hard. Ever yours

Oscar F. O'F. Wills Wilde

Wilde continued the outdoor life at Illaunroe Lodge in Connemara at the end of August 1876.

Illaunroe Lodge, Connemara

Dear Bouncer, I am very glad you like *Aurora Leigh*. I think it simply *"intense"* in every way. I am deep in a review of Symonds's last book whenever I can get time and the weather is too bright for fishing. Mahaffy has promised to look it over before publication. Up to this however I am glad to say that I have been too much *occupied with rod and gun for the handling of the quill* (neat and Pope-like?).

I have only got one salmon as yet but have had heaps of seatrout which give great play. I have not had a blank day yet. Grouse are few but I have got a lot of hares so have had a capital time of it. I hope next year that you and the Kitten will come and stay a (lunar) month with me. I am sure you would like this wild mountainous country, close to the Atlantic and teeming with sport of all kinds. It is in every way magnificent and makes me years younger than actual history records.

I hope you are reading hard; if you don't get your First the examiners ought to be sent down.

Write like a good boy to Moytura House, Cong, County Mayo, as I will be leaving here this week.

With kind regards to your mother and sisters, ever yours

Oscar F. O'F. Wills Wilde

I have Frank Miles with me. He is delighted with all.

This letter written in 1877 refers to the death of Wilde's "cousin" Dr. Henry Wilson who died at thirty-nine of pneumonia. He was, in fact, Wilde's half brother, one of Dr. William Wilde's many illegitimate children. Oscar and his brother Willie were the mourners at Wilson's funeral, although Oscar was virtually left out of Henry Wilson's will.

Oscar Wilde flirted with Catholicism for most of his life, outraging his Protestant family. He finally converted to Roman Catholicism shortly before his death of meningitis in Paris in 1900.

To Reginald Harding
MS. HYDE (H. M.)

[Circa 16 June 1877]   *1 Merrion Square North*

My dear Kitten, Many thanks for your delightful letter. I am glad you are in the midst of beautiful scenery and *Aurora Leigh*.

I am very much down in spirits and depressed. A cousin of ours to whom we were all very much attached has just died— quite suddenly from some chill caught riding. I dined with him on Saturday and he was dead on Wednesday. My brother and I were always supposed to be his heirs but his will was an unpleasant surprise, like most wills. He leaves my father's hospital about £8,000, my brother £2,000, and me £100 on condition of my being a Protestant!

He was, poor fellow, bigotedly intolerant of the Catholics and seeing me "on the brink" struck me out of his will. It is a terrible disappointment to me; you see I suffer a good deal from my Romish leanings, in pocket and mind.

My father had given him a share in my fishing lodge in Connemara, which of course ought to have reverted to me on his death; well, even this I lose "if I become a Roman Catholic for five years" which is very infamous.

Fancy a man going before "God and the Eternal Silences" with his wretched Protestant prejudices and bigotry clinging still to him.

However, I won't bore you with myself any more. The world seems too much out of joint for me to set it right.

I send you a little notice of Keats's grave I have just written which may interest you. I visited it with Bouncer and Dunskie.

If you would care to see my views on the Grosvenor Gallery send for the enclosed, and write soon to me. Ever yours

Oscar Wilde

I heard from little Bouncer from Constantinople lately: he said he was coming home. Love to Puss.

Wilde planned to return to Illaunroe Lodge in 1877 and tried to convince his friend William Ward to join him. In this letter he enumerates the lures of Connemara.

1 Merrion Square North

Dear old Boy, I hear you are back: did you get my telegram at the Lord Warden? Do write and tell me about the Turks. I like their attitude towards life very much, though it seems strange that the descendants of the wild Arabs should be the Sybarites of our day.

I sent you two mags, to Frenchay: one with a memoir of Keats, the other religious.

Do you remember our delightful visit to Keats's grave, and Dunskie's disgust. Poor Dunskie: I know he looks on me as a renegade; still I have suffered very much for my Roman fever in mind and *pocket* and happiness.

I am going down to Connemara for a month or more next week to try and read. I have not opened a book yet, I have been so bothered with business and other matters. I shall be quite alone. Will you come? I will give you fishing and scenery—and bring your books—*and some notebooks for me.* I am in despair about "Greats."

It is roughing it, you know, but you will have
(1) bed
(2) table and chair
(3) knife and fork
(4) fishing
(5) scenery—sunsets—bathing—heather—mountains—lakes
(6) whisky and salmon to eat. Write and say when you can come, and also send me please *immediately* the name and address of Miss Fletcher whom I rode with at Rome, and of her stepfather. I have never sent her some articles of Pater's I promised her.

I want you to read my article on the Grosvenor Gallery in the *Dublin University Magazine* of July—my first art-essay.

I have had such delightful letters from many of the painters, and from Pater *such sympathetic praise.* I must send you his letter: or rather do so, but return it in *registered letter* by next post: don't forget. Ever yours

Oscar

On the brink of leaving Ireland for good, Wilde in late 1878 wrote to Florence Balcombe who was about to marry Bram Stoker. Stoker, a young Irish civil servant, wrote the horror novel Dracula *in 1897.*

1 Merrion Square North

Dear Florrie, As I shall be going back to England, probably for good, in a few days, I should like to bring with me the little gold cross I gave you one Christmas morning long ago.

I need hardly say that I would not ask it from you if it was anything you valued, but worthless though the trinket be, to me it serves as a memory of two sweet years—the sweetest of all the years of my youth—and I should like to have it always with me. If you would care to give it to me yourself I could meet you any time on Wednesday, or you might hand it to Phil, whom I am going to meet that afternoon.

Though you have not thought it worth while to let me know of your marriage, still I cannot leave Ireland without sending you my wishes that you may be happy; whatever happens I at least cannot be indifferent to your welfare: the currents of our lives flowed too long beside one another for that.

We stand apart now, but the little cross will serve to remind me of the bygone days, and though we shall never meet again, after I leave Ireland, still I shall always remember you at prayer. Adieu and God bless you.

Oscar

Writing from London in early 1880, Wilde sets out the specifications of his fishing lodge for an unnamed potential renter.

13 Salisbury Street

Dear Sir, My Fishing Lodge is situated on Lough Fee near Leenane and the Killary Bay, and three miles from the sea: it is a small two-storied cottage, furnished in bachelor fashion for *three* persons, but would accommodate more. My servant, an excellent fisherman, and his wife, a good cook, are in charge of it. There are boats etc. belonging to the house.

The fishing extends over Lough Fee 2½ miles, Lough Muck 1 mile, River Calfin 2 miles, salmon and white trout.

A public car by which letters and provisions can be brought passes *every day* within one mile of the house. Leenane is 5 miles off, Westport 30 miles.

The rent is £40 for one month, £70 for two, £90 for season. Truly yours

Oscar Wilde

Munster

ANNABEL DAVIS-GOFF

(193?–)

Annabel Davis-Goff was born to Anglo-Irish gentry between the two world wars. Her memoir Walled Gardens *tells a bittersweet story of her family's attempt to keep up appearances after the loss of its fortunes. The Goffs lived in Glenville, an estate near Waterford with enviable gardens, stables, two lodges, and a main house—but not enough heat to prevent chilblains. Glenville was a financial albatross around the family's fragile structure. Surprisingly, it was Davis-Goff's mother who broke out of the rigid façade of faded nobility. After nearly twenty years of marriage, she left her husband, four children, and a respectable life for a liaison with her business partner. Because of the Irish ban on divorce, she forfeited all rights to her children.*

At seventeen Davis-Goff left Ireland for England and a career in film and television in London and eventually in Hollywood. She now lives in New York. Her most recent novel is The Dower House, *a coming-of-age story set in Ireland and London, published in 1999.*

GLENVILLE

from WALLED GARDENS

It is possible, without stretching the imagination overmuch, to think that we had found, in the factory-desecrated ruins of our home, a kind of open coffin. A contrast to my father, sealed in a stark, pale wooden box. Everything at the cathedral neat and controlled, everything at Glenville random and jumbled and broken, with the uncontrolled illogic of a daytime nightmare.

Glenville was an Italianate mid-nineteenth-century house about a mile and a half outside Waterford, overlooking the river Suir. It was not architecturally beautiful in the way many Irish houses are. Its date was wrong for that, but it was large and pleasant. Apart from the main house and the walled garden, there were two lodges—one at the front gate, one at the back—a couple of fruit gardens, good stabling, small kennels and enough paddocks and grazing for a few hunters and a cow or two. It was not an estate or even a farm. It was a carefully thought-out, upper-middle-class residence for a family that had had civilized tastes and plenty of money to indulge them. A gentleman's property, but one which bore none of the responsibility which went with the estates of the landowning aristocracy. An estate in Ireland meant a house set on a piece of land large enough to support a working, though not necessarily commercial, farm. It implies tenants and some position of authority held by the owner of the house, which would have been built considerably before Glenville was. Glenville produced nothing which was not consumed by its owners and any land not used for horses, cows, poultry and tennis was landscaped.

Although Ireland is on a parallel with Labrador and the southern part of Hudson Bay, the Gulf Stream and North Atlantic currents touch her southwest coast and modify the climate. This condition, in combination with a cheap labor force and a comparatively affluent moment in the fortunes of the Anglo-Irish around the turn of the century, resulted in an enthusiasm for landscaping, often executed with a combination of knowledge and taste which had dramatic and beautiful results.

As the period of affluence ended (virtually overnight in our family), even the cheap labor became unaffordable and the imported plants and shrubs were left to become both a metaphor for the new, drastically reduced and unprotected state of the Anglo-Irish and a short-term experiment in Darwin's theory. By the time I was a child the result had a dreamlike quality. We played in woods containing eucalyptus trees and rhododendrons which had grown big enough for a child to climb up into and which still blossomed in bright improbable colors. The three ponds were another favorite playground. There had been two large oval ponds with a small round one between them. One of the oval ones had leaked and was full of marsh plants. It had a tiny island in the middle. The other two ponds were still intact and beside the larger one, on warm summer afternoons, we would sometimes have a family picnic. Three generations would gather on an overgrown grassy patch beside the water, surrounded by oversized plants whose inappropriate tropical lushness created a scene somewhere between a photograph from a Russian family scrapbook and a minor Rousseau. The water from this pond poured over a waterfall which took it underground for a while, then into a stream, another waterfall, a large ornamental pool, another waterfall, then down to the river below. Bamboo, which had been planted many years before, had proliferated and provided a tall dense jungle with just enough space between plants to allow children to creep sideways. A field of daffodils which had taken over in the same way was an even more beautiful backdrop to our games but contained fewer possibilities. Among the daffodils there was a walnut tree and a large chestnut, and in autumn we would roast chestnuts in the glowing embers and grey ash of the library fire.

In front of the house was a lawn, part of which had once been a tennis court. Closer to the house stood the large and beautiful weeping ash. Between the driveway and the lawn was a short but steep bank down whose grassy slope we would slide on tea trays or roll down and lie, dizzy, at the bottom, in the sweet smell of newly cut grass. My father used to mow this lawn. It was hard work; the lawn was large and lawn mowers were not the sophisticated machines they have now become. Nevertheless, he used to buy and then abandon quite a large selection of mowers. Mowing the lawn to keep up the appearance of the house and working in the greenhouses to pay for it took a large part of my father's leisure time and also a good deal of energy. He must have been all too well aware of the contrast between the life he then led and his memories of childhood. I never heard him make the comparison. "The good old days" was a phrase I often heard as a child, but never from my parents. We knew that the cheap and plentiful labor came not only from the poor working class but, in the original upkeep of the grounds at Glenville, through an arrangement with the local insane asylum. One of the first clues I had as a small child that the world could be cruel was the sight of truckloads of men from the asylum pulling sugar beets from a local farmer's wintery field and my mother's expression of pity when she explained to us who they were.

The climate and the rich earth and the constant rain helped keep up appearances in the gardens and grounds of large Irish houses long after the houses themselves had started to disintegrate.

Glenville was not the house in which my father had been born. His family had lived next door in a similar house called Maypark (which wasn't the family home either; that had been Horetown in County Wexford, built on land given to an ancestor by Richard Cromwell). Maypark was divided from Glenville only by fields and the immediate grounds and lawns of both houses. It had become a nursing home run by nuns. We used to meet the nuns during our afternoon walks. They, too, would take a little stroll after lunch and were the occasional source of boiled sweets which would be unwrapped from handkerchiefs taken out of secret pockets in their habits. They were quiet, calm, patient women and I was a little surprised that, having made the momentous decision they had, there was not a greater sense of conviction or aura of passion about them.

Glenville had a front gate and a back gate. The front-gate lodge was where the gardener lived. The driveway came from the front gate directly up to the house, where there was a gravel area large enough for a car or a pony and trap to turn, then con-

tinued past the ponds, the bamboo, the rhododendrons, over-
grown patches of lawn with York and Lancaster roses struggling
through the grass and weeds, to the stables and the coachman's
house. The driveway continued, on one side the stable build-
ings, henhouses and, on the other, a large black-currant garden,
to the back gate. Both gates opened out onto the lane.

The Little House, as the coachman's house was called after
the last coachman moved out and our family moved in, was
where my parents lived when I was born. The main house had
been closed up as an economy measure some time before. The
Little House was two stories high and built out of brick. The
house, stables, barn and kennels were all part of one large,
square, fortresslike construction. Except for the coachman's
house, which occupied one corner and had a normal front door
and windows, the rest faced inward. There were no windows on
the ground level and the only access was from the front, through
two separate sets of solid wooden double doors. The house and
stables had been built during a time of political unrest, and
while it had been impossible to build a house that was both
pleasant to look at and secure, measures had been taken to pro-
tect horses, dogs, grooms and motorcars.

The best thing about the house was the magnolia tree, which
grew on the courtyard side. Its heavy dark greenness against the
red brick gave a feeling of absorbed and retained warmth,
unusual and sensuously luxurious in so northern a climate. The
worst thing was the layout of the house, although perhaps the
way we utilized it added to the problem. At some time, probably
when it had ceased to be servant accommodation and became
the family home, it had been expanded and a bathroom and two
other rooms had been added. Since the house was not freestand-
ing, it had been necessary to add the new rooms on the ground
level and to attach them to the existing kitchen. The main bed-
room, dressing room and bathroom were behind the kitchen
and the nursery quarters were upstairs. It is possible that there
were good reasons for allocating space in this way, but it is also

possible that using the top floor for nurseries (as belowstairs was used for kitchen activities) prevented anyone indulging in lateral thinking when deciding who should sleep where.

This added a complication to my mother's already harried existence when, at some unsatisfactory moment in his life, one or the other of my father's two younger brothers would come to stay and have to sleep in the dressing room of the main bedroom.

Most of my adult life had been spent in or near the theatrical community. Show-business people pride themselves on their temperament and sensitivity. It is generally accepted that to succeed in this curiously structured and transitory line of work one has to have a taste for intrigue and competition, to understand betrayal and to possess nerves of steel and a poker face. My guess is that the emotional temperature or the neurotic possibilities of high-powered behind-the-scenes life never come close to those of a household which includes: a marriage, two or more generations of family members, and a sprinkling of unrelated personnel whose terms of employment require them to live under the same roof.

If downstairs was full of worries about brothers-in-law, money, domestic staff and my father's business problems, life abovestairs was also not without dramatic possibilities. In a modest way I, too, was able to make a contribution toward the emotional temperature of the Little House. I was a morbid child. The British tradition of reserve was well instilled in me by the age of four and I found it impossible to communicate or voice my fears. These repressed feelings would occasionally burst out in appalling tantrums. My mother still well remembers, as I do, a tantrum which manifested itself in a hysterical rage ostensibly because my nanny had gone upstairs before me. No one ever inquired or, as far as I know, wondered what it was really about, possibly because it had an unpleasant hint of assumed social superiority, which would have been embarrassing and hard to deal with.

My nanny's name was Nelly. I knew even then that she wasn't

a healthy influence, but of course at the time I never discussed her with my parents. Julia, being first a baby and then a small child during Nelly's reign, was even less likely to blow the whistle. Discipline was maintained by a series of threats and promises, none ever being fulfilled. If we were naughty or bold, as she, Nelly, would have said, she would threaten to lock us in the black closet at the top of the stairs. In fairness, the threat was clearly an idle one and carried little weight.

At some stage, Nelly became emotionally disturbed and it became apparent that she would have to go. My father took the position that firing nannies was women's work. It seems a little unfair. He was fifteen years older than my mother and would have been able to perform the deed with a fraction of the anxiety and—not too strong a word—the fear my mother felt. It had to do with the way he'd been brought up. He was more comfortable dealing with employees or servants than she was. He perceived the relationship in a different and less personal way. Oddly enough, his distant attitude often worked better than her more humane approach. Both parties appeared to feel more comfortable, or at least to recognize the ground rules.

My mother later told me that my father calmly continued to read a book while she took a stiff drink and fired Nelly. Tears, I imagine, ensued. Mine certainly did. "Nelly's gone" were soon, my father said, the saddest words in the English language. Despite experiencing a strong sense of loss, I don't remember feeling much, if any, affection for her. But I do remember an awful visit to her family. They lived in a cottage on the road to Woodstown, where she used to bicycle on her day off. Once when we were staying with my great-grandmother and great-great-aunt, who lived in Woodstown, she took me to see her family, incorporating the visit into our afternoon walk. It was a small cottage for a large Catholic-sized family. I only saw the main room, but I doubt if there were many more. Certainly not an indoor bathroom. The main room was a combined kitchen and living room. Her father sat at the hob beside the kitchen fire. The room was murky, lit by oil lamps. He told me that they were poor. I don't know if he wanted to make me, a junior member of the so-called privileged Protestant upper class, guilty, or whether he thought I would pass on this information to my father, who would do something for them or give Nelly a pay rise. Or maybe I was just a fresh audience for a running complaint. With that clarity reserved for childhood incidents horribly outside one's control, I remember his clinching argument. He took me to a cupboard where they kept their supplies and showed me an almost empty sugar bowl, not entirely clean—someone had helped himself to sugar with a tea-wet spoon—and said that that was all the sugar they had. I was used to the idea of shortages because of rationing, and used to the idea that almost no one we knew had enough money, but this was something different.

I have no memory of the move from the Little House to Glenville proper, or of the reasons for the move; still less did I understand that we were fulfilling some kind of Anglo-Irish destiny. I suppose we moved because our circumstances had improved slightly, or because the crowded atmosphere of the coachman's house had become impossible. Or a combination of the two. It was a very Anglo-Irish choice—to move into a large house without the means to make it comfortable or to live in it with comparative financial peace of mind. It was certainly not an ignorant choice. We were surrounded by examples of people stuck in large impossible houses when we voluntarily moved into ours. We didn't, of course, do anything as foolish as buying one. Glenville stood empty and in fairly good repair and the space must have seemed like a rationale for the move.

It is not a choice I would now make. The thought of all those not-quite-met responsibilities gives me a knot of anxiety, but I operate on a different value system, one geared toward freedom through simplification, whereas the society in which my parents (or at least my father) lived looked constantly over its shoulder. Few did it more gracefully than my father.

Glenville was built facing the lawn with its large and beautiful weeping ash. To the right of the house were the greenhouses and beyond them the walled garden. Each of the main rooms— the drawing room, dining room and library and, on the next floor, my parents' bedroom and the other two largest bed- rooms—had a gently curved wall, into which regular, not bay, windows were set. In each, the window which sat square to the room looked out over the row of ornamental ponds and behind them, some way below, the river. The curved wall allowed a slightly different view from the secondary windows, so that the library also looked over one end of the lawn, edged with a row of red-hot pokers (Kniphotia Uvaria), and the dining room had one window facing an unusually large and beautiful laburnum, behind which lay the densely packed bamboo jungle, which seemed too dense, exotic, threatening. Vandals at the gates of Rome.

The house had a double hallway, the inner part double-height, and, on the upper level, there was a gallerylike landing and a corridor off which lay the main bedrooms. The layout of the house, topped off with a glass dome, made it impossible to heat.

At one point, a large stove was installed in the hall. We called it Pingo. Pingo was the Edwardian nickname of Sir Terence Langrishe, whose real name carried all the weight of literary and upper-class associations one man could be expected to bear. He was a friend of my parents' and had been, in some way, instru- mental in our acquiring the stove. He may actually have sold it to us. Unless one was standing within a radius of four feet, the heat, which shot upward to the icy glass roof, eluded one entirely.

The cold and the dark shadows and the orange-red glow which came through the transparent but, to me, miraculously uninflammable windows on the front of Pingo were all part of one winter scene I remember. Julia and I were very small, Alice not yet born, when a party of carol singers from the Waterford Protestant cathedral came to Glenville. They had been expected all evening, and Julia and I had become more excited and more anxious as the evening wore on, our bedtime approached, and

the carolers did not materialize. Our bedtime, never late, was
slightly postponed and still no lights appeared on the driveway
and there was no sound of cars on the gravel. Eventually, disap-
pointed but not complaining, we allowed ourselves to be shooed
up the stairs. We were far too excited to sleep, but lay in bed
alert, with ears strained for the sound of visitors. Eventually they
arrived and our mother came upstairs and told us to put on our
dressing gowns and to watch from the gallery. It was too late and
too cold for us to get dressed again and I suppose also that,
although we were not sleepy, we must have been tired. Julia and
I both had pink dressing gowns, each with a white bunny rabbit
stitched on the pocket, and, wearing them over our night-
dresses, we crouched in the dark gallery peering through the
banisters, able to see and hear everything below. There is no
rational explanation why two children, covered from neck to
ankle in conventional nightclothes, should not have been able to
go downstairs and join their parents to listen to Christmas carols,
but the conventions of the time made it impossible. Two sepa-
rate conventions came into play here; I am not sure which was
the dominant. One had to do with dress. No one ever came
downstairs in a dressing gown. Breakfast was eaten, fully dressed,
in the dining room. In a well-run house a tray would have earlier
been sent up to one's bedroom with a pot of tea and a couple of
slices of toast. This snack was called "early morning tea." The
other convention was left over from the almost complete separa-
tion of adults from children a generation before. In those days,
parents who could afford to do so had their children cared for by
nannies and governesses and would frequently see them for less
than half an hour a day. Phrases like "Children should be seen
and not heard," not necessarily said as a joke, were common
even when I was growing up. (When Robert Gregory, about
whom Yeats wrote "An Irish Airman Foresees His Death," went
off to war in 1917, his wife and a maid watched him leave from
outside the hall door, while his two small daughters watched
from an upstairs window.) As occasionally happened, these con-
ventions worked in our favor that night. My mother, whose

most dominant emotion was probably slight embarrassment, remembers nothing of that evening. Julia and I, benefiting from the dim light, the distance, the atmosphere of secrecy as we concealed ourselves, remember it as magical, theatrical, beautiful. It is almost certainly Julia's earliest memory. When the singing ended my parents gave the carolers money and mugs of hot tomato soup (from a can, not homemade, which in Julia's and my eyes made it a luxury). The scene's resemblance to a Christmas card was further enhanced since, very wisely, none of the carolers took off his coat or muffler.

We all dressed warmly, with lots of home-knitted sweaters. I didn't suffer much from the cold, but my mother, who has poor circulation, was wretched during the winter, as was Julia, who used to develop the kind of incapacitating chilblains one wouldn't expect to meet outside a polar expedition.

Although it was not possible to keep a house such as Glenville warm, it was necessary to keep it dry and in winter we varied the rooms in which we sat so that the study and library alternately had the benefit of our fire. Heating throughout the house, to the extent it existed at all, was provided on a room-to-room basis, and it was a mad dash at mealtimes from living room to dining room. All the main rooms, however, had large old-fashioned and unused radiators—another relic of an age of cheap labor and cheap fuel.

The furnishing of the house was varied. Most things left over from the past were fine and, I suppose, valuable. China, silver, glass and furniture were often old and beautiful, although I don't remember any good paintings. What had been added in the way of beds and other household furniture was inexpensive department-store stuff—I don't think there was much in the way of good modern design then, and if there had been, we couldn't have afforded it.

Today, spending part of my time in rural Connecticut, I sometimes see my nursery plates for sale as valuable antiques, or a soap dish identical to those I remember from a maid's bedroom at Glenville priced at two hundred dollars, and I have a fantasy involving time and space. If I could have gone forward in time and sideways across the Atlantic bearing almost any everyday household object, sold it and returned with the money, it would have accomplished more than a year's worth of market gardening.

Julia and I, like most children, gravitated to the kitchen, not in search of delicious morsels—the kitchen did not have provisions for picking and snacking. We did not have a refrigerator or a cookie jar and most edible treats were found in the garden or the greenhouses. What we were after was gossip and drama, women's magazines and the wireless, as we called the radio. My father disliked the wireless, and used to say that most people played it at a volume in inverse proportion to their intelligence, so the only source of music as light entertainment was in the so-called servants' hall. (All my childhood rooms had grander names than the functions they had come to serve. When my father had been a boy it had been a servants' hall and no one had ever thought to change the name even though the only remaining trace of old-fashioned service was a numbered board with a bell and indicators to show in which room the summoning bell had been rung.) If one of us were sick and confined to bed for several days, the wireless would be moved across to our bedroom, but the rest of the time it was tuned to Radio Eireann and used only by the maids and any child who might be lurking about eavesdropping. The two exceptions were Christmas afternoon, when we listened, liverish and faintly embarrassed to, in early childhood, the King's Speech and, later, the Queen's Speech, and the great sporting events of the year, the English and Irish Grand Nationals and the English and Irish Derbies. The horse races evoked less complicated emotions, but while I can remember no highlights from the Queen's speeches, I am still familiar with the winners of the races from the time I was six until I left home. My father might have had a small bet on these occasions, but the importance and excitement of the races far transcended personal gain. One year, when I was eight, a local horse called Freebooter was entered in the English Grand

National and the level of excitement was higher than ever before. It was discovered that Madigan, the gardener, had placed a substantial bet on the local entry. Protocol, his shyness and muddy boots did not allow him to join us in the library while we listened to the race, but a happy compromise was reached. The library window was opened, the volume turned up, and Madigan stood outside among the camellias, overjoyed as his horse won.

We loved to listen to kitchen gossip, though I, at least, instinctively knew that, however fascinating, it wouldn't travel as far as the dining room. I would never have asked, as did Julia, still saucer-eyed from a belowstairs crash course on miracles: "What is Lourdes?" My father, his thoughts and maybe even his conversation elsewhere, replied without a moment's hesitation: "It's where they play cricket in London." This tiny incident illustrates the distance between kitchen and dining room but should not be taken as a suggestion that there was a gap in understanding, only in interests. We all read *Some Experiences of an Irish R.M.,* an entertaining novel in which a well-meaning but slightly pompous English Resident Magistrate is constantly, but not unaffectionately, made a fool of by the Irish, but the joke wasn't on us. Lourdes or Lord's, you took your pick. The difference was based on background and choice, not misunderstanding.

FRANK McCOURT

(1930–   )

"Worse than the ordinary miserable childhood is the miserable Irish childhood," wrote Frank McCourt in Angela's Ashes, *"and worse yet is the miserable Irish Catholic childhood." Born in Brooklyn of Irish parents, McCourt, his parents, and brother reemigrated to Ireland during the depression. Life had been hard for the family in New York, but scrabbling for food and housing in Limerick was poverty of another dimension.*

Frank McCourt came back to New York when he was nineteen and taught in the New York City public schools for nearly thirty years. It is only lately that he has been returning to Ireland. "I used to go back with a chip on my shoulder," he said, "but now I wrote the book and I've got this toxic stuff out of my system."

Catholicism and Irish nationalism were the twin pillars of McCourt's youth. "The master says it's a glorious thing to die for the Faith and Dad says it's a glorious thing to die for Ireland," he wrote. "I wonder if there is anyone in the world who would like us to live." An Irish boy's First Communion was marked by The Collection, a parading of the communicant in front of friends and neighbors who gave candy and money, and a trip to the Lyric Cinema to watch James Cagney. In this excerpt, McCourt's First Communion goes terribly awry.

from ANGELA'S ASHES

First Communion day is the happiest day of your life because of The Collection and James Cagney at the Lyric Cinema. The night before I was so excited I couldn't sleep till dawn. I'd still be sleeping if my grandmother hadn't come banging at the door.

Get up! Get up! Get that child outa the bed. Happiest day of his life an' him snorin' above in the bed.

I ran to the kitchen. Take off that shirt, she said. I took off the shirt and she pushed me into a tin tub of icy cold water. My mother scrubbed me, my grandmother scrubbed me. I was raw, I was red.

They dried me. They dressed me in my black velvet First Communion suit with the white frilly shirt, the short pants, the white stockings, the black patent leather shoes. Around my arm they tied a white satin bow and on my lapel they pinned the Sacred Heart of Jesus, a picture of the Sacred Heart, with blood dripping from it, flames erupting all around it and on top a nasty-looking crown of thorns.

Come here till I comb your hair, said Grandma. Look at that mop, it won't lie down. You didn't get that hair from my side of the family. That's that North of Ireland hair you got from your father. That's the kind of hair you see on Presbyterians. If your mother had married a proper decent Limerickman you wouldn't have this standing up, North of Ireland, Presbyterian hair.

She spat twice on my head.

Grandma, will you please stop spitting on my head.

If you have anything to say, shut up. A little spit won't kill you. Come on, we'll be late for the Mass.

We ran to the church. My mother panted along behind with Michael in her arms. We arrived at the church just in time to see the last of the boys leaving the altar rail where the priest stood with the chalice and the host, glaring at me. Then he placed on my tongue the wafer, the body and blood of Jesus. At last, at last.

It's on my tongue. I draw it back.

It stuck.

I had God glued to the roof of my mouth. I could hear the master's voice, Don't let that host touch your teeth for if you bite God in two you'll roast in hell for eternity.

I tried to get God down with my tongue but the priest hissed at me, Stop that clucking and get back to your seat.

God was good. He melted and I swallowed Him and now, at last, I was a member of the True Church, an official sinner.

When the Mass ended there they were at the door of the church, my mother with Michael in her arms, my grandmother. They each hugged me to their bosoms. They each told me it was the happiest day of my life. They each cried all over my head and after my grandmother's contribution that morning my head was a swamp.

Mam, can I go now and make The Collection?

She said, After you have a little breakfast.

No, said Grandma. You're not making no collection till you've had a proper First Communion breakfast at my house. Come on.

We followed her. She banged pots and rattled pans and complained that the whole world expected her to be at their beck and call. I ate the egg, I ate the sausage, and when I reached for more sugar for my tea she slapped my hand away.

Go aisy with that sugar. Is it a millionaire you think I am? An American? Is it bedecked in glitterin' jewelry you think I am? Smothered in fancy furs?

The food churned in my stomach. I gagged. I ran to her backyard and threw it all up. Out she came.

Look at what he did. Thrun up his First Communion break-
fast. Thrun up the body and blood of Jesus. I have God in me
backyard. What am I goin' to do? I'll take him to the Jesuits for
they know the sins of the Pope himself.

She dragged me through the streets of Limerick. She told the
neighbors and passing strangers about God in her backyard. She
pushed me into the confession box.

In the name of the Father, the Son, the Holy Ghost. Bless
me, Father, for I have sinned. It's a day since my last confession.

A day? And what sins have you committed in a day, my child?

I overslept. I nearly missed my First Communion. My grand-
mother said I have standing up, North of Ireland, Presbyterian
hair. I threw up my First Communion breakfast. Now Grandma
says she has God in her backyard and what should she do.

The priest is like the First Confession priest. He has the heavy
breathing and the choking sounds.

Ah . . . ah . . . tell your grandmother to wash God away with
a little water and for your penance say one Hail Mary and one
Our Father. Say a prayer for me and God bless you, my child.

Grandma and Mam were waiting close to the confession box.
Grandma said, Were you telling jokes to that priest in the con-
fession box? If 'tis a thing I ever find out you were telling jokes
to Jesuits I'll tear the bloody kidneys outa you. Now what did he
say about God in me backyard?

He said wash Him away with a little water, Grandma.

Holy water or ordinary water?

He didn't say, Grandma.

Well, go back and ask him.

But, Grandma . . .

She pushed me back into the confessional.

Bless me, Father, for I have sinned, it's a minute since my last
confession.

A minute! Are you the boy that was just here?

I am, Father.

What is it now?

My grandma says, Holy water or ordinary water?

Ordinary water, and tell your grandmother not to be bothering me again.

I told her, Ordinary water, Grandma, and he said don't be bothering him again.

Don't be bothering him again. That bloody ignorant bogtrotter.

I asked Mam, Can I go now and make The Collection? I want to see James Cagney.

Grandma said, You can forget about The Collection and James Cagney because you're not a proper Catholic the way you left God on the ground. Come on, go home.

Mam said, Wait a minute. That's my son. That's my son on his First Communion day. He's going to see James Cagney.

No he's not.

Yes he is.

Grandma said, Take him then to James Cagney and see if that will save his Presbyterian North of Ireland American soul. Go ahead.

She pulled her shawl around her and walked away.

Mam said, God, it's getting very late for The Collection and you'll never see James Cagney. We'll go to the Lyric Cinema and see if they'll let you in anyway in your First Communion suit.

We met Mikey Molloy on Barrington Street. He asked if I was going to the Lyric and I said I was trying. Trying? he said. You don't have money?

I was ashamed to say no but I had to and he said, That's all right. I'll get you in. I'll create a diversion.

What's a diversion?

I have the money to go and when I get in I'll pretend to have the fit and the ticket man will be out of his mind and you can slip in when I let out the big scream. I'll be watching the door and when I see you in I'll have a miraculous recovery. That's a diversion. That's what I do to get my brothers in all the time.

Mam said, Oh, I don't know about that, Mikey. Wouldn't that be a sin and surely you wouldn't want Frank to commit a sin on his First Communion day.

Mikey said if there was a sin it would be on his soul and he wasn't a proper Catholic anyway so it didn't matter. He let out his scream and I slipped in and sat next to Question Quigley and the ticket man, Frank Goggin, was so worried over Mikey he never noticed. It was a thrilling film but sad in the end because James Cagney was a public enemy and when they shot him they wrapped him in bandages and threw him in the door, shocking his poor old Irish mother, and that was the end of my First Communion day.

GEORGE MOORE

(1852–1933)

George Moore's parents were Catholic landowners with peasant sympathies. Moore was reared in County Mayo in wealth, educated at boarding schools, and at the age of twenty-one he went to Paris to study painting. Shortly after arriving in Paris he abandoned art for literature. Influenced by Flaubert and Zola, he wrote many novels and acquired a reputation as one of the major writers of his time.

It surprised many when Moore returned to Ireland in 1898 to take part in the Irish Literary Revival. For more than ten years he worked with Yeats, Edward Martyn, and Lady Gregory on the foundation of the Irish Literary Theater, a forerunner of the Abbey. Moore thought he would be embraced as a messiah. Instead, other Irish writers ridiculed him for his Continental airs, French accent, and impeccable dress. A contemporary described him as looking like an "artful, middle-aged baby" with a profile that was "melting in outline, as if he had no bones."

Disillusioned, Moore again left Ireland, this time for London. He wrote a well-received three-volume autobiography, Hail and Farewell, *an account of the Irish Literary Revival. "Homesickness" is from his short story collection* The Untilled Field. *Frank O'Connor said this was his favorite story by Moore. Moore died in London in 1933.*

HOME SICKNESS

from THE UNTILLED FIELD

He told the doctor he was due in the barroom at eight o'clock in the morning; the barroom was in a slum in the Bowery; and he had only been able to keep himself in health by getting up at five o'clock and going for long walks in the Central Park.

"A sea voyage is what you want," said the doctor. "Why not go to Ireland for two or three months? You will come back a new man."

"I'd like to see Ireland again."

And he began to wonder how the people at home were getting on. The doctor was right. He thanked him, and three weeks after he landed in Cork.

As he sat in the railway carriage he recalled his native village, built among the rocks of the large headland stretching out into the winding lake. He could see the houses and the streets, and the fields of the tenants, and the Georgian mansion and the owners of it; he and they had been boys together before he went to America. He remembered the villagers going every morning to the big house to work in the stables, in the garden, in the fields—mowing, reaping, digging, and Michael Malia building a wall; it was all as clear as if it were yesterday, yet he had been thirteen years in America; and when the train stopped at the station the first thing he did was to look round for any changes that might have come into it. It was the same blue limestone station as it was thirteen years ago, with the same five long miles between it and Duncannon. He had once walked these miles gaily, in little over an hour, carrying a heavy bundle on a stick, but he did not feel strong enough for the walk today, though the evening tempted him to try it. A car was waiting at the station, and the boy, discerning from his accent and his dress that Bryden had come from America, plied him with questions, which Bryden answered rapidly, for he wanted to hear who was still living in the village, and if there was a house in which he could get a clean lodging. The best house in the village, he was told, was Mike Scully's, who had been away in a situation for many years, as a coachman in the King's County, but had come back and built a fine house with a concrete floor. The boy could recommend the loft, he had slept in it himself, and Mike would be glad to take in a lodger, he had no doubt. Bryden remembered that Mike had been in a situation at the big house. He had intended to be a jockey, but had suddenly shot up into a fine tall man, and had become a coachman instead, and Bryden tried to recall his face, but could only remember a straight nose and a somewhat dusky complexion.

So Mike had come back from King's County, and had built himself a house, had married—there were children for sure running about; while he, Bryden, had gone to America, but he had come back; perhaps he, too, would build a house in Duncannon, and—his reverie was suddenly interrupted by the carman.

"There's Mike Scully," he said, pointing with his whip, and Bryden saw a tall, finely built, middle-aged man coming through the gates, who looked astonished when he was accosted, for he had forgotten Bryden even more completely than Bryden had forgotten him; and many aunts and uncles were mentioned before he began to understand.

"You've grown into a fine man, James," he said, looking at Bryden's great width of chest. "But you're thin in the cheeks, and you're very sallow in the cheeks, too."

"I haven't been very well lately—that is one of the reasons I've come back; but I want to see you all again."

"And thousand welcome you are."

Bryden paid the carman, and wished him Godspeed. They divided the luggage, Mike carrying the bag and Bryden the bundle, and they walked round the lake, for the townland was at the back of the domain; and while walking he remembered the woods thick and well forested; now they were wind worn, the drains were choked, and the bridge leading across the lake inlet was falling away. Their way led between long fields where herds of cattle were grazing, the road was broken—Bryden wondered how the villagers drove their carts over it, and Mike told him that the landlord could not keep it in repair, and he would not allow it to be kept in repair out of the rates, for then it would be a public road, and he did not think there should be a public road through his property.

At the end of many fields they came to the village, and it looked a desolate place, even on this fine evening, and Bryden remarked that the county did not seem to be as much lived in as it used to be. It was at once strange and familiar to see the chickens in the kitchen; and, wishing to reknit himself to the old customs, he begged of Mrs. Scully not to drive them out, saying they reminded him of old times.

"And why wouldn't they?" Mike answered, "he being one of ourselves bred and born in Duncannon, and his father before him."

"Now, is it truth ye are telling me?" and she gave him her hand, after wiping it on her apron, saying he was heartily welcome, only she was afraid he wouldn't care to sleep in a loft.

"Why wouldn't I sleep in a loft, a dry loft! You're thinking a good deal of America over here," he said, "but I reckon it isn't all you think it. Here you work when you like and you sit down when you like; but when you've had a touch of blood-poisoning as I had, and when you have seen young people walking with a stick, you think that there is something to be said for old Ireland."

"You'll take a sup of milk, won't you? You must be dry," said Mrs. Scully.

And when he had drunk the milk Mike asked him if he would like to go inside or if he would like to go for a walk.

"Maybe resting you'd like to be."

And they went into the cabin and started to talk about the wages a man could get in America, and the long hours of work.

And after Bryden had told Mike everything about America that he thought of interest, he asked Mike about Ireland. But Mike did not seem to be able to tell him much. They were all very poor—poorer, perhaps, than when he left them.

"I don't think anyone except myself has a five-pound note to his name."

Bryden hoped he felt sufficiently sorry for Mike. But after all Mike's life and prospects mattered little to him. He had come back in search of health, and he felt better already; the milk had done him good, and the bacon and the cabbage in the pot sent forth a savory odor. The Scullys were very kind, they pressed him to make a good meal; a few weeks of country air and food, they said, would give him back the health he had lost in the Bowery; and when Bryden said he was longing for a smoke, Mike said there was no better sign than that. During his long illness he had never wanted to smoke, and he was a confirmed smoker.

It was comfortable to sit by the mild peat fire watching the smoke of their pipes drifting up the chimney, and all Bryden wanted was to be left alone; he did not want to hear of anyone's misfortunes, but about nine o'clock a number of villagers came in, and Bryden remembered one or two of them—he used to know them very well when he was a boy; their talk was as depressing as their appearance, and he could feel no interest whatever in them. He was not moved when he heard that Higgins the stonemason was dead; he was not affected when he heard that Mary Kelly, who used to go to do the laundry at the Big House, had married; he was only interested when he heard she had gone to America. No, he had not met her there; America is a big place. Then one of the peasants asked him if he

remembered Patsy Carabine, who used to do the gardening at
the Big House. Yes, he remembered Patsy well. He had not been
able to do any work on account of his arm; his house had fallen
in; he had given up his holding and gone into the poorhouse. All
this was very sad, and to avoid hearing any further unpleasant-
ness, Bryden began to tell them about America. And they sat
round listening to him; but all the talking was on his side; he
wearied of it; and looking round the group he recognized a
ragged hunchback with grey hair; twenty years ago he was a
young hunchback and, turning to him, Bryden asked him if he
were doing well with his five acres.

"Ah, not much. This has been a poor season. The potatoes
failed; they were watery—there is no diet in them."

These peasants were all agreed that they could make nothing
out of their farms. Their regret was that they had not gone to
America when they were young; and after striving to take an
interest in the fact that O'Connor had lost a mare and a foal
worth forty pounds, Bryden began to wish himself back in the
slum. And when they left the house he wondered if every
evening would be like the present one. Mike piled fresh sods on
the fire, and he hoped it would show enough light in the loft for
Bryden to undress himself by.

The cackling of some geese in the street kept him awake, and
he seemed to realize suddenly how lonely the country was, and
he foresaw mile after mile of scanty fields stretching all round
the lake with one little town in the far corner. A dog howled in
the distance, and the fields and the boreens between him and the
dog appeared as in a crystal. He could hear Michael breathing by
his wife's side in the kitchen, and he could barely resist the
impulse to run out of the house, and he might have yielded to
it, but he wasn't sure that he mightn't awaken Mike as he came
down the ladder. His terror increased, and he drew the blanket
over his head. He fell asleep and awoke and fell asleep again, and
lying on his back he dreamed of the men he had seen sitting
round the fireside that evening, like specters they seemed to him

in his dream. He seemed to have been asleep only a few minutes when he heard Mike calling him. He had come halfway up the ladder, and was telling him that breakfast was ready.

"What kind of a breakfast will he give me?" Bryden asked himself as he pulled on his clothes. There were tea and hot grid-dle cakes for breakfast, and there were fresh eggs; there was sun-light in the kitchen, and he liked to hear Mike tell of the work he was going to be at in the farm—one of about fifteen acres, at least ten of it was grass; he grew an acre of potatoes, and some corn, and some turnips for his sheep. He had a nice bit of meadow, and he took down his scythe, and as he put the whet-stone in his belt Bryden noticed a second scythe, and he asked Mike if he should go down with him and help him to finish the field.

"It's a long time since you've done any mowing, and it's heav-ier work than you think for. You'd better go for a walk by the lake." Seeing that Bryden looked a little disappointed he added, "if you like you can come up in the afternoon and help me to turn the grass over." Bryden said he would, and the morning passed pleasantly by the lakeshore—a delicious breeze rustled in the trees, and the reeds were talking together, and the ducks were talking in the reeds; a cloud blotted out the sunlight, and the cloud passed and the sun shone, and the reed cast its shadow again in the still water; there was a lapping always about the shingle; the magic of returning health was sufficient distraction for the convalescent; he lay with his eyes fixed upon the castles, dreaming of the men that had manned the battlements; when-ever a peasant driving a cart or an ass or an old woman with a bundle of sticks on her back went by, Bryden kept them in chat, and he soon knew the village by heart. One day the landlord from the Georgian mansion set on the pleasant green hill came along, his retriever at his heels, and stopped surprised at finding somebody whom he didn't know on his property. "What, James Bryden!" he said. And the story was told again how ill health had overtaken him at last, and he had come home to Duncannon to recover. The two walked as far as the pinewood, talking of the county, what it had been, the ruin it was slipping into, and as they parted Bryden asked for the loan of a boat.

"Of course, of course!" the landlord answered, and Bryden rowed about the islands every morning; and resting upon his oars looked at the old castles, remembering the prehistoric raiders that the landlord had told him about. He came across the stones to which the lake dwellers had tied their boats, and these signs of ancient Ireland were pleasing to Bryden in his present mood.

As well as the great lake there was a smaller lake in the bog where the villagers cut their turf. This lake was famous for its pike, and the landlord allowed Bryden to fish there, and one evening when he was looking for a frog with which to bait his line he met Margaret Dirken driving home the cows for the milking. Margaret was the herdsman's daughter, and lived in a cottage near the Big House; but she came up to the village whenever there was a dance, and Bryden had found himself opposite to her in the reels. But until this evening he had had little opportunity of speaking to her, and he was glad to speak to someone, for the evening was lonely, and they stood talking together.

"You're getting your health again," she said, "and will be leaving us soon."

"I'm in no hurry."

"You're grand people over there; I hear a man is paid four dollars a day for his work."

"And how much," said James, "has he to pay for his food and for his clothes?"

Her cheeks were bright and her teeth were small, white, and beautifully even; and a woman's soul looked at Bryden out of her soft Irish eyes. He was troubled and turned aside, and catching sight of a frog looking at him out of a tuft of grass, he said:

"I have been looking for a frog to put upon my pike line."

The frog jumped right and left, and nearly escaped in some bushes, but he caught it and returned with it in his hand.

"It is just the kind of frog a pike will like," he said. "Look at its great white belly and its bright yellow back."

And without more ado he pushed the wire to which the hook was fastened through the frog's fresh body, and dragging it through the mouth he passed the hooks through the hind legs and tied the line to the end of the wire.

"I think," said Margaret, "I must be looking after my cows; it's time I got them home."

"Won't you come down to the lake while I set my line?"

She thought for a moment and said:

"No, I'll see you from here."

He went down to the reedy tarn, and at his approach several snipe got up, and they flew above his head uttering sharp cries. His fishing rod was a long hazel stick, and he threw the frog as far as he could in the lake. In doing this he roused some wild ducks; a mallard and two ducks got up, and they flew towards the larger lake in a line with an old castle; and they had not disappeared from view when Bryden came towards her, and he and she drove the cows home together that evening.

They had not met very often when she said: "James, you had better not come here so often calling to me."

"Don't you wish me to come?"

"Yes, I wish you to come well enough, but keeping company isn't the custom of the country, and I don't want to be talked about."

"Are you afraid the priest would speak against us from the altar?"

"He has spoken against keeping company, but it is not so much what the priest says, for there is no harm in talking."

"But if you're going to be married there is no harm in walking out together."

"Well, not so much, but marriages are made differently in these parts; there isn't much courting here."

And next day it was known in the village that James was going to marry Margaret Dirken.

His desire to excel the boys in dancing had caused a stir of gaiety in the parish, and for some time past there had been dancing in every house where there was a floor fit to dance upon;

and if the cottager had no money to pay for a barrel of beer, James Bryden, who had money, sent him a barrel, so that Margaret might get her dance. She told him that they sometimes crossed over into another parish where the priest was not so averse to dancing, and James wondered. And next morning at Mass he wondered at their simple fervor. Some of them held their hands above their head as they prayed, and all this was very new and very old to James Bryden. But the obedience of these people to their priest surprised him. When he was a lad they had not been so obedient, or he had forgotten their obedience; and he listened in mixed anger and wonderment to the priest, who was scolding his parishioners, speaking to them by name, saying that he had heard there was dancing going on in their homes. Worse than that, he said he had seen boys and girls loitering about the road, and the talk that went on was of one kind—love. He said that newspapers containing love stories were finding their way into the people's houses, stories about love, in which there was nothing elevating or ennobling. The people listened, accepting the priest's opinion without question. And their pathetic submission was the submission of a primitive people clinging to religious authority, and Bryden contrasted the weakness and incompetence of the people about him with the modern restlessness and cold energy of the people he left behind him.

One evening, as they were dancing, a knock came to the door, and the piper stopped playing, and the dancers whispered:

"Someone has told on us: it is the priest."

And the awestricken villagers crowded round the cottage fire, afraid to open the door. But the priest said that if they didn't open the door he would put his shoulder to it and force it open. Bryden went towards the door, saying he would allow no one to threaten him, priest or no priest, but Margaret caught his arm and told him that if he said anything to the priest, the priest would speak against them from the altar, and they would be shunned by the neighbors.

"I've heard of your goings-on," he said—"of your beer

drinking and dancing. I'll not have it in my parish. If you want that sort of thing you had better go to America."

"If that is intended for me, sir, I'll go back tomorrow. Margaret can follow."

"It isn't the dancing, it's the drinking I'm opposed to," said the priest, turning to Bryden.

"Well, no one has drunk too much, sir," said Bryden.

"But you'll sit here drinking all night," and the priest's eyes went to the corner where the women had gathered, and Bryden felt that the priest looked on the women as more dangerous than the porter. "It's after midnight," he said, taking out his watch.

By Bryden's watch it was only half past eleven, and while they were arguing about the time, Mrs. Scully offered Bryden's umbrella to the priest, for in his hurry to stop the dancing the priest had gone out without his; and, as if to show Bryden that he bore him no ill will, the priest accepted the loan of the umbrella, for he was thinking of the big marriage fee that Bryden would pay him.

"I shall be badly off for the umbrella tomorrow," Bryden said, as soon as the priest was out of the house. He was going with his father-in-law to a fair. His father-in-law was learning him how to buy and sell cattle. The country was mending, and a man might become rich in Ireland if he only had a little capital. Margaret had an uncle on the other side of the lake who would give twenty pounds, and her father would give another twenty pounds. Bryden had saved two hundred pounds. Never in the village of Duncannon had a young couple begun life with so much prospect of success, and some time after Christmas was spoken of as the best time for the marriage; James Bryden said that he would not be able to get his money out of America before the spring. The delay seemed to vex him, and he seemed anxious to be married, until one day he received a letter from America, from a man who had served in the bar with him. This friend wrote to ask Bryden if he were coming back. The letter was no more than a passing wish to see Bryden again. Yet Bryden stood looking at it, and everyone wondered what could be in the letter. It seemed momentous, and they hardly believed him when he said it was from a friend who wanted to know if his health were better. He tried to forget the letter, and he looked at the worn fields, divided by walls of loose stones, and a great longing came upon him.

The smell of the Bowery slum had come across the Atlantic, and had found him out in his western headland; and one night he awoke from a dream in which he was hurling some drunken customer through the open doors into the darkness. He had seen his friend in his white duck jacket throwing drink from glass into glass amid the din of voices and strange accents; he had heard the clang of money as it was swept into the till, and his sense sickened for the barroom. But how should he tell Margaret Dirken that he could not marry her? She had built her life upon this marriage. He could not tell her that he would not marry her . . . yet he must go. He felt as if he were being hunted; the thought that he must tell Margaret that he could not marry her hunted him day after day as a weasel hunts a rabbit. Again and again he went to meet her with the intention of telling her that he did not love her, that their lives were not for one another, that it had all been a mistake, and that happily he had found out it was a mistake soon enough. But Margaret, as if she guessed what he was about to speak of, threw her arms about him and begged him to say he loved her, and that they would be married at once. He agreed that he loved her, and that they would be married at once. But he had not left her many minutes before the feeling came upon him that he could not marry her—that he must go away. The small of the barroom hunted him down. Was it for the sake of the money that he might make there that he wished to go back? No, it was not the money. What then? His eyes fell on the bleak country, on the little fields divided by bleak walls; he remembered the pathetic ignorance of the people, and it was these things that he could not endure. It was the priest who came to forbid the dancing. Yes, it was the priest.

As he stood looking at the line of the hills the barroom seemed by him. He heard the politicians, and the excitement of politics was in his blood again. He must go away from this place—he must get back to the barroom. Looking up, he saw the scanty orchard, and he hated the spare road that led to the village, and he hated the little hill at the top of which the village began, and he hated more than all other places the house where he was to live with Margaret Dirken—if he married her. He could see it from where he stood—by the edge of the lake, with twenty acres of pasture land about it, for the landlord had given up part of his demesne land to them.

He caught sight of Margaret, and he called her to come through the stile.

"I have just had a letter from America."

"About the money?"

"Yes, about the money. But I shall have to go over there."

He stood looking at her, wondering what to say; and she guessed that he would tell her that he must go to America before they were married.

"Do you mean, James, you will have to go at once?"

"Yes," he said, "at once. But I shall come back in time to be married in August. It will only mean delaying our marriage a month."

They walked on a little way talking, and every step he took James felt that he was a step nearer the Bowery slum. And when they came to the gate Bryden said:

"I must walk on or I shall miss the train."

"But," she said, "you are not going now—you are not going today?"

"Yes, this morning. It is seven miles. I shall have to hurry not to miss the train."

And then she asked him if he would ever come back.

"Yes," he said, "I am coming back."

"If you are coming back, James, why don't you let me go with you?"

"You couldn't walk fast enough. We should miss the train."

"One moment, James. Don't make me suffer; tell me the truth. You are not coming back. Your clothes—where shall I send them?"

He hurried away, hoping he would come back. He tried to think that he liked the country he was leaving, that it would be better to have a farmhouse and live there with Margaret Dirken than to serve drinks behind a counter in the Bowery. He did not think he was telling her a lie when he said he was coming back. Her offer to forward his clothes touched his heart, and at the end of the road he stood and asked himself if he should go back to her. He would miss the train if he waited another minute, and he ran on. And he would have missed the train if he had not met a car. Once he was on the car he felt himself safe—the country was already behind him. The train and the boat at Cork were mere formulae; he was already in America.

And when the tall skyscraper stuck up beyond the harbor he felt the thrill of home that he had not found in his native village and wondered how it was that the smell of the bar seemed more natural than the smell of fields, and the roar of crowds more welcome than the silence of the lake's edge. He entered into negotiations for the purchase of the barroom. He took a wife, she bore him sons and daughters, the barroom prospered, property came and went; he grew old, his wife died, he retired from business, and reached the age when a man begins to feel there are not many years in front of him, and that all he has had to do in life has been done. His children married, lonesomeness began to creep about him in the evening, and when he looked into the firelight, a vague tender reverie floated up, and Margaret's soft eyes and name vivified the dusk. His wife and children passed out of mind, and it seemed to him that a memory was the only real thing he possessed, and the desire to see Margaret again grew intense. But she was an old woman, she had married, maybe she was dead. Well, he would like to be buried in the village where he was born.

There is an unchanging, silent life within every man that none knows but himself, and his unchanging silent life was his memory of Margaret Dirken. The barroom was forgotten and all that concerned it, and the things he saw most clearly were the green hillside, and the bog lake and the rushes about it, and the greater lake in the distance, and behind it the blue line of wandering hills.

EDNA O'BRIEN

(1932–   )

"I do not see into male sensibility as clearly as into female," said Edna O'Brien. Most of O'Brien's fiction and poetry explores the problems of Irish women in a repressed society. O'Brien's female characters try to communicate with each other and with men, but their efforts often come up against brutality and hypocrisy.

Born in County Clare and trained as a pharmacist, O'Brien moved to London in 1959 with her husband, the Irish writer Ernest Gebler. Her first novel, The Country Girls, *was published in 1960. Many followed:* The High Road, Time and Tide, Night *among them. Her most recent book,* Down by the River, *is based on the true case of a fourteen-year-old Irish girl who was prevented from leaving the country to obtain an abortion. O'Brien sympathizes with the victim and her allies, and lashes out at the Catholic community that condemns and isolates them. One reviewer wrote that her stories "stare you down and tear you apart like a wolf—and then, miraculously and tenderly, bring you back to life again, stronger and better than before."*

Ireland has often banned O'Brien's work because of its frank sexuality. The following short story, "My Mother's Mother," was first published in 1984 in her collection A Fanatic Heart.

MY MOTHER'S MOTHER

from A FANATIC HEART

I loved my mother, yet I was glad when the time came to go to her mother's house each summer. It was a little house in the mountains and it commanded a fine view of the valley and the great lake below. From the front door, glimpsed through a pair of very old binoculars, one could see the entire Shannon Lake studded with various islands. On a summer's day this was a thrill. I would be put standing on a kitchen chair, while someone held the binoculars, and sometimes I marveled though I could not see at all, as the lenses had not been focused properly. The sunshine made everything better, and though we were not down by the lake, we imagined dipping our feet in it, or seeing people in boats fishing and then stopping to have a picnic. We imagined lake water lapping.

I felt safer in that house. It was different from our house, not so imposing, a cottage really, with no indoor water and no water closet. We went for buckets of water to the well, a different well each summer. These were a source of miracle to me, these deep cold wells, sunk into the ground, in a kitchen garden, or a paddock, or even a long distance away, wells that had been divined since I was last there. There was always a tin scoop nearby so that one could fill the bucket to the very brim. Then of course the full bucket was an occasion of trepidation, because one was supposed not to spill. One often brought the bucket to the very threshold of the kitchen and then out of excitement or clumsiness some water would get splashed onto the concrete floor and

there would be admonishments, but it was not like the admon-
ishments in our house, it was not calamitous.

My grandfather was old and thin and hoary when I first saw
him. His skin was the color of a clay pipe. After the market day
he would come home in the pony and trap drunk, and then as
soon as he stepped out of the trap he would stagger and fall into
a drain or whatever. Then he would roar for help, and his grand-
son, who was in his twenties, would pick him up, or rather, drag
him along the ground and through the house and up the stairs to
his feather bed, where he moaned and groaned. The bedroom
was above the kitchen, and in the night we would be below,
around the fire, eating warm soda bread and drinking cocoa.
There was nothing like it. The fresh bread would only be an
hour out of the pot and cut in thick pieces and dolloped with
butter and greengage jam. The greengage jam was a present
from the postmistress, who gave it in return for the grazing of a
bullock. She gave marmalade at a different time of year and a
barmbrack at Halloween. He moaned upstairs, but no one was
frightened of him, not even his own wife, who chewed and
chewed and said, "Bad cess to them that give him the drink."
She meant the publicans. She was a minute woman with a
minute face and her thin hair was pinned up tightly. Her little
face, though old, was like a bud, and when she was young she
had been beautiful. There was a photo of her to prove it.

SITTING WITH THEM at night I thought that maybe I
would not go home at all. Maybe I would never again lie in bed
next to my mother, the two of us shivering with expectancy and
with terror. Maybe I would forsake my mother.

"Maybe you'll stay here," my aunt said, as if she had guessed
my thoughts.

"I couldn't do that," I said, not knowing why I declined,
because indeed the place had definite advantages. I stayed up as
late as they did. I ate soda bread and jam to my heart's content, I
rambled around the fields all day, admiring sally trees, elder

bushes, and the fluttering flowers, I played "shop" or I played teaching in the little dark plantation, and no one interfered or told me to stop doing it. The plantation was where I played secrets, and always I knew the grownups were within shouting distance, if a stranger or a tinker should surprise me there. It was pitch dark and full of young fir trees. The ground was a carpet of bronzed fallen fir needles. I used to kneel on them for punishment, after the playing.

Then when that ritual was done I went into the flower garden, which being full of begonias and lupines was a mass of bright brilliant colors. Each area had its own color, as my aunt planned it that way. I can see them now, those bright reds, like nail varnish, and those yellows like the gauze of a summer dress and those pale blues like old people's eyes, with the bees and the wasps luxuriating in each petal, or each little bell, or each flute, and feel the warmth of the place, and the drone of the bees, and see again tea towels and gray flannelette drawers that were spread out on the hedge to dry. The sun garden, they called it. My aunt got the seeds and just sprinkled them around, causing marvelous blooms to spring up. They even had tulips, whereas at home we had only a diseased rambling rose on a silvered arch and two clumps of devil's pokers. Our garden was sad and windy, the wind had made holes and indentations in the hedges, and the dogs had made further holes where they slept and burrowed. Our house was larger, and there was better linoleum on the floor, there were brass rods on the stairs, and there was a flush lavatory, but it did not have the same cheeriness and it was imbued with doom.

Still, I knew that I would not stay in my grandmother's forever. I knew it for certain when I got into bed and then desperately missed my mother, and missed the little whispering we did, and the chocolate we ate, and I missed the smell of our kind of bedclothes. Theirs were gray flannel, which tickled the skin, as did the loose feathers, and their pointed ends kept irking one. There was a gaudy red quilt that I thought would come to life and turn into a sinister Santa Claus. Except that they had told me that there was no Santa Claus. My aunt told me that, she insisted.

There was my aunt and her two sons, Donal and Joe, and my grandmother and grandfather. My aunt and Joe would tease me each night, say that there was no Santa Claus, until I got up and stamped the floor, and in contradicting them welled up with tears, and then at last, when I was on the point of breaking down, they would say that there was. Then one night they went too far. They said that my mother was not my real mother. My real mother, they said, was in Australia and I was adopted. I could not be told that word. I began to hit the wall and screech, and the more they insisted, the more obstreperous I became. My aunt went into the parlor in search of a box of snaps to find a photo of my real mother and came out triumphant at having found it. She showed me a woman in knickerbockers with a big floppy hat. I could have thrown it in the fire so violent was I. They watched for each new moment of panic and furious disbelief, and then they got the wind up when they saw I was getting out of control. I began to shake like the weather conductor on the chapel chimney and my teeth chattered, and before long I was just this shaking creature, unable to let out any sound, and seeing the room's contents swim away from me, I felt their alarm almost as I felt my own. My aunt took hold of my wrist to feel my pulse, and my grandmother held a spoonful of tonic to my lips, but I spilled it. It was called Parishes Food and was the color of cooked beetroot. My eyes were haywire. My aunt put a big towel around me and sat me on her knee, and as the terror lessened, my tears began to flow and I cried so much that they thought I would choke because of the tears going back down the throat. They said I must never tell anyone and I must never tell my mother.

"She is my mother," I said, and they said, "Yes, darling," but I knew that they were appalled at what had happened.

That night I fell out of bed twice, and my aunt had to put chairs next to it to keep me in. She slept in the same room, and often I used to hear her crying for her dead husband and beg-

ging to be reunited with him in heaven. She used to talk to him
and say, "Is that you, Michael, is that you?" I often heard her
arms striking against the headboard, or heavy movements when
she got up to relieve herself. In the daytime we used the fields,
but at night we did not go out for fear of ghosts. There was a
gutter in the back kitchen that served as a channel, and twice a
week she put disinfectant in it. The crux in the daytime was
finding a private place and not being found or spied on by any-
one. It entailed much walking and then much hesitating so as
not to be seen.

The morning after the fright, they pampered me, scrambled
me an egg, and sprinkled nutmeg over it. Then along with that
my aunt announced a surprise. Our workman had sent word by
the mail-car man that he was coming to see me on Sunday and
the postman had delivered the message. Oh, what a glut of hap-
piness. Our workman was called Carnero and I loved him too. I
loved his rotting teeth and his curly hair and his strong hands and
his big stomach, which people referred to as his "corporation."
He was nicknamed Carnero after a boxer. I knew that when he
came he would have bars of chocolate, and maybe a letter or a
silk hanky from my mother, and that he would lift me up in his
arms and swing me around and say "Sugarbush." How many
hours were there until Sunday, I asked.

Yet that day, which was Friday, did not pass without event.
We had a visitor—a man. I will never know why but my grand-
father called him Tim, whereas his real name was Pat, but my
grandfather was not to be told that. Tim, it seems, had died and
my grandfather was not to know, because if any of the locals
died, it brought his own death to his mind and he dreaded death
as strenuously as did all the others. Death was some weird jour-
ney that you made alone and unbefriended, once you had
embarked on it. When my aunt's husband had died, in fact had
been shot by the Black and Tans, my aunt had to conceal the
death from her own parents, so irrational were they about the
subject. She had to stay up at home the evening her husband's
remains were brought to the chapel, and when the chapel bell

rang out intermittently, as it does for a death, and they asked who it was, again and again, my poor aunt had to conceal her own grief, be silent about her own tragedy, and pretend that she did not know. Next day she went to the funeral on the excuse that it was some forester whom her husband knew. Her husband was supposed to be transferred to a barracks a long way off, and meanwhile she was going to live with her parents and bring her infant sons until her husband found accommodation. She invented a name for the district where her husband was supposed to be, it was in the North of Ireland, and she invented letters that she had received from him, and the news of the Troubles up there. Eventually, I expect, she told them, and I expect they collapsed and broke down. In fact, the man who brought these imaginary letters would have been Tim, since he had been the postman, and it was of his death my grandfather must not be told. So there in the porch, in a worn suit, was a man called Pat answering to the name of Tim, and the news that a Tim would have, such as how were his family and what crops had he put in and what cattle fairs had he been to. I thought that it was peculiar that he could answer for another, but I expect that everyone's life story was identical.

SUNDAY AFTER MASS I was down by the little green gate skipping and waiting for Carnero. As often happens, the visitor arrives just when we look away. The cuckoo called, and though I knew I would not see her, I looked in a tree where there was a ravaged bird's nest, and at that moment heard Carnero's whistle. I ran down the road, and at once he hefted me up onto the crossbar of his bicycle.

"Oh, Carnero," I cried. There was both joy and sadness in our reunion. He had brought me a bag of tinned sweets, and the most glamorous present—as we got off the bicycle near the little gate he put it on me. It was a toy watch—a most beautiful red, and each bit of the bracelet was the shape and color of a raspberry. It had hands, and though they did not move, that did not matter. One could pull the bracelet part by its elastic thread and cause it to snap in or out. The hands were black and curved like an eyelash. He would not say where he had got it. I had only one craving, to stay down there by the gate with him and admire the watch and talk about home. I could not talk to him in front of them because a child was not supposed to talk or have any wants. He was puffing from having cycled uphill and began to open his tie, and taking it off, he said, "This bloody thing." I wondered who he had put it on for. He was in his Sunday suit and had a fishing feather in his hat.

"Oh, Carnero, turn the bike around and bring me home with you."

Such were my unuttered and unutterable hopes. Later my grandfather teased me and said it was in his backside I saw Carnero's looks, and I said no, in every particle of him.

THAT NIGHT AS we were saying the Rosary my grandfather let out a shout, slouched forward, knocking the wooden chair and hitting himself on the rungs of it, then falling on the cement floor. He died delirious. He died calling on his Maker. It was ghastly. Joe was out and only my grandmother and aunt were there to assist. They picked him up. His skin was purple, the exact color of the iron tonic, and his eyes rolled so that they were seeing every bit of the room, from the ceiling, to the whitewashed wall, to the cement floor, to the settle bed, to the cans of milk, seeing and bulging. He writhed like an animal and then let out a most beseeching howl, and that was it. At that moment my aunt remembered I was there and told me to go into the parlor and wait. It was worse in there, pitch dark, and I in a place where I did not know my footing or my way around. I'd only been in there once, to fetch a teapot and a sugar tongs when Tim came. Had it been in our own house I would have known what to cling to, the back of a chair, the tassel of a blind, the girth of a plaster statue, but in there I held on to nothing and thought how the thing he dreaded had come to pass and now he was finding out those dire things that all his life his mind had shirked from.

"May he rest in peace, may the souls of the faithful departed rest in peace."

It was that for two days, along with litanies and mourners smoking clay pipes, plates being passed around and glasses filled. My mother and father were there, among the mourners. I was praised for growing, as if it were something I myself had caused to happen. My mother looked older in black, and I wished she had worn a Georgette scarf, something to give her a bit of brightness around the throat. She did not like when I said that, and sent me off to say the Confiteor and three Hail Marys. Her eyes were dry. She did not love her own father. Neither did I. Her sister and she would go down into the far room and discuss whether to bring out another bottle of whiskey or another porter cake, or whether it was time to offer the jelly. They were reluctant, the reason being that some provisions had to be held over for the next day, when the special mourners would come up after the funeral. Whereas that night half the parish was there. My grandfather was laid out upstairs in a brown habit. He had stubble on his chin and looked like a frosted plank lying there, gray-white and inanimate. As soon as they had paid their respects, the people hurried down to the kitchen and the parlor, for the eats and the chat. No one wanted to be with the dead man, not even his wife, who had gone a bit funny and was asking my aunt annoying questions about the food and the fire, and how many priests were going to serve at the High Mass.

"Leave that to us," my mother would say, and then my grandmother would retell the world what a palace my mother's house was, and how it was the nicest house in the countryside, and my mother would say "Shhhh," as if she were being disgraced. My father said, "Well, missy," to me twice, and a strange man gave me sixpence. It was a very thin, worn sixpence and I thought it would disappear. I called him Father, out of reverence, because he looked like a priest, but he was in fact a boatman.

The funeral was on an island on the Shannon. Most of the

people stayed on the quay, but we, the family, piled into two rowboats and followed the boat that carried the coffin. It was a jolty ride, with big waves coming in over us and our feet getting drenched. The island itself was full of cows. The sudden arrivals made them bawl and race about, and I thought it was quite improper to see that happening while the remains were being lowered and buried. It was totally desolate, and though my aunt sniffled a bit, and my grandmother let out ejaculations, there was no real grief, and that was the saddest thing.

Next day they burned his working clothes and threw his muddy boots on the manure heap. Then my aunt sewed black diamonds of cloth on her clothes, on my grandmother's, and on Joe's. She wrote a long letter to her son in England, and enclosed black diamonds of cloth for him to stitch onto his effects. He worked in Liverpool in a motorcar factory. Whenever they said Liverpool, I thought of a whole mound of bloodied liver, but then I would look down at my watch and be happy again and pretend to tell the time. The house was gloomy. I went off with Joe, who was mowing hay, and sat with him on the mowing machine and fell slightly in love. Indoors was worst, what with my grandmother sighing and recalling old times, such as when her husband tried to kill her with a carving knife, and then she would snivel and miss him and say, "The poor old creature, he wasn't prepared . . ."

OUT IN THE fields Joe fondled my knee and asked was I ticklish. He had a lovely long face and a beautiful whistle. He was probably about twenty-four, but he seemed old, especially because of a slouchy hat and because of a pair of trousers that were several times too big for him. When the mare passed water he nudged me and said, "Want lemonade?" and when she broke wind he made disgraceful plopping sounds with his lips. He and I ate lunch on the headland and lolled for a bit. We had bread and butter, milk from a flask, and some ginger cake that was left over from the funeral. It had gone damp. He sang, "You'll be

lonely, little sweetheart, in the spring," and smiled a lot at me,
and I felt very privileged. I knew that all he would do was tickle
my knees, and the backs of my knees, because at heart he was
shy and not like some of the local men who would want to
throw you to the ground and press themselves over you so that
you would have to ask God for protection. When he lifted me
onto the machine, he said that we would bring out a nice little
cushion on the morrow so that I would have a soft seat. But on
the morrow it rained and he went off to the sawmill to get
shelving, and my aunt moaned about the hay getting wet and
perhaps getting ruined and possibly there being no fodder for
cattle next winter.

That day I got into dire disaster. I was out in the fields play-
ing, talking, and enjoying the rainbows in the puddles, when all
of a sudden I decided to run helter-skelter toward the house in
case they were cross with me. Coming through a stile that led to
the yard, I decided to do a big jump and landed head over heels
in the manure heap. I fell so heavily onto it that every bit of
clothing got wet and smeared. It was a very massive manure
heap, and very squelchy. Each day the cow house was cleaned
out and the contents shoveled there, and each week the straw
and old nesting from the hen house were dumped there, and so
was the pigs' bedding. So it was not like falling into a sack of hay.
It was not dry and clean. It was a foul spot I fell into, and as soon
as I waded out, I decided it was wise to undress. The pleated
skirt was ruined and so was my blouse and my navy cardigan.
Damp had gone through to my bodice, and the smell was dread-
ful. I was trying to wash it off under an outside tap, using a fist of
grass as a cloth, when my aunt came out and exclaimed, "Jesus,
Mary, and Joseph, glory be to the great God today and tonight,
but what have you done to yourself!" I was afraid to tell her that
I fell, so I said I was doing washing and she said in the name of
God what washing, and then she saw the ruin on the garments.
She picked up the skirt and said why on earth had she let me
wear it that day, and wasn't it the demon that came with me the
day I arrived with my attaché case. I was still trying to wash and

not answer this barrage of questions, all beginning with the word "why." As if I knew why! She got a rag and some pumice stone, plus a can of water, and stripped to the skin, I was washed and reprimanded. Then my clothes were put to soak in the can, all except for the skirt, which had to be brought in to dry, and then cleaned with a clothes brush. Mercifully my grandmother was not told.

My aunt forgave me two nights later when she was in the dairy churning and singing. I asked if I could turn the churn handle for a jiff. It was changing from liquid to solid and the handle was becoming stiff. I tried with all my might, but I was not strong enough.

"You will, when you're big," she said, and sang to me. She sang "Far Away in Australia" and then asked what I would like to do when I grew up. I said I would like to marry Carnero, and she laughed and said what a lovely thing it was to be young and carefree. She let me look into the churn to see the mound of yellow butter that had formed. There were drops of water all over its surface, it was like some big bulk that had bathed but had not dried off. She got two sets of wooden pats, and together we began to fashion the butter into dainty shapes. She was quicker at it than I. She made little round balls of butter with prickly surfaces, then she said wouldn't it be lovely if the curate came up for tea. He was a new curate and had rimless spectacles.

THE NEXT DAY she went to the town to sell the butter and I was left to mind the house along with my grandmother. My aunt had promised to bring back a shop cake, and said that, depending on the price, it would be either a sponge cake or an Oxford Lunch, which was a type of fruit cake wrapped in beautiful dun silverish paper. My grandmother donned a big straw hat with a chin strap and looked very distracted. She kept thinking that there was a car or a cart coming into the back yard and had me looking out windows on the alert. Then she got a flush and I had to conduct her into the plantation and sit on the bench next to her, and we were scarcely there when three huge fellows walked in and we knew at once that they were tinkers. The fear is indescribable. I knew that tinkers took one off in their cart, hid one under shawls, and did dire things to one. I knew that they beat their wives and children, got drunk, had fights among themselves, and spent many a night cooling off in the barracks. I jumped up as they came through the gate. My grandmother's mouth fell wide open with shock. One of them carried a shears and the other had a weighing pan in his hand. They asked if we had any sheep's wool and we both said no, no sheep, only cattle. They had evil eyes and gamey looks. There was no knowing what they would do to us. Then they asked if we had any feathers for pillows or mattresses. She was so crazed with fear that she said yes and led the way to the house. As we walked along, I expected a strong hand to be clamped on my shoulder. They were dreadfully silent. Only one had spoken and he had a shocking accent, what my mother would call "a gurrier's." She sent me upstairs to get the two bags of feathers out of the wardrobe, and I knew that she stayed below so that they would not steal a cake or bread or crockery or any other things. She was agreeing on a price when I came down, or rather, requesting a price. The talking member said it was a barter job. We would get a lace cloth in return. She asked how big this cloth was, and he said very big, while his companion put his hand into the bag of feathers to make sure that there was not anything else in there, that we were not trying to fob them off with grass or sawdust or something. She asked where was the cloth. They laughed. They said it was down in the caravan, at the crossroads, ma'am. She knew then she was being cheated, but she tried to stand her ground. She grabbed one end of the bag and said, "You'll not have these."

"D'you think we're mugs?" one of them said, and gestured to the others to pick up the two bags, which they did. Then they looked at us as if they might mutilate us, and I prayed to St. Jude and St. Anthony to keep us from harm. Before going, they insisted on being given new milk. They drank in great slugs.

"Are you afraid of me?" one of the men said to her.

He was the tallest of the three and his shirt was open. I could see the hair on his chest, and he had a very funny look in his eyes as if he was not thinking, as if thinking was beyond him. His eyes had a thickness in them. For some reason he reminded me of meat.

"Why should I be afraid of you," she said, and I was so proud of her I would have clapped, but for the tight shave we were in.

She blessed herself several times when they'd gone and decided that what we did had been the practical thing to do, and in fact our only recourse. But when my aunt came back and began an intensive cross-examination, the main contention was how they learned in the first place that there were feathers in the house. My aunt reasoned that they could not have known unless they had been told, they were not fortune-tellers. Each time I was asked, I would seal my lips, as I did not want to betray my grandmother. Each time she was asked, she described them in detail, the holes in their clothes, the safety pins instead of buttons, their villainous looks, and then she mentioned the child, me, and hinted about the things they might have done and was it not the blessing of God that we had got rid of them peaceably! My aunt's son joked about the lace cloth for weeks. He used to affect to admire it, by picking up one end of the black oilcloth on the table and saying, "Is it Brussels lace or is it Carrickmackross?"

SUNDAY CAME AND my mother was expected to visit. My aunt had washed me the night before in an aluminum pan. I had to sit in it, and was terrified lest my cousin should peep in. He was in the back kitchen shaving and whistling. It was a question of a "Saturday splash for Sunday's dash." My aunt poured a can of water over my head and down my back. It was scalding hot. Then she poured rainwater over me and by contrast it was freezing. She was not a thorough washer like my mother, but all the time she kept saying that I would be like a new pin.

My mother was not expected until the afternoon. We had washed up the dinner things and given the dogs the potato skins and milk when I started in earnest to look out for her. I went to the gate where I had waited for Carnero, and seeing no sign of her, I sauntered off down the road. I was at the crossroads when I realized how dangerous it was, as I was approaching the spot where the tinkers said their caravan was pitched. So it was back at full speed. The fuchsia was out and so were the elderberries. The fuchsia was like dangling earrings and the riper elderberries were in maroon smudges on the road. I waited in hiding, the better to surprise her. She never came. It was five, and then half past five, and then it was six. I would go back to the kitchen and lift the clock that was face down on the dresser, and then hurry out to my watch post. By seven it was certain that she would not come, although I still held out hope. They hated to see me sniffle, and even hated more when I refused a slice of cake. I could not bear to eat. Might she still come? They said there was no point in my being so spoiled. I was imprisoned at the kitchen table in front of this slice of seed cake. In my mind I lifted the gate hasp a thousand times and saw my mother pass by the kitchen window, as fleeting as a ghost; and by the time we all knelt down to say the Rosary, my imagination had run amuck. I conceived of the worst things, such as she had died, or that my father had killed her, or that she had met a man and eloped. All three were unbearable. In bed I sobbed and chewed on the blanket so as not to be heard, and between tears and with my aunt enjoining me to dry up, I hatched a plan.

On the morrow there was no word or no letter, so I decided to run away. I packed a little satchel with bread, my comb, and, daftly, a spare pair of ankle socks. I told my aunt that I was going on a picnic and affected to be very happy by humming and doing little reels. It was a dry day and the dust rose in whirls under my feet. The dogs followed and I had immense trouble getting them to go back. There were no tinkers' caravans at the crossroads and because of that I was jubilant. I walked and then ran, and then I would have to slow down, and always when I slowed down, I looked back in case someone was following me. While I was running I felt I could elude them, but there was no eluding the loose stones and the bits of rock that were wedged into the dirt road. Twice I tripped. If, coming toward me, I saw two people together, I then felt safe, but if I saw one person it boded ill, as that one person could be mad, or drunk, or likely to accost. On three occasions I had to climb into a field and hide until that one ominous person went by. Fortunately, it was a quiet road, as not many souls lived in that region.

When I came off the dirt road onto the main road, I felt safer, and very soon a man came by in a pony and trap and offered me a lift. He looked a harmless enough person, in a frieze coat and a cloth cap. When I stepped into the trap I was surprised to find two hens clucking and agitating under a seat.

"Would you be one of the Linihans?" he asked, referring to my grandmother's family.

I said no and gave an assumed name. He plied me with questions. To get the most out of me, he even got the pony to slow down, so as to lengthen the journey. We dawdled. The seat of black leather was held down with black buttons. He had a tartan rug over him. He spread it out over us both. Quickly I edged out from under it, complaining about fleas and midges, neither of which there were. It was a desperately lonely road with only a house here and there, a graveyard, and sometimes an orchard. The apples looked tempting on the trees. To see each ripening apple was to see a miracle. He asked if I believed in ghosts and told me that he had seen the riderless horse on the moors.

"If you're a Minnogue," he said, "you should be getting out here," and he pulled on the reins.

I had called myself a Minnogue because I knew a girl of that name who lived with her mother and was separated from her father. I would like to have been her.

"I'm not," I said, and tried to be as innocent as possible. I then had to say who I was, and ask if he would drop me in the village.

"I'm passing your gate," he said, and I was terrified that I would have to ask him up, as my mother dreaded strangers, even dreaded visitors, since these diversions usually gave my father the

inclination to drink, and once he drank he was on a drinking bout
that would last for weeks, and that was notorious. Therefore I
had to conjure up another lie. It was that my parents were both
staying with my grandmother and that I had been dispatched
home to get a change of clothing for us all. He grumbled at not
coming up to our house, but I jumped out of the trap and said
we would ask him to a card party for sure, in December.

There was no one at home. The door was locked and the big
key in its customary place under the pantry window. The
kitchen bore signs of my mother having gone out in a hurry, as
the dishes were on the table, and on the table, too, were her
powder puff, a near-empty powder box, and a holder of papier-
mâché in which her toiletries were kept. Had she gone to the
city? My heart was wild with envy. Why had she gone without
me? I called upstairs, and then hearing no reply, I went up with a
mind that was buzzing with fear, rage, suspicion, and envy. The
beds were made. The rooms seemed vast and awesome com-
pared with the little crammed rooms of my grandmother's. I
heard someone in the kitchen and hurried down with renewed
palpitations. It was my mother. She had been to the shop and got
some chocolate. It was rationed because of its being wartime, but
she used to coax the shopkeeper to give her some. He was a bach-
elor. He liked her. Maybe that was why she had put powder on.

"Who brought you home, my lady?" she said stiffly.

She hadn't come on Sunday. I blurted that out. She said did
anyone ever hear such nonsense. She said did I not know that I
was to stay there until the end of August till school began. She
was even more irate when she heard that I had run away. What
would they now be thinking but that I was in a bog hole or
something. She said had I no consideration and how in heaven's
name was she going to get word to them, an SOS.

"Where's my father?" I asked.

"Saving hay," she said.

I gathered the cups off the table so as to make myself useful in
her eyes. Seeing the state of my canvas shoes and the marks on
the ankle socks, she asked had I come through a river or what.

All I wanted to know was why she had not come on Sunday as promised. The bicycle got punctured, she said, and then asked did I think that with bunions, corns, and welts she could walk six miles after doing a day's work. All I thought was that the homecoming was not nearly as tender as I hoped it would be, and there was no embrace and no reunion. She filled the kettle and I laid clean cups. I tried to be civil, to contain the pique and misery that was welling up in me. I told her how many trams of hay they had made in her mother's house, and she said it was a sight more than we had done. She hauled some scones from a colander in the cupboard and told me I had better eat. She did not heat them on the top of the oven, and that meant she was still vexed. I knew that before nightfall she would melt, but where is the use of a thing that comes too late?

I sat at the far end of the table watching the lines on her brow, watching the puckering, as she wrote a letter to my aunt explaining that I had come home. I would have to give it to the mail-car man the following morning and ask the postman to deliver it by hand. She said, God only knows what commotion there would be all that day and into the night looking for me. The ink in her pen gave out, and I held the near-empty ink bottle sideways while she refilled it.

"Go back to your place," she said, and I went back to the far end of the table like someone glued to her post. I thought of fields around my grandmother's house and the various smooth stones that I had put on the windowsill, I thought of the sun garden, of the night my grandfather had died and my vigil in the cold parlor. I thought of many things. Sitting there, I wanted both to be in our house and to be back in my grandmother's missing my mother. It was as if I could taste my pain better away from her, the excruciating pain that told me how much I loved her. I thought how much I needed to be without her so that I could think of her, dwell on her, and fashion her into the perfect person that she clearly was not. I resolved that for certain I would grow up and one day go away. It was a sweet thought, and it was packed with punishment.

MURIEL RUKEYSER

(1913–1980)

The Orgy *by Muriel Rukeyser was originally published as a novel. In 1997, after several decades out of print,* The Orgy *was reprinted as what it truly is—a memoir. In this work Rukeyser recorded her experiences at the Puck Fair in County Kerry, the pagan festival of the goat. As a 1930s radical, a Jewish single mother, and a New York poet, Rukeyser is an unusual participant in this orgy of drink and sex. But it is the author's sense of "otherness" that makes her vision so clear, and her frankness that shocked readers when the work was first published in 1965.*

Rukeyser was used to shocking people. Her poetry was entwined with her political causes: the Spanish Civil War, women's rights, the War in Vietnam. Rukeyser lived most of her life in New York City and taught at Sarah Lawrence, Vassar, and Columbia and was the mentor to Alice Walker. She wrote fifteen books of poetry, two biographies, and only one "novel," The Orgy. *Rukeyser based* The Orgy *on her experiences at the Puck Fair in 1958 when she was working on a research project for the filmmaker Paul Rotha. Sharon Olds wrote in the preface to the Paris Press Edition, "*The Orgy *has layers and secrets. It refers to things it's not going to tell and tells us it's not going to tell. It is a message in a bottle—a brilliant packet of messages in a far traveled bottle."*

from THE ORGY

A word went over the crowd, a sound like a strange note in music that quieted them, and opened the roaring of the air to another note, higher, intense, reaching the center of the body and seeming to travel outward to the ears. It was the bagpipes. The spanned music—the high piercing cry and the underdrone, stabbing and wringing, reached us as we stood at the Nolans' window. We looked out at the people through whom we had made our way to the barracks' door. And then upstairs to the rooms, and all the children—Stephanie, the eldest, with Nicholas beside me, and the baby held on Liadain's lap, starting and calling to the piper's music. The Square was filled; packed tight against each other, with the children invisible in the crush, it was impossible for them to move or turn; but they did move, slowly and with enormous difficulty opening a way. At the sides, there were the calls of women pushed against the plate-glass windows. The pipers outcried all. Led by a small boy, saffron-kilted, and wearing a green tartan, his face white and concentrated in tense pride, they thrust their knees out, ringing, snarling, driving their music through the air.

Behind them, rising up from the river, the amazing procession came. Following the pipers, an open truck pushed inch by inch up the hill. Standing just behind the red cab, four young boys in white and green held their spears up and forward toward us; and at the back of the truck, on a bridge of planks, stood the platform—the throne—of the white goat. Four more boys, guardians, spear-bearers, rode the planks; two more stood on the floor of the truck, holding their spears fierce and straight. Two more stood in the corners, at the back. Long strings of pennants rose up from the headlights to poles in the truck, and stretched backward, saffron, white, green and red.

The boys' trousers are green, and their ties; their skirts are white; so are the spears white and green, with silver spearheads made at home. They are all boys of the same size, a size meaning a stage just before puberty or else a small man, ancient and small, a size not seen in northern countries since neolithic times.

The goat is vastly changed. An hour ago, in the shed, he was uncertain, vibrating. Now his time has begun, although he has not yet achieved his place. He stands on his roofed platform, wearing his robe, a green blanket bound and corded with red.

Still and firm, he stands, long white waterfalls of fur cover him
to his ankles. As he approaches dominion, his white head is held
up; the white mane curls forward over his forehead; a cord of
great round bells stretches in a curve from horn to horn.

The second truck seems empty for a moment. Then it moves
from under the green pennants. A little girl, dressed as a queen,
sits there; she makes a center of silence. Receptive, lovely, she is
the Green Queen, in green robe and mantle over her shoulders,
and her brown hair down her back in little waves and sepia mist.
She wears a broad gold crown with big jewels—almost as large
as the goat's bells—spaced around, and in front a harp over her
round brow. Around the child's waist is the wide girdle of a
queen, with gold tab pendant to back and right, coming to
points that point down her loins. She is attended by a lady-in-
waiting, in green too. This is a young woman.

The goat has begun to take on his new life. A curious shudder
goes through the crowd, in recognition. Now they are not
watching, they are part of this requirement in the air, where the
presence of the Puck, the receptive presence of his Queen,
demand acknowledgment.

The music is right before the tower, breaking over all in shrill
ripples, an underdrone like a repeated wave, a sort of shudder-
ing. The pipers turn off the Square, and the third truck can be
seen.

Bright red, a loud clap of red, the stiff and hieratic bird
spreads out his wings. Eagle-beaked, horn-headed, his white eye
flame-shaped, he holds out the separate feathers. At his feet rise
flames, the same red as he; bright blood, bright fire, and the fire
raging up like thorns which could never reach him. I feel myself
start, hard against Hilliard's arm, and the points of my breasts
stand up: I can see the big word below the red creature. It says
PHOENIX, below the painted bird. It is all there: king, queen, and
resurrection.

The bird truck swerves, following the goat, the Green
Queen, and the pipers. There is a smaller phoenix painted on its
door. Then I can see what it is. Grinning, the men in the truck,

young and triumphant, stand over brown barrels banded with silver. They grin, they wave their hands; they beg the crowd to wait, while the shallow amber pools on top of the barrels slop over. The truck turns the corner, brimming with ale.

I laugh at myself; Nicholas is saying, "I never heard of Phoenix Ale."

The phoenix is still there, red and eternal.

THE PROCESSION FORCES open the crowd and heads for the Oisin Ballroom. In the Square, the feeling has changed. Short waves of movement disturb the surface, as the impatience builds. A few hand-lettered I.R.A. signs bob up, sink, rise again.

Suddenly—if anything in that slow, tight body could be sudden—a surge develops at the Bank corner, and a Morris appears among the arms and shoulders. Incredibly, it turns into the Square and heads toward the tower. Its wheels cannot turn without crushing the feet of twenty people. Around it, a kind of crunching of space takes place; there must be, between layers of clothing, air layers that can still be compressed. And between flesh, flesh. And joints and sockets. The Morris does advance. The procession is making its way around the town. As the pipes are finally heard again, a double sound, part laugh, part groan, comes from those pressed around the car. Someone has opened its hood, five men throw themselves on it bodily until it becomes invisible and a woman sits her baby on the corner over the taillight.

Sergeant Nolan and Looby are firmly making their way through impossibility to the car. They prevail upon the people who now cover it entirely to lean away from its tail and toward its headlights, create a continuous opening through which it is pushed back to the Bank corner, and around it, as the procession reaches the blue tower.

The step dancing, the accordion display from the States, even the renewal of the sale of tickets for the Miniature Sweeps, cannot quiet the crowd in the Square. The loudspeakers are turned

up farther, and the photographers push forward on the platform.
Mr. Houlihan leans out from the platform to the truck with the
white goat. "All right, boys!" he says, and the goat, shed and all,
is slid over the planks on which it rested and onto the lower
stage of the tower.

From the microphone, the first lines of a song are magnified
frightfully:

> Your eyes
> Are the eyes
> Of a woman in love—

and then cut off.

The speaker begins. "This, according to ancient tradition, is
the finest, most majestic he-goat to be found on the slopes of
the MacGillycuddy's Reeks. Some say that this is a Cromwellian
goat, who saved the town of Cill Lorgan when it was a hamlet
of thatched huts. But we know that Cromwell and his generals
never set foot in County Kerry.

"Some say the origins of this festival belong in the mists of
antiquity, that the area around Killorglin was the scene of many
of the legendary exploits of Diarmiud and Graine, and that it
was in their time that the first goat ruled from his tower. We
need scarcely say that there is nothing on record to support the
belief of a pre-Christian origin.

"No; more likely that the story as we have it is the real one,
the story of Dan O'Connell and the local landlord Blennerhas-
set, here in 1808, Mr. Harman Blennerhasset, and how the Lib-
erator helped Blennerhasset to levy the tolls, even though the
Viceroy of Dublin had made the tolls unlawful."

One cheer, like hysteria, from the pink doorway of Stephens
Champ. The photographers are climbing up. The I.R.A. signs
have vanished.

The speaker continues: he wishes to thank those responsi-
ble . . . he begins lovingly to read the names of the Committee.
The sky has turned bruise-purple over the gray, where the

crowd slopes downhill; far over and across, the field on the other side of the Laune is a fever green, vibrating yellow and red. Black cattle in a constellation.

He is finishing. A man in a blue serge suit begins to climb the tower with something in his hand. It lengthens behind him, the rope to raise the goat. He turns at the second stage and smiles thickly down. The tower sways from side to side of a plane, like a creature on water skis.

The speaker is introducing the Green Queen: "Kathleen Corkery, our ten-year-old Queen, and her lady-in-waiting, the ever-charming Miss Nuala O'Sullivan, Queen of the festival." Up in our window Stephanie says to me, "That's my friend, that's Kathleen."

The lady-in-waiting looks desperate; her face goes crooked in an embarrassed one-sided simper at the photographers. She is thinking only of herself.

But the Green Queen, with a young and powerful gesture, takes the tall crown from the hands of her lady-in-waiting. The crown had never been offered. She is giving it, the Queen has assumed the potency of the gift. She looks at the goat. She gives his head the high crown, buckling it about the base of his horns. The power of her clear voice carries high and young; she says, "I crown you King Puck."

"The only king of Ireland!" sings out the chairman. "Hip, hip—" and the cheer arrives.

I LOOKED AT the men as they began to pull on the ropes. Almost everybody had cleared away from the lowest floor of the tower; no girl pipers, no twins from the States. There were five men involved in the Elevation of the King. One of them was now standing near a microphone, lifting one foot and then the other in a quickened rhythm, a step dance hastening on as the goat's platform began to rise. The dancer shut his eyes, his dance was fast now and he was lost in it. His back was to the mike and its long cord dwindled away from him in silence. I watched him dance, his knees lifting as his body stayed almost still and his feet went free, up and down.

Two other men were pulling on the rope that went up past the second floor of the tower to the pulley wheel above the third floor. The first floor was solid, the men were pulling against the wood beneath them and against the rope, whose end still coiled in slack circles at their feet. The second floor had an oblong opening cut in it, just big enough to let the goat and his platform rise up through it as through a doorway. The third and highest floor was not a floor at all; or it was a floor of air, with a double cross of planks running over it. At the meeting-place of this cross the king would stand. The timbers were not new. They were freshly painted and bright blue, but you could see the nail holes of other years. And the three ladders, set against each floor, looked well-used and familiar.

Two more men stood steadying the platform, one on each side as it began to rise. It swayed, about four feet above the flooring. I was looking down at the white King, his green robe over his back and the bells slung between his great horns swaying from side to side. He backed two small steps, as far as he could move, backing in time with the dancer beneath him. He was backed against the railing of his platform. I could see his short tail tremble, and then go firm as the swaying stopped. He was rising, smoothly, in strong pulsations. Circle after circle of rope fell as he rose, like the coils of music as a great bell rings. No sound came from the Square. We watched him rise in the strong silence, as the dancer paced the rising, and the men pulled hard on their rope, drinking the rope down to earth as the King went up.

He was before my eyes now. What is wrong? I thought suddenly, in clumsiness of soul. Is there something the matter with him that they are so large, so heavy? Surely they would not choose a Puck who had something the matter with his sex.

The huge white balls were before my eyes, great in their power and whiteness. The life of the King was in them, making reasons for the eye's glint, the curl of lip, the hard spread of bone lifting out of his forehead. Energy bulged here, a double bulge robed in the smoothness of white fur, hidden and trumpeting, open and recondite, worlds creating worlds, something secret and understood. I laughed at myself in pleasure and triumph. Wrong! He swung there, strong, white, the crowned world rising up through worlds, crowned by a girl's arm, still and held in his kingship, with the great bells ringing slung between his horns, the great testicles slung between his legs.

They lifted their eyes in silence, all of us looking, looking, as some strength poured out upon the air. Everyone looking up at the King on his tower; all but one woman whose face was fastened sideways, staring across all the faces at someone with a camera. I looked up again at him. He was larger than before, braced and powerful. He turned his head from side to side, and around backwards to where we watched from the windows. His eyes glinted yellow. A long strong scent, a great pennant of smell of goat, goat of the world and the world of goat in his kingship, on his height, streamed across all of us, flowing on air. The huge cheer went up: "King! Puck!" Up, on the air, a sound that was a tower around a tower, in the filled and male upper air of the King.

WALLACE STEVENS

(1879–1955)

The image of the rock was a recurring symbol in the poetry of Wallace Stevens. Especially toward the end of his life, Stevens mused about the origins of the Earth and the relationship of man to the Earth. He searched for what endured; the Cliffs of Moher on the west coast of Ireland, majestically "rising out of present time and place, above the wet, green grass."

Ironically, Stevens never saw the Cliffs of Moher, never visited Ireland nor even went to Europe. Stevens led a circumscribed life and traveled mostly in his imagination. A graduate of Harvard and the New York University Law School, he joined the Hartford Accident Indemnity Company in 1916, became vice president in 1934, and stayed in that position until his death. He published his first volume of poetry, Harmonium, *in 1923 and then was silent for a decade. He resumed writing in the mid-1930s and published his second volume,* Ideas of Order, *in 1936. Books then appeared at regular intervals, culminating in* The Collected Poems *in 1954, winner of the National Book Award and the Pulitzer Prize.*

In his later works, Stevens wrestled with the place of poetry in the modern world. This vice president of an insurance company was Walt Whitman's unlikely heir, for both men shared a belief in poetry as religion. Stevens wrote, "In an age of disbelief . . . in a time that is largely humanistic, in one sense or the other, it is for the poet to supply the satisfactions of belief. . . . I think of it as a role of the utmost seriousness. It is, for one thing, a spiritual role."

THE IRISH CLIFFS OF MOHER

Who is my father in this world, in this house,
At the spirit's base?

My father's father, his father's father, his—
Shadows like winds

Go back to a parent before thought, before speech,
At the head of the past.

They go to the cliffs of Moher rising out of the mist,
Above the real,

Rising out of present time and place, above
The wet, green grass.

This is not landscape, full of the somnambulations
Of poetry

And the sea. This is my father or, maybe,
It is as he was,

A likeness, one of the race of fathers: earth
And sea and air.

PAUL THEROUX
(1941–   )

Novelist and travel writer Paul Theroux does not like to travel. "It's uncomfortable. It's tedious. It's repetitive," he said in an interview. "And in order to achieve the epiphanies of travel—the vistas, the experiences—you have to go through an awful lot of hell and high water."

Despite his objections, there are few places in the world that Theroux has not journeyed. He started his career as a teacher in postcolonial Africa and began a tormented friendship with novelist V. S. Naipaul, later documented in Sir Vidia's Shadow: A Friendship Across Five Continents (1998). In the 1970s Theroux traveled by train through Europe and Asia (The Great Railway Bazaar) and through South America (The Old Patagonian Express). He has written eight travel books and almost three times as many novels, several of them autobiographical.

Whatever the subject, locale, or form, Theroux writes with a caustic pen. He has been accused of being irascible, but he defends his prickliness as a form of misunderstood humor. Theroux says that he is merely a realist. Travel writing, he says, is fraught with "sweetness and light"—the literary equivalent of a merry postcard that says, "Everything's fine. Wish you were here."

"Discovering Dingle" is from Theroux's collection Sunrise with Seamonsters.

DISCOVERING DINGLE

from SUNRISE WITH SEAMONSTERS

The nearest thing to writing a novel is traveling in a strange country. Travel is a creative act—not simply loafing and inviting your soul, but feeding the imagination, accounting for each fresh wonder, memorizing and moving on. The discoveries the traveler makes in broad daylight—the curious problems of the eye he solves—resemble those that thrill and sustain a novelist in his solitude. It is fatal to know too much at the outset: boredom comes as quickly to the traveler who knows his route as to the novelist who is overcertain of his plot. And the best landscapes, apparently dense or featureless, hold surprises if they are studied patiently, in the kind of discomfort one can savor afterward. Only a fool blames his bad vacation on the rain.

A strange country—but how strange? One where the sun bursts through the clouds at ten in the evening and makes a sunset as full and promising as dawn. An island which on close inspection appears to be composed entirely of rabbit droppings. Gloomy gypsies camped in hilarious clutter. People who greet you with "Nice day" in a pelting storm. Miles of fuchsia hedges, seven feet tall, with purple hanging blossoms like Chinese lanterns. Ancient perfect castles that are not inhabited; hovels that are. And dangers: hills and beach-cliffs so steep you either hug them or fall off. Stone altars that were last visited by Druids, storms that break and pass in minutes, and a local language that sounds like Russian being whispered and so incomprehensible that the attentive traveler feels, in the words of a native writer, "like a dog listening to music."

It sounds as distant and bizarre as The Land Where the Jumblies Live, and yet it is the part of Europe that is closest in miles to America, the thirty mile sausage of land on the southwest coast of Ireland that is known as the Dingle Peninsula. Beyond it is Boston and New York, where many of its people have fled. The land is not particularly fertile. Fishing is dangerous and difficult. Food is expensive; and if the Irish Government did not offer financial inducements to the natives they would probably shrink inland, like the people of Great Blasket Island who simply dropped everything and went ashore to the Dingle, deserting their huts and fields and leaving them to the rabbits and the ravens.

It is easy for the casual traveler to prettify the place with romantic hyperbole, to see in Dingle's hard weather and exhausted ground the Celtic Twilight, and in its stubborn hopeful people a version of Irishness that is to be cherished. That is the patronage of pity—the metropolitan's contempt for the peasant. The Irish coast, so enchanting for the man with the camera, is murder for the fisherman. For five of the eight days I was there the fishing boats remained anchored in Dingle Harbor, because it was too wild to set sail. The dead seagulls, splayed out like old-fangled ladies' hats below Clogher Head, testify to the furious winds; and never have I seen so many sheep skulls bleaching on hillsides, so many cracked bones beneath bushes.

Farming is done in the most clumsily primitive way, with horses and donkeys, wagons and blunt plows. The methods are traditional by necessity—modernity is expensive, gas costs more than Guinness. The stereotype of the Irishman is a person who spends every night at the local pub, jigging and swilling; in the villages of this peninsula only Sunday night is festive and the rest are observed with tea and early supper.

"I don't blame anyone for leaving here," said a farmer in Dunquin. "There's nothing for young people. There's no work, and it's getting worse."

After the talk of the high deeds of Finn MacCool and the fairies and leprechauns, the conversation turns to the price of spare parts, the cost of grain, the value of the Irish pound which has sunk below the British one. Such an atmosphere of isolation is intensified and circumscribed by the language—there are many who speak only Gaelic. Such remoteness breeds political indifference. There is little talk of the guerrilla war in Northern Ireland, and the few people I tried to draw on the subject said simply that Ulster should become part of Eire.

Further east, in Cork and Killarney, I saw graffiti reading BRITS OUT or UP THE IRA. It is not only the shortage of walls or the cost of spray cans that keep the Irish in Dingle from scrawling slogans. I cannot remember any people so quickly hospitable or easier to meet. Passers-by nod in greeting, children wave at cars: it is all friendliness. At almost three thousand feet the shepherd salutes the climbers and then marches on with his dogs yapping ahead of him.

Either the people leave and go far—every Irishman I met had a relative in America—or they never stir at all. "I've lived here my whole life," said an old man in Curraheen on Tralee Bay; and he meant it—he had always sat in that chair and known that house and that tree and that pasture. But his friend hesitated. "Well, yes," this one said, "not here exactly. After I got married I moved further down the road." It is the outsider who sees Dingle whole; the Irish there live in solitary villages. And people who have only the vaguest notion of Dublin or London, and who have never left Ballydavid or Inch, show an intimate knowledge of American cities, Boston, Springfield, Newark or San Diego. The old lady in Dunquin, sister of the famous "Kruger" Kavanagh—his bar remains, a friendly ramshackle place with a dark side of bacon suspended over one bar and selling peat bricks, ice cream, shampoo, and corn flakes along with the Guinness and the rum—that old lady considered Ventry (her new homestead, four miles away) another world, and yet she used her stern charm on me to recommend a certain bar on Cape Cod.

*   *   *

I DID NOT find, in the whole peninsula, an inspired meal or a great hotel; nor can the peninsula be recommended for its weather. We had two days of rain, two of mist, one almost tropical, and one which was all three, rain in the morning, mist in the afternoon, and sun that appeared in the evening and didn't sink until eleven at night—this was June. "Soft evening," says the fisherman; but that is only a habitual greeting—it might be raining like hell. In general, the sky is overcast, occasionally the weather is unspeakable: no one should go to that part of Ireland in search of sunny days. The bars, two or three to a village, are musty with rising damp and woodworm, and the pictures of President Kennedy—sometimes on yellowing newsprint, sometimes picked out daintily in needlepoint on framed tea-towels—do little to relieve the gloom. The English habit of giving bars fanciful names, like The Frog and Nightgown or The White Hart, is virtually unknown in Ireland. I did not see a bar in any village that was not called simply Mahoney's, or Crowley's, or Foley's or O'Flaherty's: a bar is a room, a keg, an Irish name over the door, and perhaps a cat asleep on the sandwiches.

The roads are empty but narrow, and one—the three miles across the Conair Pass—is, in low cloud, one of the most dangerous I have ever seen, bringing a lump to my throat that I had not tasted since traversing the Khyber. The landscape is utterly bleak, and sometimes there is no sound but the wind beating the gorse bushes or the cries of gulls which—shrill and frantic—mimic something tragic, like a busload of schoolgirls careering off a cliff. The day we arrived my wife and I went for a walk, down the meadow to the sea. It was gray. We walked fifty feet. It rained. The wind tore at the outcrops of rock. We started back, slipping on seaweed, and now we could no longer see the top of the road, where we had begun the walk. It was cold; both of us were wet, feebly congratulating ourselves that we had remembered to buy rubber boots in Killarney.

Then Anne hunched and said, "It's bloody cold. Let's make this a one-night stand."

But we waited. It rained the next day. And the next. The third was misty, but after so much rain the mist gave us the illusion of good weather: there was some promise in the shifting clouds. But, really, the weather had ceased to matter. It was too cold to swim and neither of us had imagined sunbathing in Ireland. We had started to discover the place on foot, in a high wind, fortified by stout and a picnic lunch of crab's claws (a dollar a pound) and cheese and soda bread. Pausing, we had begun to travel.

There is no detailed guidebook for these parts. Two choices are open: to buy Sheet 20 of the Ordnance Survey Map of Ireland, or climb Mount Brandon and look down. We did both, and it was odd how, standing in mist among ecclesiastical-looking cairns (the mountain was a place of pilgrimage for early Christian monks seeking the intercession of St Brendan the Navigator), we looked down and saw that Smerwick and Ballyferriter were enjoying a day of sunshine, Brandon Head was rainy, and Mount Eagle was in cloud. Climbing west of Dingle is deceptive, a succession of false summits, each windier than the last; but from the heights of Brandon the whole peninsula is spread out like a topographical map, path and road, cove and headland. Down there was the Gallarus Oratory, like a perfect boathouse in stone to which no one risks assigning a date (but probably ninth century), and at a greater distance Great Blasket Island and the smaller ones with longer names around it. The views all over the peninsula are dramatic and unlikely, as anyone who has seen *Ryan's Daughter* knows—that bad dazzling movie was made in and around the fishing hamlet of Dunquin. The coastal cliffs are genuinely frightening, the coves echoic with waves that hit the black rocks and rise—foaming, perpendicular—at the fleeing gannets; and the long Slieve Mish Mountains and every valley— thirty miles of them—are, most weirdly, without trees.

We had spotted Mount Eagle. The following day we wandered from the sandy, and briefly sunny, beach at Ventry, through tiny farms to the dark sloping lake that is banked like a sink a thousand feet up the slope—more bones, more rabbits, and a mountain wall strafed by screeching gulls. We had begun to enjoy the wind and rough weather, and after a few days of it saw Dingle Town as too busy, exaggerated, almost large, without much interest, and full of those fairly grim Irish shops which display in the front window a can of beans, a fan belt, a pair of boots, two chocolate bars, yesterday's newspaper and a row of plastic crucifixes standing on fly-blown cookie boxes. And in one window—that of a shoe store—two bottles of "Guaranteed Pure Altar Wine"—the guarantee was lettered neatly on the label: "Certified by the Cardinal Archbishop of Lisbon and Approved by his Lordship the Most Reverend Dr Eamonn Casey, Bishop of Kerry."

But no one mentions religion. The only indication I had of the faith was the valediction of a lady in a bar in Ballyferriter, who shouted, "God Bless ye!" when I emptied my pint of Guinness.

On the rainiest day we climbed down into the cove at Coumeenoole, where—because of its unusual shape, like a ruined cathedral—there was no rain. I sent the children off for driftwood and at the mouth of a dry cave built a fire. It is the bumpkin who sees travel in terms of dancing girls and candle-light dinners on the terrace; the city-slicker's triumphant holiday is finding the right mountain-top or building a fire in the rain or recognizing the wildflowers in Dingle: foxglove, heather, blue-bells.

And it is the city-slicker's conceit to look for untrodden ground, the five miles of unpeopled beach at Stradbally Strand, the flat magnificence of Inch Strand, or the most distant frontier of Ireland, the island off Dunquin called Great Blasket.

Each day, she and her sister-islands looked different. We had seen them from the cliffside of Slea Head, and on that day they had the appearance of sea monsters—high backed creatures making for the open sea. Like all offshore islands, seen from the mainland, their aspect changed with the light: they were lizard-like, then muscular, turned from gray to green, acquired highlights that might have been huts. At dawn they seemed small, but they grew all day into huge and fairly fierce-seeming mountains in the water, diminishing at dusk into pink beasts and finally only hindquarters disappearing in the mist. Some days they were not there at all; on other days they looked linked to the peninsula.

It became our ambition to visit them. We waited for a clear day, and it came—bright and cloudless. But the boat looked frail, a rubber dinghy with an outboard motor. The children were eager; I looked at the high waves that lay between us and Great Blasket and implored the boatman for reassurance. He said he had never overturned—but he was young. On an impulse I agreed and under a half-hour later we arrived at the foreshore on the east of the main island, soaking wet from the spray.

No ruin in Ireland prepared us for the ruins on Great Blasket. After many years of cozy habitation—described with good humor by Maurice O'Sullivan in *Twenty Years A-Growing* (1933)—the villagers were removed to the mainland in 1953. They could no longer support themselves: they surrendered their island to the sneaping wind. And their houses, none of them large, fell down. Where there had been parlors and kitchens and vegetable gardens and fowl-coops there was now bright green moss. The grass and moss and wildflowers combine to create a cemetery effect in the derelict village, the crumbled hut walls like old gravemarkers.

I think I have never seen an eerier or more beautiful island. Just beyond the village which has no name is a long sandy beach called White Strand, which is without a footprint; that day it shimmered like any in Bali. After our picnic we climbed to Sorrowful Cliff and discovered that the island which looked only steep from the shore was in fact precipitous. "Sure, it's a wonderful place to commit suicide," a man told me in Dunquin. A narrow path was cut into the slope on which we walked single file—a few feet to the right and straight down were gulls and the dull sparkle of the Atlantic. We were on the windward side, heading for Fatal Cliff; and for hundreds of feet straight up rabbits were defying gravity on the steepness. The island hill becomes such a sudden ridge and so sharp that when we got to the top of it and took a step we were in complete silence: no wind, no gulls, no surf, only a green-blue vista of the coast of Kerry, Valencia Island and the soft headlands. Here on the lee side the heather was three feet thick and easy as a mattress. I lay down, and within minutes my youngest child was asleep on his stomach, his face on a cushion of fragrant heather. And the rest of the family had wandered singly to other parts of the silent island, so that when I sat up I could see them prowling alone, in detached discovery, trying—because we could not possess this strangeness—to remember it.

VIRGINIA WOOLF

(1882–1941)

Virginia Woolf started a diary at the age of fifteen as part of her training to be a professional writer. Idiosyncratic and impressionistic, her journal was the companion of her troubled lifetime. Woolf once wrote, "Life is not a series of gig-lamps symmetrically arranged; life is a luminous halo, a semi-transparent envelope surrounding us from the beginning of consciousness to the end." Eventually edited into five volumes, her diaries are a window into her aesthetic process.

On Friday, April 27, 1934, Virginia and Leonard Woolf sailed overnight from England to the Irish Free State. She recorded her impressions of their not quite two-week journey on twenty-five loose-leaf pages that she inserted into Diary XXII. The Woolfs' first stop was Bowen's Court, Kildorrery, an eighteenth-century mansion inherited by the Anglo-Irish writer Elizabeth Bowen. Bowen lived in the house for part of the year with her husband Alan Cameron, who was the secretary for education in the City of Oxford.

Woolf's Irish journey was interrupted by the news of the death of her half-brother George Duckworth, one of three children from her mother's first marriage. Duckworth had made inappropriate sexual advances to her during her youth. The extent of his intrusion into Woolf's life is a matter of debate, but her diary reflects her conflicting feelings.

In addition to diaries and collected letters, Woolf produced what are now considered feminist classics of fiction, including A Room of One's Own, Mrs. Dalloway, To the Lighthouse, *and* Orlando. *In 1941 Woolf filled her pockets with stones, wrote two letters to her husband and one to her sister, walked into the River Ouse near her home, and drowned.*

from THE DIARY OF VIRGINIA WOOLF

[MONDAY 30 APRIL]

Glengariff

This is the 30th of April, Monday, so I think, foreign travel not leading to thought. A mixture of Greece, Italy & Cornwall; great loneliness; poverty & dreary villages like squares cut out of West Kensington. Not a single villa or house a-building; great stretches of virgin sea shore; the original land that Cornwall & much of England was in Elizabethan times. And a sense that life is receding. At Lismore the Tchekov innkeeper said They're all going away & leaving their houses; nothing's kept up since the war. So the old man on the island here said today—the very sad gentle old man who longed to talk.[1] All gone—What good did the war do anyone? Only the Americans. And crooned & moaned leaning on the rake with which he was heaping up some kind of weed. Yes there is great melancholy in a deserted land, though the beauty remains untouched—miles & miles of Killarney—the lake water lapping the stones, the butterflies flitting, & not a Cockney there. Today, sitting on the verandah after lunch, the German lawyer having been forced to go to the Island—a string of touts loaf about pressing poetry & boats on one—after they had gone, the invalid, who reminds me of Nelly Cecil began to talk as they all begin to talk; & said she came from Limerick & when we asked if one could get a house there,

1. The old man was one of the O'Sullivan brothers, caretakers for the Bryce family who owned Garnish Island and planted its locally celebrated gardens.

she said—she laughed a great deal yet seems hopelessly crippled—"You can get plenty, but it's not so nice when you have one." "Servant difficulties?" I asked. "Ah; all that" she said, & one can see, after Bowen's Court, how ramshackle & half squalid the Irish life is, how empty & poverty stricken. There we spent one night, unfortunately with baboon Connolly & his gollywog slug wife Jean to bring in the roar of the Chelsea omnibus,[2] & it was all as it should be—pompous & pretentious & imitative & ruined—a great barrack of grey stone, 4 storeys & basements, like a town house, high empty rooms, & a scattering of Italian plasterwork, marble mantelpieces, inlaid with brass & so on. All the furniture clumsy solid cut out of single wood— the wake sofa, on wh. the dead lay—carpets shrunk in the great rooms, tattered farm girls waiting, the old man of 90 in his cabin who wdn't let us go—E[lizabe]th had to say Yes The Ladies are very well several times.[3] And we went to the wishing well, where there are broken cups as offerings & half a rosary & L. wished that Pinka might not smell, which made me laugh; & then I talked to the cook, & she showed me the wheel for blowing the fire in the windy pompous kitchen, half underground— rather like the Bride of Lammermuir—Caleb showing the guests nothing[4]—no there was a fine turkey but everywhere desolation & pretention cracked grand pianos, faked old portraits, stained walls—& yet with character & charm, looking on to a meadow where the trees stand in a ring called Lamb's Cradle. Talk too much of the Chelsea bar kind, owing to C.'s— about starting a society called Bostocks, about Ireland with

2. Cyril Vernon Connolly (1903–1974), later editor of the literary periodical *Horizon,* at this time reviewed fiction for the *NS&N;* his first wife Jean, *née* Bakewell, was American.

3. The garrulous "old man of 90" was Patsy Hennessy who lived in a cabin near St Geoffrey's Well, the waters of which were said to be beneficial to the eyes.

4. Caleb Balderstone was the officious butler in Sir Walter Scott's novel who was determined to uphold the honour and conceal the impoverished circumstances of the Ravenswood family.

Alan, a good humoured bolt eyed fat hospitable man.[5] So on here over the mountains. And pray God the C.'s dont show their gorilla faces at dinner or invade the old Squires library in which we sit.

TUESDAY 1 MAY

Waterville [*Butler Arms Hotel*]

Too like its name; blowing the spray & the rain over a flat land, & a scattering of hideous 1850 watering place houses. Mist today, wind tonight; & L. opening the first Times to come our way, said George Duckworth is dead.[6] So he is. And I feel the usual incongruous shades of feeling, one from this year, one from that—how great a part he used to play & now scarcely any. But I remember the genuine glow, from last summer when I went to see him—the thing that always made me laugh & yet was marked in him. But how little he meant, after his marriage—& how childhood goes with him—the batting, the laughter, the treats, the presents, taking us for bus rides to see famous churches, giving us tea at City Inns, & so on—that was the best which oddly enough returned of late years a little, with the Lincoln sausages, the bottles of eau de Cologne, the great bunch of flowers. Margaret I remember playing round him, & I thought how happy in their way they were. But this is all happening far off. Here I sit on my bed in the windy seaside hotel, & wait for dinner, with this usual sense of time shifting & life becoming unreal, so soon to vanish while the world will go on millions upon millions of years.

5. Alan Charles Cameron (1893–1952), whom Elizabeth Bowen married in 1923, was Secretary for Education in the City of Oxford and was soon to become Secretary to the Central Council of School Broadcasting at the BBC.
6. Sir George Duckworth died on 27 April at Freshwater, Isle of Wight, aged sixty-six; the announcement of his death was in *The Times* of 28 April.

WEDNESDAY 2 MAY

Glenbeith [*Glenbeigh Hotel*]

On again, after an extremely interesting encounter at the windy hotel with Ireland—that is Mr & Mrs Rowlands; he is a giant, very shapely, small head, obliterated features; she small, abrupt, vivacious. They began directly, & so we talked,—they accepted us as their sort, & were gentry, Irish gentry, very much so, he with a house 500 years old, & no land left. "But I love my King & Country. Whatever they ask me to do I'd do it"—this with great emotion. "Oh yes, we believe in the British Empire; we hate the madman de Valéra."[7] There they live, 14 miles from Cork, hunting, with an old retriever dog, & go to bazaars miles & miles away. "Thats the way we live—no nonsense about us— not like the English people. Now I'll give you my name, & I'll write to my friend & she'll tell you of a house—& I hope you'll live in Ireland. We want people like ourselves. But wait, till the budget." This she said, with all the airs of the Irish gentry: something very foreign about her, like old Lady Young,[8] & yet in slave to London; of course everyone wants to be English. We think Englands talking of us—not a bit. No said the obliterated Greek torso, for such he was, when I was courting my wife— she lived in Liverpool—the young chaps used to say "now Paddy tell us one of your stories" but now they dont take any interest in us. But I'd do anything for my King & Country, though youve always treated us very badly.

So we got on to the Bowens; & established ourselves as of their sort. Yes I felt this is the animal that lives in the shell. These

7. Mr & Mrs A. Rowlands of Ballinacurra House, Midleton, co. Cork. Éamonn de Valéra (1882–1975), the Irish Republican leader and President of the Fianna Fail party, was from 1932–37 President of the Executive Council of the Irish Free State, and the Minister for External Affairs.

8. The Youngs, of Formosa Fishery, Cookham, were old family friends of the Stephens; Lady Young (d. 1922) was born Alice Eacy, daughter of Evory Kennedy MD of Belgard Castle, Dublin.

are the ways they live—he hunting all day, & she bustling about
in her old car, & everybody knowing everybody & laughing &
talking & picnicking, & great poverty & some tradition of gen-
tle birth, & all the sons going away to make their livings & the
old people sitting there hating the Irish Free State & recalling
Dublin & the Viceroy.

On to Tralee & saw the gipsies coming down the road &
thought of G. being buried.[9]

9. The Woolfs drove from Waterville to Tralee to pick up their letters, and
then to Glenbeigh. Sir George Duckworth's funeral was at his local church, St
Margaret's, West Hoathly, on 2 May.

Leinster

SAMUEL BECKETT

(1906–1989)

Next to James Joyce, Samuel Beckett was the best-known Irish expatri-
ate in post–World War I Paris. Despite a twenty-four-year age differ-
ence, the two were close friends, and Joyce's writing often provided a
literary model for Beckett's work. Both men had shed their religion—
Joyce, his mother's devout Catholicism; Beckett, his family's Protes-
tantism—and left their homeland for France.

Beckett seemed to embrace his adopted homeland more than Joyce
did—much of Beckett's work is in French and he was very active in the
French Resistance during World War II—but Ireland often reoccurs in
his work. This passage from the novel Mercier and Camier, *translated*
from the French by the author himself, reflects his feelings about the
mountains around Dublin. Beckett had powerful memories of walking
those mountains with his father. He wrote in Worstward Ho, *"Backs*
turned both bowed with equal plod they go. The child hand raised to
read the holding hand. Hold the old holding hand. Hold and be held."
The mountains are barren with ruins, turf-bogs. Both the city and the
sea are close by, but not always visible. The Dublin mountains are
strangely isolated.

from MERCIER AND CAMIER

A road still carriageable climbs over the high moorland. It cuts
across vast turf bogs, a thousand feet above sea-level, two thousand
if you prefer. It leads to nothing any more. A few ruined forts, a
few ruined dwellings. The sea is not far, just visible beyond the

valleys dipping eastward, pale plinth as pale as the pale wall of
sky. Tarns lie hidden in the folds of the moor, invisible from the
road, reached by faint paths, under high overhanging crags. All
seems flat, or gently undulating, and there at a stone's throw
these high crags, all unsuspected by the wayfarer. Of granite
what is more. In the west the chain is at its highest, its peaks exalt
even the most downcast eyes, peaks commanding the vast cham-
paign land, the celebrated pastures, the golden vale. Before the
travellers, as far as eye can reach, the road winds on into the
south, uphill, but imperceptibly. None ever pass this way but
beauty-spot hogs and fanatical trampers. Under its heather mask
the quag allures, with an allurement not all mortals can resist.
Then it swallows them up or the mist comes down. The city is
not far either, from certain points its lights can be seen by night,
its light rather, and by day its haze. Even the piers of the harbour
can be distinguished, on very clear days, of the two harbours,
tiny arms in the glassy sea outflung, known flat, seen raised. And
the islands and promontories, one has only to stop and turn at
the right place, and of course by night the beacon lights, both
flashing and revolving. It is here one would lie down, in a hol-
low bedded with dry heather, and fall asleep, for the last time, on
an afternoon, in the sun, head down among the minute life of
stems and bells, and fast fall asleep, fast farewell to charming
things. It's a birdless sky, the odd raptor, no song. End of
descriptive passage.

JOHN BETJEMAN

(1906–1984)

John Betjeman wrote the poetry of nostalgia. He revered the time before supermarkets, modernism, and democratic socialism. As both an architecture critic and a poet, he produced work that was enormously popular—his Collected Poems *(1948) sold 100,000 copies alone—and the literary elite were automatically suspicious of his work. But his deceptively simple poetry has a serious aesthetic. Critics called Betjeman a "topographical poet." His aim was not social commentary, but the wistful evocation of place.*

Betjeman was cherished in postwar Britain. Appearing on television to promote his architectural causes, he was a familiar champion of Gothic architecture. He was once described as looking like a "highly intelligent muffin: a small, plump, rumpled man with luminous soft eyes, a chubby face topped by wisps of white hair and imparting a distinct air of absentmindedness." His avuncular looks belied a lifelong battle with depression, occasionally manifested in his work, a feeling that he described as "good old English melancholy, like Hardy, Hood and Tennyson—solid village gloom."

In Ireland, Betjeman found a less spoiled England. This poem is sometimes called "Sunday in Ireland."

IRELAND WITH EMILY

from SELECTED POEMS

Bells are booming down the bohreens,
   White the mist along the grass.
Now the Julias, Maeves and Maureens
   Move between the fields to Mass.
Twisted trees of small green apple
Guard the decent whitewashed chapel,
Gilded gates and doorways grained,
Pointed windows richly stained
   With many-coloured Munich glass.

See the black-shawled congregations
   On the broidered vestment gaze,
Murmur past the painted stations
   As Thy Sacred Heart displays
Lush Kildare of scented meadows,
Roscommon, thin in ash-tree shadows,
And Westmeath the lake-reflected,
Spreading Leix the hill-protected,
   Kneeling all in silver haze?

In yews and woodbine, walls and guelder,
   Nettle-deep the faithful rest,
Winding leagues of flowering elder,
   Sycamore with ivy dressed,
Ruins in demesnes deserted,
Bog-surrounded, bramble-skirted—
Townlands rich or townlands mean as

These, oh, counties of them screen us
   In the Kingdom of the West.

Stony seaboard, far and foreign,
   Stony hills poured over space,
Stony outcrop of the Burren,
   Stones in every fertile place,
Little fields with boulders dotted,
Grey-stone shoulders saffron-spotted,
Stone-walled cabins thatched with reeds,
Where a Stone Age people breeds
   The last of Europe's stone age race.

Has it held, the warm June weather?
   Draining shallow sea-pools dry,
Where we bicycled together
   Down the bohreens fuchsia-high.
Till there rose, abrupt and lonely,
A ruined abbey, chancel only,
Lichen-crusted, time-befriended,
Soared the arches, splayed and splendid,
   Romanesque against the sky.

There in pinnacled protection
   One extinguished family waits
A Church of Ireland resurrection
   By the broken, rusty gates.
Sheepswool, straw and droppings cover
Graves of spinster, rake and lover,
Whose fantastic mausoleum
Sings its own seablown Te Deum
   In and out the slipping slates.

ELIZABETH BOWEN

(1899–1973)

Often compared to Henry James, Elizabeth Bowen was an Anglo-Irish short story writer and novelist. She was born at Bowen's Court, her family's eighteenth-century ancestral home outside of Dublin, which she eventually inherited. But much of her youth was spent traveling on the Continent. After her marriage in 1923 to Alan Cameron, she settled in London. She published her first short stories shortly after her marriage. Much of her early work was set in London, but like many Irish-born writers she eventually returned in theme and setting to the place of her birth.

Whether her fiction was set in London or Dublin, her Irish childhood is marked indelibly on her writing. She claimed that she "found" her characters, rather than created them, and she termed her genre "transformed biography." Eudora Welty wrote, "Elizabeth Bowen's sense of place, of where she was, *seemed to approach the seismic. It was equaled only by her close touch, the passage, the pulse, of time."*

In addition to short stories and novels, Bowen wrote many books of nonfiction, including Bowen's Court, *a history of her family estate, and* Seven Winters: Memories of a Dublin Childhood.

UNWELCOME IDEA

from COLLECTED STORIES

Along Dublin bay, on a sunny July morning, the public gardens along the Dalkey tramline look bright as a series of parasols. Chalk-blue sea appears at the ends of the roads of villas turning downhill—but these are still the suburbs, not the seaside. In the distance, floating across the bay, buildings glitter out of the heat-haze on the neck to Howth, and Howth Head looks higher veiled. After inland Ballsbridge, the tram from Dublin speeds up; it zooms through the residential reaches with the gathering steadiness of a launched ship. Its red velvet seating accommodation is seldom crowded—its rival, the quicker bus, lurches ahead of it down the same road.

After Ballsbridge, the ozone smell of the bay sifts more and more through the smell of chimneys and pollen and the July-darkened garden trees as the bay and line converge. Then at a point you see the whole bay open—there are nothing but flats of grass and the sunk railway between the running tram and the still sea. An immense glaring reflection floods through the tram. When high terraces, backs to the tramline, shut out the view again, even their backs have a salted, marine air: their cotton window-blinds are pulled half down, crooked; here and there an inner door left open lets you see a flash of sea through a house. The weathered lions on gate posts ought to be dolphins. Red, low-lying villas have been fitted between earlier terraces, ornate, shabby, glassy hotels, bow-fronted mansions all built in the first place to stand up over spaces of grass. Looks from trams and voices from public gardens invade the old walled lawns with their grottos and weeping willows. Spit-and-polish alternates with decay. But stucco, slate and slate-fronts, blotched Italian pink-wash, dusty windows, lace curtains and dolphin-lions seem to be the eternity of this tram route. Quite soon the modern will sag, chip, fade. Change leaves everything at the same level. Nothing stays bright but mornings.

The tram slides to stops for its not many passengers. The Blackrock bottleneck checks it, then the Dun Laoghaire. These are the shopping centres strung on the line: their animation congests them. Housewives with burnt bare arms out of their cotton dresses mass blinking and talking among the halted traffic, knocking their shopping-bags on each other's thighs. Forgotten Protestant ladies from "rooms" near the esplanade stand squeezed between the kerb and the shops. A file of booted children threads its way through the crush, a nun at the head like a needle. Children by themselves curl their toes in their plimsoles and suck sweets and disregard everything. The goods stacked in the shops look very static and hot. Out from the tops of the shops or brackets stand a number of clocks. As though wrought up by the clocks the tram-driver smites his bell again and again, till the checked tram noses its way through.

By half-past eleven this morning one tram to Dalkey is not far on its way. All the time it approaches the Ballsbridge stop Mrs Kearney looks undecided, but when it does pull up she steps aboard because she has seen no bus. In a slither of rather ungirt parcels, including a dress-box, with a magazine held firmly between her teeth, she clutches her way up the stairs to the top. She settles herself on a velvet seat: she is hot. But the doors at each end and the windows are half-open, and as the tram moves air rushes smoothly through. There are only four other people and no man smokes a pipe. Mrs Kearney has finished wedging her parcels between her hip and the side of the tram and is intending to look at her magazine when she stares hard ahead and shows interest in someone's back. She moves herself and everything three seats up, leans forward and gives a poke at the back. "Isn't that you?" she says.

Miss Kevin jumps round so wholeheartedly that the brims of the two hats almost clash. "Why, for goodness' sake! . . . Are you on the tram?" She settled round in her seat with her elbow hooked over the back—it is bare and sharp, with a rubbed joint: she and Mrs Kearney are of an age, and the age is about thirty-five. They both wear printed dresses that in this weather stick close to their backs; they are enthusiastic, not close friends but as close as they are ever likely to be. They both have high, fresh, pink colouring; Mrs Kearney could do with a little less weight and Miss Kevin could do with a little more.

They agree they are out early. Miss Kevin has been in town for the July sales but is now due home to let her mother go out. She has parcels with her but they are compact and shiny, having been made up at the counters of shops. "They all say, buy now. You never know." She cannot help looking at Mrs Kearney's parcels, bursting out from their string. "And aren't you very laden, also," she says.

"I tell you what I've been doing," says Mrs Kearney. "I've been saying goodbye to my sister Maureen in Ballsbridge, and who knows how long it's to be for! My sister's off to County Cavan this morning with the whole of her family and the maid."

"For goodness' sake," says Miss Kevin. "Has she relatives there?"

"She has, but it's not that. She's evacuating. For the holidays they always go to Tramore, but this year she says she should evacuate." This brings Mrs Kearney's parcels into the picture. "So she asked me to keep a few of her things for her." She does not add that Maureen has given her these old things, including the month-old magazine.

"Isn't it well for her," says Miss Kevin politely. "But won't she find it terribly slow down there?"

"She will, I tell you," says Mrs Kearney. "However, they're all driving down in the car. She's full of it. She says we should all go somewhere where we don't live. It's nothing to her to shift when she has the motor. But the latest thing I hear they say now in the paper is that we'll be shot if we don't stay where we are. They say now we're all to keep off the roads—and there's my sister this morning with her car at the door. Do you think they'll halt her, Miss Kevin?"

"They might," says Miss Kevin. "I hear they're very suspicious. I declare, with the instructions changing so quickly it's better to take no notice. You'd be upside down if you tried to follow them all. It's of the first importance to keep calm, they say, and however would we keep calm doing this, then that? Still, we don't get half the instructions they get in England. I should think they'd really pity themselves. . . . Have you earth in your house, Mrs Kearney? We have, we have three buckets. The warden's delighted with us: he says we're models. We haven't a refuge, though. Have you one?"

"We have a kind of pump, but I don't know it is much good. And nothing would satisfy Fergus till he turned out the cellar."

"Well, you're very fashionable!"

"The contents are on the lawn, and the lawn's ruined. He's crazy," she says glumly, "with A.R.P."

"Aren't men very thorough," says Miss Kevin with a virgin detachment that is rather annoying. She has kept thumbing her sales parcels, and now she cannot resist undoing one. "Listen," she says, "isn't this a pretty delaine?" She runs the end of a fold between her finger and thumb. "It drapes sweetly. I've enough for a dress and a bolero. It's French: they say we won't get any more now."

"And that Coty scent—isn't that French?"

Their faces flood with the glare struck from the sea as the tram zooms smoothly along the open reach—wall and trees on its inland side, grass and bay on the other. The tips of their shingles and the thoughts in their heads are for the minute blown about and refreshed. Mrs Kearney flutters in the holiday breeze, but Miss Kevin is looking inside her purse. Mrs Kearney thinks she will take the kids to the strand. "Are you a great swimmer, Miss Kevin?"

"I don't care for it: I've a bad circulation. It's a fright to see me go blue. They say now the sea's full of mines," she says, with a look at the great, innocent bay.

"Ah, they're tethered; they'd never bump you."

"I'm not nervous at any time, but I take a terrible chill."

"My sister Maureen's nervous. At Tramore she'll never approach the water: it's the plage she enjoys. I wonder what will she do if they stop the car—she has all her plate with her in the back with the maid. And her kiddies are very nervous: they'd never stand it. I wish now I'd asked her to send me a telegram. Or should I telegraph her to know did she arrive? . . . Wasn't it you said we had to keep off the roads?"

"That's in the event of invasion, Mrs Kearney. In the event of not it's correct to evacuate."

"She's correct all right, then," says Mrs Kearney, with a momentary return to gloom. "And if nothing's up by the finish she'll say she went for the holiday, and I shouldn't wonder if she still went to Tramore. Still, I'm sure I'm greatly relieved to hear what you say. . . . Is that your father's opinion?"

Miss Kevin becomes rather pettish. "Him?" she says, "oh gracious, I'd never ask him. He has a great contempt for the whole war. My mother and I daren't refer to it—isn't it very mean of him? He does nothing but read the papers and roar away to himself. And will he let my mother or me near him when he has the news on? You'd think," Miss Kevin says with a clear laugh, "that the two of us originated the war to spite him: he doesn't seem to blame Hitler at all. He's really very unreasonable when he's not well. We'd a great fight to get in the buckets of earth, and now he makes out they're only there for the cat. And to hear the warden praising us makes him sour. Isn't it very mean to want us out of it all, when they say the whole country is drawn together? He doesn't take any pleasure in A.R.P."

"To tell you the truth I don't either," says Mrs Kearney. "Isn't it that stopped the Horse Show? Wouldn't that take the heart out of you—isn't that a great blow to national life? I never yet missed a Horse Show—Sheila was nearly born there. And isn't that a terrible blow to trade? I haven't the heart to look for a new hat. To my mind this war's getting very monotonous: all the interest of it is confined to a few . . . Did you go to the Red Cross Fête?"

The tram grinds to a halt in Dun Laoghaire Street. Simultaneously Miss Kevin and Mrs Kearney move up to the window ends of their seats and look closely down on the shop windows and shoppers. Town heat comes off the street in a quiver and begins to pervade the immobile tram. "I declare to goodness," exclaims Miss Kevin, "there's my same delaine! French, indeed! And watch the figure it's on—it would sicken you."

But with parallel indignation Mrs Kearney has just noticed a clock. "Will you look at the time!" she says, plaintively. "Isn't this an awfully slow tram! There's my morning gone, and not a thing touched at home, from attending evacuations. It's well for her! She expected me on her step by ten—'It's a terrible parting,' she says on the p.c. But all she does at the last is to chuck the parcels at me, then keep me running to see had they the luncheon basket and what had they done with her fur coat. . . . I'll be off at the next stop, Miss Kevin dear. Will you tell your father and mother I was inquiring for them?" Crimson again at the very notion of moving, she begins to scrape her parcels under her wing. "Well," she says, "I'm off with the *objets d'art*." The heels of a pair of evening slippers protrude from a gap at the end of the dress box. The tram-driver, by smiting his bell, drowns any remark Miss Kevin could put out: the tram clears the crowd and moves down Dun Laoghaire Street, between high flights of steps, lace curtains, gardens with round beds. "Bye-bye, now," says Mrs Kearney, rising and swaying.

"Bye-bye to you," said Miss Kevin. "Happy days to us all."

Mrs Kearney, near the top of the stairs, is preparing to bite on the magazine. "Go on!" she says. "I'll be seeing you before then."

MAEVE BRENNAN

(1917–1993)

In 1934 Robert Brennan was appointed Ireland's first ambassador to Washington. He brought his family with him, including his seventeen-year-old daughter Maeve. At the end of his term the Brennan family returned to Ireland, except for Maeve who stayed in America for the rest of her life. "I don't know whether in Ireland she is considered an Irish writer or an American," wrote William Maxwell, her editor at The New Yorker. *"In fact, she is both, and both countries ought to be proud to claim her."*

Maeve Brennan *wrote for* The New Yorker *for most of her life, and the magazine accommodated her eccentricity. She contributed to "Talk of the Town" for fifteen years under "communications from our friend, the long-winded lady." Much of her work at* The New Yorker *was about Manhattan, but Brennan's finest writing was about Ireland. She wrote a series of stories, considered her best work, about a middle-class couple, Rose and Hubert Derdon, who live in a suburb of Dublin and age from young marrieds to a disaffected couple in their fifties.*

Brennan's last years were spent battling sometimes violent psychotic episodes. Her New Yorker *family bailed her out financially and emotionally. She lived in seedy neighborhoods, the Algonquin Hotel and, once, set up housekeeping in the ladies room at the magazine's office. "The Morning After the Big Fire" is from her posthumous collection* The Springs of Affection: Stories of Dublin.

THE MORNING AFTER THE BIG FIRE

from THE SPRINGS OF AFFECTION

From the time I was almost five until I was almost eighteen, we lived in a small house in a part of Dublin called Ranelagh. On our street, all of the houses were of red brick and had small back gardens, part cement and part grass, separated from one another by low stone walls over which, when we first moved in, I was unable to peer, although in later years I seem to remember looking over them quite easily, so I suppose they were about five feet high. All of the gardens had a common end wall, which was, of course, very long, since it stretched the whole length of our street. Our street was called an avenue, because it was blind at one end, the farthest end from us. It was a short avenue, twenty-six houses on one side and twenty-six on the other. We were No. 48, and only four houses from the main road, Ranelagh Road, on which trams and buses and all kinds of cars ran, making a good deal of noisy traffic.

Beyond the end wall of our garden lay a large tennis club, and sometimes in the summer, especially when the tournaments were on, my little sister and I used to perch in an upstairs back window and watch the players in their white dresses and white flannels, and hear their voices calling the scores. There was a clubhouse, but we couldn't see it. Our view was partly obstructed by a large garage building that leaned against the end wall of our garden and the four other gardens between us and Ranelagh Road. A number of people who lived on our avenue kept their cars in the garage, and the people who came to play tennis parked their cars there. It was a very busy place, the garage, and I had never been in there, although we bought our groceries in a shop that was connected with it. The shop fronted on Ranelagh Road, and the shop and the garage were the property of a red-faced, gangling man and his fat, pink-haired wife, the McRorys. On summer afternoons, when my sister and I went around to the shop to buy little paper cups of yellow water ice, some of the players would be there, refreshing themselves with ices and also with bottles of lemonade.

Early one summer morning, while it was still dark, I heard my father's voice, sounding very excited, outside the door of the room in which I slept. I was about eight. My little sister slept in the same room with me. "McRory's is on fire!" my father was saying. He had been awakened by the red glare of the flames against his window. He threw on some clothes and hurried off to see what was going on, and my mother let us look at the fire from a back window, the same window from which we were accustomed to view the tennis matches. It was a really satisfactory fire, with leaping flames, thick, pouring smoke, and a steady roar of destruction, broken by crashes as parts of the roof collapsed. My mother wondered if they had managed to save the cars, and this made us all look at the burning building with new interest and with enormous awe as we imagined the big shining cars being eaten up by the galloping fire. It was very exciting. My mother hurried us back to our front bedroom, but even there the excitement could be felt, with men calling to one another on the street and banging their front doors after them as they raced off to see the fun. Since she had decided there was no danger to our house, my mother tucked us firmly back into bed, but I could not sleep, and as soon as it grew light, I dressed myself and trotted downstairs. My father had many stories to tell. The garage was a ruin, he said, but the shop was safe. Many cars had been destroyed. No one knew how the fire had started. Some of the fellows connected with the garage had been very brave, dashing in to rescue as many cars as they could reach. The part of the building that overlooked our garden appeared charred, frail, and empty because it no longer had much in the way of a roof and its insides were gone. The air smelled very burnt.

I WANDERED QUIETLY out onto the avenue, which was deserted because the children had not come out to play and it was still too early for the men to be going to work. I walked up the avenue in the direction of the blind end. The people living there were too far from the garage to have been disturbed by the blaze. A woman whose little boy was a friend of mine came to her door to take in the milk.

"McRory's was burnt down last night!" I cried to her.

"What's that?" she said, very startled.

"Burnt to the ground," I said. "Hardly a wall left standing. A whole lot of people's cars burnt up, too."

She looked back over her shoulder in the direction of her kitchen, which, since all the houses were identical, was in the same position as our kitchen. "Jim!" she cried. "Do you hear this? McRory's was burnt down last night. The whole place. Not a stick left. . . . We slept right through it," she said to me, looking as though just the thought of that heavy sleep puzzled and unsettled her.

Her husband hurried out to stand beside her, and I had to tell the whole story again. He said he would run around to McRory's and take a look, and this enraged me, because I wasn't allowed around there and I knew that when he came back he would be a greater authority than I. However, there was no time to lose. Other people were opening their front doors by now, and I wanted everyone to hear the news from me.

"Did you hear the news?" I shouted, to as many as I could catch up with, and, of course, once I had their ear, they were fascinated by what I had to tell. One or two of the men, hurrying away to work, charged past me with such forbiddingly closed faces that I was afraid to approach them, and they continued in their ignorance down toward Ranelagh Road, causing me dreadful anguish, because I knew that before they could board their tram or their bus, some officious busybody would be sure to treat them to my news. Then one woman, to whom I always afterward felt friendly, called down to me from her front bedroom window. "What's that you were telling Mrs. Pearce?" she asked me, in a loud whisper.

"Oh, just that McRory's was burnt to the ground last night. Nearly all the cars burnt up, too. Hardly anything left, my father says." By this time I was being very offhand.

"You don't tell me," she said, making a delighted face, and the next thing I knew, she was opening her front door, more eager for news than anybody.

However, my hour of glory was short. The other children came out—some of them were actually allowed to go around and view the wreckage—and soon the fire was mine no longer, because there were others walking around who knew more about it than I did. I pretended to lose interest, although I was glad when someone—not my father—gave me a lump of twisted, blackened tin off one of the cars.

The tennis clubhouse had been untouched, and that afternoon the players appeared, as bright and immaculate in their snowy flannels and linens as though the smoking garage yard and the lines of charred cars through which they had picked their way to the courts could never interfere with them or impress them. It was nearing tournament time, and a man was painting the platform on which the judge was to sit and from which a lady in a wide hat and a flowered chiffon dress would present cups and medals to the victors among the players. Now, in the sunshine, they lifted their rackets and started to play, and their intent and formal cries mingled with the hoarse shouts of the men at work in the dark shambles of the garage. My little sister and I, watching from our window, could imagine that the rhythmical thud of the ball against the rackets coincided with the unidentifiable sounds we heard from the wreckage, which might have been groans or shrieks as the building, unable to recover from the fire, succumbed under it.

*   *   *

IT WAS NOT long before the McRorys put up another garage, made of silvery corrugated-metal stuff that looked garish and glaring against our garden wall; it cut off more of our view than the old building had. The new garage looked very hard and lasting, as unlikely to burn as a pot or a kettle. The beautiful green courts that had always seemed from our window to roll comfortably in the direction of the old wooden building now seemed to have turned and to be rolling away into the distance, as though they did not like the unsightly new structure and would have nothing to do with it.

My father said the odds were all against another fire there, but I remembered that fine dark morning, with all the excitement and my own importance, and I longed for another just like it. This time, however, I was determined to discover the blaze before my father did, and I watched the garage closely, as much of it as I could see, for signs that it might be getting ready to go up in flames, but I was disappointed. It stood, and still was standing, ugly as ever, when we left the house years later. Still, for a long time I used to think that if some child should steal around there with a match one night and set it all blazing again, I would never blame her, as long as she let me be the first with the news.

OLIVER GOLDSMITH

(1731–1774)

At first glance, Oliver Goldsmith typifies the Irish immigrant who leaves for England and is absorbed into British culture. After leaving Ireland in 1752, he never returned and seldom corresponded with the family he left behind. Thackeray once wrote that Goldsmith, author of the novel Citizen of the World and the brilliant comedy She Stoops to Conquer, was the "most beloved of English writers." Yeats wrote that Goldsmith had given up his Irishness and become "part of the English system."

But Goldsmith's correspondence shows that he longed for his village of Lissoy. He wrote to his friend Daniel Hodson, "If I go to the opera where Signora Colomba pours out all the mazes of melody; I sit and sigh for Lishoy fireside, and 'Johnny Armstrong's Last Good Night' from Peggy Golden. If I climb Flamstead hill where nature never exhibited a more magnificent prospect; I confess it fine but then I had rather be placed on the little mount before Lishoy gate, and take in, to me, the most pleasing horizon in nature."

Critics generally agree that "The Deserted Village" is an amalgam of Goldsmith's cultures. Auburn in its happy days is probably based on a hamlet in Kent; Auburn in its decay is an Irish village, perhaps one remembered from his Leinster childhood. In presenting the "two villages," Goldsmith is painting an incendiary portrait of the relative wealth of England compared to the lack thereof in Ireland. In this excerpt Goldsmith catalogues the decay of "Auburn." The selection ends with the poet's declaration that he still hopes that he will return "and die at home at last."

from THE DESERTED VILLAGE

Sweet smiling village, loveliest of the lawn,
Thy sports are fled, and all thy charms withdrawn;
Amidst thy bowers the tyrant's hand is seen,
And desolation saddens all thy green:
One only master grasps the whole domain,
And half a village stints thy smiling plain:
No more thy glassy brook reflects the day,
But, choked with sedges, works its weedy way:
Along thy grades, a solitary guest,
The hollow-sounding bittern guards its nest;
Amidst thy desert walks the lapwing flies,
And tires their echoes with unvaried cries:
Sunk are thy bowers in shapeless ruin all,
And the long grass o'ertops the mouldering wall;
And, trembling, shrinking from the spoiler's hand,
Far, far away; thy children leave the land.

Ill fares the land, to hastening ills a prey,
Where wealth accumulates, and men decay.
Princes and lords may flourish, or may fade;
A breath can make them, as a breath has made;
But a bold peasantry, their country's pride,
When once destroyed, can never be supplied.

A time there was, ere England's griefs began,
When every rood of ground maintained its man;
For him light labour spread her wholesome store,
Just gave what life required, but gave no more:
His best companions, innocence and health;
And his best riches, ignorance of wealth.

But times are altered; trade's unfeeling train

Usurp the land, and dispossess the swain;
Along the lawn, where scattered hamlets rose,
Unwieldy wealth and cumbrous pomp repose;
And every want to luxury allied,
And every pang that folly pays to pride.
Those gentle hours that plenty bade to bloom,
Those calm desires that asked but little room,
Those healthful sports that graced the peaceful scene,
Lived in each look and brightened all the green;
These, far departing, seek a kinder shore,
And rural mirth and manners are no more.

   Sweet Auburn! parent of the blissful hour,
Thy glades forlorn confess the tyrant's power.
Here, as I take my solitary rounds,
Amidst thy tangling walks and ruined grounds,
And, many a year elapsed, return to view
Where once the cottage stood, the hawthorn grew,
Remembrance wakes with all her busy train,
Swells at my breast and turns the past to pain.

   In all my wanderings through this world of care,
In all my griefs—and God has given my share—
I still had hopes, my latest hours to crown,
Amidst these humble bowers to lay me down;
To husband out life's taper at the close,
And keep the flame from wasting by repose:
I still had hopes, for pride attends us still,
Amidst the swains to show my book-learned skill,
Around my fire an evening group to draw,
And tell of all I felt and all I saw;
And, as a hare, whom hounds and horns pursue,
Pants to the place from whence at first she flew,
I still had hopes, my long vexations past,
Here to return—and die at home at last.

JAMES JOYCE

(1882–1941)

*James Joyce left Ireland, but Ireland never left him. The country he re-
jected was the setting for all his writing, including the novels* Ulysses *and*
Finnegans Wake *and the short story collection* Dubliners, *from which
this selection is taken. The son of a dissolute Dublin civil servant, Joyce
was the eldest of ten children. Despite his family's poverty, Joyce received
a classical education at Jesuit schools, including University College Dublin
where his first essays were published. Joyce broke with the Church in col-
lege. He also rejected the cause of Irish nationalism, and at the age of
twenty he left Ireland.*

In A Portrait of the Artist as a Young Man *Joyce's alter-ego
Stephen Dedalus says, "I will not serve that in which I no longer believe
whether it call itself my home, my fatherland, or my church: and I will
try to express myself in some mode of life or art as freely as I can, using
for my defence the only arms I allow myself to use—silence, exile, and
cunning." Except for brief visits to Ireland, Joyce lived in Paris, Trieste,
Rome, and Zurich with Nora Barnacle, a Dublin chambermaid whom
he eventually married. Joyce supported his wife and two children by giv-
ing language lessons and doing clerical work.*

*Joyce made little money from his writing until the end of his life. His
work was banned, burned, pirated, and misunderstood. Fellow Irishman
George Bernard Shaw wrote, "[Ulysses] is a revolting record of a dis-
gusting phase of civilization, but it is a truthful one."*

*Joyce was once asked if he was proud of being Irish, and he replied,
"I regret the temperament it gave me." Joyce died in 1941 at the age of
fifty-eight in Zurich.*

A LITTLE CLOUD

from DUBLINERS

Eight years before he had seen his friend off at the North Wall and wished him godspeed. Gallaher had got on. You could tell that at once by his traveled air, his well-cut tweed suit, and fearless accent. Few fellows had talents like his and fewer still could remain unspoiled by such success. Gallaher's heart was in the right place and he had deserved to win. It was something to have a friend like that.

Little Chandler's thoughts ever since lunchtime had been of his meeting with Gallaher, of Gallaher's invitation and of the great city London where Gallaher lived. He was called Little Chandler because, though he was but slightly under the average stature, he gave one the idea of being a little man. His hands were white and small, his frame was fragile, his voice was quiet and his manners were refined. He took the greatest care of his fair silken hair and moustache and used perfume discreetly on his handkerchief. The half-moons of his nails were perfect and when he smiled you caught a glimpse of a row of childish white teeth.

As he sat at his desk in the King's Inns he thought what changes those eight years had brought. The friend whom he had known under a shabby and necessitous guise had become a brilliant figure on the London Press. He turned often from his tiresome writing to gaze out of the office window. The glow of a late autumn sunset covered the grass plots and walks. It cast a shower of kindly golden dust on the untidy nurses and decrepit old men who drowsed on the benches; it flickered upon all the moving figures—on the children who ran screaming along the gravel paths and on everyone who passed through the gardens. He watched the scene and thought of life; and (as always happened when he thought of life) he became sad. A gentle melancholy took possession of him. He felt how useless it was to struggle against fortune, this being the burden of wisdom which the ages had bequeathed to him.

He remembered the books of poetry upon his shelves at home. He had bought them in his bachelor days and many an evening, as he sat in the little room off the hall, he had been tempted to take one down from the bookshelf and read out something to his wife. But shyness had always held him back; and so the books had remained on their shelves. At times he repeated lines to himself and this consoled him.

When his hour had struck he stood up and took leave of his desk and of his fellow-clerks punctiliously. He emerged from under the feudal arch of the King's Inns, a neat modest figure, and walked swiftly down Henrietta Street. The golden sunset was waning and the air had grown sharp. A horde of grimy children populated the street. They stood or ran in the roadway or crawled up the steps before the gaping doors or squatted like mice upon the thresholds. Little Chandler gave them no thought. He picked his way deftly through all that minute vermin-like life and under the shadow of the gaunt spectral mansions in which the old nobility of Dublin had roistered. No memory of the past touched him, for his mind was full of a present joy.

He had never been in Corless's but he knew the value of the name. He knew that people went there after the theatre to eat oysters and drink liqueurs; and he had heard that the waiters there spoke French and German. Walking swiftly by at night he had seen cabs drawn up before the door and richly dressed ladies, escorted by cavaliers, alight and enter quickly. They wore noisy dresses and many wraps. Their faces were powdered and they caught up their dresses, when they touched earth, like alarmed Atalantas. He had always passed without turning his head to look. It was his habit to walk swiftly in the street even by day and whenever he found himself in the city late at night he hurried on his way apprehensively and excitedly. Sometimes, however, he courted the causes of his fear. He chose the darkest and narrowest streets and, as he walked boldly forward, the silence that was spread about his footsteps troubled him, the wandering, silent figures troubled him; and at times a sound of low fugitive laughter made him tremble like a leaf.

He turned to the right towards Capel Street. Ignatius Gallaher on the London Press! Who would have thought it possible eight years before? Still, now that he reviewed the past, Little Chandler could remember many signs of future greatness in his friend. People used to say that Ignatius Gallaher was wild. Of course, he did mix with a rakish set of fellows at that time, drank freely and borrowed money on all sides. In the end he had got mixed up in some shady affair, some money transaction: at least, that was one version of his flight. But nobody denied him talent. There was always a certain . . . something in Ignatius Gallaher that impressed you in spite of yourself. Even when he was out at elbows and at his wits' end for money he kept up a bold face. Little Chandler remembered (and the remembrance brought a slight flush of pride to his cheek) one of Ignatius Gallaher's sayings when he was in a tight corner:

"Half time now, boys," he used to say lightheartedly. "Where's my considering cap?"

That was Ignatius Gallaher all out; and, damn it, you couldn't but admire him for it.

Little Chandler quickened his pace. For the first time in his life he felt himself superior to the people he passed. For the first time his soul revolted again the dull inelegance of Capel Street. There was no doubt about it: if you wanted to succeed you had to go away. You could do nothing in Dublin. As he crossed Grattan Bridge he looked down the river towards the lower quays and pitied the poor stunted houses. They seemed to him a band of tramps, huddled together along the river-banks, their old coats covered with dust and soot, stupefied by the panorama of sunset and waiting for the first chill of night to bid them arise, shake themselves and begone. He wondered whether he could write a poem to express his idea. Perhaps Gallaher might be able to get it into some London paper for him. Could he write something original? He was not sure what idea he wished to express but the thought that a poetic moment had touched him took life within him like an infant hope. He stepped onward bravely.

Every step brought him nearer to London, farther from his own sober inartistic life. A light began to tremble on the horizon of his mind. He was not so old—thirty-two. His temperament might be said to be just at the point of maturity. There were so many different moods and impressions that he wished to express in verse. He felt them within him. He tried to weigh his soul to see if it was a poet's soul. Melancholy was the dominant note of his temperament, he thought, but it was a melancholy tempered by recurrences of faith and resignation and simple joy. If he could give expression to it in a book of poems perhaps men would listen. He would never be popular: he saw that. He could not sway the crowd but he might appeal to a little circle of kindred minds. The English critics, perhaps, would recognise him as one of the Celtic school by reason of the melancholy tone of his poems; besides that, he would put in allusions. He began to invent sentences and phrases from the notice which his book would get. *"Mr. Chandler has the gift of easy and graceful verse."* . . . *"A wistful sadness pervades these poems."* . . . *"The Celtic note."* It was a pity his name was not more Irish-looking. Perhaps it would be better to insert his mother's name before the surname: Thomas Malone Chandler, or better still: T. Malone Chandler. He would speak to Gallaher about it.

He pursued his revery so ardently that he passed his street and had to turn back. As he came near Corless's his former agitation began to overmaster him and he halted before the door in indecision. Finally he opened the door and entered.

The light and noise of the bar held him at the doorways for a

few moments. He looked about him, but his sight was confused
by the shining of many red and green wine-glasses. The bar
seemed to him to be full of people and he felt that the people
were observing him curiously. He glanced quickly to right and
left (frowning slightly to make his errand appear serious), but
when his sight cleared a little he saw that nobody had turned to
look at him: and there, sure enough, was Ignatius Gallaher lean-
ing with his back against the counter and his feet planted far
apart.

"Hallo, Tommy, old hero, here you are! What is it to be?
What will you have? I'm taking whisky: better stuff than we get
across the water. Soda? Lithia? No mineral? I'm the same. Spoils
the flavour . . . Here, *garçon,* bring us two halves of malt whisky,
like a good fellow. . . . Well, and how have you been pulling
along since I saw you last? Dear God, how old we're getting! Do
you see any signs of aging in me—eh, what? A little grey and
thin on the top—what?"

Ignatius Gallaher took off his hat and displayed a large closely
cropped head. His face was heavy, pale and clean-shaven. His
eyes, which were of bluish slate-colour, relieved his unhealthy
pallor and shone out plainly above the vivid orange tie he wore.
Between these rival features the lips appeared very long and
shapeless and colourless. He bent his head and felt with two
sympathetic fingers the thin hair at the crown. Little Chandler
shook his head as a denial. Ignatius Gallaher put on his hat again.

"It pulls you down," he said. "Press life. Always hurry and
scurry, looking for copy and sometimes not finding it: and then,
always to have something new in your stuff. Damn proofs and
printers, I say, for a few days. I'm deuced glad, I can tell you, to
get back to the old country. Does a fellow good, a bit of a holi-
day. I feel a ton better since I landed again in dear dirty
Dublin . . . Here you are, Tommy. Water? Say when."

Little Chandler allowed his whiskey to be very much diluted.

"You don't know what's good for you, my boy," said Ignatius
Gallaher. "I drink mine neat."

"I drink very little as a rule," said Little Chandler modestly. "An odd half-one or so when I meet any of the old crowd: that's all."

"Ah, well," said Ignatius Gallaher, cheerfully, "here's to us and to old times and old acquaintance."

They clinked glasses and drank the toast.

"I met some of the old gang to-day," said Ignatius Gallaher. "O'Hara seems to be in a bad way. What's he doing?"

"Nothing," said Little Chandler. "He's gone to the dogs."

"But Hogan has a good sit, hasn't he?"

"Yes; he's in the Land Commission."

"I met him one night in London and he seemed to be very flush. . . . Poor O'Hara! Boose, I suppose?"

"Other things, too," said Little Chandler shortly.

Ignatius Gallaher laughed.

"Tommy," he said, "I see you haven't changed an atom. You're the very same serious person that used to lecture me on Sunday mornings when I had a sore head and a fur on my tongue. You'd want to knock about a bit in the world. Have you never been anywhere even for a trip?"

"I've been to the Isle of Man," said Little Chandler.

Ignatius Gallaher laughed.

"The Isle of Man!" he said. "Go to London or Paris: Paris, for choice. That'd do you good."

"Have you seen Paris?"

"I should think I have! I've knocked about there a little."

"And is it really so beautiful as they say?" asked Little Chandler.

He sipped a little of his drink while Ignatius Gallaher finished his boldly.

"Beautiful?" said Ignatius Gallaher, pausing on the word and on the flavour of his drink. "It's not so beautiful, you know. Of course, it is beautiful. . . . But it's the life of Paris; that's the thing. Ah, there's no city like Paris for gaiety, movement, excitement . . ."

Little Chandler finished his whisky and, after some trouble, succeeded in catching the barman's eye. He ordered the same again.

"I've been to the Moulin Rouge," Ignatius Gallaher continued when the barman had removed their glasses, "and I've been to all the Bohemian cafés. Hot stuff! Not for a pious chap like you, Tommy."

Little Chandler said nothing until the barman returned with two glasses: then he touched his friend's glass lightly and reciprocated the former toast. He was beginning to feel somewhat disillusioned. Gallaher's accent and way of expressing himself did not please him. There was something vulgar in his friend which he had not observed before. But perhaps it was only the result of living in London amid the bustle and competition of the Press. The old personal charm was still there under this new gaudy manner. And, after all, Gallaher had lived, he had seen the world. Little Chandler looked at his friend enviously.

"Everything in Paris is gay," said Ignatius Gallaher. "They believe in enjoying life—and don't you think they're right? If you want to enjoy yourself properly you must go to Paris. And, mind you, they've a great feeling for the Irish there. When they heard I was from Ireland they were ready to eat me, man."

Little Chandler took four or five sips from his glass.

"Tell me," he said, "is it true that Paris is so . . . immoral as they say?"

Ignatius Gallaher made a catholic gesture with his right arm.

"Every place is immoral," he said. "Of course you do find spicy bits in Paris. Go to one of the students' balls, for instance. That's lively, if you like, when the *cocottes* begin to let themselves loose. You know what they are, I suppose?"

"I've heard of them," said Little Chandler.

Ignatius Gallaher drank off his whisky and shook his head.

"Ah," he said, "you may say what you like. There's no woman like the Parisienne—for style, for go."

"Then it is an immoral city," said Little Chandler, with timid insistence—"I mean, compared with London or Dublin?"

"London!" said Ignatius Gallaher. "It's six of one and half-a-dozen of the other. You ask Hogan, my boy. I showed him a bit about London when he was over there. He'd open your eye. . . . I say, Tommy, don't make punch of that whisky: liquor up."

"No, really . . ."

"O, come on, another one won't do you any harm. What is it? The same again, I suppose?"

"Well . . . all right."

"*François,* the same again . . . Will you smoke, Tommy?"

Ignatius Gallaher produced his cigar-case. The two friends lit their cigars and puffed at them in silence until their drinks were served.

"I'll tell you my opinion," said Ignatius Gallaher, emerging after some time from the clouds of smoke in which he had taken refuge, "it's a rum world. Talk of immorality! I've heard of cases—what am I saying?—I've know them: cases of . . . immorality . . ."

Ignatius Gallaher puffed thoughtfully at his cigar and then, in a calm historian's tone, he proceeded to sketch for his friend some pictures of the corruption which was rife abroad. He summarised the vices of many capitals and seemed inclined to award the palm to Berlin. Some things he could not vouch for (his friends had told him), but of others he had had personal experience. He spared neither rank nor caste. He revealed many of the secrets of religious houses on the Continent and described some of the practices which were fashionable in high society and ended by telling, with details, a story about an English duchess—a story which he knew to be true. Little Chandler was astonished.

"Ah well," said Ignatius Gallaher, "here we are in old jog-along Dublin where nothing is known of such things."

"How dull you must find it," said Little Chandler, "after all the other places you've seen!"

"Well," said Ignatius Gallaher, "it's a relaxation to come over here, you know. And, after all, it's the old country, as they say, isn't it? You can't help having a certain feeling for it. That's human nature. . . . But tell me something about yourself. Hogan told me you had . . . tasted the joys of connubial bliss. Two years ago, wasn't it?"

Little Chandler blushed and smiled.

"Yes," he said. "I was married last May twelve months."

"I hope it's not too late in the day to offer my best wishes," said Ignatius Gallaher. "I didn't know your address or I'd have done so at the time."

He extended his hand, which Little Chandler took.

"Well Tommy," he said, "I wish you and yours every joy in life, old chap, and tons of money, and may you never die till I shoot you. And that's the wish of a sincere friend, an old friend. You know that?"

"I know that," said Little Chandler.

"Any youngsters?" said Ignatius Gallaher.

Little Chandler blushed again.

"We have one child," he said.

"Son or daughter?"

"A little boy."

Ignatius Gallaher slapped his friend sonorously on the back.

"Bravo," he said, "I wouldn't doubt you, Tommy."

Little Chandler smiled, looked confusedly at his glass and bit his lower lip with three childishly white front teeth.

"I hope you'll spend an evening with us," he said, "before you go back. My wife will be delighted to meet you. We can have a little music and—"

"Thanks awfully, old chap," said Ignatius Gallaher. "I'm sorry we didn't meet earlier. But I must leave to-morrow night."

"To-night, perhaps . . . ?"

"I'm awfully sorry, old man. You see I'm over here with another fellow, clever young chap he is too, and we arranged to go to a little card party. Only for that . . ."

"O, in that case . . ."

"But who knows?" said Ignatius Gallaher considerately. "Next year I may take a little skip over here now that I've broken the ice. It's only a pleasure deferred."

"Very well," said Little Chandler, "the next time you come
we must have an evening together. That's agreed now, isn't it?"

"Yes, that's agreed," said Ignatius Gallaher. "Next year if I
come, *parole d' honneur.*"

"And to clinch the bargain," said Little Chandler, "we'll just
have one more now."

Ignatius Gallaher took out a large gold watch and looked at it.

"Is it to be the last?" he said. "Because you know, I have an
a.p."

"O, yes, positively," said Little Chandler.

"Very well, then," said Ignatius Gallaher, "let us have another
one as a *deoc an doruis*—that's good vernacular for a small whisky,
I believe."

Little Chandler ordered the drinks. The blush which had
risen to his face a few moments before was establishing itself. A
trifle made him blush at any time: and now he felt warm and
excited. Three small whiskies had gone to his head and Galla-
her's strong cigar had confused his mind, for he was a delicate
and abstinent person. The adventure of meeting Gallaher after
eight years, of finding himself with Gallaher in Corless's sur-
rounded by lights and noise, of listening to Gallaher's stories and
of sharing for a brief space Gallaher's vagrant and triumphant
life, upset the equipoise of his sensitive nature. He felt acutely
the contrast between his own life and his friend's, and it seemed
to him unjust. Gallaher was his inferior in birth and education.
He was sure that he could do something better than his friend
had ever done, or could ever do, something higher than mere
tawdry journalism if he only got the chance. What was it that
stood in his way? His unfortunate timidity! He wished to vindi-
cate himself in some way, to assert his manhood. He saw behind
Gallaher's refusal of his invitation. Gallaher was only patronising
him by his friendliness just as he was patronising Ireland by his
visit.

The barman brought their drinks. Little Chandler pushed
one glass towards his friend and took up the other boldly.

"Who knows?" he said, as they lifted their glasses. "When

you come next year I may have the pleasure of wishing long life
and happiness to Mr. and Mrs. Ignatius Gallaher."

Ignatius Gallaher in the act of drinking closed one eye
expressively over the rim of his glass. When he had drunk he
smacked his lips decisively, set down his glass and said:

"No blooming fear of that, my boy. I'm going to have my
fling first and see a bit of life and the world before I put my head
in the sack—if I ever do."

"Some day you will," said Little Chandler calmly.

Ignatius Gallaher turned his orange tie and slate-blue eyes full
upon his friend.

"You think so?" he said.

"You'll put your head in the sack," repeated Little Chandler
stoutly, "like everyone else if you can find the girl."

He had slightly emphasised his tone and he was aware that he
had betrayed himself; but, though the colour had heightened in
his cheek, he did not flinch from his friend's gaze. Ignatius Gal-
laher watched him for a few moments and then said:

"If ever it occurs, you may bet your bottom dollar there'll be
no mooning and spooning about it. I mean to marry money.
She'll have a good fat account at the bank or she won't do for
me."

Little Chandler shook his head.

"Why, man alive," said Ignatius Gallaher, vehemently, "do
you know what it is? I've only to say the word and to-morrow I
can have the woman and the cash. You don't believe it? Well, I
know it. There are hundreds—what am I saying?—thousands of
rich Germans and Jews, rotten with money, that'd only be too
glad. . . . You wait a while, my boy. See if I don't play my cards
properly. When I go about a thing I mean business, I tell you.
You just wait."

He tossed his glass to his mouth, finished his drink and
laughed loudly. Then he looked thoughtfully before him and
said in a calmer tone:

"But I'm in no hurry. They can wait. I don't fancy tying
myself up to one woman, you know."

He imitated with his mouth the act of tasting and made a wry face.

"Must get a bit stale, I should think," he said.

LITTLE CHANDLER SAT in the room off the hall, holding a child in his arms. To save money they kept no servant but Annie's young sister Monica came for an hour or so in the morning and an hour or so in the evening to help. But Monica had gone home long ago. It was a quarter to nine. Little Chandler had come home late for tea and, moreover, he had forgotten to bring Annie home the parcel of coffee from Bewley's. Of course she was in a bad humour and gave him short answers. She said she would do without any tea but when it came near the time at which the shop at the corner closed she decided to go out herself for a quarter of a pound of tea and two pounds of sugar. She put the sleeping child deftly in his arms and said:

"Here. Don't waken him."

A little lamp with a white china shade stood upon the table and its light fell over a photograph which was enclosed in a frame of crumpled horn. It was Annie's photograph. Little Chandler looked at it, pausing at the thin tight lips. She wore the pale blue summer blouse which he had brought her home as a present one Saturday. It had cost him ten and elevenpence; but what an agony of nervousness it had cost him! How he had suffered that day, waiting at the shop door until the shop was empty, standing at the counter and trying to appear at his ease while the girl piled ladies' blouses before him, paying at the desk and forgetting to take up the odd penny of his change, being called back by the cashier, and finally, striving to hide his blushes as he left the shop by examining the parcel to see if it was securely tied. When he brought the blouse home Annie kissed him and said it was very pretty and stylish; but when she heard the price she threw the blouse on the table and said it was a regular swindle to charge ten and elevenpence for it. At first she wanted to take it back but when she tried it on she was delighted with it, especially with the make of the sleeves, and kissed him and said he was very good to think of her.

Hm! . . .

He looked coldly into the eyes of the photograph and they answered coldly. Certainly they were pretty and the face itself was pretty. But he found something mean in it. Why was it so unconscious and ladylike? The composure of the eyes irritated him. They repelled him and defied him: there was no passion in them, no rapture. He thought of what Gallaher had said about rich Jewesses. Those dark Oriental eyes, he thought, how full they are of passion, of voluptuous longing! . . . Why had he married the eyes in the photograph?

He caught himself up at the question and glanced nervously round the room. He found something mean in the pretty furniture which he had bought for his house on the hire system. Annie had chosen it herself and it reminded him of her. It too was prim and pretty. A dull resentment against his life awoke within him. Could he not escape from his little house? Was it too late for him to try to live bravely like Gallaher? Could he go to London? There was the furniture still to be paid for. If he could only write a book and get it published, that might open the way for him.

A volume of Byron's poems lay before him on the table. He opened it cautiously with his left hand lest he should waken the child and began to read the first poem in the book:

> Hushed are the winds and still the evening gloom,
>   Not e'en a Zephyr wanders through the grove,
> Whilst I return to view my Margaret's tomb
>   And scatter flowers on the dust I love.

He paused. He felt the rhythm of the verse about him in the room. How melancholy it was! Could he, too, write like that, express the melancholy of his soul in verse? There were so many things he wanted to describe: his sensation of a few hours before on Grattan Bridge, for example. If he could get back again into that mood. . . .

The child awoke and began to cry. He turned from the page and tried to hush it: but it would not be hushed. He began to rock it to and fro in his arms but its wailing cry grew keener. He rocked it faster while his eyes began to read the second stanza:

> Within this narrow cell reclines her clay,
>   That clay where once . . .

It was useless. He couldn't read. He couldn't do anything. The wailing of the child pierced the drum of his ear. It was useless, useless! He was a prisoner for life. His arms trembled with anger and suddenly bending to the child's face he shouted:

"Stop!"

The child stopped for an instant, had a spasm of fright and began to scream. He jumped up from his chair and walked hastily up and down the room with the child in his arms. It began to sob piteously, losing its breath for four or five seconds, and then bursting out anew. The thin walls of the room echoed the sound. He tried to soothe it but it sobbed more convulsively. He looked at the contracted and quivering face of the child and began to be alarmed. He counted seven sobs without a break between them and caught the child to his breast in fright. If it died! . . .

The door was burst open and a young woman ran in, panting.

"What is it? What is it?" she cried.

The child, hearing its mother's voice, broke out into a paroxysm of sobbing.

"It's nothing, Annie . . . it's nothing. . . . He began to cry . . ."

She flung her parcels on the floor and snatched the child from him.

"What have you done to him?" she cried, glaring into his face.

Little Chandler sustained for one moment the gaze of her eyes and his heart closed together as he met the hatred in them. He began to stammer:

"It's nothing. . . . He . . . he began to cry. . . . I couldn't . . . I didn't do anything. . . . What?"

Giving no heed to him she began to walk up and down the room, clasping the child tightly in her arms and murmuring:

"My little man! My little mannie! Was 'ou frightened, love? . . . There now, love! There now! . . . There now! . . . Lambabaun! Manna's little lamb of the world! . . . There now!"

Little Chandler felt his cheeks suffused with shame and he stood back out of the lamplight. He listened while the paroxysm of the child's sobbing grew less and less; and tears of remorse started to his eyes.

JAN MORRIS

(1926–   )

Travel writer Jan Morris has had two writing lives—as James Humphrey Morris, the fearless foreign correspondent for the London Times *and the Manchester* Guardian *who covered Sir Edmund Hillary's assault on Mt. Everest, and as Jan Morris, the English matron and the inveterate travel writer. In 1972 Morris underwent a sex change operation because he felt the "victim of a genetic mix-up." The experience is detailed in the book* Conundrum *(1974).*

One need only read two of Morris's essays on Dublin to contrast her changed writing sensibility. On James Morris's first trip, he wrote peckishly of the place, allowing only that it was "agreeable" and the people "delightfully unsophisticated." "Compared with this city," he wrote, "Reykjavik feels go-ahead, Oslo feels luxurious, even Prague feels almost hopeful." When Jan Morris returned to Dublin in 1974 (as detailed in the following article, "Do You Think Should He Have Gone Over?" from the anthology Among the Cities*), she fretted about buying a proper dress for the installation of Ireland's president, found the city "truly exotic," and called Ireland's new president a "dear man."*

Oxford educated, Morris is an extraordinarily well-informed traveler. Her writing is peppered with historic, architectural facts, thrown off casually among passages of brilliant description. Morris's travel books include Manhattan '45 *(1987),* Locations *(1992), and* Fifty Years of Europe *(1997).*

"DO YOU THINK SHOULD HE HAVE
GONE OVER?"

1974 was a bad year for Anglo-Irish relations, and as I flew from London to Dublin to write this piece the Aer Lingus hostess said, "Now you'll be sure to write something nice about the old place, won't you?" I did, and when the essay appeared the Irish Government offered me a free week's holiday in Connemara—"down to the last Guinness"—to say thank you. I accepted without a qualm—the nearest I have ever got to corruption.

When I went to Dublin once, I found that the very next morning the fifth President of the Irish Republic, the *Uachtarán*, was to be installed in the Hall of St. Patrick in Dublin Castle. Hastening out to buy myself a proper dress ("I congratulate you," said the maid at my hotel in some surprise, "you've got excellent taste"), and procuring an official pass (*Preas, Insealbhu an Uchtaráin*), promptly in the morning I presented myself at the Castle gates, made my way through the confusion of soldiery, officialdom and diplomacy that filled the old yard, and found my place beside the dais in the elegantly decorated hall ("No place for purple prose," murmured my cicerone pointedly, "more the Ionian white and gold").

It was a delightful occasion. All Eire was there, among the massed banners and crests of the ancient Irish provinces, beneath the stern gaze of the trumpeters poised for their fanfare in the minstrels' gallery. All the Ministers were there, with their invisible portfolios. All the Ambassadors were there, with their distinctly visible wives. *Both* Primates of All Ireland were there, side by side in parity. There were judges and surgeons, old revolutionaries and new politicians, clerics by the hundred, professors by the score. There was Conor Cruise O'Brien. There was John Lynch. There was Sean MacBride the Nobel Laureate. There was Cyril Cusack the actor. It was like seeing the Irish Republic encapsulated, dressed in its newest fineries, sworn to its best behaviour, and deposited in the building which, more than any other in Ireland, speaks of Irish history.

The new President, Cearbhall O'Dálaigh, seemed a dear man indeed, and gave us a gentle rambling speech much concerned with what the removal men said when they packed his possessions for the move. Some of it was in Gaelic, some in French, some in English, and I confess my mind did wander now and then, towards the Ruritanian Ambassadress's fur coat, towards the twin smiles of the Archbishops, towards the fierce survey of the bandmaster high above, who might easily have stepped from the ranks of the old Connaught Rangers. One phrase in particular, though, and not alas the President's own, caught my attention. It was a quotation from Thoreau, and it ran thus: "If a man does not keep pace with his companions, perhaps it is because he hears a different drummer."

A different drummer! What drummer beat in Dublin now, I wondered, where the best were always out of step? What pace would the bandmaster set today? Was the drumbeat different still, in this most defiantly different of capitals?

THAT EVENING, WHEN the dignitaries, officials and soldiers had dispersed to their celebratory banquets (all except the poor military policeman who, vainly trying to kick his motor bike to life, was left forlorn in the Castle yard to a universal sigh of sympathy), I drove along the coast to Howth, and then the Joyceness of Dublin, the Yeatsness, the pubness, the tramness, the Liffeyness, the Behanness, in short the stock Dublinness of the place seemed to hang like a vapour over the distant city. It was one of those Irish evenings, when the points of the compass seem to have been confused, and their climates with them. A bitter east wind swayed the palm trees along the promenade, a quick northern air sharpened that slightly Oriental languor, that Celtic *dolce far niente,* which habitually blurs the intentions of Dublin. Over the water the city lay brownish below the Wicklow Mountains, encrusted it seemed with some tangible patina of legend and literature, and fragrant of course with its own *vin du pays,* Guinness.

This is everyone's Dublin, right or wrong, and if it is partly myth, it is substance too. There is no such thing as a stage Dubliner: the characters of this city, even at their most theatrical, are true and earnest in their kind, and Dublin too, even today, lives up to itself without pretence. Are there any urchins like Dublin urchins, grubby as sin and bouncy as ping-pong balls? Are there any markets like Dublin markets, sprawling all over the city streets like gypsy jumble sales? Are there any buses so evocative as Dublin buses lurching in dim-lit parade towards Glasnevin?

Certainly there are few more boisterous streets on earth than O'Connell Street on a Saturday night, when a salt wind gusts up from the sea, making the girls giggle and the young men clown about, driving the Dublin litter helter-skelter here and there, and eddying the smells of beer, chips and hot-dogs all among the back streets. And there is no café more tumultuous than Bewley's Oriental Café in Grafton Street, with its mountains of buns on every table, with its children draped over floors and chairs, with its harassed waitresses scribbling, its tea-urns hissing, its stained glass and its tiled floors, its old clock beside the door, the high babel of its Dublin chatter and its haughty Dublin ladies, all hats and arched eyebrows, smoking their cigarettes loftily through it all.

It is an all too familiar rhythm, but it beats unmistakably still, hilariously and pathetically, and makes of Dublin one of the most truly exotic cities in the world. One still finds shawled beggar women on the Liffey bridges at night, huddling their babies close, attended by wide-eyed small boys and holding cardboard boxes for contributions. One still hears the instant give-and-take in Dublin pubs and parlours. "Ah, me rheumatism's cured," says the old lady, quick as a flash when the landlord pats her kindly on the knee, "you should advertise your healing powers." "Sure it was only my left hand too," says the landlord. "Well and it was only my left knee—try the other one, there's a good man." I experienced the tail-end of a bank robbery in Dublin one day, and only in this city, I thought, could I observe the principal witness of a crime interviewed by the police in a butcher's shop—between whose ranks of hanging turkeys, from the pavement outside, I could glimpse his blood-streaked face enthusiastically recalling the horror of it all.

Dublin's gay but shabby recklessness, too, which so infuriated its English overlords, brazenly survives. If there is a public clock that works in Dublin, I have yet to find it, and I was not in the least surprised when, calling at a restaurant at a quarter to five to arrange a table for dinner, I found several jolly parties concluding their lunch. The Irish honour their own priorities still. "It's not very satisfactory just to tell your customers," I overheard a lady complaining at the GPO, "that the mail's gone with a bomb, it's not very satisfactory at all." "He'll make a fine President," somebody said to me of Cearbhall O'Dálaigh, "nobody knows what his name is." "Enjoy yourself now!" everybody says in Dublin, and they mean enjoy yourself *notwithstanding.*

Dublin is very old—old in history, old in style. If there is no such thing as a stage Dubliner, in a curious way there is no such thing as a young one, either. The dry scepticism of the Dublin manner, the elliptical nature of its conversations, the dingy air of everything, the retrospection—all conspire to give this city a sense of elderly collusion. Everyone seems to know everyone else, and all about him too. Go into any Dublin company, somebody suggested to me one day, and present the cryptic inquiry: "Do you think should he have gone over?" Instantly, whatever the circumstances, there will be a cacophony of replies. "Sure he should, but not without telling his wife"—"And why shouldn't he have, was he not the elected representative?"—"Well it wasn't so far as it looked"—"It didn't surprise me, his father went too, remember." Such is the accumulated familiarity of the city that to any inquiry, about anybody, about anything, every Dubliner—every true Dubberlin man, as the vernacular has it— possesses an infallible response, usually wrong.

Such a sense of commonality curdles easily into conspiracy, and of course history has helped to fuse your Dubliners, making them feel far more homogeneous than the people of most Western capitals. This is not only a classless society, at least in externals, it is an indigenous one too. Your Italian waiter, your Chinese take-away *restaurateur,* your Jamaican bus conductor, even your Nigerian student of computer technology are all rare figures in Dublin still, and the consequent unity of method and temper gives the city much of its exuberant punch.

It also gives a special pride, for this is not only the capital of a nation, but the capital of an idea. The idea of Irishness is not universally beloved. Some people mock it, some hate it, some fear it. On the whole, though, I think it fair to say the world interprets it chiefly as a particular kind of happiness, a happiness sometimes boozy and violent, but essentially innocent: and this ineradicable spirit of merriment informs the Dublin genius to this day, and is alive and bubbling still, for all the miseries of the Irish Problem, in this jumbled brown capital across the water.

SOMETIMES I COULD hear other drummers, though. I rang up the *Dáil* one day and asked if there was anything interesting to observe that evening. "There's always me," said the usher, "I'm interesting." For if on one level Dublin is a world capital, to which subjects from Melbourne to the Bronx pay a vicarious or morganatic allegiance, on another it is the day-to-day capital of a little state. In this it is very modern. Ireland seems to me the right size for a country, the truly contemporary size, the size at which regionalism properly becomes nationhood, and the parliamentary usher answers the telephone himself. Small

units within a large framework offer a sensible pattern for the
world's future, and beneath the fustiness of the old Dublin, the
world's Dublin, a much more contemporary entity exists.

Old Dublin is averse to change, but this smaller, inner Dublin
welcomes it. "If we know the Brits," said a genial enthusiast at a
Ballsbridge party, holding my hand and talking about London,
"they'll soon be having St. Paul's down to make way for a new
ghastly office block." Well, the Micks are not much better when
it comes to urban development. Visual taste is hardly their forte,
and they have done little to improve the look of Dublin since
the end of the Ascendancy. Wide areas of the Liberties are in
that melancholy state of unexplained decay that generally pre-
cedes "improvement," there are frightful plans for the Liffey
quays, the Central Bank is building itself a structure which is not
only grossly out of scale with the time and the city, but seems in
its present state of completion to be made of Meccano—"an
awful thing in itself," as a bystander observed to me, "and terri-
ble by implication."

More often the implications of change are merely sad. They
imply a deliberate, functional rejection not perhaps of tradition
or principle, but of habit. Gone is many an ancient pub, anom-
alous perhaps to a condition of progress, but beloved in itself.
Crippled is many a Georgian square. Doomed and derelict is J. J.
Byrne the fish shop ("This Is The Place"). Fearful ring roads
threaten. No good looking in for Dublin Bay prawns at the old
Red Bank: it was long ago converted into a Catholic chapel,
where in the Dublin manner the local girls slip in for a moment's
supplication before rejoining their boy friends on the pavement
outside for a stout in the corner bar.

There are worse things to worry about, too. There are the
Troubles, those endemic mysteries of Ireland, which are inescap-
able in Dublin if only by suggestion—*Beál Feirste,* as the road
signs say, is only 100 miles to the north. A fairly muzzy security
screen protects the offices of the Irish Government, and sends
the unsuspecting visitor backwards and forwards between the
guards—"Did you not see this young lady when she came in?"

"I did not, she must have walked by like a ghost." When I saw a big black car with two big men in it, standing outside my host's surburban house, I knew a Minister was calling, and I looked more than once over my shoulder before, in a spirit of pure inquiry, I entered the house in Parnell Square where they sell Christmas cards and *objets d'art* made by the internees of Ulster.

But far more immediate than the bomber is the rising price. In Britain inflation is merely another blow to the punch-drunk: in Ireland it is an unfair decision. For so many centuries a loser, in recent years Eire has found a winning streak, finding its feet at last, establishing its place in the world, evolving a mean between the practical and the ideal, forgiving and even half-forgetting the tragedies of the past. With change, it seemed, prosperity was coming. Many of the new buildings of Dublin might be unlovely, but at least they were earnests of success.

Now the poor Dubliners find themselves haunted once again by the prospect of failure. The Irish economy is less than hefty, and couldn't long resist a world recession. Then the brief holi-day would be over, the cars would be sold, the colour televisions sold, the plump young Dublin executive would no longer be lunching at a quarter to five. You might not guess the possibility from the Grafton Street stores, which are among the most charming and fastidious in Europe, but your Dubberlin man sees it plain enough, and often speaks of it with cheerful foreboding, as he chooses a third sticky cake at Bewley's, or summons a sec-ond bottle of hock.

For luckily Dublin's rueful optimism survives, and pervades the Republic too. They said some fairly gloomy things in the *Dáil* that evening, and discussed some daunting prospects, but when they adjourned for a vote, and the deputies hung over the rail of the Chamber waiting for the tellers, with their rubicund laughing faces, their stocky country frames, their irrepressible chatter and their elbows on the rail, I thought they looked for all the world like convivial farmers at a cattle sale, looking down towards the Speaker's chair as towards the auctioneer, and wait-ing for the next Friesian to be led in from the robing chamber.

"Didja enjoy yourself now?" said the usher when I left, and the security man in his little lodge waggled his fingers at me as I passed.

I suppose there are terrorists plotting in Dublin, and bombers preparing their fuses, but it remains, all the same, pre-eminently the innocent capital of a star-crossed state—for the luck of the Irish is a wish more than a characteristic. There are only three million people in Eire, scarcely more than there are in Wales, but Dublin has its diplomatic corps and its Government departments, its *Uachtarán,* in *Taoiseach* and all the trappings of a sovereign capital. Irish pictures, Irish plays, Irish artifacts, Irish heroes—Dublin is obsessed with itself and its hinterland, giving the little capital a character introspective perhaps but undeniably authoritative, for it is certainly the last word on itself.

Half its pleasure lies in its pride. Ten columns of the Dublin telephone book are needed to list the 660 institutions which boast the prefix "Irish." Like the Welsh and Scots, but unlike the hapless English, the Irish are still frankly affectionate towards their nationality, and this gives Dubliners an unexpected balance or serenity. I went one night to the Abbey Theatre, where Mr. Cusack was playing the Vicar of Wakefield as to the manner born, and thought as I looked at the audience around me how enviably *natural* they looked. The burden of their history did not show, and they were not entangled by inhibitions of power or prestige. They had never been citizens of a Great Power, and never would be. They talked in no phoney accents, pined for no lost empires, and laughed at Goldsmith's gentle humour without much caring whether the world laughed too.

For if Dublin is parochial, it is not provincial exactly, for it remains original. British influences are ubiquitous, it is true, from the Aldershot drill of the Presidential guard to "Coronation Street" on Monday evening, but there is no sense of copycat. Dubliners are their own men still. Even when a concern is foreign owned, as so many in Dublin are, it acquires a distinctively Irish flavour, so that even Trust House Fortes' Airport Hotel coffee-shop, physically a carbon of every airport coffee-

shop ever built anywhere, will give you eggs and bacon at lunch time if you ask nicely, "for sure the chef's a kindly man."

And though it is small, still Dublin feels like a true capital. Like Edinburgh, it deserves sovereignty. It is a fine thing to walk through the Dublin streets on a Sunday morning, say, when the sun is rising brilliantly out of the Bay, and to see the monuments of Irish pride around you—the fire on Parnell's column, O'Connell the Liberator on his plinth, the great columns of the Customs House, the delicate dome of the Four Courts. Over the great bridge you go, where the wind off the Bay sweeps up-river to blow your hair about, and there is Trinity before you, where Congreve and Swift and Burke were educated, where Goldsmith stands on his pedestal and the *Book of Kells* lies for ever open in its case. On your right is the old Irish Parliament, on the left is the City Hall, and soon, turning the cobbled cor-ner at the top, you are—

Soon you are where? Why, back in the yard of Dublin Castle, where Presidents of Eire are installed indeed, but where for 800 years, in a presence far more monstrous, far more stately, the power of the English inexorably resided.

FOR LIKE IT or not, whatever your opinions, the drums of tragedy sound still in Dublin, muffled but unavoidable, as they sound nowhere else on earth. For eight centuries the Irish strug-gled against the dominion of the English, and it takes more than fifty uneasy years to silence the echoes.

The most compelling of all the figures at that Presidential occasion was that of Eamon de Valera, who arrived in an aged Rolls, and whose stiff blind figure, depending upon the arm of a veteran officer, leaning slightly backward as the blind sometimes do, and tapping with his stick between the silent lines of the diplomatic corps, cast a somewhat macabre hush upon the assembly. "The skeleton at the feast," whispered an irreverent observer somewhere near me, but I found the spectacle very moving; and when with difficulty the old rebel climbed the dais

and sat ramrod-stiff on his chair a few feet away from me, hold-
ing his stick between his knees and sometimes decorously
applauding, I envisaged all he had seen in the progress of the lit-
tle state, the Easter Rising, the war against the British, the horri-
ble Civil War, and so by way of plot and revolution, obstinacy
and courage, deviousness and boldness, to the installation of the
fifth *Uachtarán* there on the bright blue carpets of St Patrick's
Hall.

When I first knew Dublin, in the early 1960s, I thought the
old fervours of revolution were fading, and that the memories
of that sad struggle would die with its own generation. But the
drum beats still, a drum to the treble of the Ulster fifes, and the
presence there of Mr de Valera did not seem an anachronism to
me, only a grave reminder. The terrible beauty lingers still,
tainted perhaps but inescapable. That evening, after dinner, I
wandered alone among the back streets behind the General Post
Office, where little more than fifty years ago the fated visionar-
ies of the Rising fought and died among the blazing ruins.

It is smart in Dublin to denigrate the Easter Rising now, and
to say that it achieved nothing after all, but still those streets
seemed haunted ground to me. The glow of the burning Post
Office lit the night sky still, the Soldier's Song sounded above
the traffic, and at the end of every street I could see the barri-
cades of the British, and hear the clatter of their rifles and the
clink of their tea-mugs. Sometimes machine-guns rattled, and
the awful smell of war, of death and dirt and cordite, hung all
about the buildings. I wept as I remembered that old tragedy,
and thought of those brave men so soon to be shot at dawn, and
of the ignorant homely English at their guns behind their sand-
bags, and I turned towards home in a sad despair, contemplating
the deceits of glory.

But when I turned into O'Connell Street I looked up into
the plane trees, swaying above me in the night wind, and dimly I
discerned there the grey shapes of the pied wagtails, those
miraculous familiars of Dublin. Every winter those loyal coun-
try birds come back to roost in the trees of O'Connell Street,

settling down each day at dusk, fluttering away to mountain and moorland when the dawn breaks. They calmed and comforted me at once, and I saw in their silent presence a figure of my own gratitude—for the gaiety that takes me back to Dublin year after year, for the melody that sounds always above the drums and bombs of Ireland, and for the old comradeship of this city, which transcends all bitterness, ignores time, and is the truest of Dublin's contradictory truths.

GEORGE BERNARD SHAW

(1856–1950)

George Bernard Shaw was foremost an Irishman. Born in Dublin, he emigrated to England when he was twenty and did not return for twenty-nine years. But he never lost his allegiance to Ireland or failed to be interested and exasperated by his native country. "Eternal is the fact that the human creature born in Ireland and brought up in its air is Irish," he wrote in 1948. "I have lived for twenty years in Ireland and for seventy-two in England; but the twenty came first, and in Britain I am still a foreigner and shall die one."

Shaw had a lifelong dialogue with Ireland. In character, he was patriotic and patronizing, critical and inconsistent. Although he was a Protestant, Shaw rejected the concept of the Anglo-Irish. According to Shaw, an Irishman of whatever religion or region was incapable of forming an amalgam. The Irish are Irish, he insisted, wherever they live they maintain an inalienable identity. Yet he despised the teaching of Gaelic and the artificial resuscitation of a dead language. Although he did not like partition, Shaw disliked the rabid partisanship of Irish nationalism. Shaw was like a distant relative participating in a family quarrel, exasperated by the circumstances, critical of the participants, but unable to either stop or ignore the fight.

Both Shaw and James Joyce left Ireland at about the same age. Ireland remained the palette of Joyce's art; Shaw wrote only one play set in Ireland, John Bull's Other Island, commissioned by Yeats for the Abbey Theater. But in articles, essays, pamphlets, and speeches Shaw demonstrated that Ireland was never far from his thoughts. On Shaw's ninety-fourth, and last, birthday, Britain officially recognized its first Irish ambassador.

TOURING IN IRELAND

from THE MATTER WITH IRELAND

In Ireland a protuberance like Primrose Hill, or, at most, Hindhead, looks like a mountain haunted by giants. You may be fresh from surmounting every pass in the Tyrol, but when you are faced by a trumpery lane through the Kerry mountains, you are filled with vague terrors: it seems dangerous to venture in and impossible to get out, even if you do not meet another car on a track that looks a tight fit for one. In Galway, south of the bay, you find stone fields instead of grass ones, and in those fields cattle gravely crop the granite and seem to thrive on it. You travel on roads that are far more like the waves of the sea than the famous billowy pavement of St Mark's in Venice.

In the north there are no stone fields, but you come to a common green one with a little stagnant pool in the corner, and from that magic pool you are amazed to see a rush of waters through a narrow, deep, sinuous ditch, which ditch is the mighty Shannon emerging from the underworld. Rivers in Ireland duck like porpoises and then come to the surface and charge along it for a space and duck again. If you are afraid to penetrate a country so full of marvels, you can stay in a hotel in Dublin and yet be within half an hour's drive by car of moors as wild as you have often traveled many hundreds of miles from London to reach in the remotest parts of Scotland, and of coast scenery after which most English "seaside resorts" will seem mere dust heaps on the banks of a dirty canal. On the west coast you can struggle for an hour and a half up an endless succession of mountain brows, each of which looks like the top until you get there and see the next one towering above you; and when you are at last exhausted and filled with a conviction that you are enchanted and doomed to climb there forever, you suddenly recoil from a sheer drop of two thousand feet to the Atlantic, with nothing but salt water between you and America. You can watch affrightedly a bull's mouth of which the grinders are black, merciless rocks and the boiling spittle Atlantic rollers. You can make strange voyages to uncanny islands which carry to its highest the curious power of Ireland to disturb and excite the human imagination; and if one of these voyages leads you in an open boat through seven or eight miles of ocean waves and tide races to Skellig Michael,[1] no experience that the conventional tourist travel can bring you will stick in your memory so strangely; for Skellig Michael is not after the fashion of this world.

To the unfortunate man who has to live in Ireland all these things are only part of the daily horror of his lot. But to the English or American tourist, whose retreat is secured, and who only screws himself up for the moment to peep at these wonders as he screws himself up to take a flight in an aeroplane, there is no place like Ireland. You do the most commonplace and safe things with a sense of adventure and a doubt whether you will come out of them alive. Even if you have no imagination, and simply like pretty scenery, you can have in Ireland all the color of the Mediterranean coast without its hard brilliance and absence of mystery and distance, and all the veiling atmosphere and fairy sunset of the land of mountain and flood without its darkness and harshness. Only you must avoid places which describe themselves as "the Irish Biarritz." If you don't you will be astonished to see men consenting to spend a second day in

---

1. An enormous mass of precipitous rock rising out of the sea eight miles off the coast of County Kerry, containing the remains of an early Christian monastic settlement.

them when they have every convenience for drowning them-
selves.

Irish roads are not so good as English roads, but rather better
than French ones. When they are not rolled, and the stones lie
loose in the lanes, get off the road on to the rocks when your car
begins to refuse. In Ireland you must clear your mind from the
cockney illusion that an artificial road is the only surface a car
will travel on.

Another novel driving experience is to rush a little slope not
thirty yards long nor steeper than one in twelve, and when you
have just reached the brow flying, find the road, with your car
on it, sink blissfully down as into a feather bed laid on a founda-
tion of sponge. That is bog. The road is "a trifle soft." You get
over that as best you can, usually at an ignominious crawl, dodg-
ing about in search of hard bits. Or you may come to a splendid
stretch of perfectly straight, flat road with a good white surface,
and let your car go all out on it until you find it bounding up
and tossing the car as in a blanket. That means that the road is a
mere peat pontoon floating on a bog. As they say, it is "springy."

Hotels in Ireland are like hotels everywhere, very various.
Inland hotels of moderate pretensions in all countries are now
apt to be bad within fifty miles of the capital, because the com-
mercial travelers, whose custom keeps such hotels up to the
mark, prefer to push for home when they are as near it as that.
Ireland is no exception to this rule. The custom of the motorist
does not alter it, for he too makes for Dublin or Kingstown or
Bray from outside the fifty-mile radius. Otherwise I consider the
ordinary inland country-town hotels less depressing in Ireland
than in England. If there is a castle in the town, and if the assize
judge has to be entertained occasionally, you often find well-
trained maids and a tradition of serving "the quality" which
makes the motorist who is able to play up to that conception of
him much more comfortable than an experienced tourist expects
to be in an out-of-the-way place. But the main stand-by of the
tourist in Ireland is the fishing hotel.

Ireland is one of the great fishing countries of the world: the Shannon, which comes down the middle of it, is a string of lakes rather than a river; and I have known Irishmen who would starve rather than eat salmon, because they had once had to eat it every day for three months. Consequently, if you are a sensible person, and can get on with a moderately tidy bachelor sort of accommodation, and enjoy breakfasts of ham and eggs and tea, lunches of mutton chops, and dinners of plain joints, you will find that these hotels will suit you extremely well. But avoid Irish clear soups. They still believe in Ireland that soup means water in which bones have been boiled; and unless your taste is sepulchral you will not like it.

Of course, if you want to dine in evening dress confronted with a bediamonded wife and flanked by daughters in the very latest, if you demand six-course dinners, and feel injured if you have to open a door for yourself, or if "Boots" occasionally gives up brown leather as a bad job, then you will be unhappy in Ireland; for just in proportion to the efforts made by an Irish hotel to meet your views is it sure to be a bad one. Ireland cannot afford that game, and would not know how to play it if she could; for an Irish gentleman is passing rich with two or three thousand dollars a year. Of course, there are exceptions. The golfing hotels like Rosapenna in Donegal and Lahinch in Clare, the Killarney hotels, the hotels at Parknasilla and Waterville in Kerry, and, generally, the first-class hotels are like first-class hotels anywhere else: in fact, that is the only complaint one makes of them. But no experienced tourist wants to be reassured about these. It is the cheaper stopping places that matter; and after a large experience of Continental touring I cannot recall, at worst, any experience at an Irish hotel more disagreeable than I have had to endure on quite main lines of travel in France and Italy, to say nothing of Britain.

Irish people in Ireland do not play up to English romantic illusions concerning them, as they are apt to do in England when they want to make themselves popular or to borrow money. There may still be a tradition among Irish carmen plying

between Bray and the show places in the County Wicklow that they should entertain English tourists with impersonations of Myles na Coppaleen and Micky Free,[2] just as there may possibly be a tradition among Venetian gondoliers that they should recite Tasso to the compatriots of Lord Byron. I do not know: the carmen never try it on me, because I am an Irishman. All such performances are pure humbug and the anecdotes are learned and repeated without sense.

Irish people are, like most country people, civil and kindly when they are treated with due respect. But anyone who, under the influence of the stage Irishman and the early novels of Lever, treats a tour in Ireland as a lark, and the people as farce actors who may be addressed as Pat and Biddy, will have about as much success as if he were to paint his nose red and interrupt a sermon in Westminster Abbey by addressing music-hall patter to the dean. Also there are certain bustling nuances of manner which are popular in a busy place like England because they save time and ceremony, but which strike an Irishman as too peremptory and too familiar, and are resented accordingly. You need be no more ceremonious in word or gesture than in England; but your attitude had better be the Latin attitude which you have learned in Italy and France, and not the Saxon attitude learned in England and Bavaria. It is as well to know, by the way, that there are no Celts in Ireland and never have been, though there are many Iberians. The only European nation where the typical native is also a typical Celt is Prussia.

As an illustration of the sort of police activity which is peculiar to Ireland, I will give an experience of my own. One evening in the south of Donegal it was getting dark rapidly, and, after being repeatedly disappointed of finding our destination round the next corner, as tired people will expect, we had at last grown desperate and settled down to drive another twenty miles as fast as the road would let us before the light failed altogether.

2. Colourful fictional characters; the first appears in Gerald Griffin's *The Collegians* (1829), the second in Charles Lever's *Charles O'Malley* (1841).

The result was that we came suddenly round a bend and over a bridge right into the middle of the tiny town before we supposed our selves to be within five miles of it. The whole population had assembled in the open for evening gossip, and we dashed through them at a speed considerably in excess of the ten-mile limit. They scattered in all directions, and a magnificent black retriever charged us like a wolf, barking frantically. My chauffeur, who was driving, made a perilous swerve and just saved the dog by a miracle of dexterity. Then we drew up at the porch of the hotel, and I looked anxiously back at the crowd, hoping it did not include a member of the R.I.C.[3] Alas, it did, and he was a stern-faced man whose deliberate stalk in our direction could have only one object. The crowd, which had taken our rush with the utmost goodhumor, did not gather to witness our discomfiture as a city crowd would have done. It listened, but pretended not to, as a matter of good breeding. The inspector inspected us up and down until we shrank into mere guilty worms. He then addressed my chauffeur in these memorable words: "What sort of a man are you? Here you come into a village where there's a brute of a dog that has nearly ate two childer, and is the curse and terror of this countryside, and when you get a square chance of killing him you twist your car out of the way and nearly upset it. What sort of a man are you at all?"

My own opinion is that any Briton who does not need at least a fortnight in Ireland once a year to freshen him up has not really been doing his duty.

3. Royal Irish Constabulary.

JONATHAN SWIFT

(1667–1745)

The Irish people recognized Jonathan Swift, born of English parents, as their defender. In "A Modest Proposal" and other essays he championed Ireland's cause. In 1713 Queen Anne appointed Swift dean of the Protestant St. Patrick's Cathedral in Dublin. Despite his position, Swift continued to write anonymous political pamphlets, including "The Drapier's Letters," rallying the Irish against a new British coinage that would have debased their currency. A reward of three hundred pounds was offered for the name of the author. Although it was well-known that Swift had written "The Letters," he was so loved that the bounty was never collected. From then on, bonfires and bell ringing in Dublin marked Swift's birthday.

In addition to essays and novels (including Gulliver's Travels) Swift wrote hundreds of poems, many about Ireland. "An Answer to the Ballyspellin Ballad" was a reply to a ballad written by Sheridan. Swift wrote, "[Sheridan] sent us in print a ballad upon Ballyspellin which he has employed all the rhymes he could find to that word; but we have found fifteen more and employed them in abusing his ballad and Ballyspellin too." The Irish spa of Ballyspellin was known for its restorative drinking waters.

Swift is buried in Dublin in St. Patrick's. He composed his own epitaph.

Here lies the body of Jonathan Swift, D.D. dean of this cathedral, where burning indignation can no longer lacerate his heart. Go, traveler, and imitate if you can a man who was an undaunted champion of liberty.

AN ANSWER TO THE
BALLYSPELLIN BALLAD

Dare you dispute,
You saucy brute,
And think there's no refelling
Your scurvy lays,
And senseless praise
You give to Ballyspellin.

Howe'er you bounce,
I here pronounce
You medicine is repelling,
Your water's mud,
And sours the blood
When drunk at Ballyspellin.

Those pocky drabs
To cure their scabs
You thither are compelling,
Will back be sent
Worse than they went
From nasty Ballyspellin.

Llewellyn! why,
As well may I
Name honest Doctor Pelling;
So hard sometimes
You tug for rhymes
To bring in Ballyspellin.

No subject fit
To try your wit
When you went colonelling,
But dull intrigues
'Twixt jades and teagues
That met at Ballyspellin.

Our lasses fair
Say what you dare,
Who sowens make with shelling;
At Market Hill
More beaux can kill
Than yours at Ballyspellin.

Would I was whipped
When Sheelah stripped
To wash herself our well in;
A bum so white
Ne'er came in sight
At paltry Ballyspellin.

Your mawkins there
Smocks hempen wear;
For Holland, not an ell in;
No, not a rag,
Whate'er you brag,
Is found at Ballyspellin.

But Tom will prate
At any rate,
All other nymphs expelling;
Because he gets
A few grisettes
At lousy Ballyspellin.

There's bonny Jane
In yonder lane,
Just o'er against the Bell Inn;
Where can you meet

A lass so sweet
Round all your Ballyspellin?

We have a girl
Deserves an earl,
She came from Enniskillen;
So fair, so young,
No such among
The belles of Ballyspellin.

How would you stare
To see her there,
The foggy mists dispelling,
That cloud the brows
Of every blowze
Who lives at Ballyspellin.

Now, as I live,
I would not give
A stiver or a skilling
To touse and kiss
The fairest miss
That leaks at Ballyspellin.

Whoe'er will raise
Such lies as these
Deserves a good cudgelling;
Who falsely boasts
Of belles and toasts
At dirty Ballyspellin.

Our rhymes are gone
To all but one,
Which is, our trees are felling;
As proper quite
As those you write
To force in Ballyspellin.

WILLIAM TREVOR

(1928–   )

Even before he left Ireland, William Trevor saw his homeland from afar. As a Protestant child raised by restless parents in Irish Catholic farm country, Trevor has the lucidity of an alien's view of his birthplace. Books were an antidote for his rootless life. "As a child I was certain I would grow up to be a writer," he once said. "I never read children's books. I read thrillers, mysteries, detective fiction—anything I could get my hands on."

Trevor resisted the writer's call. He worked as a teacher first in Northern Ireland and then in England. Then he supported himself as an advertising copywriter in London while also creating sculpture, working in wood, terra-cotta, and metal. As his art became more abstract, Trevor realized that he missed the humanity of writing. His first novel, A Standard of Behavior, was published in 1958.

William Trevor's novels and short stories are set in England, Ireland, and, increasingly, Italy. His British stories—or those about the British in Ireland—have a lacerating thrust, a vicious humor. But his Irish stories—populated by characters both Catholic and Protestant—are sympathetic, tragic, and tender. Trevor now lives in Dorset countryside. "Autumn Sunshine" is from William Trevor: The Collected Stories, *published in 1993.*

AUTUMN SUNSHINE

from THE COLLECTED STORIES

The rectory was in County Wexford, eight miles from Enniscorthy. It was a handsome eighteenth-century house, with Virginia creeper covering three sides and a tangled garden full of buddleia and struggling japonica which had always been too much for its incumbents. It stood alone, seeming lonely even, approximately at the centre of the country parish it served. Its church—St Michael's Church of Ireland—was two miles away, in the village of Boharbawn.

For twenty-six years the Morans had lived there, not wishing to live anywhere else. Canon Moran had never been an ambitious man; his wife, Frances, had found contentment easy to attain in her lifetime. Their four girls had been born in the rectory, and had become a happy family there. They were grown up now, Frances's death was still recent: like the rectory itself, its remaining occupant was alone in the countryside. The death had occurred in the spring of the year, and the summer had somehow been bearable. The clergyman's eldest daughter had spent May and part of June at the rectory with her children. Another one had brought her family for most of August, and a third was to bring her newly married husband in the winter. At Christmas nearly all of them would gather at the rectory and some would come at Easter. But that September, as the days drew in, the season was melancholy.

Then, one Tuesday morning, Slattery brought a letter from Canon Moran's youngest daughter. There were two other letters

as well, in unsealed buff envelopes which meant that they were either bills or receipts. Frail and grey-haired in his elderliness, Canon Moran had been wondering if he should give the lawn in front of the house a last cut when he heard the approach of Slattery's van. The lawn-mower was the kind that had to be pushed, and in the spring the job was always easier if the grass had been cropped close at the end of the previous summer.

"Isn't that a great bit of weather, Canon?" Slattery remarked, winding down the window of the van and passing out the three envelopes. "We're set for a while, would you say?"

"I hope so, certainly."

"Ah, we surely are, sir."

The conversation continued for a few moments longer, as it did whenever Slattery came to the rectory. The postman was young and easy-going, not long the successor to old Mr O'Brien, who'd been making the round on a bicycle when the Morans first came to the rectory in 1952. Mr O'Brien used to talk about his garden; Slattery talked about fishing, and often brought a share of his catch to the rectory.

"It's a great time of year for it," he said now, "except for the darkness coming in."

Canon Moran smiled and nodded; the van turned round on the gravel, dust rising behind it as it moved swiftly down the avenue to the road. Everyone said Slattery drove too fast.

He carried the letters to a wooden seat on the edge of the lawn he'd been wondering about cutting. Deirdre's handwriting hadn't changed since she'd been a child; it was round and neat, not at all a reflection of the girl she was. The blue English stamp, the Queen in profile blotched a bit by the London postmark, wasn't on its side or half upside down, as you might possibly expect with Deirdre. Of all the Moran children, she'd grown up to be the only difficult one. She hadn't come to the funeral and hadn't written about her mother's death. She hadn't been to the rectory for three years.

I'm sorry, she wrote now. *I couldn't stop crying actually. I've never known anyone as nice or as generous as she was. For ages I didn't even want to believe she was dead. I went on imagining her in the rectory and doing the flowers in church and shopping in Enniscorthy.*

Deirdre was twenty-one now. He and Frances had hoped she'd go to Trinity and settle down, but although at school she'd seemed to be the cleverest of their children she'd had no desire to become a student. She'd taken the Rosslare boat to Fishguard one night, having said she was going to spend a week with her friend Maeve Coles in Cork. They hadn't known she'd gone to England until they received a picture postcard from London telling them not to worry, saying she'd found work in an egg-packing factory.

Well, I'm coming back for a little while now, she wrote, *if you could put up with me and if you wouldn't find it too much. I'll cross over to Rosslare on the 29th, the morning crossing, and then I'll come on to Enniscorthy on the bus. I don't know what time it will be but there's a pub just by where the bus drops you so could we meet in the small bar there at six o'clock and then I won't have to lug my cases too far? I hope you won't mind going into such a place. If you can't make it, or don't want to see me, it's understandable, so if you don't turn up by half six I'll see if I can get a bus on up to Dublin. Only I need to get back to Ireland for a while.*

It was, as he and Slattery had agreed, a lovely autumn. Gentle sunshine mellowed the old garden, casting an extra sheen of gold on leaves that were gold already. Roses that had been ebullient in June and July bloomed modestly now. Michaelmas daisies were just beginning to bud. Already the crab-apples were falling, hydrangeas had a forgotten look. Canon Moran carried the letter from his daughter into the walled vegetable garden and leaned against the side of the greenhouse, half sitting on a protruding ledge, reading the letter again. Panes of glass were broken in the greenhouse, white paint and putty needed to be renewed, but inside a vine still thrived, and was heavy now with black ripe fruit. Later that morning he would pick some and drive into Enniscorthy, to sell the grapes to Mrs Neary in Slaney Street.

Love, Deirdre: the letter was marvellous. Beyond the rectory the fields of wheat had been harvested, and the remaining stubble had the same tinge of gold in the autumn light; the beech trees and the chestnuts were triumphantly magnificent. But decay and rotting were only weeks away, and the letter from Deirdre was full of life. *"Love, Deirdre"* were words more beautiful than all the season's glories. He prayed as he leaned against the sunny greenhouse, thanking God for this salvation.

FOR ALL THE years of their marriage Frances had been a help. As a younger man, Canon Moran hadn't known quite what to do. He'd been at a loss among his parishioners, hesitating in the face of this weakness or that: the pregnancy of Alice Pratt in 1954, the argument about grazing rights between Mr Willoughby and Eugene Dunlevy in 1960, the theft of an altar cloth from St Michael's and reports that Mrs Tobin had been seen wearing it as a skirt. Alice Pratt had been going out with a Catholic boy, one of Father Gowan's flock, which made the matter more difficult than ever. Eugene Dunlevy was one of Father Gowan's also, and so was Mrs Tobin.

"Father Gowan and I had a chat," Frances had said, and she'd had a chat as well with Alice Pratt's mother. A month later Alice Pratt married the Catholic boy, but to this day attended St Michael's every Sunday, the children going to Father Gowan. Mrs Tobin was given Hail Marys to say by the priest; Mr Willoughby agreed that his father had years ago granted Eugene Dunlevy the grazing rights. Everything, in these cases and in many others, had come out all right in the end: order emerged from the confusion that Canon Moran so disliked, and it was Frances who had always begun the process, though no one ever said in the rectory that she understood the mystery of people as well as he understood the teachings of the New Testament. She'd been a freckle-faced girl when he'd married her, pretty in her way. He was the one with the brains.

Frances had seen human frailty everywhere: it was weakness in people, she said, that made them what they were as much as strength did. And she herself had her own share of such frailty, falling short in all sorts of ways of the God's image her husband preached about. With the small amount of housekeeping money she could be allowed she was a spendthrift, and she said she was lazy. She loved clothes and often overreached herself on visits to Dublin; she sat in the sun while the rectory gathered dust and the garden became rank; it was only where people were concerned that she was practical. But for what she was her husband had loved her with unobtrusive passion for fifty years, appreciating her conversation and the help she'd given him because she could so easily sense the truth. When he'd found her dead in the garden one morning he'd felt he had lost some part of himself.

Though many months had passed since then, the trouble was that Frances hadn't yet become a ghost. Her being alive was still too recent, the shock of her death too raw. He couldn't distance himself; the past refused to be the past. Often he thought that her fingerprints were still in the rectory, and when he picked the grapes or cut the grass of the lawn it was impossible not to pause and remember other years. Autumn had been her favourite time.

"OF COURSE I'D come," he said. "Of course, dear. Of course."

"I haven't treated you very well."

"It's over and done with, Deirdre."

She smiled, and it was nice to see her smile again, although it was strange to be sitting in the back bar of a public house in Enniscorthy. He saw her looking at him, her eyes passing over his clerical collar and black clothes, and his quiet face. He could feel her thinking that he had aged, and putting it down to the death of the wife he'd been so fond of.

"I'm sorry I didn't write," she said.

"You explained in your letter, Deirdre."

"It was ages before I knew about it. That was an old address you wrote to."

"I guessed."

In turn he examined her. Years ago she'd had her long hair cut. It was short now, like a black cap on her head. And her face had lost its chubbiness; hollows where her cheeks had been made her eyes more dominant, pools of seaweed green. He remembered her child's stocky body, and the uneasy adolescence that had spoilt the family's serenity. Her voice had lost its Irish intonation.

"I'd have met you off the boat, you know."

"I didn't want to bother you with that."

"Oh, now, it isn't far, Deirdre."

She drank Irish whiskey, and smoked a brand of cigarettes called Three Castles. He'd asked for a mineral himself and the woman serving them had brought him a bottle of something that looked like water but which fizzed up when she'd poured it. A kind of lemonade he imagined it was, and didn't much care for it.

"I have grapes for Mrs Neary," he said.

"Who's that?"

"She has a shop in Slaney Street. We always sold her the grapes. You remember?'

She didn't, and he reminded her of the vine in the greenhouse. A shop surely wouldn't be open at this hour of the evening, she said, forgetting that in a country town of course it would be. She asked if the cinema was still the same in Enniscorthy, a cement building halfway up a hill. She said she remembered bicycling home from it at night with her sisters, not being able to keep up with them. She asked after her sisters and he told her about the two marriages that had taken place since she'd left: she had in-laws she'd never met, and nephews and a niece.

They left the bar, and he drove his dusty black Vauxhall straight to the small shop he'd spoken of. She remained in the car while he carried into the shop two large chip-baskets full of grapes. Afterwards Mrs Neary came to the door with him.

"Well, is that Deirdre?" she said as Deirdre wound down the window of the car. "I'd never know you, Deirdre."

"She's come back for a little while," Canon Moran explained, raising his voice a little because he was walking round the car to the driver's seat as he spoke.

"Well, isn't that grand?" said Mrs Neary.

Everyone in Enniscorthy knew Deirdre had just gone off, but it didn't matter now. Mrs Neary's husband, who was a red-cheeked man with a cap, much smaller than his wife, appeared beside her in the shop doorway. He inclined his head in greeting, and Deirdre smiled and waved at both of them. Canon Moran thought it was pleasant when she went on waving while he drove off.

In the rectory he lay wakeful that night, his mind excited by Deirdre's presence. He would have loved Frances to know, and guessed that she probably did. He fell asleep at half past two and dreamed that he and Frances were young again, that Deirdre was still a baby. The freckles on Frances's face were out in profusion, for they were sitting in the sunshine in the garden, tea things spread about them, the children playing some game among the shrubs. It was autumn then also, the last of the September heat. But because he was younger in his dream he didn't feel part of the season himself, or sense its melancholy.

A WEEK WENT by. The time passed slowly because a lot was happening, or so it seemed. Deirdre insisted on cooking all the meals and on doing the shopping in Boharbawn's single shop or in Enniscorthy. She still smoked her endless cigarettes, but the peakiness there had been in her face when she'd first arrived wasn't quite so pronounced—or perhaps, he thought, he'd become used to it. She told him about the different jobs she'd had in London and the different places she'd lived in, because on the postcards she'd occasionally sent there hadn't been room to go into detail. In the rectory they had always hoped she'd managed to get a training of some sort, though guessing she hadn't. In fact, her jobs had been of the most rudimentary kind: as well as her spell in the egg-packing factory, there'd been a factory that made plastic earphones, a cleaning job in a hotel near Euston, and a year working for the Use-Us Office Cleansing Service. "But you can't have liked any of that work, Deirdre?" he suggested, and she agreed she hadn't.

From the way she spoke he felt that that period of her life was over: adolescence was done with, she had steadied and taken stock. He didn't suggest to her that any of this might be so, not wishing to seem either too anxious or too pleased, but he felt she had returned to the rectory in a very different frame of mind from the one in which she'd left it. He imagined she would remain for quite a while, still taking stock, and in a sense occupying her mother's place. He thought he recognized in her a loneliness that matched his own, and he wondered if it was a feeling that their loneliness might be shared which had brought her back at this particular time. Sitting in the drawing-room while she cooked or washed up, or gathering grapes in the greenhouse while she did the shopping, he warmed delightedly to this theme. It seemed like an act of God that their circumstances should interlace this autumn. By Christmas she would know what she wanted to do with her life, and in the spring that followed she would perhaps be ready to set forth again. A year would have passed since the death of Frances.

"I have a friend," Deirdre said when they were having a cup of coffee together in the middle of one morning. "Someone who's been good to me."

She had carried a tray to where he was composing next week's sermon, sitting on the wooden seat by the lawn at the front of the house. He laid aside his exercise book, and a pencil and a rubber. "Who's that?" he inquired.

"Someone called Harold."

He nodded, stirring sugar into his coffee.

"I want to tell you about Harold, Father. I want you to meet him."

"Yes, of course."

She lit a cigarette. She said, "We have a lot in common. I mean, he's the only person . . ."

She faltered and then hesitated. She lifted her cigarette to her lips and drew on it.

He said, "Are you fond of him, Deirdre?"

"Yes, I am."

Another silence gathered. She smoked and drank her coffee. He added more sugar to his.

"Of course I'd like to meet him," he said.

"Could he come to stay with us, Father? Would you mind? Would it be all right?"

"Of course I wouldn't mind. I'd be delighted."

HAROLD WAS SUMMONED, and arrived at Rosslare a few days later. In the meantime Deirdre had explained to her father that her friend was an electrician by trade and had let it fall that he was an intellectual kind of person. She borrowed the old Vauxhall and drove it to Rosslare to meet him, returning to the rectory in the early evening.

"How d'you do?" Canon Moran said, stretching out a hand in the direction of an angular youth with a birthmark on his face. His dark hair was cut very short, cropped almost. He was wearing a black leather jacket.

"I'm fine," Harold said.

"You've had a good journey?"

"Lousy, 'smatter of fact, Mr Moran."

Harold's voice was strongly Cockney, and Canon Moran wondered if Deirdre had perhaps picked up some of her English vowel sounds from it. But then he realized that most people in London would speak like that, as people did on the television and the wireless. It was just a little surprising that Harold and Deirdre should have so much in common, as they clearly had from the affectionate way they held one another's hand. None of the other Moran girls had gone in so much for holding hands in front of the family.

He was to sit in the drawing-room, they insisted, while they made supper in the kitchen, so he picked up the *Irish Times* and did as he was bidden. Half an hour later Harold appeared and said that the meal was ready: fried eggs and sausages and bacon, and some tinned beans. Canon Moran said grace.

Having stated that County Wexford looked great, Harold didn't say much else. He didn't smile much, either. His afflicted face bore an edgy look, as if he'd never become wholly reconciled to his birthmark. It was like a scarlet map on his left cheek, a shape that reminded Canon Moran of the toe of Italy. Poor fellow, he thought. And yet a birthmark was so much less to bear than other afflictions there could be.

"Harold's fascinated actually," Deirdre said, "by Ireland."

Her friend didn't add anything to that remark for a moment, even though Canon Moran smiled and nodded interestedly. Eventually Harold said, "The struggle of the Irish people."

"I didn't know a thing about Irish history," Deirdre said. "I mean, not anything that made sense."

The conversation lapsed at this point, leaving Canon Moran greatly puzzled. He began to say that Irish history had always been of considerable interest to him also, that it had a good story to it, its tragedy uncomplicated. But the other two didn't appear to understand what he was talking about and so he changed the subject. It was a particularly splendid autumn, he pointed out.

"Harold doesn't go in for anything like that," Deirdre replied.

During the days that followed Harold began to talk more, surprising Canon Moran with almost everything he said. Deirdre had been right to say he was fascinated by Ireland, and it wasn't just a tourist's fascination. Harold had read widely: he spoke of ancient battles, and of the plantations of James I and Elizabeth, of Robert Emmet and the Mitchelstown martyrs, of Pearse and de Valera. "The struggle of the Irish people" was the expression he most regularly employed. It seemed to Canon Moran that the relationship between Harold and Deirdre had a lot to do with Harold's fascination, as though his interest in Deirdre's native land had somehow caused him to become interested in Deirdre herself.

There was something else as well. Fascinated by Ireland,

Harold hated his own country. A sneer whispered through his voice when he spoke of England: a degenerate place, he called it, destroyed by class-consciousness and the unjust distribution of wealth. He described in detail the city of Nottingham, to which he appeared to have a particular aversion. He spoke of unnecessary motorways and the stupidity of bureaucracy, the stifling presence of a Royal family. "You could keep an Indian village," he claimed, "on what those corgis eat. You could house five hundred homeless in Buckingham Palace." There was brain-washing by television and the newspaper barons. No ordinary person had a chance because pap was fed to the ordinary person, a deliberate policy going back into Victorian times when educa-tion and religion had been geared to the enslavement of minds. The English people had brought it on themselves, having lost their spunk, settling instead for consumer durables. "What bet-ter can you expect," Harold demanded, "after the hypocrisy of that empire the bosses ran?"

Deirdre didn't appear to find anything specious in this line of talk, which surprised her father. "Oh, I wonder about that," he said himself from time to time, but he said it mildly, not wishing to cause an argument, and in any case his interjections were not acknowledged. Quite a few of the criticisms Harold levelled at his own country could be levelled at Ireland also and, Canon Moran guessed, at many countries throughout the world. It was strange that the two neighbouring islands had been so picked out, although once Germany was mentioned and the point made that developments beneath the surface there were a hope-ful sign, that a big upset was on the way.

"We're taking a walk," Harold said one afternoon. "She's going to show me Kinsella's Barn."

Canon Moran nodded, saying to himself that he disliked Harold. It was the first time he had admitted it, but the feeling was familiar. The less generous side of his nature had always emerged when his daughters brought to the rectory the men they'd become friendly with or even proposed to marry. Emma, the eldest girl, had brought several before settling in the end for

Thomas. Linda had brought only John, already engaged to him. Una had married Carley not long after the death, and Carley had not yet visited the rectory: Canon Moran had met him in Dublin, where the wedding had taken place, for in the circumstances Una had not been married from home. Carley was an older man, an importer of tea and wine, stout and flushed, certainly not someone Canon Moran would have chosen for his second-youngest daughter. But, then, he had thought the same about Emma's Thomas and about Linda's John.

Thomas was a farmer, sharing a sizeable acreage with his father in Co. Meath. He always brought to mind the sarcasm of an old schoolmaster who in Canon Moran's distant schooldays used to refer to a gang of boys at the back of the classroom as "farmers' sons," meaning that not much could be expected of them. It was an inaccurate assumption but even now, whenever Canon Moran found himself in the company of Thomas, he couldn't help recalling it. Thomas was mostly silent, with a good-natured smile that came slowly and lingered too long. According to his father, and there was no reason to doubt the claim, he was a good judge of beef cattle.

Linda's John was the opposite. Wiry and suave, he was making his way in the Bank of Ireland, at present stationed in Waterford. He had a tiny orange-coloured moustache and was good at golf. Linda's ambition for him was that he should become the Bank of Ireland's manager in Limerick or Galway, where the insurances that went with the position were particularly lucrative. Unlike Thomas, John talked all the time, telling jokes and stories about the Bank of Ireland's customers.

"Nothing is perfect," Frances used to say, chiding her husband for an uncharitableness he did his best to combat. He disliked being so particular about the men his daughters chose, and he was aware that other people saw them differently: Thomas would do anything for you, John was fun, the middle-aged Carley laid his success at Una's feet. But whoever the husbands of his daughters had been, Canon Moran knew he'd have felt the same. He was jealous of the husbands because ever since his daughters had been born he had loved them unstintingly. When he had prayed after Frances's death he'd felt jealous of God, who had taken her from him.

"There's nothing much to see," he pointed out when Harold announced that Deirdre was going to show him Kinsella's Barn. "Just the ruin of a wall is all that's left."

"Harold's interested, Father."

They set off on their walk, leaving the old clergyman ashamed that he could not like Harold more. It wasn't just his griminess: there was something sinister about Harold, something furtive about the way he looked at you, peering at you cruelly out of his afflicted face, not meeting your eye. Why was he so fascinated about a country that wasn't his own? Why did he refer so often to "Ireland's struggle" as if that struggle particularly concerned him? He hated walking, he had said, yet he'd just set out to walk six miles through woods and fields to examine a ruined wall.

Canon Moran had wondered as suspiciously about Thomas and John and Carley, privately questioning every statement they made, finding hidden motives everywhere. He'd hated the thought of his daughters being embraced or even touched, and had forced himself not to think about that. He'd prayed, ashamed of himself then, too. "It's just a frailty in you," Frances had said, her favourite way of cutting things down to size.

He sat for a while in the afternoon sunshine, letting all of it hang in his mind. It would be nice if they quarrelled on their walk. It would be nice if they didn't speak when they returned, if Harold simply went away. But that wouldn't happen, because they had come to the rectory with a purpose. He didn't know why he thought that, but he knew it was true: they had come for a reason, something that was all tied up with Harold's fascination and with the kind of person Harold was, with his cold eyes and his afflicted face.

*   *   *

IN MARCH 1798 an incident had taken place in Kinsella's Barn, which at that time had just been a barn. Twelve men and women, accused of harbouring insurgents, had been tied together with ropes at the command of a Sergeant James. They had been led through the village of Boharbawn, the Sergeant's soldiers on horseback on either side of the procession, the Sergeant himself bringing up the rear. Designed as an act of education, an example to the inhabitants of Boharbawn and the country people around, the twelve had been herded into a barn owned by a farmer called Kinsella and there burned to death. Kinsella, who had played no part either in the harbouring of insurgents or in the execution of the twelve, was afterwards murdered by his own farm labourers.

"Sergeant James was a Nottingham man," Harold said that evening at supper. "A soldier of fortune who didn't care what he did. Did you know he acquired great wealth, Mr Moran?"

"No, I wasn't at all aware of that," Canon Moran replied.

"Harold found out about him," Deirdre said.

"He used to boast he was responsible for the death of a thousand Irish people. It was in Boharbawn he reached the thousand. They rewarded him well for that."

"Not much is known about Sergeant James locally. Just the legend of Kinsella's Barn."

"No way it's a legend."

Deirdre nodded; Canon Moran did not say anything. They were eating cooked ham and salad. On the table there was a cake which Deirdre had bought in McGovern's in Enniscorthy, and a pot of tea. There were several bunches of grapes from the greenhouse, and a plate of wafer biscuits. Harold was fond of salad cream, Canon Moran had noticed; he had a way of hitting the base of the jar with his hand, causing large dollops to spurt all over his ham. He didn't place his knife and fork together on the plate when he'd finished, but just left them anyhow. His fingernails were edged with black.

"You'd feel sick," he was saying now, working the salad cream again. "You'd stand there looking at that wall and you'd feel a revulsion in your stomach."

"What I meant," Canon Moran said, "is that it has passed into local legend. No one doubts it took place; there's no question about that. But two centuries have almost passed."

"And nothing has changed," Harold interjected. "The Irish people still share their bondage with the twelve in Kinsella's Barn."

"Round here of course—"

"It's not round here that matters, Mr Moran. The struggle's world-wide; the sickness is everywhere actually."

Again Deirdre nodded. She was like a zombie, her father thought. She was being used because she was an Irish girl; she was Harold's Irish connection, and in some almost frightening way she believed herself in love with him. Frances had once said they'd made a mistake with her. She had wondered if Deirdre had perhaps found all the love they'd offered her too much to bear. They were quite old when Deirdre was a child, the last expression of their own love. She was special because of that.

"At least Kinsella got his chips," Harold pursued, his voice relentless. "At least that's something."

Canon Moran protested. The owner of the barn had been an innocent man, he pointed out. The barn had simply been a convenient one, large enough for the purpose, with heavy stones near it that could be piled up against the door before the conflagration. Kinsella, that day, had been miles away, ditching a field.

"It's too long ago to say where he was," Harold retorted swiftly. "And if he was keeping a low profile in a ditch it would have been by arrangement with the imperial forces."

When Harold said that, there occurred in Canon Moran's mind a flash of what appeared to be the simple truth. Harold was an Englishman who had espoused a cause because it was one through which the status quo in his own country might be damaged. Similar such Englishmen, read about in newspapers, stirred in the clergyman's mind: men from Ealing and Liverpool and Wolverhamption who had changed their names to Irish names, who had even learned the Irish language, in order to ingratiate themselves with the new Irish revolutionaries. Such men dealt out death and chaos, announcing that their conscience insisted on it.

"Well, we'd better wash the dishes," Deirdre said, and Harold rose obediently to help her.

THE WALK TO Kinsella's Barn had taken place on a Saturday afternoon. The following morning Canon Moran conducted his services in St Michael's, addressing his small Protestant congregation, twelve at Holy Communion, eighteen at morning service. He had prepared a sermon about repentance, taking as his text St Luke, 15:32: *for this thy brother was dead, and is alive again; and was lost, and is found.* But at the last moment he changed his mind and spoke instead of the incident in Kinsella's Barn nearly two centuries ago. He tried to make the point that one horror should not fuel another, that passing time contained its own forgiveness. Deirdre and Harold were naturally not in the church, but they'd been present at breakfast, Harold frying eggs on the kitchen stove, Deirdre pouring tea. He had looked at them and tried to think of them as two young people on holiday. He had tried to tell himself they'd come to the rectory for a rest and for his blessing, that he should be grateful instead of fanciful. It was for his blessing that Emma had brought Thomas to the rectory, that Linda had brought John. Una would bring Carley in November. "Now, don't be silly," Frances would have said.

"The man Kinsella was innocent of everything," he heard his voice insisting in his church. "He should never have been murdered also."

Harold would have delighted in the vengeance exacted on an innocent man. Harold wanted to inflict pain, to cause suffering and destruction. The end justified the means for Harold, even if the end was an artificial one, a pettiness grandly dressed up. In his sermon Canon Moran spoke of such matters without mentioning Harold's name. He spoke of how evil drained people of their humour and compassion, how people pretended even to themselves. It was worse than Frances's death, he thought as his voice continued in the church: it was worse that Deirdre should be part of wickedness.

He could tell that his parishioners found his sermon odd, and he didn't blame them. He was confused, and naturally distressed. In the rectory Deirdre and Harold would be waiting for him. They would all sit down to Sunday lunch while plans for atrocities filled Harold's mind, while Deirdre loved him.

"Are you well again, Mrs Davis?" he inquired at the church door of a woman who suffered from asthma.

"Not too bad, Canon. Not too bad, thank you."

He spoke to all the others, inquiring about health, remarking on the beautiful autumn. They were farmers mostly and displayed a farmer's gratitude for the satisfactory season. He wondered suddenly who'd replace him among them when he retired or died. Father Gowan had had to give up a year ago. The young man, Father White, was always in a hurry.

"Goodbye so, Canon," Mr Willoughby said, shaking hands as he always did, every Sunday. It was a long time since there'd been the trouble about Eugene Dunlevy's grazing rights; three years ago Mr Willoughby had been left a widower himself. "You're managing all right, Canon?" he asked, as he also always did.

"Yes, I'm all right, thank you, Mr Willoughby."

Someone else inquired if Deirdre was still at the rectory, and he said she was. Heads nodded, the unspoken thought being that that was nice for him, his youngest daughter at home again after all these years. There was forgiveness in several faces, forgiveness of Deirdre, who had been thoughtless to go off to an egg-packing factory. There was the feeling, also unexpressed, that the young were a bit like that.

"Goodbye," he said in a general way. Car doors banged, engines started. In the vestry he removed his surplice and his cassock and hung them in a cupboard.

*   *   *

"WE'LL PROBABLY GO tomorrow," Deirdre said during lunch.

"Go?"

"We'll probably take the Dublin bus."

"I'd like to see Dublin," Harold said.

"And then you're returning to London?"

"We're easy about that," Harold interjected before Deirdre could reply. "I'm a tradesman, Mr Moran, an electrician."

"I know you're an electrician, Harold."

"What I mean is, I'm on my own; I'm not answerable to the bosses. There's always a bob or two waiting in London."

For some reason Canon Moran felt that Harold was lying. There was a quickness about the way he'd said they were easy about their plans, and it didn't seem quite to make sense, the logic of not being answerable to bosses and a bob or two always waiting for him. Harold was being evasive about their movements, hiding the fact that they would probably remain in Dublin for longer than he implied, meeting other people like himself.

"It was good of you to have us," Deirdre said that evening, all three of them sitting around the fire in the drawing-room because the evenings had just begun to get chilly. Harold was reading a book about Che Guevara and hadn't spoken for several hours. "We've enjoyed it, Father."

"It's been nice having you, Deirdre."

"I'll write to you from London."

It was safe to say that: he knew she wouldn't because she hadn't before, until she'd wanted something. She wouldn't write to thank him for the rectory's hospitality, and that would be quite in keeping. Harold was the same kind of man as Sergeant James had been: it didn't matter that they were on different sides. Sergeant James had maybe borne an affliction also, a humped back or a withered arm. He had ravaged a country that existed then for its spoils, and his most celebrated crime was neatly at hand so that another Englishman could make matters worse by attempting to make amends. In Harold's view the trouble had always been that these acts of war and murder died beneath the weight of print in history books, and were forgotten. But history could be rewritten, and for that Kinsella's Barn was an inspiration: Harold had journeyed to it as people make journeys to holy places.

"Yes?" Deirdre said, for while these reflections had passed through his mind he had spoken her name, wanting to ask her to tell him the truth about her friend.

He shook his head. "I wish you could have seen your mother again," he said instead. "I wish she were here now."

The faces of his three sons-in-law irrelevantly appeared in his mind: Carley's flushed cheeks, Thomas's slow good-natured smile, John's little moustache. It astonished him that he'd ever felt suspicious of their natures, for they would never let his daughters down. But Deirdre had turned her back on the rectory, and what could be expected when she came back with a man? She had never been like Emma or Linda or Una, none of whom smoked Three Castles cigarettes and wore clothes that didn't seem quite clean. It was impossible to imagine any of them becoming involved with a revolutionary, a man who wanted to commit atrocities.

"He was just a farmer, you know," he heard himself saying. "Kinsella."

Surprise showed in Deirdre's face. "It was Mother we were talking about," she reminded him, and he could see her trying to connect her mother with a farmer who had died two hundred years ago, and not being able to. Elderliness, he could see her thinking. "Only time he wandered," she would probably say to her friend.

"It was good of you to come, Deirdre."

He looked at her, far into her eyes, admitting to himself that she had always been his favourite. When the other girls were busily growing up she had still wanted to sit on his knee. She'd had a way of interrupting him no matter what he was doing, arriving beside him with a book she wanted him to read to her.

"Goodbye, Father," she said the next morning while they waited in Enniscorthy for the Dublin bus. "Thank you for everything."

"Yeah, thanks a ton, Mr Moran," Harold said.

"Goodbye, Harold. Goodbye, my dear."

He watched them finding their seats when the bus arrived and then he drove the old Vauxhall back to Boharbawn, meeting Slattery in his postman's van and returning his salute. There was shopping he should have done, meat and potatoes, and tins of things to keep him going. But his mind was full of Harold's afflicted face and his black-rimmed fingernails, and Deirdre's hand in his. And then flames burst from the straw that had been packed around living people in Kinsella's Barn. They burned through the wood of the barn itself, revealing the writhing bodies. On his horse the man called Sergeant James laughed.

Canon Moran drove the car into the rectory's ramshackle garage, and walked around the house to the wooden seat on the front lawn. Frances should come now with two cups of coffee, appearing at the front door with the tray and then crossing the gravel and the lawn. He saw her as she had been when first they came to the rectory, when only Emma had been born; but the grey-haired Frances was somehow there as well, shadowing her youth. "Funny little Deirdre," she said, placing the tray on the seat between them.

It seemed to him that everything that had just happened in the rectory had to do with Frances, with meeting her for the first time when she was eighteen, with loving her and marrying her. He knew it was a trick of the autumn sunshine that again she crossed the gravel and the lawn, no more then pretence that she handed him a cup and saucer. "Harold's just a talker," she said. "Not at all like Sergeant James."

He sat for a while longer on the wooden seat, clinging to these words, knowing they were true. Of course it was cowardice that ran through Harold, inspiring the whisper of his sneer when he spoke of the England he hated so. In the presence of a befuddled girl and an old Irish clergyman England was an easy target, and Ireland's troubles a kind of target also.

Frances laughed, and for the first time her death seemed far away, as her life did too. In the rectory the visitors had blurred her fingerprints to nothing, and had made of her a ghost that could come back. The sunshine warmed him as he sat there, the garden was less melancholy than it had been.

Ulster

BRENDAN BEHAN

(1923–1964)

When he was not in jail or in a pub, Brendan Behan was writing. Behan was born in the slums of Dublin. At the time of his birth, his father was in a British compound because of his involvement with the IRA. Young Brendan followed suit at an early age, joining an IRA youth organization at the age of nine. By the time he was in his late teens he was a messenger boy for the organization. At fifteen Behan was put in the Borstal Reform School in England for trying to blow up a British battleship in Liverpool harbor. His experience was captured in his book Borstal Boy.

After his release, Behan returned to Ireland, but he was arrested in 1942 for the attempted murder of two detectives. He was released under a general amnesty in 1946, but was arrested many more times, either for his political activities or for public drunkenness. He spent the rest of his life in London, Dublin, New York, and Paris.

Behan's work is autobiographical and several of his books were banned in Ireland during his lifetime. His plays, The Quare Fellow, The Hostage, *and* The Big House, *combined song and dance and direct addresses to the audience. In the end, even Brendan Behan could not live the life of Brendan Behan. He died at forty-one of the effects of alcoholism.*

I'M A BRITISH OBJECT,
SAID THE BELFAST-MAN

from HOLD YOUR HOUR AND HAVE ANOTHER

"I'm a British object," said this elderly Belfast-man to me, one Twelfth of July, a long time ago. We were in the little village of Millisle, near Donaghadee in the County Down. We had gone out there to pass the beautiful day of high summer like true Irishmen, locked in the dark snug of a public house.

The Belfast-man was an inebriate of some standing, whose politics were purely alcoholic. He was what they call in the North-East a wine victim, and carried his affection for things British to drinking port from the vineyards of Hoxton, and sherry from Tooting Bec, at five shillings the ten-glass bottle. He had come down for the day from the city and scandalized the assembled Orangemen by his reluctance to drink porter.

That lovely summer's day I'll remember too for the singing of an old man from Millisle. *The Bright Silvery Light of the Moon* and the *Yellow Rose of Texas* he sang, and disappointed me because he didn't sing something more Orange. The nearest he got to "party politics" was a song about the Crimean War that went to the air of *The Rakes of Mallow:*

> All drawn up, Britannia's sons
> Faced the Russian tyrant's guns,
> And bravely dared his shells and bombs,
> On the Bonny Heights of Alma.

We had a great day of singing and drinking and eating, and though I did feel a bit shamed by the bright sunshine when we came out blinking into it at closing-time, it wasn't long before we got indoors again.

Next morning I didn't feel so good, but in the summer-time nothing lasts long, and I was swimming around the harbour like a two-year-old and was shortly joined by a young man from the Shankill, who confided in me that he could always "tell a Fenian."

"And how," said I, lying on the sea, *bolg anairde,*[1] and looking up at the sun, "do you manage that?"

"Ah know them be their wee button noses."

I felt my own snitcher, and reflected that it would make a peculiar surrealistic sort of wee button.

The British Object was not so politically unaware as I'd thought. He too appeared, ready for the waves, dressed in a high-necked black costume that bore some resemblance to a habit, and emblazoned with an enormous orange crest with the inscription "True to You," and surmounted not as you might expect by a ten-glass bottle of Liverpool champagne, but by a head of the late King Edward the Seventh.

He dived in and thrashed about like a man in the jigs, and I confidently expected the sea to become wine-coloured after him, like "the wine-coloured ocean" of Homer.

I'd not have believed a person if they'd told me that summer would never end, or I'd have believed them as one believes a mathematical proposition, from the mind out only.

It seems years ago since the summer when we were crowded jam-tight from Merrion to Seapoint, and half doped from the sun when the pavements of Grafton Street were like the top of an oven, and you had to dodge into Mac's and get yourself on the high stool for the safety of the soles of your feet.

Is it only a short time ago that I stood at ten o'clock of an

1. Belly upwards.

evening in the little town of Callan, and went over to read the inscription over the house of Humphrey O'Sullivan, the Gaelic diarist and poet, now most appropriately a fish-and-chip shop?

Poets are great one-and-one men. I don't know about diarists.

I'd sample the chips another time, with a bit of ray, but that evening I had eaten at Mrs. Coady's, and after her huge rounds of prime beef and fresh vegetables you wouldn't be in humour of anything for a good while.

I'd come out from her place trying to remember the name, and getting mixed up, muttering in a daze of good living, like an incantation, charm or spell, the words "Mrs. Callan of Coady," I mean "Mrs. Coady of Callan."

And the Guard I met, that told me of raiding a pub after hours and finding three men in it. And the publican starts "ah-sure-ing" him that they're only friends that he wants to give a farewell drink to, because they're off to Lourdes the following day.

The Guard says all right, and not be too long and, going out, meets three others on their way to the hall door.

Regretting his previous mildness, he enquires sarcastically:

"And I suppose you three are going to Lourdes, too?"

"Musha no, sergeant, *a mhic,* we're going to Knock."[2]

---

2. Knock: a place of Irish pilgrimage.

EAMON GRENNAN

(1941–)

A critic once called Eamon Grennan "a Celtic amphibian, at home both in Ireland and America." Like the poets Seamus Heaney and Paul Muldoon, Grennan teaches at an American university, and much of his work is an attempt to reconcile his bifurcated Irish-American life. His poems written in the present tense often capture his American experience, while his verses written in the past tense are reminiscences of Ireland.

Grennan published his first books in Ireland, but it was not until the 1989 American publication of What Light There Is and Other Poems *that he received significant attention. His work has been collected in* Relations: New and Selected Poems *(1998), which includes "Facts of Life, Ballymoney," presented here. This poem illustrates Grennan's minute attention to the visual and aural, what one critic called his "ear for the most reclusive sound . . . his eye for the elusive detail." In midlife Grennan is still wrestling with the value and nature of "home." Edward Hirsch wrote in* The New Republic, *"His quiet, well-crafted poems are painterly, sensible, shapely; they are eager, unrhetorical, straightforward, melodic. They are never extreme."*

FACTS OF LIFE, BALLYMONEY

I would like to let things be:

The rain comes down on the roof
The small birds come to the feeder
The waves come slowly up the strand.

Three sounds to measure
My hour here at the window:
The slow swish of the sea
The squeak of hungry birds
The quick ticking of rain.

Then of course there are the trees.
Bare for the most part.
The grass wide open to the rain
Clouds accumulating over the sea
The water rising and falling and rising
Herring-gulls bobbing on the water.

They are killing cuttlefish out there,
One at a time without fuss.
With a brisk little shake of the head
They rinse their lethal beaks.

Swollen by rain, the small stream
Twists between slippery rocks.
That's all there's to it, spilling
Its own sound onto the sand.

In one breath one wink all this
Melts to an element in my blood.
And still it's possible to go on
Simply living
As if nothing had happened.

Nothing has happened:
Rain inching down the window,
Me looking out at the rain.

BERNARD MacLAVERTY

(1942–   )

Born in Belfast, Bernard MacLaverty claims that he took up writing at the age of nineteen to have something to do "after the dot disappeared on the tv set." After taking his A-level exams in chemistry and English, MacLaverty worked as a laboratory technician. At twenty-eight he left the lab to return to school and study English at Queens University. MacLaverty moved to Scotland to teach school in Edinburgh and Glasglow until he left teaching in 1981 to write full-time.

MacLaverty's work examines family relationships. Perhaps because his own father died when he was twelve, he is especially interested in the bond between fathers and sons. "Some Surrender," from MacLaverty's collection The Great Profundo and Other Stories, *was published in 1987 and records the conversation between a grown man and his father as they walk the hills around Belfast.*

Several of MacLaverty's novels have been made into films, including Lamb *and* Cal. *His most recent novel, the first in fourteen years,* Grace Notes *(1997), was short-listed for the Booker Prize. Bernard MacLaverty lived with his wife and four children on the Isle of Islay, but has returned to Glasgow.*

SOME SURRENDER

from THE GREAT PROFUNDO AND
OTHER STORIES

Two figures move slowly up the steep angle of the Hill, waist deep in gorse and bracken. The man taking up the rear, by far the younger of the two, is dressed in anorak and climbing boots while his companion wears a light sports-jacket, collar and tie and ordinary brightly polished shoes. The older man walks with his arms swinging, leaning into the slope. Strung tightly over his shoulder is the strap of a binocular case which raps and bobs against his back. There is a spring in his step and he tends to climb the narrow path on his toes. The more bulky man behind is breathing heavily and placing his hands on his thighs and pushing against them for leverage. At this point the Hill is like a staircase, the path worn brown and notched with footholds. They come to a flat area at the top of the staircase and the younger man flops on to the grass.

"Jesus, Dad, take a break."

"Are you serious?"

The old man is breathing normally. He stands with his back to the panorama of the city while his son gets his breath back.

"Look at that view," says the son.

"I save it till I get to the top. Then I take it all in."

"You're some machine. How do you keep so fit?"

"I walk a lot. I've done this climb since you were small."

"Think I don't remember. The tears and the sore legs and the nettle stings."

The old man smiles.

"Roy, I'm not as fit as I look. There's bits of the system not in full working order."

"Like what?"

"When I put too much pressure on the legs I tend to blow off," he laughs. "Like a horse at the trot."

The son gets to his feet.

"In that case, if you don't mind, I'll go first."

Roy leads the way up the next section, his father speaking to him from behind.

"There's a design fault built into Man."

"What's that?"

"Age. The teeth are beginning to go."

"At seventy-five I'm not surprised."

"Loosening. I've lost two big, back molars on both sides. That means their opposite numbers overgrow. Nothing to grind against. So they get sensitive. I can't eat ice-cream—or lollipops."

The son laughs, "I've never seen you eat an ice-cream in your life."

"You haven't been around much lately."

"Whose fault was that?"

The path widens and they are able to walk side by side. There is silence for a while except for Roy's breathing and the slithering noises his anorak makes with each step. The old man says, "Would you not come and see her?"

"No."

"I suppose I take your point. A lot of people don't get on with your mother. But there's nobody else I'd rather be with."

"She has got to ask me back."

"It's not off the ground you lick it—you're both stubborn."

"I don't want to see her. Anyway, in twenty years she's hardly crossed my mind."

"Liar."

They come to the edge of a wood which covers most of the

slope of the Cave Hill and sit down on a large stepped rock. The old man crosses his legs and Roy sits down at his feet. The day is bright but occasionally clouds pass in front of the sun. Shadows chase across the landscape.

"Remember the first time we met at the Ireland-Scotland game? Afterwards I told her. I said, 'I met Roy on the terraces today,' and she said, 'Roy who?' "

There is a long silence. Roy says, "I like looking into a wood like that," he jabs his hand towards it. "The way you see in under the trees, like a colonnade. The way the birds echo."

"I like seeing out. Being in a wood, seeing out to a field in the sun through trees."

"You'd argue a black crow white."

"I would—if it was."

Roy laughs and digs into his anorak pocket and produces a camera. He opens the bellows and begins to photograph the woods again and again.

"That's a brave old-fashioned job."

"A Leica," says Roy with his eye to it, pressing the shutter. "I got it in a junkshop in London. It's great for this kind of work. Feels like a favourite paintbrush." He winds the film on with his thumb and changes the camera to the upright position. "There's a lovely lens in it." Roy turns and looks up at his father. From where he sits he can see the sinews taut in his neck. He raises the camera to his eye and focuses. The old man sees what he is doing and looks away into the woods.

"Don't start that nonsense." The shutter clicks.

"Portrait of retired, famous architect on his seventy-fifth birthday."

"Put that thing away."

"But I've never taken any pictures of you."

"Keep it like that."

The old man begins to pluck moss from the rock he is sitting on and crosses his legs the other way revealing his thin white shin.

Roy closes the camera with a snap, returns it to his pocket and laughs, "Forty-four years of age and I'm still looking up to you." His father gives a snort. "No, really. Even then . . ."

"When?"

"When you didn't come out on my side."

"You must always remember that I chose your mother. I didn't choose you."

Roy gives a sigh which is meant to be heard and stands up.

"I mean that philosophically—that you can't choose your children. It's not to say that I wouldn't have picked you. It's a bit like 'Old Maid'—you pick and then see what you've got. There's the appearance of choice."

They begin walking again, leaving the woods behind. On the open ground the birdsong changes from a blackbird to larks. The old man stops and looks up narrowing his eyes. He says, "What's your own son doing?"

"Still at Aberdeen, so far as I know. At least he was before Christmas."

"What's he like?"

"Aw—Damien, he's great. I'm very fond of him—yet there's no particular reason to be. As you say, you can't choose them. Every time I see him . . . he's gauche, unsure of himself, a bit brilliant—and sometimes he makes me laugh out loud."

"An oddly Romish name for a grandson of mine. What's he studying?"

"Law. Aberdeen has a good reputation and it's what his mother wanted him to do."

"You and I know that doesn't count for much."

"I didn't even have the qualifications to get in."

"You failed because you didn't work hard enough."

"For fucksake, Dad, don't start. We're talking about twenty-five years ago."

"Even though we're on a mountain there's no need for language. Save it for the terraces."

"Do you not even give me credit for doing okay now?"

"I do."

"It doesn't seem like it. I did all my studying a generation after everybody else."

"At a London Poly."

"Come on Dad, you make it sound like some sort of Craft School for the Less Able."

"No-oo, you've got me wrong. I see your postcards all over the place. Supermarkets even."

"And there's the possibility of a book."

"Congratulations. I didn't know."

"There's a lot to catch up on. Photographers who get books are few and far between."

"What's it about?"

"Belfast. Belfast people. But I wrote the text myself."

"Are you happy with it?"

"What?"

"The book?"

"The pictures—okay. The text I'm not sure of. The best one in the whole thing is from down by the Markets. A white horse rearing up in front of the knacker's yard. You only realize afterwards, in the darkroom, that you've got it all in the frame."

"My father was a man who knew the value of education. His ambition for me was to get a job indoors." The old man laughs and climbs in silence for a while.

"Why did you come back, Roy? And to Dublin of all places?"

"I got an offer of sharing some darkroom space there. In London the warring parties would have seen too much of each other. I suppose that's why Belfast was out, as well. With you and Mother."

On the exposed side of the Hill the wind is fresher and blows his father's white hair about. He keeps trying to smooth it down with his hand.

Roy clears his throat and says, "What galls me the most is you were right."

"Hard to admit."

"But it was for the wrong reasons. She wasn't even a good Catholic."

"Thank God."

"She gave the whole thing up after a couple of years in England."

"But I bet she insisted on sending your boy to a Roman Catholic school." Roy nods.

"It's ingrained deep in them."

"That's a tautology. If it's ingrained it must be deep."

"Thank you for pointing this out to me. My life will never be the same again."

"Religion has f . . . nothing to do with it. She and I were . . . we just didn't get on—fought like weasels in a hole. You go through the whole bit, 'It's best to stay together for the sake of the boy.' But when it came to a boxing match I thought I'd better go."

"Did you ever get married?"

"After the baby was born."

"In a Roman Catholic church?"

"It's what she wanted at the time. Very, very quiet. There were only about five of us. We went to a pub in the afternoon for our honeymoon." Roy laughs and his father looks quizzically at him. "We had to arrange an all-day babysitter."

"I don't find it funny, even yet. Your mother has been known to cry if the subject is raised."

"Come on, people who get married nowadays are the exception."

"We're not talking about nowadays, we're talking about the mid-sixties. But that's only part of it. Your mother was more offended by . . ." The old man pauses and begins to gesture with his hands. "You know the way you feel about Jews?"

"I don't feel anything about Jews."

"Well, the way most people feel about them. That's what we think of Roman Catholics. There's something spooky about them. As my father said, 'Neither employ them nor play with them.' "

"Doesn't leave much."

"That's the idea," he pauses again, then says, "Taigs."

"Do you know what that word means?"

"Fenians. Catholics."

"I know *that*. But it's Gaelic—the word means poet."

"So what?"

"We use it as a term of abuse—dirty taig—and all the time it means poet."

"You're learning too much south of the border. And none of it's good for you."

"We lack culture. Sashes and marches."

"Nobody ever survived on poems. Hard work and thrift. People that speak their mind—that's a culture. I'm proud to be part of it—and so should you be."

"You don't understand."

"Why?"

Roy laughs. "You're an oul bigot."

"I'm a man who knows what's right and if that's being a bigot, then I am one."

Roy stops walking and his father looks over his shoulder at him. Roy makes a fist and shakes it in the air.

"Catholics have too many children. Their eyes are too close together. They keep coal in the bath."

His old man grins. "Tell me something new."

"Let's talk about something else. This is beginning to annoy me."

"You're aisy annoyed."

They walk on, saying nothing. Every so often Roy glances over his shoulder at the view but the old man strides on looking neither right nor left.

AHEAD OF THEM and slightly to their right they can see Napoleon's Nose, a cliff face dropping away for several hundred feet. Set back a little from the edge is a concrete beacon which from this distance looks like a wart on the nose. When they reach it Roy stands leaning against it, panting. It is covered in graffiti, the most prominent of which is a red NO SURRENDER. His father stands beside him shaking his head.

"Can you imagine carrying a spray can the whole way up here just to do that?"

"Shows Ulster determination, I suppose."

His father goes over to the edge. A crow flaps across the space beneath him.

"You're high up when you can look down on the birds."

"Careful," says Roy. "Don't stand so near the edge. In your condition one fart would propel you over." Roy stands at a safe distance and takes out his camera. He snaps the panorama, moving a little to the right each time. The blue Lough lies like a wedge between the Holywood hills at the far side and the grey mass of the city at his feet and to his right. Spires and factory chimneys poke up in equal numbers. Soccer pitches appear as green squares with staples for goalposts.

The old man shouts over the wind. "You could read registration plates in Carnmoney on a day like that."

"But who'd want to be in Carnmoney?"

"Good one, Roy." He laughs and comes over to his son who is crouching, threading a new film into his camera. He clicks the back shut and takes three quick exposures of his feet, each time winding on with a flick of his thumb.

He looks up at his father and says, "This was the place the United Irishmen took an oath to overthrow the English. They were all Prods as well."

"History, Roy. It's not the way things are now." He plucks up the knees of his trousers and sits down on the plinth of the beacon. "It's never been worse."

"The design fault here is the border."

"What do you mean?"

"I think we should at least consider the island being one country."

"Roy, please." He shakes his head as if to rid himself of the idea, then goes on, "The British Government are on the same side as the terrorists now. They're beating us with the stick *and* the bloody carrot. God knows where we'll be in ten years' time."

"I'd like to see a new slogan, SOME SURRENDER."

"Never."

"When Ireland score a try at Landsdowne Road, father— don't tell me you've no feeling for it."

"Peripheral. That's all peripheral. What matters is our identity. We've been here from the sixteenth century."

"A minute ago you dismissed history." Roy reaches out and punches his father on the shoulder. The old man smiles. Roy says, "History in Ireland is what the other side have done to you. People have got to stop killing each other and talk."

"I read a good quote in Sunday's paper. Let me get it right. 'For evil to flourish all that need happen . . .' "

" 'Is that good men do nothing.' That was Burke. We must read the same paper."

"That's how the Civil Rights and the IRA got a foothold. The good men of Ulster sat back and did nothing."

"Rubbish. The IRA probably say exactly the same thing."

"What do you mean?"

"They see the Prods and the Brits as an evil force. Reagan used it as an excuse to bomb Libya. It *sounds* like a good phrase . . . but . . . good and evil are very personal—like false teeth, they don't transfer easily."

"But there must be standards. Rules."

"That's the Catholic way. Do you want me to get you an introduction?"

"Catch yourself on."

HIS FATHER TAKES out the binoculars and rests his elbows on his knees to scan the distance.

"I have to do it like this. Shaky hands."

"Let's have a look."

"In a minute."

When the old man looks through the glasses his mouth opens. He focuses and swings farther to the right.

"They're clearing the site," he says and passes the binoculars to Roy.

"What's this?"

"You can see the lorries and the JCBs. Over there, towards the Shore Road." Roy raises the binoculars and finds where his father is pointing.

"That was the multi-storey block they demolished? I saw it on the News," he says, without taking the glasses from his eyes. "It was pretty spectacular coming down. Slow motion. Wallop!"

"Lagan Point. It was one of mine."

"I didn't know that."

"There's a lot to catch up on."

Roy lowers the binoculars.

His father smiles. "The people that lived in it had a better name for it. No Point." The old man grunts and rises to his feet. He stands with his hands joined behind his back looking down on the city.

"I got a prize for it, too. There was a plaque on the wall at the front door. It occurred to me to salvage it but the ironies were too obvious." He begins to rock backwards and forwards on his feet. "The other two I built are due to come down over the next couple of years. Just as soon as they can get the people housed."

"Jesus."

"That's almost the complete works."

Roy looks at his taut back and asks, "Is it structural?"

"It's everything." The old man lifts his shoulders, then drops them. "The whole idea came from Morocco or somewhere. A steel skeleton with cladding. But nobody took into account the Belfast climate. The continual rain got into the bolts no matter how well they were sealed. Shortcuts were taken. At the time we were looking for cheap housing for a lot of people. Quickly. It seemed to be the answer."

"I took some of the pictures for this book in Divis Flats.

They're pretty terrible—the Flats, not the pictures. Nobody should be asked to live in such conditions."

"Divis is not mine." He leans back against the concrete and looks at the sky. "The principle of living stacked is a perfectly sound one. Look what van der Rohe did in Chicago. And Le Corbusier. What they hadn't reckoned with was the Belfast working-class."

"Bollicks, Dad. You can't shift the blame that way."

"I suppose not. But the concept works with a different population. Put security on the door, good maintenance and fill the place with pensioners. Bob's your uncle."

"That's like saying Northern Ireland would be fine without the extremists. You must take account of what is. Would you like to live in one?"

"We're living in sheltered housing at the moment. . . ."

"Have you sold the house?"

"Three years ago."

"God—after the matches I thought you were going back home." Roy shakes his head. "That's really thrown me. I pictured you going back to mother in our house. The place I knew." He shakes his head again. "Why should that worry me?"

"Best thing we ever did—to get rid of that barracks. Your mother wasn't up to it and it was expensive to heat."

"I can't think of you anywhere else."

"We've moved into this sheltered place. It's fine. You get your shopping done—if anyone takes ill you just press the buzzer. I have a bit of a garden, my 'defensible space,' which keeps me amused. If you came up I could give you some broccoli."

"And I'd get to meet Mother." The old man shrugs his shoulders again.

"I was *never* keen on talking to her. When she'd take me into town to get shoes or something I kept thinking, 'What'll I talk about—I don't know what to say.' At the age of twelve I talked to my mother on the bus *about the weather.* Because I felt I had to say something."

The old man laughed a little, nodding.

"You're not the only one."

"I remember on one of these jaunts she bought me a treat of currant squares. When we came out of the shop I was so delighted I swung the bag round and the weight of the things tore through the bottom and they ended up all over the wet street."

"Aw poor Roy!"

"If it had happened to me as a parent I'd have bought another bagful, but not Mother."

"Maybe at the time we couldn't afford it."

"Aw come on! She was training me in thrift."

"No bad thing, if it was true." The old man paused. "Did you ever feel that about me?"

"What?"

"Having to make up things to say."

"No. You always seemed to be busy. I had to fight to get talking to you. Listening to you with Charlie Burgess or Billy Muir I used to be amazed at the stories you could tell. Why didn't you tell them to me? All you'd talk to me about was filling the coalscuttle and school. And just when it was getting interesting Mother would always say, 'I think Roy should be in bed.'"

"Why're we able to talk now?"

"God knows. I suppose . . . . I don't know. There was a gap—for a long time—and it couldn't have been worse."

"And here we are again."

"Yeah, here we are again. But I'll forgo the broccoli, if you don't mind. Broccoli as Trojan horse. Speaking of gifts . . ."

Roy puts his hand in another of his anorak pockets and takes out a small wrapped package. "Happy birthday," he says.

The old man is genuinely surprised.

"I was going to give it to you when we reached the top."

"Well, we're here—so what's different?" His father begins to unpick the sellotape then gives up and tears off the wrapping paper. "It seems like . . . after what you've just told me . . . like a kind of consolation prize."

"Damn the bit."

It is a silver hip-flask. He weighs it in his hand, then shakes it close to his ear listening to the tiny glugging noise.

"It's full."

"For the terraces."

The old man unscrews the cap and sniffs.

"Is there water in it?"

"Come on, Dad. I've been to three matches with you."

The old man puts the flask to his mouth and tips it up. Afterwards he makes a face. Roy says, "It's hall-marked."

"I didn't know they could do that with whisky. Thanks, I'm delighted with this. How did you remember?"

Roy laughs.

"We made a date—after the Scotland game. You said why don't you drive to Belfast and we'll climb the Hill on my birthday."

"That's right. Of course." His father taps his temple. "When's the next one?"

"Saturday three weeks. Against the English."

"I'll be there." He clenches his fist and shakes it at the sky. With his other hand he offers Roy the hip-flask.

"No thanks, I'll stick to the beer. I've never liked the taste of whisky."

"That's what has you the shape you are."

Roy rummages in his anorak and takes out a can of beer. He jerks at the ring pull. A small explosion of beer sprays over his father who jumps sideways. Roy laughs and apologizes.

"I forgot it would be all shook up." He takes a hanky from his pocket and reaches toward his father. The old man ducks away.

"It's clean." Roy dabs at the beads of beer. "Wait—it's all over your tie."

"Your mother'll accuse me of smelling like a brewery when I go in."

"She'd be right." Roy sits down to finish what is left of his can. "For once."

His father looks away in another direction.

"Would you not come back with me?"

Roy sighs and shakes his head.

"What would be the harm?"

"You're making it out to be a big thing," says Roy. "It's not. I'm not keen on talking to her—that's all."

"But you might come round to it—some day?"

"Who knows?"

His father folds the torn wrapping paper and puts it in his pocket. Roy says, "More thrift."

"No. I'm anti-litter as well as everything else." He takes up the binoculars again and looks towards the Lough.

"The constructive thing to get into these days is demolition." He lowers the glasses and his head turns slowly from left to right. "When I die bury me here for the view." There is a long silence between them. Roy breaks it by laughing.

"Sure thing," he says.

THE TWO MEN go back the way they came.

"That's when you know your age."

"What?" says Roy.

"When going down is harder than coming up." Roy goes in front and offers his hand as they come down the steep, stepped part of the path. The old man ignores it and instead leans his weight on Roy's shoulder. Guiding him between two rocks the son puts his hand on his father's back and is startled to feel his shoulder-blades, the shape of butterfly wings, through the thin material of his jacket.

BRIAN MOORE

(1921–1999)

Brian Moore was a writer's writer, better known among his peers than among the general public. He was short-listed for the Booker Prize three times but never won. Few of the titles of his twenty novels are familiar, except the two that were made into films, The Lonely Passion of Judith Hearne *and* Black Robe. *Yet Graham Greene called Moore his "favorite living novelist . . . Each book of his is dangerous, unpredictable and amusing. He treats the novel as a trainer treats a wild beast."*

The son of a Belfast doctor, Moore had a nomadic career. He worked in films, notably with Alfred Hitchcock, Claude Chabrol, and Bruce Beresford. Like many Irish writers, he taught in American universities, including UCLA. He traveled restlessly between Europe, Canada, and the United States, but, as this essay notes, he was at heart an Irishman. His novels, though not always set in Ireland, often dealt with themes of ancestral isolation, Catholic doubt, and divided loyalties.

This was the last essay that Brian Moore wrote before his death. Originally commissioned by Granta, *it was published posthumously in* The New York Times.

GOING HOME

A few years ago on holiday in the west of Ireland I came upon a field which faced a small strand and, beyond it, the Atlantic Ocean. Ahead of me five cows raised their heads and stared at the intruder. And then behind the cows I saw a few stone crosses, irregular, askew as though they had been thrown there in a game of pitch-and-toss. This was not a field but a graveyard. I walked among the graves and came to a path which led to the sandy shore below. There, at the edge of this humble burial ground, was a headstone unlike the others, a rectangular slab of white marble laid flat on the ground:

BULMER HOBSON
1883–1969

I stared at this name, the name of a man I had never known, yet familiar to me as a member of my family. I had heard it spoken again and again by my father in our house in Clifton Street in Belfast and by my uncle, Eoin MacNeill, when during school holidays I spent summers in his house in Dublin. For my uncle and my father, Bulmer Hobson was both a friend and in some sense a saint. A Quaker, he, like my uncle, devoted much of his life to the cause of Irish independence, becoming in the early years of this century an exemplary patriot whose nonviolent beliefs made our tribal animosities seem brutal and mean. That his body lay here in this small Connemara field, facing the ocean under a simple marker, was somehow emblematic of his life.

Proust says of our past: "It is a labor in vain to try to recapture it: all the efforts of our intellect are useless. The past is hidden somewhere outside its own domain in some material object which we never suspected. And it depends on chance whether or not we come upon it before we die."

I believe now that the "material object" was, for me, that gravestone in Connemara, a part of Ireland which I had never known in my youth. And as I stood staring at Bulmer Hobson's name, my past as a child and adolescent in Belfast surged up, vivid and importunate, bringing back a life which ended forever when I sailed to North Africa on a British troopship in the autumn of 1943.

There are those who choose to leave home vowing never to

return and those who, forced to leave for economic reasons, remain in thrall to a dream of the land they left behind. And then there are those stateless wanderers who, finding the larger world into which they have stumbled vast, varied and exciting, become confused in their loyalties and lose their sense of home.

I am one of those wanderers. After the wartime years in North Africa and Italy, I worked in Poland for the United Nations, then emigrated to Canada, where I became a citizen before moving on to New York, and at last to California, where I have spent the greater part of my life.

And yet in all the years I have lived in North America I have never felt that it is my home. Annually, in pilgrimage, I go back to Paris and the French countryside and to London, the city which first welcomed me as a writer. And if I think of re-emigrating it is to France or England, not to the place where I was born.

For I know that I cannot go back. Of course, over the years I have made many return visits to my native Belfast. But Belfast, its configuration changed by the great air raids of the blitz, its inner city covered with a carapace of flyovers, its new notoriety as a theater of violence, armed patrols and hovering helicopters, seems another city, a distant relative to that Belfast which in a graveyard in Connemara filled my mind with a jumbled kaleidoscope of images fond, frightening, surprising and sad.

— My pet canary is singing in its cage above my father's head as he sits reading *The Irish News* in the breakfast room of our house in Belfast —

— A shrill electric bell summons me to Latin class in the damp, hateful corridors of St. Malachy's College. I have forgotten the declension and hear the swish of a rattan cane as I hold out my hand for punishment —

— In Fortstewart, where we spent our summer holidays, I have been all day on the sands, building an elaborate sand sculpture in hopes of winning the Cadbury contest first prize, a box of chocolates —

— Alexandra Park, where, a seven-year-old, I walk beside my sister's pram holding the hand of my nurse, Nellie Ritchie, who at that time I secretly believed to be my real mother —

— I hear the terrified squeal of a pig dragged out into the yard for butchery on my uncle's farm in Donegal —

— I stand with my brothers and sisters singing a ludicrous Marian hymn in St. Patrick's Church at evening devotions:

> O Virgin pure, O spotless maid,
> We sinners send our prayers to thee,
> Remind thy Son that He has paid
> The price of our iniquity —

— I hear martial music, as a regimental band of the British Army marches out from the military barracks behind our house. I see the shining brass instruments, the drummers in tiger-skin aprons, the regimental mascot, a large horned goat. Behind that imperial panoply long lines of poor recruits are marched through the streets of our native city to board ship for India, a journey from which many will never return —

— Inattentive and bored, I kneel at the Mass amid the stench of unwashed bodies in our parish church, where 80 percent of the female parishioners have no money to buy overcoats or hats and instead wear black woolen shawls which cover head and shoulders, marking them as "Shawlies," the poorest of the poor —

— We, properly dressed in our middle-class school uniforms sitting in a crosstown bus, move through the poor streets of Shankill and the Falls, where children without shoes play on the cobbled pavements —

— The front gates of the Mater Infirmorum Hospital, where my father, a surgeon, is medical superintendent. As he drives out of those gates, a man so poor and desperate that he will court minor bodily injury to be given a bed and food for a few days steps in front of my father's car —

— An evening curfew is announced following Orange

parades and the clashes which invariably follow them. The curfew, my father says, is less to prevent riots than to stop the looting of shops by both Catholic and Protestant poor —

— Older now, I sit in silent teen-age rebellion as I hear my elders talk complacently of the "Irish Free State" and the differences between the Fianna Fail and Fine Gael parties who compete to govern it. Can't they see that this Catholic theocratic "grocer's republic" is narrow-minded, repressive and no real alternative to the miseries and injustices of Protestant Ulster? —

— Unbeknownst to my parents I stand on Royal Avenue hawking copies of a broadsheet called *The Socialist Appeal*, although I have refused to join the Trotskyite party which publishes it. Belfast and my childhood have made me suspicious of faiths, allegiances, certainties. It is time to leave home —

The kaleidoscope blurs. The images disappear. The past is buried until, in Connemara, the sight of Bulmer Hobson's grave brings back those faces, those scenes, those sounds and smells which now live only in my memory. And in that moment I know that when I die I would like to come home at last to be buried here in this quiet place among the grazing cows.

H. V. MORTON

(1892–1979)

*Henry Canova Vollam Morton was born and educated in Birmingham,
England. At eighteen he began a career in journalism as an assistant
editor at the* Birmingham Gazette. *His writing career was interrupted
by army service in France during World War I. After the war he went to
the London* Evening Standard *as a member of the editorial staff. The
success of his first book,* The Heart of London *(1925), gave him the
impetus to leave his job for freelance travel writing. At first Morton con-
centrated on England, then Scotland, and by 1930 he branched out to
Ireland (with* In Search of Ireland *from which this selection is
excerpted). By the end of his career he had covered most of Europe and
the Holy Land.*

*Morton's series of travel books was read by millions who vicariously
toured with him in his bullnosed Morris. His publisher wrote, "Morton
has imagination of two kinds. He can project himself back into history
and capture distant events and the actors on stage at a particular place he
visits. And when the people he meets are contemporaries of the twentieth
century, he understands them and their work with a sympathy they
repay. This is just what we would like to manage on our own travels."*

from IN SEARCH OF IRELAND

*I cross into Northern Ireland, see the only frontier post in the British
Isles, walk the walls of Derry, hear about the siege and remember
Columcille, go on into Antrim, explore Belfast, see the mountains of
Mourne and—say farewell to Ireland on the Hill of Tara.*

I

When I said good-bye to Donegal I went south into Northern Ireland. An English reader who has not studied the map will wonder how I performed such an unnatural feat. It is simple.

Donegal, the most northerly county in Ireland and topographically in Ulster, is not in Northern Ireland! It is Free State territory. When the Irish Free State was established six of the nine counties of Ulster expressed themselves ready to die rather than become part of it. They decided to form themselves into a political entity with a parliament of their own. And this is Northern Ireland.

The six counties that compose it are Fermanagh, Tyrone, Londonderry, Antrim, Down, and Armagh. The three Ulster counties under the Free State flag are Donegal, Cavan, and Monaghan. The last two, forming, as they do, the southern boundary of Ulster, melt naturally into the Free State, but Donegal in the north is cut off in the most untidy and inconvenient manner from her parent. She looks almost like an orphan or a foundling. There is a little back door to her on the south about five miles wide (from Bundoran to Belleek) but the rest of her eastern boundary is on the frontier.

It thus happens that when you are in Donegal you can look south into Northern Ireland, and when you are in either Londonderry, Tyrone, or Fermanagh you can look north into Southern Ireland! This is no doubt an excellent joke except to those who have to live in it! It must be exasperating to find yourself barred by a customs barrier from the county town in which you have always enjoyed free trading.

But as long as it profits the Free State to build up her enterprises behind a tariff wall, or as long as Northern Ireland remains outside the Free State (which, I am told, will be for ever), this inconvenient and costly boundary with its double line of officials will remain, the only frontier in the British Isles.

*   *   *

As I approached Strabane, which is one of Northern Ireland's frontier towns, the Free State customs stopped me, groped about in the car for contraband goods, smiled at me in a friendly way when they discovered that I was not a smuggler, and took me into a tin hut to settle the one serious annoyance which faces the motorist in the Free State. If you take a car into this country you have to deposit a third of its value with the customs, and similarly if you remove it from the country, as you do technically when you take it over the boundary into Northern Ireland. Although motoring and tourist organizations will settle this for you in London, it is a tiresome law which, I suggest, if lifted in favour of those who are travelling for pleasure would react to the advantage of the Free State.

What a queer sight it was, this North-and-South Border line. Five or six cars were halted by the road-side waiting to be searched. An omnibus came along. It pulled up. Its passengers got out. Their brown paper parcels were prodded. I looked at the women and wondered how many wore more than one skirt. Several passengers were wearing new boots. They had left their old boots behind a hedge in Northern Ireland!

There was something rather funny about it. I have crossed frontier lines all over the world, but this was unlike any of them. We were going out of one English-speaking country into a part of the same English-speaking country. It would seem more probable if the Free State would make its customs officials speak Gaelic! As it is, the Irish Boundary has all the elements of a game—"Come on, let's play at being foreigners; you be French and I'll be German."

A few yards farther down the road I encountered the officials of Northern Ireland. They were a good advertisement for the manners and cheerfulness of the northern province.

After this ordeal I felt that I deserved a large whisky and soda. I was given one in an hotel full of gloomy Victorian mahogany and equally gloomy commercial travellers. Some sat writing their orders in the little compartments fitted up with sides to prevent cribbing; and others sat about with bags, reading news-papers and waiting for a train.

"How's trade?" I asked the least mournful one.

"Rotten," he said.

"When is this idiotic frontier going to disappear?"

"When the Free State income tax is a bob in the pound," he replied bluntly.

"You don't mean that?"

"Well, what the hell do you think I mean?"

"I thought you were making a joke."

"I don't make jokes."

"I'm sorry for you."

"I didn't ask for your sympathy."

"Will you have a drink?"

"I don't mind if I do."

This man told me quite a lot of things. He was a hard, embit-tered cynic. Some of his opinions I believed and tucked away for future reference; others I abandoned as the illusions of one con-demned for ever to wander the face of the earth with some utterly stupid commodity for which he could feel no respect.

2

As I went on into Northern Ireland a strange thing happened to me.

When I landed months ago in the Free State I adopted the attitude of foreigner in a foreign land. I had been, I hope, respectful, unargumentative, observant, anxious to understand and to be pleased. Now I realized as I went through towns and villages in Ulster that perhaps the boundary was not so nebulous as I had thought it. For I seemed to be in England again. There were war memorials quite as bad as those at home. I saw a Union Jack flying on a railway station. The pillar-boxes were red. The postmen were like English postmen. All trivial things, but after the Free State, which is trying to make itself as Irish as possible, they printed themselves on the mind with agreeable sharpness. In the south the deeds of the Irish troops in the Great War are never mentioned and no stone infantrymen remind one of the dead, but in Ulster every town and village is proud of the Ulster Division, and their war memorials stand beside the road as in towns and villages all over England, Scotland, and Wales. I had to look at the hills to convince myself that I had not, in some miraculous way, crossed the Irish Sea; but the hills were, beyond question, the hills of Ireland.

I ARRIVED IN Londonderry—or Derry as it is called—in the late afternoon. I saw a large city on a slight hill beside a wide river, the Foyle. The slim spire of the cathedral lifted itself above the buildings on the crest of the rise; and at the back, in the distance, was a ridge of low hills.

There are only two other cities in Great Britain as easy to see at a glance: York and Chester. The walls of Derry, like those of York and Chester, are complete. They form a rough parallelogram which encloses Old Derry, but, like all walled cities, modern Derry has broken its ancient confines and now spreads beyond the walls on every side.

What a magnificent walk this is, not as beautiful perhaps as a walk round the walls of York, but finer, in my opinion, than the walls of Chester. These walls are wider than those of York or Chester. They are about twenty-five feet high and in a magnificent state of preservation.

The story of Derry, as of Ulster, is one of the most heroic pages in the book of Ireland. The hatred of Celt and Saxon was complicated and deepened during Elizabethan times by the Reformation: religious hatred was now added to racial hatred. The consistent rebellion against English government went on, and as each one was crushed by the armies of Elizabeth the lands of the rebels were confiscated and handed over to English "undertakers," or settlers who undertook to live in Ireland and anglicize it. Walter Raleigh was an undertaker; so was Edmund

Spenser. Raleigh received 42,000 confiscated Irish acres, and Spenser received Kilcolman Castle, County Cork, where during the years 1586 to 1590 he wrote the *Faerie Queene.*

The last great armed struggle of the Irish Nation until modern times began in Ulster in 1598. It was inspired by one of the most gallant warriors who ever opposed the might of England—Hugh O'Neill, Earl of Tyrone. He was educated in England under the eye of Elizabeth; and this handsome Irishman seems to have pleased the queen, who was never too busy to notice a fine young man. Hugh O'Neill returned to Ireland, apparently the friend of England but in reality to plot against her. He set himself to that most difficult of all tasks, the healing of clan quarrels. He ended for ever the bitter feud that had existed between his own clan, the O'Neills, and the O'Donnells by marrying the sister of Red Hugh O'Donnell. Gradually and cunningly he brought the tribes together and trained them in up-to-date warfare. When his wife died he eloped with an English lady, Mabel Bagenal, sister of Sir Henry Bagenal, Chief Marshal of Ireland. From that time onward Bagenal was Hugh O'Neill's implacable foe.

The rebel clans now made war and fought a number of minor engagements, sometimes winning and sometimes losing. Spain sent three ships with arms and troops. The English generals decided to march on Ulster by three different routes and crush the clans. They were beaten back and the war dragged on for two years.

In August 1598, by one of those melodramatic chances so frequent in Irish history, O'Neill found himself at a place called the Mouth of the Yellow Ford, about two miles from Armagh, facing an English army commanded by his still implacable brother-in-law, Sir Henry Bagenal, Chief Marshal.

Sharpshooters picked off the English infantry as they advanced. Bagenal flung his heavy cavalry into the battle, but O'Neill, remembering Bannockburn, perhaps, had dug pits covered with grass into which the heavily armed horsemen fell in a ghastly tangle of lamed animals and dying men. The Irish light horse charged the English cavalry as they struggled in the pits. Bagenal then called up his cannon and drove back the Irish slightly, whereupon O'Neill ordered a general advance, and the Irish army—horse, foot, and guns—came on in a mad rush that must have been rather like the last charge of the Scottish clans at Culloden. The battle was now a hand-to-hand struggle. The English ranks were broken and were giving way. Just at the critical moment as English and Irish were locked together in the fight, a careless English gunner exploded a quantity of gunpowder which created terrible confusion. Sir Henry Bagenal, in an attempt to rally his army, raised the visor of his helmet and an Irish musket-ball shot him through the head. When the English saw the Chief Marshal fall from his horse the army wavered, gave way and fled, pursued by the clansmen.

The English general, twenty-three of his high commanders, and 2,500 rank and file lay dead on the field. The Irish army captured thirty-four banners, the artillery, money and baggage trains of the enemy. Their own losses were only 200 killed and 600 wounded.

This battle of the Yellow Ford was the greatest overthrow of the English since they had set foot in Ireland. O'Neill was hailed as the deliverer of his country. All over Ireland the clans rose to drive the English into the sea. O'Neill had set the heather alight.

Elizabeth, learning of the defeat of her army in Ireland, sent over the greatest expeditionary force that had ever landed in that country under the command of her favourite, the Earl of Essex. He had with him 20,000 foot and 2,000 horse. He behaved with unusual stupidity, patched up a peace with O'Neill, and returned to England, where, soon after, he suffered disgrace and death.

His successor was a vastly different man, the crafty Charles Blount, Lord Mountjoy. He sent forged letters among the Irish chiefs and sowed discord and mutual distrust among the clans, thus splitting up his enemies. The decisive battle was fought at Kinsale in September 1601.

A force of 3,000 Spaniards occupied Kinsale. An English army of 17,000 besieged them. The Irish clans under O'Neill and

Red Hugh O'Donnell made two magnificent forced marches to come to the rescue of the Spaniards. One of Ireland's most notorious traitors, a person called Brian MacMahon, sold the plan of campaign to the English for a bottle of whisky! On a dark night the English armies surprised the Irish and utterly routed them.

But Hugh O'Neill fought a losing fight for another two years. It was no good. His cause was lost. At Mellifont in Meath the great chieftain fell upon his knees and implored the mercy of the English queen. He was permitted to retain his title and part of his lands.

This is how Professor G. M. Trevelyan in his brilliant *History of England* sums up the Elizabethan Age in Ireland:

The policy of colonization was favoured by government as the only means of permanently holding down the natives, who were growing more hostile every year. This opened the door to a legion of "gentlemen-adventurers" and "younger sons" from the towns and manor houses of England. It has been said that the Elizabethan eagles flew to the Spanish Main while the vultures swooped down on Ireland; but they were in many cases one and the same bird. Among the conquerors and exploiters of Ireland were Humphrey Gilbert, Walter Raleigh, Grenville of the *Revenge,* and the high-souled author of the *Faerie Queene.* They saw in America and Ireland two new fields of equal importance and attraction, where private fortunes could be made, public service rendered to their royal mistress, and the cause of true religion upheld against Pope and Spaniard. When Raleigh and Spenser were stone-blind to the realities of the Irish racial and religious problem under their eyes, it was not likely that the ordinary Englishman at home would comprehend it for centuries to come.

And so in the last years of Elizabeth's reign, Irish history, till then fluid, ran into the mould where it hardened for three hundred years. The native population conceived a novel enthusiasm for the Roman religion, which they identified with a passionate hatred of the English. On the other hand the new colonists, as distinguished from the old Anglo-Irish nobility, identified

Protestantism with their own racial ascendancy, to retain which they regarded as a solemn duty to England and to God. Ireland has ever since remained the most religious part of the British Islands.

In such circumstances the Irish tribes finally became welded into the submerged Irish nation. The union of hatred against England, and the union of religious observance and enthusiasm became strong enough to break down at last the clan divisions of dateless antiquity, which the English were also busily destroying from outside. The abolition of the native upper class to make room for Irish landlords, began under the Tudors and completed under Cromwell, left this peasant nation with no leaders but the priests and no sympathizers but the enemies of England.

And now the walls of Derry rise out of history. When the O'Neill begged mercy from Elizabeth she had been dead (although they did not know in Ireland) for six days. Already Sir Robert Carey had ridden through the wild March weather from London to Edinburgh to offer the Crown to the King of Scotland, James VI (and I of England), the mean-spirited son of Mary, Queen of Scots, and Darnley.

James decided to "plant" the north of Ireland with English and Scottish farmers. The first thing to do was to get rid of the Ulster chieftains, the O'Neill, Earl of Tyrone, and Red Hugh's brother, Rory O'Donnell, Earl of Tyrconnell. A trumped-up charge of conspiracy was brought against them and they, seeing that a defence would be useless, decided to fly from Ireland.

On a September day in 1607 a ship put out from Rathmullan on Lough Swilly and set its course for France. The two earls saw the green hills of Donegal go down into the sea; and so, like countless sons of their country, known and unknown, they went away in order to live.

The "Flight of the Earls" decided the fate of Northern Ireland. The moment they had turned their backs on their country Protestant Ulster was born. O'Donnell died the following year, and the O'Neill in nine years' time, in a city that has soothed many a broken heart—Rome.

So ended an old song.

3

Now, said James and his ministers, was the time to try the experiment of a "plantation" on a grand scale. Over three and three-quarter million acres in Ulster were declared forfeit to the Crown, or practically the whole of the six counties of Donegal, Derry, Tyrone, Fermanagh, Cavan and Armagh.

Every inch of ground owned by the earls was promptly confiscated. In Irish eyes this land was not the property of the earls: it belonged to their clansmen. That did not matter to James or his ministers. They pressed forward their scheme for a solid Protestant colony in the north. The Corporation of London was approached by the Lords of the Privy Council with the suggestion that the rich City Companies might care to acquire land in Ulster. This is how the conquered territory was described to the merchants of London:

The country is well watered, generally, by abundance of springs, brooks, and rivers; and plenty of fuel, either by means of wood, or where that is wanting of good and wholesome turf. It yieldeth store of all necessary for man's sustenance, in such measure as may not only maintain itself, but also furnish the City of London, yearly, with manifold provisions, especially for their fleets; namely with beef, pork, fish, rye, bere, peas, and beans, which will also in some years help the dearth of the city and country about, and the storehouses appointed for the relief of the poor. As it is fit for all sorts of husbandry, so for breeding of mares and increase of cattle it doth excel, whence may be expected plenty of butter, cheese, hides and tallow.

English sheep will breed abundantly in Ireland, the seacoast, and the nature of the soil, being very wholesome for them; and, if need be, wool might be had cheaply and plentifully out of the west parts of Scotland. It is held to be good in many places for madder, hops and woad. It affordeth fells of all sorts, in great quantity, red-deer, foxes, sheep, lamb, rabbits, martins, squirrels, etc. Hemp and flax do more naturally grow there than elsewhere; which being well regarded, might give great provision for canvas, cable, cording, and such like requisites for shipping, besides thread, linen cloth, and all stuffs made of linen yarn, which is more plentiful there than in all the rest of the kingdom.

Materials for building—timber, stone of all sorts, limestone, slate, and shingle—are afforded in most parts of the country; and the soil is good for brick and tile. The harbour of the river of Derry is exceedingly good; and the road of Portrush and Lough Swilly, not far distant from the Derry, tolerable. The sea fishing of that coast very plentiful of all manner of usual sea fish, especially herrings and eels; there being yearly, after Michaelmas, for taking of herrings, above seven or eight score sail of his Majesty's subjects and strangers for lading, besides an infinite number of boats for fishing and killing. . . .

The coasts be ready for traffic with England and Scotland and for supply of provisions from or to them; and do lie open and convenient for Spain and the Straits, and the fittest and nearest for Newfoundland.

The City of London, approached by this auctioneers' circular, wisely sent four "grave and discreet" citizens to spy out the land. Their report was favourable. On March 29, 1613, the Irish Society was formed under the title "The Society of the Governor and Assistants of London of the new Plantation in Ulster within the Realm of Ireland." The land was divided into twelve parts which the companies drew by lot.

It is not unnatural that in the events which followed the prefix London should have been tacked on to the ancient name of Derry. Only the map-makers and the tourists, however, call it Londonderry. The older name persists.

It is, to a Londoner, strange to walk round the splendid walls of Derry and be told by any lounger how the Skinners or the Merchant Taylors did this or that and how the Grocers gave this gun and the Haberdashers that one; for old cannon still point their black noses above the Derry walls. You look from the ramparts down the chimneys of the city, you can pry into a thousand back yards, you gaze down into streets and squares, you pass over massive gateways which must be rather like the vanished gates of London Wall; and you come at length to a veteran of the Siege called Roaring Meg, an old cannon which made a great noise at that time. It was provided by the Fishmongers of London!

So London merchants built an Anglo-Scottish bulwark in the north. The "plantation" went on. The country of the clans was split up and redistributed. Many of the dispossessed Irish were allowed to enlist in foreign armies—a trial flight of the Wild Geese.

From this time dates the title of Baronet. James, who was full of schemes for raising money, had the happy idea of creating a new order of chivalry and conferring the dignity on certain men who paid for it by maintaining thirty armed men in Ulster at eightpence a day for three years. I have been told that the Act authorizing the creation of baronets has never been repealed, so that anyone who can prove that he is a gentleman by birth, not in trade, and possessing property valued at £1,000 a year can theoretically become a baronet if he can find men-at-arms willing to serve in Ulster for eightpence a day!

By a grim touch of irony baronets use the Red Hand of O'Neill as the mark of their rank.

4

I imagine that no other city, except perhaps Limerick, has such a single-minded memory of its history as Londonderry. You cannot live even for a few hours in this city without hearing the story of the Closing of the Gates of Derry.

It is, thanks to Macaulay, the only incident in Irish history which is thoroughly well known in England. Here they tell it all over again with just pride: how the thirteen 'prentice boys shut the gates of Derry in the face of a Catholic army sent to win the town for James II; how Derry declared for William of Orange; how the town endured the worst horrors of starvation and disease for one hundred and five days; how the Jacobite army placed a great boom of fir logs bound with cable across the River Foyle to prevent the relief of the city from the sea; and

how, on a Sunday night in August 1689, the starving garrison
saw two ships loaded with food break through the barrier and
sail right up to the walls of Derry.

It was one of the most gallant defences in the history of siege
warfare. It links Derry with Limerick. But Derry was holding
greater stakes. The siege of Limerick was fought on the old
racial quarrel between Irish and English; the siege of Derry
lifted the curtain on greater issues: the survival or defeat of
Protestantism in Western Europe. Ireland for the first time in her
history had become a European battle-field, and the thirteen
'prentice boys of Derry shut the gate on some one more dan-
gerous to England than James: they shut it on Louis XIV.

Few Catholics seem aware, by the way, that the Pope knew
of, and approved, William's Protestant Armada. Innocent XI had
himself urged all Catholics to resist the French Jesuits and the
Gallican Church, so that when William of Orange set sail from
Hellevoetsluis on a November day in 1688 he took with him,
paradoxically, the blessing of the Holy See and the united hopes
of Protestant Europe! In a similar way Gustavus Adolphus,
struggling against Spain and Austria, had been helped by Catholic
France and by the Pope.

The gallant defenders of Derry must have known the utmost
horrors possible to a beleaguered town. Three days before the
boom was broken and the food-ships came up a member of the
garrison compiled a list of food and prices. A rat cost a shilling.
A cat cost four and sixpence. No money would buy a small fish
from the river. It would be exchanged only for a quantity of
meal. A quart of horse blood cost a shilling. There is one savage
entry in the list:

A quarter of a dog, five and sixpence (fattened by eating the
bodies of the slain Irish.)

The men of Derry take you to the lofty Doric column
erected to the memory of the hero of the defence, the Rev.
George Walker, who later died at the Battle of the Boyne. They

take you to the cathedral and show you the graves of the
defenders, a bomb which was hurled over the walls with a pro-
posal of surrender, two white flags and a red flag.

And in the evening, even when the streets of Derry are full of
young small girls, plump and thin ones, who make shirts and
control the purse-strings in these bad times when so many men
are out of work, it is never possible to feel that Derry is an ordi-
nary city. Look where you will and you see the wall and a peep-
ing cannon. The memory of 1688-1689 is as vivid as though the
smoke of Roaring Meg was still blowing from the Walls.

5

One evening I mounted the Walls of Derry and looked down
over the city with its clustered chimneys. I stood there a long
time, dreaming of that far-off time in the history of Ireland
when the twin lamps of faith and learning went out one by one
all over Europe until only in Ireland was there the Light.

> For the end of the world was long ago
>   When the ends of the world waxed free,
> When Rome was sunk in a waste of slaves
>   And the sun drowned in the sea.
>
> When Caesar's sun fell out of the sky
>   And whoso hearkened right
> Could only hear the plunging
>   Of the nations in the night.
>
> When the ends of the earth came marching in
>   To torch and cresset gleam,
> And the roads of the world that lead to Rome
> Were filled with faces that moved like foam,
>   Like faces in a dream. . . .
>
> Misshapen ships stood on the deep
>   Full of strange gold and fire,

And hairy men as huge as sin,
With horned heads, came wading in
   Through the long, low sea mire.

Our towns were shaken of tall kings
   With scarlet beards like blood;
The world turned empty where they trod,
They took the kindly cross of God
   And cut it up for wood.[1]

In this time, when the barbarian armies marched and counter-marched across Europe, gathering like vultures round the corpse of Rome, this little island in the West knew its Golden Age. The weeds pushed apart the Roman pavements all over England. The nettles and the bramble grew on London Wall. The wild Saxon war bands halted outside London and blew their horns, but there was no answer. Roman London was dead.

In France, in Spain, in Germany the barbaric cavalry of Vandal and Hun swept to the four corners of the world; and there was no sound in Europe but the whistle of swords and the death-cry of civilization.

Then the great army of Irish saints set out to rekindle the Faith of Europe. Century after century saw them sailing off into sunrise or sunset to clothe the land with Christ. St. Fridolin, "the traveller," crossed the Rhine and set up the Cross at Seckingen; St. Kilian converted Gozbert, duke of Wurzburg; St. Columbanus of Bobbio went through Burgundy with twelve other Irish monks and founded the monasteries of Luxeuil and Fontaines; St. Gall, one of his monks, pushed on over the Alps into Switzerland and founded the monastery known by his name; St. Molaissi of Leighlin, in Carlow, journeyed to Rome where he studied for fourteen years; St. Fursa, son of a South Munster prince, passed through France and founded a monastery of Lagy, near Paris; St. Buite of Monasterboice travelled to Italy,

---

1. *The Ballad of the White Horse* by G. K. Chesterton (Methuen).

where he studied for years; Virgilius, Abbot of Aghaboe, explored France and became bishop of Salzburg.

There was St. Cataldus, educated at Lismore, who became bishop of Tarentum. There was John Scotus Erigena, the great Greek scholar, who taught philosophy in Paris at the Court of Charles the Bold. There was St. Fiacre who died at Breuil in France and gave his name to the vehicle—*fiacre*—which was used to convey pilgrims to his tomb.

And on the Walls of Derry a man remembers the best-loved of them all, Columcille, "Dove of the Church," who founded the monastery of Derry in the year 546. There could have been nothing on the hill above the Foyle but perhaps a grove of oak trees. The word *Derry,* or *Daire,* means oak or oak wood. We can imagine the young saint, for he was then only twenty-five years of age, building a little oratory of wattles and oak boughs and listening at the end of his day's labours to the wind going through the leaves. When he was far away in after years he used to think of Derry. He once wrote that the angels of God sang in the glades of Derry and that every leaf held its angel.

Even St. Patrick is not more dearly beloved by the common people of Ireland than Columcille. He is as real and vivid in the country places to-day as he was during his lifetime thirteen hundred years ago. Every age has told stories about him. Century after century has lovingly embroidered his memory so that he lives so vividly in Ireland that I believe there are many country people who would not be surprised to meet him on the road some morning.

He was born at Gartan in Donegal in 521. The royal blood of Ireland ran in his veins. He belonged to the northern Hy Neill, the descendants of Niall of the Nine Hostages. Over the green mountains of Donegal, beside a little lake, tradition has preserved a stone on which he lay. It is said that if anyone sleeps on this stone he will be saved the agonies of home-sickness. Many a pitiful journey has been made to the stone of Ráith Cnó by men and women on the eve of their exile.

His first name was Crimthann, but the children with whom

he played, watching him come from the church near the house of his fosterage, called him "Colum from the Cill"—Columcille.

The education of a child like Columcille in the Ireland of the sixth century illustrates more clearly than anything, I think, the culture of a State that had survived the wreck of Western civilization.

First the child was sent to the school of St. Finnen at Moville on Lough Foyle. This saint was of royal blood and had, as I have already mentioned, spent seven years as a student in Rome. He then went to the Leinster School of Bards which was ruled by an ancient poet, Gemman, who must have taught the boy the ancient druidic lore of Ireland. His next school was that of Aranmore, founded by St. Enna. He passed on into the great college of Clonard on the Boyne, where St. Finnen taught three thousand pupils from every part of Europe. His last school was that of Mobhi at Fin-glas—the "fair stream"—at Glasnevin, near Dublin. This school was broken up by the plague that swept Ireland in the year 544.

When we realize the powerful and ordered State behind such a remarkable system of education and such wealth of knowledge, and when we realize that at this time England was still in the nebulous, legendary period of King Arthur, does it not seem one of history's puzzles that the Irish did not invade and dominate England after the departure of the Romans?

Columcille, in order to avoid the plague, went into Ulster, where his cousin, Prince of Aileach, gave him the oak grove of Derry as his first monastery. During the next fifteen years of his life he founded monasteries at Kells, Swords, Tory Island, Lambay, near Dublin, and Durrow.

His new monastery of Durrow was the cause of his exile and the cause of the coming of Christianity to Scotland and the north of England. It happened in this way. His old master, St. Finnen of Moville, had returned from a second journey to Rome with a rare manuscript, probably the first translation of

the Vulgate of St. Jerome to reach Ireland. Finnen, like a true
bookman, valued his manuscript so highly that he did not wish
anyone to copy it. He desired to be the sole owner of it. Had
Columcille waited a while no doubt the bibliophile's enthusiasm
would have been tempered by generosity. But Columcille could
not wait. He wanted a copy of St. Jerome for his new founda-
tion. So he borrowed the book and secretly copied it, sitting up
by night and working by the light of a lamp. When Finnen
knew of this he was furious. He appealed to the High King at
Tara and brought forward the first action for violation of copy-
right. The king decided in favour of Finnen on the theory that
as every cow owns her calf so every book owns its child, or
copy. This greatly angered Columcille, who, like St. Patrick, had
a temper.

Another event complicated matters and hastened Colum-
cille's departure from Ireland. During the Festival at Tara the son
of the King of Connaught lost his temper and killed another
youth, thus violating the annual truce proclaimed at this time.
The murderer fled to Ulster and was placed under Columcille's
protection. The High King had the boy seized and, in spite of
Columcille's protests, put to death. His anger again burst out.
The saint raised his clan against the High King. A furious battle
was fought in which 3,000 lives were lost.

The legend is that in order to make penance for the battle
Columcille decided to leave Ireland and seek some desolate
place from which he could no longer see his native land. But it is
more reasonable, perhaps, to believe that he was animated
merely by the missionary zeal of his age and nation. However,
two years after the battle of Cuil Dremne, the saint set out in a
boat with a few companions to take the Word of God into hea-
then places. His sorrow in leaving Ireland expresses the centuries
of exile which this country has known. As he listened to the
sounds of the gulls on Lough Foyle, he turned to his monks and
said:

"The sound of it will not go from my ears till death."

They landed on the little, unearthly island of Iona that lies in bright blue water facing the red granite cliffs of Mull.

"It is well that our roots should pass into the earth here," said Columcille.

Nobly and eternally did they root themselves into the earth. It was from Iona that Christ went through Scotland, and from Iona that He went to Lindisfarne, off the Northumbrian coast. So Christianity came to England from Ireland.

Columcille died before the high altar of his church at the age of seventy-five and in the year 596. In the following year there landed on the south coast of England a band of forty monks, led by St. Augustine. They had been sent by Pope Gregory the Great to convert Britain. But for more than thirty years the Light from Ireland had been burning in the north.

SO ONE TURNS from the Walls of Derry as dusk falls. There is nothing now to remind one of the oak grove on the hill. But as the wind passes over Derry from Lough Foyle, as the gulls cry over the water one thinks of a boat turning from Ireland and a saint who expressed so simply the ache of exile:

"The sound of it will not go from my ears till death."

NIALL WILLIAMS
(1958–   )

CHRISTINE BREEN
(1954–   )

In 1985 Niall Williams and Christine Breen gave up promising profes-sional careers in Manhattan to live in the village of Kilmihil, County Clare, on Ireland's west coast. Williams is a Dublin native, born in Stil-lorgan; Breen grew up in suburban Westchester County in New York. They met at the University College Dublin where they were both study-ing, and married in 1981.

In many ways, Williams and Breen live the romantic Irish idyll. They renovated Breen's grandfather's cottage; he writes, she paints, and they are raising their two children. Ironically, their most profitable crop is writing about Kilmihil. Four books have chronicled their Irish life: O Come Ye Back to Ireland, The Luck of the Irish, The Pipes Are Calling, *and* When Summer's in the Meadow. *This excerpt, from* The Pipes Are Calling, *is written in two voices; Williams' voice is set in regular type, Breen's in bold.*

In 1998, Williams published a well-received first novel, Four Let-ters of Love, *described by* The New York Times *as "a delicate and graceful story." It is, of course, set in Ireland.*

from THE PIPES ARE CALLING

With the map of Ireland spread before us, we drove north toward Galway and turned off onto the Dublin road. We passed still lakewater and a handful of paddling swans. In Athlone, legendary center of Ireland, bright sailboats were moored in sunshine on the Shannon River. To the north was the inland sea of Lough Rea, and the sleepy town of Lissoy of which Oliver Goldsmith had written, "Sweet Auburn, loveliest village of the plain, where health and plenty cheered the laboring swain . . ."

We drove through the tidy but empty town of Ballymore to Mullingar and stopped for lunch: soup, chops, potatoes, and good old marrowfat peas. Good honest stuff, take it or leave it. The road took us out of County Westmeath into Meath: Clonmellon with tall trees growing in stone circle beds that were actually in the road, a few feet from the sidewalk; Kells (Ceanannus Mór in Irish), once a center of learning celebrated throughout Europe. St. Columba founded a monastery here in the year 550, leading two and a half centuries later to the superbly illustrated manuscript of the Gospels that is known as The Book of Kells. After Kells we passed through Ardee in County Louth. Here, every Irish schoolboy and girl is taught how Cuchulainn, champion of Ulster, fought from daybreak to sunset against Ferdia, his best friend, both of them retiring at nightfall to secretly bathe each other's wounds before resuming their fight in the dawn. Here in Ardee, at the bridge of Ferdia (Baile Atha Fhirdhia), Ferdia was slain.

After Ardee we drove through Dundalk. To the west was County Monaghan and the poet Paddy Kavanagh's village of

Inniskeen, to the east the Cooley Peninsula, setting for the Ulster cycle myths of Cuchulainn and the *Tain Bó Cuilainn.*

Four hours brought us across the map of Ireland, to The Border, which runs from the Atlantic coastline to the Irish Sea. In ours, as in many travelers' minds, the middle of the island had seemed more a place to traverse than to linger in. We'd preferred the coast and sea air. But bumping northeastward across the country toward Dundalk and the Belfast road, we were made newly aware of the wealth of layered history and varied geography of middle Ireland. The drive itself seemed to lead us through a constantly changing panoply of poets and saints, heroes and warriors, lakewater and blue hills, rivers, green fields, and stone walls. In this unfrequented part of the country, in pastoral peace, we found, unexpectedly, green places full of secrets and beauty. We would come again to linger; this is what travel in Ireland is about.

WE ARRIVED AT last at Ulster, The North, the Six Counties, the area that is known to the world as the place of "the Troubles." I had been there as a boy with my mother, up and down from Dublin on the train in the same day to shop in the big English department stores. English sweets, bars of chocolate, and toy English soldiers are what I remember—but that was long ago in a different age. Since 1969 all our television screens have brought us, protected, glimpses of the strife, of marches and riots, stone-throwing, fire-bombing, knee-capping, baton-charges, rubber-bullets, and tear gas. We have come to know of the Shankill and the Falls roads, read the familiar graffiti of a sectarian war, the three-letter-word daubings—IRA, UVF, and others—and to feel from the green tranquillity of southern Ireland, if only vicariously, the griefs of bombed shops, bridges, and roads "up North." But the truth is, the North is the North, and despite the two decades of internal war in Ulster, little of its anger or bloodshed has spilled into the rest of the island. That is a fact. Another, quoted in the London *Sunday Times* this March:

There were three times more people murdered in Washington, D.C., last year than in the *whole* six counties of Northern Ireland, which has a similar population. And another fact, this from the Northern Irish Tourist Board, contains an important truth: "In twenty years we've never lost a tourist yet!"

Plainly put, the struggle in Northern Ireland is, and has been, largely between the Republican and Loyalist factions of its population. No attempts are made to ambush tourists.

All this said, such is the impact of newspapers and television that Chris's and my image of what we might expect once we crossed the border was certainly colored with the faint tinge of apprehension of violence. Dan, an American friend studying at Queens University in Belfast, had called earlier in the week to assure us that it was a wonderful city and that in the years he had been working on his doctorate he had never encountered trouble. I took his word and that of others, too, and, in leaving the peace of Clare for the North, had full confidence that we would spend four tranquil days in beautiful countryside. Well, nearly full confidence—we left Deirdre behind with friends.

At the border we saw our first British soldier. Helmeted, dressed in camouflage uniform, holding a small machine gun, he stood alone beyond the customs and police officers at the place where the North began. We slowed into a line of cars and waited. I imagined other soldiers somewhere beyond the walls and the little hills of grass, routinely watching us. A green-uniformed officer in a bullet-proof vest waved the cars to him, one by one, across a series of low ramps in the road. You bumped slowly forward and were either waved on or to one side as the officer on duty decided. As we sat there, next in line, Chris rummaged for our passports. Did Irishmen and women need passports to enter the north of Ireland? For a minute I wasn't sure, and despite all the assurances of safety I felt a little anxious. Like everyone else, we, too, had heard stories of cars stopped for hours, stripped down to their innards in detailed searches by unnervingly silent or coldly polite soldiers. It was our turn. Sunshine was beating down, and under the weight of his bullet-proof vest and gunbelt the man who motioned us to him was glistening with sweat.

"Going touring, sir?"

"Yes, just for a few days."

There was a pause, his eyes traveled across the backseat, our bags, our travel books.

"Carry on." A wave of his hand, a bump over another ramp, and we were in Northern Ireland.

At once we sensed change. The road was better, the signposts were different, newer, English-style, not Irish, and the feeling of space itself was different. It is extraordinary on so small an island, but immediately we felt we were in another country. Motoring on the smooth wide surface of the M1, we arrived at Newry and for a moment lost our way. We passed a road that was cordoned off and guarded by three Security Force soldiers. That unnerved us a bit. Especially when Chris shouted out, "Wait, that's our road, B24." It was, but, fortunately, going in the other direction.

I was glad not to have had to inquire of the soldiers what detour to take. The part of Newry we drove through was depressed and unpleasant. We passed a little boy dressed in green and black, like a little IRA soldier. He stood below a telephone pole bearing a poster of Sinn Fein. We went wrong at a roundabout and drove up a street where half the shops were shuttered and closed. A siren sounded down the road behind us, and I pulled the car over in a panic. Images from the television news flashed before us, of car chases, armored vehicles, bullets. But only a fire engine went speeding past. In a pathetic way we were relieved. Anywhere else and we might not have thought twice about it, but here, not quite sure of our way, in a city that seemed shut into itself, we couldn't help feeling tense. I looked along the street, people were coming and going casually about their business. Only a fire engine.

*   *   *

ALL THE LAND from Rathfriland to Banbridge along the River Bann is Brontë territory, according to the Northern Ireland Tourist Board brochure. Patrick Brontë recounted his childhood for his children, and from his imaginative descriptions of County Down it is said that the Brontë sisters acquired their material for their novels. Another guide book says "there is hardly prettier, more welcoming countryside in which to get slightly lost."

So we took the "Brontë Homeland Drive" on our way to Belfast. I wonder what the Brontë sisters would think now if they could see the place about which their father so often reminisced. We passed under arches made of wrought iron and about fifteen feet high—"Enniskillen" to the right, "Boyne" to the left, and "No Surrender" in the center—as we drove through Ballyroney looking for the correct road. We finally stumbled upon Drumbally-roney Parish Church and School where Patrick Brontë was employed as schoolmaster before entering Cambridge. There is a British flag flying from the steeple and a little notice stating that the church was deconsecrated in 1976.

When we got to the end of the church house road, the main road forked, but there were no further signposts, only a huge red hand—the red hand of Ulster—painted in the center of the street that indicated, for us, whose territory we were really in.

We headed back toward the M1 to Belfast, only slightly reminded of Heathcliff and Cathy by the moors and rolling hills of the Bann Valley.

MRS. HAZLETT'S AT Ash-Rowan, 12 Windsor Avenue, was our destination in Belfast. On our way to Mrs. Hazlett's without an adequate map of the city, once again we turned off the motorway at the wrong exit from the roundabout. Within moments it seemed we were on a road without traffic—an empty street, ominous in itself—heading, as we discovered in panic, toward the Falls Road. "Provo Land" was scrawled in black across the street sign and, in giant lettering, IRA. We pulled over and turned back. Five minutes later we were driving, entirely lost, down a narrow street of small attached houses beneath the fluttering of a dozen red, white, and blue banners. Union Jacks flew from bedroom windows, loyalists slogans were brandished across a bus shelter: "F—— IRA," "IRA SCUM." And in front of their hall doors men and women sat, looking out on the street. Waiting. I stopped the car to ask directions of a young-looking man who was walking along the path. I got out beneath the flags in the grip of intimidation, and no sooner had I taken a step toward him than the man tensed. I saw his eyes go past me to the car, a car from the Republic; he stood, half-turned toward me. In one split second he had to decide: stand or run. What was he thinking? Of the others in their doorways watching? Of the amassed flags and banners flying over the little enclave of sectar-ian hatred, of what watchers might be thinking seeing him here on a street corner talking with a man from the Republic? Informers were shot. At the least, knee-capped.

"Turn left at the end of the street, take the next left, ask any-one then," he said and hurried on. For a hot hour we blundered about Belfast in a series of such narrow, working-class streets feeling the hostile atmosphere and driving in a tense unease past brick buildings painted with Unionist emblems of loyalty, under British flags that seemed to fly to keep strangers out rather than welcome anyone in. How dare we have come to this city at war as tourists, they seemed to say. And when we had driven at last out onto the Lisburn Road and along to Windsor Avenue, and arrived exhausted at Mrs. Hazlett's door, it was with mixed feel-ings and a dreadful anxiety at the thought of three more days of the same.

Ash-Rowan is a three-story, red-brick house in one of the quiet elegant avenues on the outskirts of Belfast City. Potted geraniums and summer annuals bloomed around the doorstep and across the front of the guest house, and when we rang the bell at the end of our six-hour drive a round-faced, genial woman of fifty came out to greet us with a warm smile.

"Ye were lost? Twice? Oh, no, come in, ye were lost, and och, it doesn't help that they've nicked me sign. Come in."

It was like going inside the home of a favorite, friendly aunt you hadn't seen for some time. She trotted up the stairs ahead of us, talking, passing a huge potted philodendron on the second floor.

"The toilet's there," she said, a little breathlessly, waving a hand at the massive plant and heading up another flight of stairs.

"The toilet's *there?* "Sorry?" I said.

"Och, I've been meaning to get that plant trimmed or have something done with it, ye can't even see the door." Mrs. Hazlett chuckled, shook her head, and climbed on. As we followed after her we saw the bathroom door, all but hidden behind the plant. We stopped at the third floor, top of the house, before a door into a shower cabinet, and another next to it into her daughter's old bedroom. And what a lovely room it was! Painted a soft yellow, with a window looking out on the Antrim hills and a church spire, it was furnished with twin deep armchairs, an old-fashioned fireplace dressed for summer with a basket of dried flowers, a big double bed with linen sheets, a big dresser with china teapot and teacups and coffee and teabags and crunchy ginger biscuits, a scattering of books and magazines, and a table and chair for writing. Mrs. Hazlett left us to it after a little speech filled with genuine welcome, and we fell on the bed, safe.

An hour later we were downstairs for dinner. On a table in the deep-pink front room by the window two plates were set for us amid a collection of Victorian antiques.

"Waldorf salad?" asked Mr. Hazlett in a strong northern accent, appearing 'round the door behind us, blue-eyed beneath a crop of silver hair.

We sat at a table that was dappled in sunlight; strains of Mozart emanated from the sitting room across the hall. There was nobody else around. Peace settled over us after the long day. By the time we had been offered and partaken of delicious roast pork on a bed of shallots with mushrooms, and were transferred for our coffee to the sitting room where Bach was now playing, it was impossible not to feel remarkably comfortable and at ease. Mrs. Hazlett, bringing in the coffee, sat herself across the arm of a chair as Chris told her about Deirdre back in Clare.

"I know, I know," she said, "people think it's so dangerous in Belfast, and it's not. Och, it's a lovely city so it is. I think so anyway. What do ye think? I mean people are so frightened to come up. We get so few tourists, mostly businessmen, but it's not the same. We used to have a restaurant. Did ye see the doll in the dining room?"

At this point she paused. Chris said she hadn't seen the doll, so Mrs. Hazlett bounced up from the chair and out. She was back in seconds with an old porcelain doll dressed in the black and white uniform of a Victorian servant girl.

"All the waitresses were dressed like this. But we stopped it. It just became too much for us. In a restaurant you don't really meet people, do you? They're just in and out and you don't get any chance to talk to them. So we opened up four rooms here in Ash-Rowan. We're only open a year. We like to think of it as a rest for friends. What do you think?"

She left us alone after giving us directions for an evening walk, and after coffee and biscuits and Bach we stepped out the front door and down the avenue.

So much of a visit to any place depends upon first impressions. In staying at Bed and Breakfast houses all over the country we had learned that our first welcome colored the impression of the larger place, the city, the village, or the countryside around it. From Mrs. Hazlett's, we walked in the glow of her friendliness. What was her religion, what were her political convictions? We didn't know and they didn't matter to us, just as ours didn't matter to her.

We seemed to be in a relatively wealthy Protestant part of the city. The streets we walked in the evening light were tree-lined

and gracious with tall, red-brick houses that glowed redder in
the sunset and ran back one after the other to the green mound
of Cave Hill. Her father always said Belfast had the most beauti-
ful setting for a city, Mrs. Hazlett had told us. "In a bowl of
green hills" was how he'd put it, she said. And it was true. Here
along Malone Road, south of the city, every street ended in a
view of a hillside. Along this road, leading down past the Ulster
Museum to the Botanic Gardens and Queens University, there
was an easygoingness, a carefree feeling that one might have
expected twenty years before. Young people clustered by a pub.
Students abounded, foreign students passed along the sidewalks.
People came and went from shops in summer clothes. The
world went on normally despite the high-pitched thrumming
noise of constantly circling army helicopters. For a moment we
were reminded that this was *Belfast,* and looking up at the heli-
copters Chris said, "It's like being in a goldfish bowl."

It was nine o'clock in the evening. We passed the Ulster
Museum with its collections of Irish and international art; Irish
furniture, glass, silver, and ceramics; and the gold and silver jew-
elry recovered from the wreck of the Spanish Armada ship
Girona. We then turned onto the path between the gates of the
Belfast Botanic Gardens and walked down the pathways by beds
of marigolds and petunias, lobelia and red salvia. Three men on
a bench were talking football in front of the famous 150-year-
old glass and wrought-iron Palm House with its dozens of rare
tropical plants, many as old as the century. Around the corner,
two ladies with walking sticks were resting themselves and talk-
ing about the good weather. Their smiles and polite friendly
nods encouraged us to bid "good evening" to them. Upon the
grass before the Palm House youths had gathered to play cricket.
Their calls and cries sounded behind us as we walked around
through the rose gardens and along two fledgling perennial
flower borders.

Was *this* Belfast then? Was this what it was like here? It was—
and it wasn't. For such is the complexity of the tragedy of
Northern Ireland that scenes of absolute tranquillity are quite

possible and even normal only minutes away from places where the blackened shells of houses, barred gates, and barbed wire bear testament to a state of war.

But in the evening streets around the Botanic Gardens and the university a different world existed in the gilded air. There were no soldiers or flags, armored trucks or sirening squad cars here, only the flowers of the gardens, the surprising smiles and hellos of passersby, tall old trees in summer leaf, the bowl of green hills, and the old-fashioned hump-backed black "London" taxis gliding by.

At Ash-Rowan on Windsor Avenue we slept deeply all night and in the morning came down for Mrs. Hazlett's "Not for the Fainthearted" breakfast fry. It included fried eggs, rashers, sausages, white pudding, black pudding, grilled tomato, fried mushrooms, fried banana, potato bread, and toast. Having stout-heartedly worked my way through most of it while Chris ate a plate of kippers, we sat back sipping coffee and told our hostess how friendly we were finding the city. But like the circling helicopters, all talk in Belfast eventually comes round to "the Troubles."

"Och, it is friendly," she said. "People just don't understand. We all wish it was all over, ye know. But my daughter's twenty now, she's just gone down to the Republic to university, and like, she's never known anything else in Belfast but the troubles. She was born with it on, ye know. And I go in the park sometimes with my grandchildren and I see little wee 'uns, four years old, shaking their fists up at the helicopters. They get it from their parents don't they; it's terrible so it is. But I think you see Belfast *is* friendly, people are lovely despite it all. We can only hope it'll end soon, isn't that it?"

We nodded and listened and later shook her hand and said our goodbyes. Leaving our car at Ash-Rowan for the morning, we walked into the city, down the Dublin Road past the Ulster hall, down Royal Avenue into the pedestrian shopping heart of Belfast. Until only recently great iron gates barred these streets and shoppers had to pass through checkpoint turnstiles and have their bags and parcels searched. But no more. The gates were wide open and in the bustle of the shopping streets there was all the energy of a living city. However trite it might sound, in every shop we went we encountered in shop assistants and shoppers alike the same friendliness and welcome we had met at Mrs. Hazlett's. These people cared that we had come to their city. They thanked us across shop counters, hoped we were enjoying our stay and that we would come back. Again and again we came from shops and turned to each other with the same surprise. Was Belfast perhaps the friendliest city in Ireland?

WE WERE GOING to tour the northern tip of Counties Antrim and Derry today.

"Niall," I said as we were driving, "do you notice anything peculiar about these cars we're passing?"

"No," he answered.

"Then it must be my imagination."

"What are you talking about?"

"Either I'm seeing sunspots, or there are a lot of *red* cars around here."

"What?" He laughed.

"Just watch," I said. "You'll see what I mean in a minute." And sure enough, within seconds, we passed seven cars, six of which were red. Then we got really curious and started to count. There wasn't a single green car that we could see. Yellow, rarely. Orange, well, who drives orange cars anyway? Some white, silver, all shades of blue, but a preponderance of red cars and vans. I would safely estimate that in the extreme northern corner of Northern Ireland every other car is a red car.

"You're right," Niall said. "It's absurd but true."

"It's weird," I said. "Why do you think it is?"

Niall reflected for a moment, scratched his graying beard in mock deliberation, and said almost in a whisper,

"It's the red hand of Ulster again."

And I think he's right. The O'Neill Red Hand is the adopted symbol of Ulster. As the story goes, rivals from an unknown land sailed to Ireland to conquer it. Warriors aboard the ships agreed that whoever touched Irish soil first would become lord. One of the leaders seized the moment by cutting off his left hand and throwing it onto the shore. Who could dispute that he had touched Irish soil first? From this man descended the O'Neills, the royal race of Ulster. The last O'Neill was "Red" Hugh O'Neill, Earl of Tyrone, who escaped to France in 1607 in the famous Flight of the Earls.

I wonder how I would have felt if we had been driving a kelly green car?

THE DRIVE FARTHER north begins at Larne. It takes you up the coast along Sir Charles Lanyon's superbly scenic road laid out in 1837. Today, a surface of smoothest tarmacadam curves in a black ribbon to the Glens of Antrim, the Irish Sea to your right beyond the kind of white seaside railing you might expect in Brighton or Blackpool. "I have seen nothing in Ireland so picturesque as this noble line of coast scenery," Thackeray wrote in 1842 when the road was newly built. It's a touring route par excellence, "reminiscent of the California coast as seen from Highway 1," says Birnbaum's *Ireland*.

The green Mull of Kintyre, Scotland, looms twelve miles out to sea and reminds you of the common links between the two countries, the Gaelic language, the pipes, and, of course, up here in Antrim, the great number of Scots transplanted to Ireland centuries earlier in Elizabeth's misguided effort to supplant the native Irish. At Glenarm begin the nine Glens of Antrim proper: Glenarm, Glencloy, Glengariff, Glenballyeamon, Glenaan, Glencorp, Glendun, Glenshesk, and Glentaisie. They run inland from the coast road, all green hills, woodlands, rivers, and waterfalls. Underneath lies what is said to be a perfect illustration of the geological history of the earth: rock layers of red sand-

stone, white chalk, basalt, and blue clay. They say people have
lived in the Glens for five thousand years. At Cushendall, one of
the prettiest villages along the sea route, neolithic ax factories
have been found, giving credence to the notion of Ulster's spirit
of industry even then, with ax heads being "exported" from
here by seafaring warriors from the north.

A few miles farther on we passed Cushendun and climbed
the narrowing, winding, and hilly coast road to Torr Head. The
cars that had streamed out along the seaside road from Larne
were all gone now. A wind blew up here on the balmiest,
mildest day in the year and the road was a lonely one. On a tip
from Mr. Hazlett, at a National Trust signpost, we turned right
driving down a tarred track by thickly wooded slopes that end in
the sandy beach of Murlough Bay. Here, in the remotest part of
Ulster, with no houses in sight, and cliffs and sheep-dotted hills
rising on either side, the tourist is catered to with a good road
and well-kept facilities. How English it all seemed to me. For
although, thanks to the National Trust, the beauty of the envi-
ronment is well safeguarded up here, I couldn't help feeling
there was a lot to be said for untamed wilderness.

Leaving the scenic coastal road of the Glens of Antrim
behind us, we drove through Ballycastle, onto the northern,
"Causeway Coast." Ballycastle is home, at the end of August, to
the Auld Lammas Fair, which, along with the Puck Fair in Kil-
lorglin and the Ballinasloe Horse Fair, is one of the oldest fairs in
the country. From Ballycastle we continued to Bushmills, home
of the oldest licensed distillery in the world, and, on a day at the
end of July, a town festooned with Union Jacks and red, white,
and blue banners. This, too, was Northern Ireland.

What was it in such places that sent shivers down my spine? I
bear no Ulster Protestant ill will; I blame the sectarian war on
the follies of history. In the north of Antrim there are virtually
no "Troubles," as such. ("And how could there be?" Chris said.
"There are no Catholics. They were driven out.") But in the
small towns with big farms of good land around them, this flag-
flying, strident loyalism didn't encourage tourism of any kind.

We were assaulted with it; there's no friendliness in the air here if you aren't flying the same flag. There must be more flags sold in the six counties of Ulster than in all of England, I thought, and drove on out of Bushmills to our guest house, feeling solemn, unwelcome, and so far from Kiltumper.

TODAY WE HAD one of those days when everything seems to be slightly askew. It took ages to find our guest house this evening. As there are virtually no B&Bs up here, I was glad that I had booked ahead, but trying to find it by its address was not easy: Black Heath House, Killeague Road, Blackhill, Coleraine. It was six o'clock when we arrived in Coleraine. "Perfect," Niall said. "Just in time for a rest before dinner." "Yes," I said. "But where is Killeague Road or Blackhill?" Two people whom we asked had no idea, so we pulled into a petrol station. The young lad told us that Blackhill was, in fact, six miles out of Coleraine. "Do you know where Garvagh is?" "No." "It's out that way." We followed the signs for Garvagh but no Blackhill. Lost once more, we pulled into another petrol station to discover that Killeague Road was just up ahead, the next right. Finally, we thought. We took the next right, which wasn't Killeague Road, and drove another mile down a lovely road with beautiful soft meadows on either side. "It sure is pretty here," I said. "I'm glad you like it; we may have to sleep in that meadow," Niall said. As it happened, the "eague" had disappeared from the sign and we *were* on the right road, now "Kill" Road, only we were going the wrong way. We had a hard time finding Black Heath House, but we finally arrived just before seven. While we were waiting to be shown to our rooms, I peeked into the breakfast room and glimpsed a cake on a table with white icing and the words "Happy Anniversary." And it was our eighth wedding anniversary.

We were greeted by a friendly enough young man who showed us to our room and quickly disappeared. It was the last we saw of anybody resembling a manager. The room, however, was lovely, with a four-poster bed. Earlier in the day, in Belfast, we had bought swimsuits as there was said to be an indoor pool at this guest house. We looked out the window to see if we could spot the building for the pool, but it was not in view.

Below, in the basement of the Black Heath House, we found a restaurant, well known in Coleraine, called Mac-Duff's. When we were seated at our table I saw a tiny centerpiece of flowers like the kind you see at weddings, with a plastic silver thing stuck on that said "Happy Anniversary." We smiled, amazed and delighted. And all during what proved to be an unfortunate meal—with respect to food and service—I had thought, all will be forgiven if that cake arrives.

But instead of the cake, the dessert menu came. Niall pointed to a table behind us, candlelit with several bowls of flowers on it for a party of eight celebrating their parents' silver anniversary. We left the restaurant a little dismayed but looking forward to a midnight swim. Our search for the pool, however, was fruitless. It either didn't exist or was superbly hidden from the guests.

We left, gladly, in the morning.

AS WE LEFT Black Heath House and drove back along the Causeway coast a fine mist was blowing in off the sea. We were almost as far from Kiltumper as it was possible to get and still be in Ireland. Giant's Causeway. The name conjures up an image of magical, majestic, grave antiquity. The Giant's Causeway is a series of strange narrow rectangular columns of stone, like steps, marching down into the sea. Weird and mysterious and, whatever your interpretation, an AONB—in British government parlance, an Area of Outstanding Natural Beauty, a perfect example of "Art in Nature." The rocks look like an extraterrestrial land-mark on earth, the result of cooled and cracked molten rock 55 million years old.

In Irish mythology, the columns are either the causeway that the giant Finn MacCoul made so his Scotch equivalent, Benan-donner, could walk across the sea to begin their fight without the minor fatigue of swimming twelve miles, or the highway he built to his giant ladylove who lived on Staffa, an island in the Hebrides. This last is a romantic interpretation, but the one I liked. In school in Dublin we had all been taught the feats of Finn MacCoul: how he could pluck thorns from his heels while running, how once he had picked up a sod of earth to throw after a fleeing enemy and the sod, landing mid-sea, became the Isle of Man, the hole it left filling with water and becoming Ire-land's largest lake, Lough Neagh. Besides all this, Chris and I had a natural penchant for giants. Kiltumper, our own townland, had been named after one, according to one story, and his grave, a mound with a circle of stones, was on the top of the hill at the back of our farm. On his holidays, had our Kiltumper giant walked this way to Scotland?

The Causeway was not "discovered" until the late seven-teenth century, when a Bishop of Derry trumpeted the news of its remarkable scenery and a stream of tourists began that hasn't stopped flowing yet. It became obligatory to see it on the Grand Irish Tour. Some, like Richard Pococke in 1754, came to mea-sure it, others, like Susannah Drury, came to make what became famous pictures. It looked like the beginning of the world according to one famous nineteenth-century writer who had to make his way past hordes of begging urchins and guides; a simi-lar experience in the same year caused the German Johannes Kohl to dub it "The Dwarf's Causeway."

Shunning the little tour bus at the top of the hill, Chris and I took the fifteen-minute walk to the strange rock formations, preferring to go guideless into the early morning mist. The nar-row black road descends steeply, disappearing into moving shrouds, and as we started down into the crash and fall of an unseen sea, it was impossible not to feel overwhelmed by the eerie atmosphere of the place. Seabirds, fulmars, gulls, and stonechats sounded below us and basalt cliffs towered overhead. Little slides of fallen stones were stopped midway between the clifftops and the water and from their fallen stillness, their perpetual balance, emanated the sense of frozen time that was the mood of the Causeway. Sleeping giant's breath, said Chris, meaning the mist that was folding and parting thickly around us, opening views down the road to the shore. In the distance a man with a black beret and a stick moved before us. From somewhere behind came the sound of children's voices.

By the time we reached the "honeycomb" (the Middle Causeway), with its yellow-and-black-colored lichen strongly marked, we found ourselves inside a landscape that had slowly changed as we walked through it. At first only bits of rock like rounded squares emerged. Then they began to grow and multiply, one on top of the other. Stacks of them. Weird, lunar, and regular; a triangle made of hundreds of hexagonal stones rising tightly together, like pipes, going out into the sea. It was Aird Snout headland. Past it, farther along the coast, are numerous and equally strange formations: the Wishing Well, The Giant's Granny, The King and His Nobles. Each one is an extraordinary sculpture of nature.

We climbed out on the little salt-sprayed peninsula of Aird's Snout, pointing toward Scotland. The sea rushed in past us. The black headland at our backs softened under a veil of mist and we sat down in that remarkable place where the surfaces of half of the stones were nicely shaped for the behinds of the seagazers but were in fact the "ball and socket" joints of fractured columns of varying heights that jutted out to sea. Here, wrapped in sea mist and bird cries, was a place that imprinted itself upon you. It was human-diminishing, dwarfing. Nature was the Giant, and upon these stones of her causeway we sat, hushed, and stared at the mysteriousness of the world.

DAVID A. WILSON

(1950–)

An assistant professor of Celtic studies at the University of Toronto, David A. Wilson takes us through Ireland on the back of his bike. His journey, chronicled in Ireland, a Bicycle, and a Tin Whistle, *follows the coastline from Island Magee to Cape Clear and from Dublin to Belfast. Wilson rides to the accompaniment of fiddles, harps, and flutes. When he stops, it is to dance jigs and reels at pubs and festivals.*

In this excerpt from Ireland, a Bicycle, and a Tin Whistle *Wilson takes the reader to remote Island Magee, one of the few Protestant areas with no Catholic residents. Wilson finds it more like Scotland than Ireland, and it leads him to muse on the Catholic and Protestant divisions. "It's like living in a world of mirror images," he writes, "where each side sees the image, but neither sees the mirror."*

SWEET CARNLOUGH BAY

from IRELAND, A BICYCLE, AND A TIN WHISTLE

And so, with the strains of "Jerusalem" still running through my mind, I left Whitehead and cycled along the country roads of green and pleasant Islandmagee, en route to Cushendall. Islandmagee is not actually an island; it is a peninsula that hooks upwards from Belfast Lough towards Larne. The Middle Road takes you through rolling hills, past well-kept farms with brambled hedges and stone gateposts that look like miniature fortresses.

If you turn off to the east, you can make your way to the path that runs beneath Gobbins Head, winding through tunnelled-out rock and stumbling over broken stones, ledged between sheer cliffs and the sea. Many years ago, with the coming of the railway, the walk attracted tourists from all over the country, even from London; there was a tubular bridge to carry you across one rift in the rocks, and a strung-together suspension bridge to take you over another. Now, hardly anyone comes here; there are no signposts, the path is crumbling into the sea, and the bridges have rusted and rotted away.

Most travellers bypass Islandmagee. The road doesn't lead anywhere except back again, and there is no car ferry to take you over the water to Larne. But it is perfect cycling country; there is little traffic, apart from the occasional Lost Soul, and the hills aren't too steep—although the drops down to Portmuck harbour and the beach at Brown's Bay will burn the rubber on your brakes and change the pressure in your ears. This is a place with a strong sense of community and cohesion. "Kick an Islandmagee man," the saying goes, "and the whole island limps." And, beneath the neat and tidy Presbyterian exterior, it is full of the unexpected; there are prehistoric, Gaelic, and Low-land Scottish roots here, twisting together in strange and surprising ways.

The most visible sign of the prehistoric past appears at the head of the peninsula, in the form of an ancient burial site known as the Druid's Altar. The stones stand incongruously in the front garden of a modern cottage, leaning together like lawn ornaments from another world. Some of the first people who settled in Ireland came into the northeast; among those who passed this way, at least a few remained huddled on these hills, gazing across the sea to the land they had left behind. A few miles to the south, there is a faint trace of another tradition that has virtually vanished from the area. As you cycle out of White-head, you pass a shop called the Rinka. The shop used to be a dance-hall; the Irish word for dancing is *rince;* the phonetic pronunciation in English is *rinka.* But apart from the occasional placename, there is nothing left in Islandmagee of the old Gaelic order that was swamped by the Ulster Scots some four centuries ago.

Elsewhere in Northern Ireland, the overlay of Protestant culture on Gaelic foundations has produced some ironic consequences. A friend of mine told me about a staunch Loyalist who was infuriated by the law that enabled Catholics to rename their streets in the Gaelic language. "Let them try that around where I live," he said, "and just see what bloody well happens." "Why, where do you live?" asked my friend. "Ballyhackamore," came the indignant reply.

There are no Catholics in Islandmagee, and there have not been since the middle of the seventeenth century. Back in 1641, there was a Catholic rising in the north of Ireland against the settlers; in Protestant culture, folk memories of the massacres and atrocities persist into the present. Then, as now, there were reprisals—including the slaughter of fifty Catholics who were living on the peninsula. In the Islandmagee imagination, the story expanded to the point where hundreds of Catholics were driven to their death over the cliffs at Gobbins Head. To this day, it is said that the nettles in the fields above the Gobbins have dark red leaves from the blood of the Catholics who were slain.

It is the myth of a community that responded to crisis by destroying the perceived enemy in its midst; the pattern is depressingly familiar. Today, in Northern Ireland, the vast majority of Protestants and Catholics live in their own communities, insulated and isolated from the other. Catholics living in Protestant housing estates have been burnt out of their homes; Protestants living in Catholic territory near the border have been forced out of their farms. Each community defines itself against the other; the land is strewn with blood-red nettles.

And yet, in their very separateness, Protestants and Catholics are much more alike than they realize; in many ways, they are divided by what they have in common. Both sides see themselves as threatened minorities—the Protestants as a minority in the island of Ireland, the Catholics as a minority in the state of

Northern Ireland. Both sides take their religion straight up, and don't want their children exposed to the "wrong" faith; the level of support for segregated education runs high across the Protestant-Catholic divide. Both sides tend to view politics as a zero-sum game, in which a victory for one side automatically means a defeat for the other, and compromise is only victory or defeat in disguise. The key words are *either* and *or,* not *both* and *together.* Even the symbols are similar. If Protestant kerbstones are painted in the red, white, and blue of the Union Jack, their Catholic counterparts are painted the green, white, and orange of the Irish Tricolor. And if Protestant graffiti proclaim FTP, the Catholics reply with FTQ. It's like living in a world of mirror images, where each side sees the image, but neither sees the mirror.

Here, in Islandmagee, there are few face-to-face encounters with real or imagined enemies. Looking out across the Irish Sea, away from the beaten track, overwhelmingly Protestant, the peninsula could easily be mistaken for a fragment of Scotland rather than a part of Ireland. Back in the seventeenth century, when King James I prevented the Irish Presbyterians from practising their religion, hundreds of them rowed back and forth across the sea to Scotland every Sunday for communion. The Scottish connection remains powerful; you can hear it in the rhythms of speech, and you can feel it in the folk traditions that permeate the place. As they crossed the sea, the people who settled in Islandmagee carried witches, fairies, spirits, and ghosts with them. "In no part of Ireland," ran a government report from the 1830s, "are the people more generally and inveterately superstitious than here."

There were stories of hauntings, fairy music, fortune-telling, magic, and counter-magic. To prevent your cows from becoming bewitched, you had to hang a "witch stone" above their heads in the byre. To protect yourself from evil spells, you had to strew your farmyard with marigolds on May Day. To cure diseases, you could call on the local "wise woman" whose charms and incantations would result in supernatural healing. Even today, it is said, the "wee folk" are about at night. They leave fairy rings, circles of dark grass around thorn bushes; if you step inside, you will be cursed. But you will receive good luck if you cross a baby's hand with silver, or if the first person entering your house on New Year's Day has dark hair.

Before they moved to Whitehead, my parents spent several years in Islandmagee, living in a farm labourer's cottage without electricity or running water. Although they were outsiders from the modern, industrial, urban world, it wasn't long before they began to succumb to the supernatural. "If ever you see a cow with two heads," my father was told, "you have come face to face with the Devil himself." He thought no more about it, until one night, walking home alone, he saw a still figure in the distance, silhouetted against the darkening sky—the shape of a cow, with a head where its head should have been, and a head where its tail should have been. "What did you do?" I asked. "I ran like hell," he said. "And I didn't stop running until I was back home with the door locked behind me, and the key safe in my pocket."

Every day, the bus would come from Belfast, wending its way through narrow roads, stopping at the different farmhouses. And every day, groups of islanders would gather at Ballydown Hill to follow its progress, to see who was coming and who was going. At first, my mother found this to be rather eccentric; living in London, she'd seen a good few buses in her time. But after a few weeks, she found herself looking forward to the event; it became one of the highlights of the day, waiting for the bus and chatting with the neighbours, and having tea and biscuits together in someone's house. When my parents bought a paraffin stove—the first one in Islandmagee, no less—they found that they were suddenly at the centre of the social scene. More and more people dropped by, ostensibly to give their regards, but actually to inspect the latest example of modern technology, to find out how well it worked and how much it cost. Between the bus and the stove, the gossip and the curiosity, rhythms were established and friendships were formed; little by little, they were being drawn into the community.

Among their friends was John Napier, a farm labourer from just down the road. "Sure your mother was just a wee bairn when she had you," he said when I called round to see him. He pulled out faded photographs, put the kettle on, and fed me a plate of sandwiches, and took me on a tour of the district. The cottage had been bulldozed away; the paraffin stove had long since given up the ghost. John decided to show me off to the neighbours and took me on a house-to-house visit. At each place, the same ritual was enacted. "D'ye recognize this fellow?" he would ask as he brought me in. The neighbours would shake their heads in embarrassment; the last time they'd seen me I was only six months old, and I'd changed a bit in the meantime. He let them dangle on the hook for a while. "You've met him before, you know," he would say; meanwhile, I was just standing there, trying not to look too stupid. Then, he would reveal his Secret Knowledge: "D'ye remember the Wilsons who lived over by Miss Ross? Well, this is their wee boy." Handshakes and smiles all round; invitations for tea. "You're raising a nice smell," John would say when the scones came out of the oven; the hosts would nod back approvingly and bring out still more. Every plate had to be finished; there was no choice in the matter. Scones, scones, and more scones: it was the Presbyterian version of the Lost Souls' drinking syndrome, an easy switch from alcoholism to foodaholism.

Still, being on a bicycle gives you a chance of working off the calories and maintaining some kind of equilibrium between the pints consumed and the miles travelled. After parting company with John Napier and his neighbours, I freewheeled down the hill, past the Druid's Altar, to take the boat to Larne. While I was waiting, one of the Islanders told me a bit about the place. Many centuries ago, he said, St. Patrick himself had passed this way, blessed the ferry, and assured his fellow travellers that no one would ever drown in the crossing. But the blessing somehow wore off during the last century; in a sudden storm, the boat capsized and all the passengers went over. Three of them managed to hold on and were rescued by a young lad who had seen the accident from the shore, and who went out to get them in his father's fishing boat. But the fourth was swept under by the tide and never came up; they found his body by Ballylumford shore, just down the road. He was sixteen years old.

Eventually, the ferry arrived—a glorified rowing boat with an outboard motor, coming across Larne Lough. "Have a good crossing, now," he said cheerfully as he strolled back to his house. I checked the sky carefully for approaching squalls, took the measure of the wind, and lowered my bicycle onto the boat. Before I knew it, I was on the other side; St. Patrick was back on form. The captain moored the boat for a year and a day, although he would be returning in an hour; one rope landward and two towards the sea, where the wind would not toss her about or sun split her or birds of the air befoul her. Then he headed for the nearest pub, "The Dragon's Head," and pointed me in the direction of the coast road.

The road here curves along the coastline, tracing a narrow path between the hills and the sea. The air is clear, and the breeze blows in from the sea, catching the spray and lifting it lightly over the road; I can almost taste the salt on my lips. As I turn past Ballygalley Head, the wind appears to drop; the pedals move faster, the gears become higher, and I suddenly have the sensation of speed and strength. Leaving the shelter of the bay, the illusion is broken; the shoulders begin to strain, thighs tighten, and I slow to an easier pace. Above, the gulls are wheeling with the wind and the clouds are drifting towards the glens. It is a day of gentle warmth, but when the clouds cover the sun, an unexpected coolness fills the air. In the distance, I can just make out Ailsa Craig off the Scottish coast; it dances in and out of focus, as if willed into existence by an act of imagination.

The road wound past Glenarm and into Carnlough Bay,

where I stopped to walk around the harbour and watch the fishing boats being readied for their next journey. "Sweet Carnlough Bay"—the song floated in from the sea:

> When winter was dawning, o'er high hills and mountains
> And dark were the clouds o'er the deep rolling sea
> I spied a fair lass as the daylight was dawning
> She was asking the road to sweet Carnlough Bay.

It has the same tune as "The Road to Dundee," an Antrim version of a Scottish song. But in the Scottish version, the couple who fall in love on the road are forced to follow separate paths; he is of low degree, her father says no, and there is wailing and gnashing of teeth all round, in the true folk tradition. In Carnlough Bay, though, all is sweetness and light. They walk together into town and wind up in Pat Hamill's for a "wee drop," where he drinks to the health of the "dear lassie" he's met. No angst, no agony, no anguish—just a fine time on a warm day.

It's a welcome change from the customary tragic theme. Most Irish love songs worth their salt have at least two suicides, one unwanted pregnancy, and maybe a murder thrown in for good measure; the characters drop like flies, the lovers usually wind up buried side by side, and the last verse generally runs something like:

> Build me a grave, both broad and deep
> A marble tombstone at my feet
> And put these words on the stone above
> To tell the world that I died for love.

The usual pattern would run as follows: he gets her drunk at Pat Hamill's and seduces her on a nearby hillside; she gets pregnant and he disowns her; she drowns herself and he dies of guilt; her parents commit suicide and Pat Hamill goes insane. But we know that this didn't happen in Carnlough Bay; had it done, the balladeer would have added at least another four verses. And bal-ladeers as a breed tend to judge the quality of a song by the quantity of its verses.

"Sweet Carnlough Bay": the song suits the day. Looking around the place, you'd never know it could be otherwise; cou-ples are walking together in the sunshine, and the beach is full of children who are charging into the coldness of the sea, shouting and laughing and shivering, and running themselves back to warmth. The melody is in my mind, but whenever I try to hum it aloud, it eludes me; perhaps the image is illusory as well. I search for Pat Hamill's, but learn that it has long since disap-peared. Someone shows me an old photograph of the place, a fine hotel on the main street, with a sign saying "Cyclists Spe-cially Catered For"—Sunday afternoons on old boneshakers, followed by plates of sandwiches and glasses of beer.

Back on the bicycle, I travel on past the short, slumped-back headland of Garron Point, where Cushendall and Cushendun come into view. Across the North Channel, the Mull of Kintyre reaches out from Scotland, bare as a bald head. The sunlight catches the windows of a large white house at Southend, on the edge of the Mull. There used to be a ferry service from Cushen-dall to the Mull a few years ago, making the trip in a couple of hours. Now, it takes a couple of days, and the wanderings are well worth the time. You cross over from Larne to Stranraer and travel northwards through the narrow roads of the Scottish coast. Just before Ayr, you pass the Electric Brae, where the Laws of Gravity have been reversed and you find yourself freewheel-ing up the hill. Further on, you take the ferry to Aran, the island of sharp-edged peaks and soft-eyed deer, until you reach Lochranza. There, in the peace and stillness of the mountain-sheltered bay, you wait for the boat to Kintyre. And you wind your way to Southend, stand by the large white house, and watch the sunset over the Glens of Antrim.

At Garron Point, I took the tin whistle from the pannier, climbed over a fence, sat down on coarse grass, and started to play. A soft tune wafts over the fields, and drifts into the spray of

the sea—a piece composed three centuries ago by the blind
harper Turlough Carolan for Fanny Power, the daughter of one
of his patrons. Then a jig, "Out on the Ocean," skipping over
the water, light as a summer's day. The music is made for mean-
dering, and the meandering depends on the mood—the state of
your mind, the direction of the wind, the sounds from the sea. A
jig or a reel will never sound quite the same way twice; the
ornamentations, elaborations, and syncopations will twist and
turn through the melody, changing its character as it is played.
There is the tune, and there is the way you play the tune; there is
the map, and there is the way you choose to travel.

You could race through Ireland in a car, sticking to the main
routes; but if you take a bicycle, breathe in the air, and wander
off into the side roads, you'd be closer to the spirit of the place.
You could learn traditional music by the book, sticking to the
main notes; but if you take a tin whistle, breathe out the air, and
wander off into the variations, you'd be closer to the spirit of
the piece. Riding a bicycle or playing a whistle, the journey
becomes more than a means to the end of reaching a destina-
tion; it becomes an end in itself, its own destination.

A slow and soothing piece, "The Lark in the Clear Air," hov-
ers over craggy hills; there is melancholy in the melody. In
ancient times, the music was said to have magical effects. It
could soften the senses and send you to sleep. It could fill the
room with laughter, quicken the pulse, set hearts racing. Or it
could sadden the soul and move you to weep. And so it still is,
from the lightest lullaby, to the liveliest jig, to the loneliest
lament. In the tin whistle there is beauty and simplicity, a narrow
range of notes and a wide range of feeling. There are slow airs
that would make the tears run down your leg, and there are
dance tunes that would make your spirits soar. Sometimes, in
sessions, the musicians will join them together and move directly
from a mournful air to a wild and wonderful set of reels, to ban-
ish misfortune with a song.

Time to move on; the tin whistle is tucked back in the pack.
Apart from anything else, it's the ideal travel instrument; it's eas-

ier to carry on a bicycle than is a guitar, say, or a piano. The whistle is also the ultimate democratic instrument; for the price of a couple of pints (the universal unit of currency for wastrels and minstrels), you can enter the world of jigs and reels, of songs and laments. And as you make the journey, you learn the music by listening to the people who play it, and you soak up the spirit by going to the places where they play it—the kitchens, the pubs, the festivals, in towns and villages all over the country.

Permissions Acknowledgments

Grateful acknowledgment is made to the following for permission to reprint previously published material.

Samuel Beckett: Excerpt from *Mercier and Camier* by Samuel Beckett, copyright © 1974 by Samuel Beckett. Reprinted by permission of Grove/Atlantic, Inc.

Brendan Behan: "I'm a British Object, Said the Belfast-Man" from *Hold Your Hour and Have Another* by Brendan Behan (now included in *The Dubbalin Man,* A and A Farmar Pubs. Ltd., Ireland), copyright © 1998 by Brendan Behan Estate. Reprinted by permission of A and A Farmar Pubs. Ltd., and Blanaid Behan.

John Betjeman: "Ireland with Emily" from *Collected Poems* by John Betjeman. Reprinted by permission of John Murray (Publishers) Ltd.

Heinrich Böll: "Mayo—God Help Us" and "Skeleton of a Human Habitation" by Heinrich Böll, translated by Leila Vennewitz, from *Irish Journal* (Northwestern University Press, 1994), copyright © 1957 by Kiepenheuer & Witsch. Reprinted by arrangement with Verlag Kiepenheuer & Witsch, Koln, care of the Joan Daves Agency as agent for the Proprietor, and Leila Vennewitz.

H. V. Morton: Chapter 12 from *In Search of Ireland* by H. V. Morton (Methuen, London). Reprinted by permission of Methuen, an imprint of Random House UK Limited, London.

Eric Newby: "To the Aran Islands" from *Round Ireland in Low Gear* by Eric Newby. Reprinted by permission of HarperCollins Publishers Ltd., London.

Edna O'Brien: "My Mother's Mother" from *A Fanatic Heart* by Edna O'Brien (Weidenfeld and Nicolson, 1984). Reprinted by permission of David Godwin Associates.

Muriel Rukeyser: Excerpt from *The Orgy* by Muriel Rukeyser (Paris Press, Ashfield, Mass., 1997), copyright © by William L. Rukeyser. Reprinted by permission of Paris Press.

Wallace Stevens: "The Irish Cliffs of Moher" from *Collected Poems* by Wallace Stevens, copyright © 1952 by Wallace Stevens. Reprinted by permission of Alfred A. Knopf, a division of Random House, Inc.

Paul Theroux: "Discovering Dingle" from *Sunrise with Seamonsters* by Paul Theroux, copyright © 1985 by Cape Cod Scriveners Co. All rights reserved. Reprinted by permission of Houghton Mifflin Co.

William Trevor: "Autumn Sunshine" from *Beyond the Pale and Other Stories* by William Trevor, copyright © 1981 by William Trevor. Reprinted by permission of Viking Penguin, a division of Penguin Putnam Inc., and Sterling Lord Literistic, Inc.

T. H. White: "Letter from a Goose Shooter" from *The Godstone and the Blackymor* by T. H. White (Penguin Putnam, New York, 1959). Reprinted by permission of David Higham Associates, London.

Oscar Wilde: Six letters from *The Complete Letters of Oscar Wilde,* edited by Merlin Holland and Sir Rupert Hart-Davis, Letters copyright © 1962, 1985, 2000 by The Estate of Oscar Wilde. Editorial matter copyright © 1962, 1985, 2000 by Sir Rupert Hart-Davis. Copyright © 2000 by Merlin Holland. Rights in Canada from *The Letters of Oscar Wilde* administered by Fourth Estate Ltd., London. Reprinted by permission of Henry Holt and Company, LLC, and Fourth Estate Ltd., London.

Niall Williams and Christine Breen: Excerpt from *The Pipes Are Calling* by Niall Williams and Christine Breen. Reprinted by permission of Soho Press, New York.

David A. Wilson: "Sweet Carnlough Bay" from *Ireland, a Bicycle, and a Tin Whistle* by David Wilson. Reprinted by permission of McGill-Queen's University Press, Montreal.

Virginia Woolf: Excerpt from *The Diary of Virginia Woolf, Volume IV, 1931–1935* by Virginia Woolf, copyright © 1982 by Quentin Bell and Angelica Garnet. Reprinted by permission of Harcourt Brace & Company and Hogarth Press, an imprint of Random House UK Limited, London, for the Executors of the Virginia Woolf Estate.